MW01245516

Wizards of the Mound

Ray Clifford Martinez II

HypnoToad Books—China, ME
Paperback ISBN: 979-8-9903341-0-6
Hardcover ISBN: 979-8-9903341-2-0
eBook ISBN: 979-8-9903341-1-3
Library of Congress Control Number: 2024906654
Title: *Wizards of the Mound*
Author: Ray Clifford Martinez II
Digital distribution | 2024
Paperback | 2024

This is a work of fiction. The characters, names, incidents, places, and dialogue are products of the author's imagination, and are not to be construed as real.

Dedication

This book is dedicated to my wife Heather. You have always supported me, in my career and pursuits. without you and your love this book would have never happened.

Prologue

Headmaster Ebus Nordau's stomach gave an unpleasant lurch. He ignored it and raised both hands, palms out, to face his opponent.

Grim Krauss was a relatively new master at the Scientia Arcana Academy. In Ebus' experience, SAA students were all flash and little payoff, which was why he'd accepted Grim's challenge. Even though he'd been feeling under-the-weather for a few days now, this Spellduel should be a simple matter.

The curved wyvern horn sounded to signal the start of the bout. Ebus easily dodged Grim's first thrust, a clumsy attempt at conjuration that flared bright orange in his mind's eye. Even without his Aursight ability, Ebus would have noticed Grim waving his hands and practically shouting the spell.

Ebus waited for that burst of magic to crash harmlessly into the sand of the Spellduel arena. Then he lifted his chin and flicked two of his fingers, lips parted to whisper the casting under his breath.

Three dark blue dragons exploded from the dirt around Grim, two meters each in size. One snapped at his head, another biting at his heels. Grim shouted in alarm, dancing out of their reach. But the creatures circled, nostrils flared. Ebus allowed himself a small, satisfied smirk. But another warning rumble in his gut soon wiped that smile away.

He winced. One of the dragons winked out of sight. The arena swam. He scanned the raised viewing seats nearby and noticed Bishop watching him, seated between Mariou and Muzud. The rest of the Wizards of the Mound Academy was there too, of course— nobody wanted to miss the chance to watch their headmaster put an SAA master in his place. But he couldn't see the rest of the stands, oddly.

In fact, he could barely see anything but those three. No, four? Bishop, Mariou, Muzud, and... His eyes narrowed. *That can't be right.*

A fourth person shimmered in and out of sight behind the other three. Almost like the illusion of dragons he'd just cast. Only, unlike the dragons, Ebus recognized this figure.

"No," he whispered, just as a burst of energy struck him hard in the chest.

Ebus flew backward. He barely felt the ground rise up to strike him. All he could see was that familiar smirk, those eyes he never thought he'd see again. Not in this lifetime, anyway…

Ebus rolled onto his side, coughing blood. All around the arena, shouts rose. Students chanted his name. Some people booed, though whether that was meant for him or his opponent, Ebus couldn't tell. With a groan, he forced himself to stand. More than just his gut rebelled now—his limbs didn't seem to want to work either. When he raised his hands to cast a fresh spell, his fingers curled in on themselves, refusing to obey.

Ebus shivered. What did Grim cast, to make his body rebel? His knees locked, his toes curling inside his boots.

This didn't feel like any spell he'd ever encountered. It certainly didn't feel like anything a Scientia Arcana master would use. It felt… *Like dying.*

Ebus ignored his own instincts and channeled his fear into another illusion. This time, pitch black night suddenly peeled across the blue sky. It shrouded the entire arena in darkness. Grim couldn't strike again if he couldn't see his target. Under the curtain of night, Ebus stumbled forward, eyes wide. His Aursight should show him his target, false night or no.

A pinprick of light caught Ebus' eye. *There.* He lifted both palms to cast, just as a fireball engulfed his vision.

It didn't hurt. It was warm, almost comforting. It lifted Ebus off his feet and dropped him to the ground again. To him, the fall felt as gentle as his mother's arms as a boy, cradling him to sleep. His eyes rolled back in his head, his hands grasping uselessly at the arena sand.

He remembered the face he'd glimpsed in the stands. The hatred in the figure's eye. His last thought, before the world slipped away, was: *Don't let him find Lazlo.*

Chapter One

Lazlo Redthorn swept the unopened letter from the Wizards of the Mound Academy into the trash. For the third time in as many years, they'd written, no doubt urging him to rejoin the on-campus faculty again.

Lazlo had no interest in ever setting foot on the academy grounds again. Too much had happened there. Too many awful memories he could never forget.

He was much happier here, in his own castle. He still tutored students—the Mound sent him the problem kids, any students with disciplinary marks against them, or who didn't fit in with the others. As an accomplished mage, he could have taught on the faculty. He'd wanted to, once.

But those days were behind him now.

Lazlo stepped out of his makeshift office into the studio he used as a classroom. His dark eyes flashed as he studied his current pupils. At the front of the room, his cat Alisa lay on his desk, licking a paw, one lazy eye on the class. Minding them, the way she always did anytime he needed to step out of the room.

Lazlo strode toward the front. As he did, Aire stopped writing and looked up. A half-elf, and more curious than did her any good, Aire had a quick tongue. She was always the first to ask questions—or to answer any he posed. Sure enough, her hand shot into the air now.

Beside her, Jub paused too, eying his desk-mate. Jub was a small-town kid, from a family of farmers. His only mistake at the Mound had been standing up to the wrong student, a bully from an influential family. Lazlo had a soft spot for Jub, although he lagged behind the others sometimes in lessons.

"What is it?" Lazlo asked.

Aire sighed loudly. "I don't understand this lesson. How can anyone possibly know what spell we're going to cast while we're still casting it?"

"Is it a different spell they cast? Maybe something to reveal our intentions?" Jub asked.

Lazlo shook his head. "Not every opponent will be able to see the auras your spells cast. But if you ever face an opponent with Aursight..." Here, Lazlo resisted the urge to shoot a glance at Kazren, tucked away in the corner over her own paper. He had a strong suspicion she possessed it, though he'd yet to officially confirm her ability. "To that opponent, any spells you cast will glow a specific color, depending on the school of magic you're using. Remember the rhyme? *Abjuration is blue, its nature protective of you. Conjuration is orange, creating objects out of...* Well, I couldn't rhyme anything with orange." He paused, while Aire snorted and went back to reading her paper.

Jub scribbled frantic notes. "So we must be aware that our opponents could know which school we're using. But will Aursight tell our opponents the exact spell too?"

Lazlo shook his head again, a faint smile appearing on his face. "That is where you must press your advantage."

Outside, wind picked up to rattle the castle windows. The sun peeked out behind the clouds as well, casting the entire room in a cozy golden hue.

Lazlo's gaze strayed to Kazren once more. The youngest of his three students, she was taciturn, subdued in both appearance and attitude. The morning Lazlo awoke to find a notification from the Wizards of the Mound Academy about her reassignment to Lazlo's castle, he'd been surprised. Kazren had been a darling of the academy, their rising star. What could have happened to make them reject her all of a sudden?

He learned the story in fits and starts—not from Kazren herself, who hated to speak about the academy or admit how badly their rejection hurt her. Instead, Lazlo had been forced to pull strings back at the Mound. Not that he had many left to pull, or much influence with anyone beyond the current headmaster, but still. A few well-placed letters to Headmaster Ebus, his old mentor, had won him an answer.

Kazren's specialty, as a half-elf, was water magic. She'd spent an entire semester building an enclosed fountain that should produce an endless supply of clean water. Her instructor kept insisting it wasn't be possible—magic was finite, and the products of spells could not be expected to last forever. But Kazren was convinced that, given enough amplifying material, she could make the fountain work.

On the day of her final exam, her instructor came to grade the fountain. Kazren hadn't tested it yet, so the instructor was about to fail her. But Kazren turned the fountain on, testing it right then and there.

It worked. Unfortunately, it worked so well that a wave of water inundated the entire room, nearly drowning her instructor in the process.

The instructor lobbied the Mound to expel her. Instead, Headmaster Ebus himself wrote to Lazlo, asking that he take on Kazren's tutelage.

She had proven a very able student. And she'd learned from her mistake with the fountain—she didn't push herself too far on the first try anymore. She grew more cautious about new spell applications, wiser about where she should or shouldn't push the boundaries of magic.

In many ways, Kazren reminded Lazlo of himself, back when he was younger. He, too, had been a self-starter. He'd discovered magic almost by accident, after stumbling across a misplaced spellbook in the library of the law school he'd attended. The few small spells he tried had worked, to his utter shock. He'd taken to practicing magic in his off-hours—during what little downtime law degree students had.

His little hobby might never have come to anything, were it not for the war.

Lazlo shook himself and focused on his classroom once more. He'd assigned them a written exercise this afternoon, since he felt they were falling behind on theory. Now, looking from their long faces to the bright sunshine outside, a prickle of guilt tugged at his conscience. Perhaps he should have given them a more practical lesson today. A sparring match, out in the yard. Or a walk through the nearby forest to practice their herbalism.

Some of Lazlo's methods were less than orthodox. His insistence on teaching his students how to recognize druidic magic as well as the eight official schools, for instance. But he couldn't help it. Firsthand experience had shown him how important it was to keep an open mind. To learn about every type of magic in the world, not just whatever the Mound insisted was important.

3

The thought of druids led him back to more pleasant memories. Short-cropped red hair, forest-dark eyes, and a quicksilver smile. He allowed himself a tiny smile, before he cleared his throat and tapped on his desk.

"How far have we all gotten on this essay?" he asked. Aire beamed. Jub groaned and buried his face in his hands. Kazren only watched him, level-eyed and curious. "Tell you what. If you agree to finish it this evening, and have the completed essay back on my desk first thing tomorrow morning, we can take a break for now. How does that sound?"

He'd barely finished speaking before Aire leapt out of her desk. Jub wasn't far behind, whooping. "Thanks, Master Lazlo," he called, already halfway to the door.

"Thanks Master!" Aire added.

Suppressing a laugh, Lazlo glanced at Kazren. She still hadn't moved from her chair. Instead, her gaze followed Alisa's feline tail as it flicked back and forth, a curious glint in her eye. "What's the matter?" Lazlo asked.

Kazren tucked a long lock of blond hair behind her ear. It was slightly pointed—the only hint at her half-elven origin. Unlike Aire, Kazren took after her human side more. "I just had a bad feeling, that's all," Kazren murmured.

Lazlo frowned. Kazren usually never complained, about anything. In fact, he often tried to get her to be more honest about her feelings, suspecting she repressed things a little too much. "What did it feel like? A premonition?" As far as he knew, Kazren didn't have any particular talent in divination. But she'd surprised him plenty of times already. He wouldn't put it past her to be hiding yet another secret talent among her arsenal.

Kazren exhaled sharply and shook her head. "No, nothing like that. My mother used to call it the tickles. She says it happens when someone walks over the site of your future grave…" Kazren forced a laugh and stood, scooping her school supplies into her saddlebag. "I apologize, Master Lazlo. I'll leave you be now."

He opened his mouth, about to tell her she need not hurry out on his account. Before he could, however, Alisa bumped his knuckles with her forehead. Lazlo glanced down at the cat. One of her liquid gold eyelids winked. So he held his tongue, nodding as Kazren departed for the day.

4

Only after the door swung shut behind her, and they were alone in the room, did Alisa transform.

Her paws bent and stretched, her tail whipping out and elongating. Wings burst from her backside with a cracking sound, unfurling to flutter in the bright light. A blink later, and in place of the cat lounging on his desk, a faerie dragon sprawled in a patch of sun. Purple stripes highlighted her violet wings and body, all the way down to the tip of her forked tail.

The only things that remained the same were her bright golden eyes, and the diamond-studded collar around her throat. A gift from Lazlo, it allowed her to transform at will.

"Well?" Lazlo asked. "Are you going to tell me what's going on with Kazren?"

"Depends." Alisa's eyes narrowed, a faint purr escaping her lips. "Are you going to tell me what has you acting so soft this afternoon? Wandering off mid-lesson on errands, releasing the students early, gazing out the window and sighing... if I didn't know any better, I'd say you were lovesick again."

Lazlo snorted. "I've never been lovesick a day in my life."

"Liar." Alisa's purr grew louder.

He ignored her. "Focus, Alisa. Do I need to be worried about Kazren?"

"No more than you ought to be worried about all of them," Alisa replied. "They're restless. The Mound promised to review their cases annually, to judge whether they're ready to be readmitted or not. The next review is coming up soon."

Lazlo grimaced. He'd almost forgotten. "Has it really been a year since Kazren got here?" She was the most recent arrival, Jub having come two years before her, and Aire the year between.

"Time flies when you're being a recluse." Alisa made a hissing sound—the equivalent of a human clicking their tongue, Lazlo had come to discover.

"I have my reasons," Lazlo snapped.

Alisa's wings quivered in apology. "I know you do. But you can't hide away here forever."

"Says who?" Lazlo arched a brow.

Alisa exhaled a steamy breath. "You do a lot of good here with these kids, I won't deny it. But you could be doing so much more. If

5

you talked to Headmaster Ebus, told him *why* you're so reluctant to go back to the Mound, I'm sure they could accommodate—"

"Ebus knows why I don't go back," Lazlo interjected. "Better than anyone. Besides, there'd be no point. My life is here now. I've dedicated myself to these students, and I will not let them down. I know I made mistakes in the past. Choices I can never take back. But this is one thing I can get right. The Mound abandoned these three, but I will not."

"Surely that could a condition of your return, though. You'll agree to join the faculty if they agree to allow those three back on campus?" Alisa watched him carefully. "They want to go back, Lazlo. I hear them talking when you're out of the room. Their lessons here are important, but they also need community, socializing. They need to be among their peers, and to—"

"Enough. I didn't rescue you so you could lecture me for the rest of my life," he muttered.

Alisa's small body tensed, her back arching. "Stubborn old..." She trailed off into grumbles, but he didn't hear the rest. He was already striding across the classroom, fists clenched.

He was doing the right thing. The Mound wasn't safe. Not for him, and certainly not for students like his.

He'd failed to protect the people he cared about too many times already. He would not make the same mistakes again.

***

Kazren followed Aire and Jub out into the afternoon air. The castle grounds spread at their feet like a welcome mat, an all-too-inviting distraction. As they walked, however, Kazren couldn't help but glance back at the castle itself. The west tower, where they studied, was four stories high. From here, she could barely make out the topmost window, where they'd been studying just now. The sun glinted from the glass panels, making the whole tower seem to blaze with an internal fire.

It set her teeth on edge, that tower. Because it was so beautiful. But regardless of its beauty, it was still a cage.

"Why do you think he let us go early?" Kazren asked. All day, she'd had a strange feeling at the back of her throat. Not a premonition—those did not run in her family, though plenty of other

6

odd abilities did. No, this was something else. Instinct, perhaps. Or what her mother liked to call *a sensitive gut.*

Something was changing. And above all else, Kazren hated change.

Aire and Jub stopped their playful shoving to glance back at her. "What did you say?" Aire called.

Kazren shook her head. "Never mind." She glanced at the others. "Our annual review is coming up soon, isn't it?"

"Is it?" Aire asked, with false nonchalance that nobody bought.

"Do you think your parents are gonna pull strings to get you back on campus?" Jub asked her.

Aire winced. They all knew her parents had been badgering the headmaster to reinstate Aire ever since she left. Or rather, ever since her quick tongue and quicker comebacks earned her more disciplinary marks than the headmaster could overlook, even for a girl from an influential family like hers.

Tall and beautiful, with long dark hair and a regal bearing, Aire carried herself like a noblewoman. Even before hearing her last name, most people guessed at first sight that she was someone to watch.

But of the three of them, Aire loved Lazlo's castle best. Lazlo spoke to her with more respect than most instructors at the Mound. More than that, though, he challenged her. When she talked back to him, he just dished it right back. She respected him, which was more than she could say for most of the crusty old masters at the academy.

Deep down, although she missed the other students and the day-to-day entertainments of campus life, Aire did not want to leave. She knew Lazlo would help her reach her true potential.

"I don't know," Aire murmured. But that was a lie. They all knew. Her parents were already trying their damndest to get her reinstated. "What about you, Jub?"

He snorted. "My parents had never even heard of the Mound until I got the acceptance letter. They wouldn't know who to complain to, much less have the gall to ask a favor of Headmaster Ebus."

"But if you could go back. Would you?" Aire blinked at him.

Jub paused for a moment. He knew the answer Aire wanted. *No, I'd stay here with you.* But he couldn't lie to her face, either. "If they offered? Yes," he said. He was in no position to turn down the status boost that would come with being a graduate of the Wizards of the

Mound Academy—much less the money he could earn in the future as a mage or a professor. Before Aire could protest, he quickly added, "But they're never going to, so don't fret. You're stuck with me."

Kazren watched the other two, gaze hooded.

"What about you, Kazren?" Jub asked, but it sounded to her like an afterthought. She'd long felt that way, ever since her arrival here. Like a third wheel, an outsider. The oddball interjected into Jub and Aire's happy little duo.

Still, she forced a smile, remaining polite. That was always her way. "I would like to go back to campus. Master Lazlo has taught me a lot, and I'm incredibly grateful for that. And grateful to have met you two, of course," she hastily added. "But... I miss the Mound. I miss lecture halls, and debates, and the *libraries*. Master Lazlo has a decent collection, but compared to the books we had access to at the Mound..." She bit her lip, trailing off. Any more of this, and she'd start to tear up.

Getting removed from the academy had been the worst day of her life. She truly was grateful to Lazlo for giving her a second chance, but the idea of spending the rest of her student days here, of never being allowed back into the libraries she'd loved, of never fulfilling her parents' dream for her education...

Kazren couldn't stand the idea of it. She needed to get back there. No matter what it took.

Chapter Two

Guerin Grayrock shook dust from his boots before he stomped up the tower to continue his morning chores. He'd served as Master Lazlo's steward ever since the king granted Master Lazlo this castle and its surrounding territory—as well as the title that came with it.

Master Lazlo had given Guerin a good life, and for a Lord, he was very low-maintenance. He paid Guerin a generous wage.

Shortly after entering Lazlo's service, he'd met a beautiful woman in the local village of Millbreach. Mia came from a family of midwives and healers, and she'd helped heal Guerin from a broken arm he'd sustained working on the keep. Love blossomed and they were inseparable. They married, and Mia was appointed Head Cook.

Lazlo was very low-maintenance for a lord. So, Guerin appreciated his post overall. Sometimes, Guerin did nurse minor resentments. Such as, for example, Master Lazlo's penchant for throwing away unopened mail without even verifying what information it contained or who might have sent it. Half the time, the castle's pending account notices wound up in Master Lazlo's trash bin, and Guerin needed to fish them out just so he could dig into the estate's coffers to pay whatever vendors they owed.

Today, it seemed, would be no exception. The first thing Guerin spotted when he entered Master Lazlo's office that morning was a shiny envelope bearing the Wizards of the Mound Academy crest, dumped right into the trash atop a pile of Alisa's half-eaten dinner from the night before.

Grimacing, Guerin fished it out and toweled off the envelope as best he could. Thankfully, the academy always wrote on thick parchment paper, so the faerie dragon's food hadn't stained the actual letter inside.

Guerin broke the wax seal and wriggled the parchment free. He felt absolutely no shame about this—long experience with Master

Lazlo taught him that it was necessary. If the letter turned out to be private correspondence, such as another missive from Headmaster Ebus begging Lazlo to return to campus, then Guerin would simply toss it away. But if it was something important, such as a letter about another problem student for Lazlo to take on, then his master would be grateful for Guerin's snooping.

Guerin helped himself to Lazlo's chair as he unfolded the letter. A stout, middle-aged man, the chair creaked under his weight. But he barely got past the first line before he leapt to his feet again, crying out in dismay.

I must find Master Lazlo at once.

Guerin hurried to the wall, where a hidden panel opened into a secret passage. Master Lazlo had had them installed when he first arrived at the castle—a leftover tactical mindset from his days as a veteran. Guerin had served too, and approved of the foresight. Only he, Mia, Lazlo and Alisa had access to these passageways, which made it easy for them to traverse the castle unseen by visitors or curious students.

Now, Guerin raced through the passages, ears peeled for the familiar sound of Master Lazlo's lecturing tone. But he didn't hear any voices in the usual classrooms. Nor did he hear anyone eating or chatting in the dining hall.

He kept moving, as fast as he could go these days. The old war wound on his knee sometimes acted up, but adrenaline helped him power through today.

The letter dampened in his fist. Finally, he caught a snatch of conversation. Was that Master Lazlo, or one of the cooks?

He paused, changing directions. The tunnel brought him to a dead end, where a tiny stone plaque marked an exterior wall of the keep. Guerin pressed an ear to the stones.

Yes. Found him.

***

"Again." Lazlo stood with his hands folded behind his back, surveying the training field. He'd done his best to imitate the dueling arena at the Mound when he'd had this constructed, only with one key difference. The stands of his arena sat flush with the dueling field, rather than raised above it on stone walls. He'd cast flexible magical barriers to protect anyone watching from the audience. He found this arrangement more effective at protecting both the viewers and the duelers.

He'd seen several Spellduels at the Mound go wrong when medical teams could not climb down from the viewing platforms quickly enough to assist injured mages.

Today, however, his precautions weren't necessary. Kazren, Aire and Jub took turns practicing simple spells while he watched. When Kazren extended her hands, whispering under her breath, as the air around her turned orange, Lazlo smiled in approval. Her conjuration was improving.

Aire cast a glittering lavender haze that signaled a transmutation spell. Before he could figure out exactly what she was doing, however, a wild-eyed Guerin burst into the arena.

He caught Lazlo's eye, then doubled over, breathing hard. Pressed against his knee was a piece of parchment, wrinkled and sweat-stained from his run.

Worry seized Lazlo at once. He hadn't seen Guerin move this fast since the campaign where they met, almost a decade ago now. "Keep practicing," he called to the students, gesturing them on. Then he jogged toward his steward. He reached for the letter in Guerin's hand, but the older man glanced at the students, then jerked his head to the side.

"Not here," Guerin panted.

Lazlo followed his old friend out of the arena. They could still hear the students' murmurs, as they continued their practice. And Alisa would keep an eye on them, alerting Lazlo if anything happened.

For now, he focused on the missive Guerin offered him. He recognized the letterhead at once—a message from the academy. "For the dozenth time," Lazlo muttered. "I've not interest in—"

"Read it," Guerin interjected.

So he did. And then he read it a second time, the world going fuzzy around the edges as the meaning of the far too formal words failed to sink in.

To the esteemed Master Lazlo Redthorn of Bacre Stronghold,

We regret to inform you that the most recent headmaster of the Wizards of the Mound Academy, Headmaster Ebus Nordau, has passed beyond the veil. We invite all masters, students, and affiliated personnel to attend his funeral. The event will be hosted here at the academy, to take place one week from the postmark of this letter.

This is a sad day for all of Cicpe, but especially for those of us who knew Headmaster Ebus personally. He was a trusted friend and advisor to many, and we mourn his passing, not just for the sake of our friendships, but for the loss of knowledge it means for our world.

Yours respectfully,

Acting Headmaster Muzud Marblebeard

Lazlo sank to his knees in the mud-speckled grass. Dimly, he was aware of Guerin saying something. Offering condolences, perhaps. He couldn't hear him. He couldn't focus on anything but that stilted first sentence. *Headmaster Ebus Nordau has passed beyond the veil...*

No explanation. No statement about what felled him. He couldn't imagine a simple illness ending Ebus' storied career. Yes, his former mentor was old—pushing three hundred—but plenty of mages with less talent had lived far longer natural lives than that. Especially mages at the Mound, which boasted the highest concentration of talented healers in the known world.

Lazlo turned the paper over, as though he might find some better explanation scribbled on the backside. But there was nothing.

He shut his eyes.

Lazlo could not imagine his life without Ebus. Without Ebus, he wouldn't be here today. He may never have even learned any more magic beyond the simple children's spells he'd taught himself. He certainly wouldn't be a master himself, teaching for the academy.

His whole life unspooled before him, the threads suddenly so obvious. He owed everything to Ebus—his position, his magic, his *life*.

He could still remember the first time they met. Ebus wasn't headmaster then—only plain Master Ebus, academy professor, deployed as an adjunct to the king's army in order to help identify potential new mages.

As for himself? At the time, Lazlo had been a nobody. A fresh graduate of law school, sure, to his parents' undying excitement. But he hadn't done anything real, hadn't yet made a name for himself.

Which was why, when Lazlo read the king's proclamation—an open invitation for anyone who believed they had magical talent to apply to join his armed forces for the coming war—he'd leapt at the chance. Deep down, he'd always believed that the random one-off spells he'd taught himself in his off-hours at law school would be useful for something greater. Now, fate had answered his prayers.

Lazlo had been nervous, riding into Plephia for the recruitment event. He'd taken a big gamble on this. His fellow graduates were busy applying for positions in merchant guilds or on town councils. His parents had expected him to come home after graduation, maybe apply for a position with the legal branch of the guild in their town. His father sat on the guild board, as one of the most successful textile merchants in the area. Lazlo's older brother had joined the guild too, though only as a member, since he'd insisted on starting his own tavern. Said he found the work more interesting than textiles, though secretly, Lazlo thought he just didn't want to wilt in their father's shadow.

But Lazlo wrote his apologies to the whole family and rode west instead. A greater destiny called.

The recruitment event was both larger and less spectacular than he'd expected. Rows upon rows of scruffy, dusty travelers lined up outside the testing tents, scraps of paper with their recruitment numbers in hand. One by one, they were called inside.

Lazlo could tell by their expressions who got favorable news, and whose dreams of becoming a king's mage had been dashed before they'd even begun.

His pulse ratcheted higher as his number neared. He recited every spell he'd ever read. When he first decided to volunteer, it had seemed to him like he already knew so many. Now, he found himself doubting. He'd only managed to find instructions on a couple dozen spells, of which he'd mastered perhaps fifteen. *They're going to laugh me out of this tent.*

He'd nearly convinced himself to give up, make a tactical retreat, when an assistant called Lazlo's number.

He stepped forward, ducking under the tent flap with his heart in his throat. Inside, the tent was dim and sparsely furnished: just a single broad table, with one man seated at the head. He beckoned Lazlo with a friendly smile. "Don't be nervous, son. There's no way to fail this test. We're just going to determine where you belong, that's all."

In the dim light of the tent, all Lazlo could make out of the man's features were his thick crop of gray hair, his matching beard, and his broad smile. He seemed more like someone's friendly grandfather than a powerful mage.

The man skimmed a document in front of him. "It says here on your application that you're self-taught. Is that right?"

Lazlo struggled to find his tongue. "I-I find a few spellbooks. In my school's library. The few spells I tried worked, but—"

"Well, now." The man's smile widened further. "That's very impressive. I couldn't do a damned thing on my own; didn't even realize I had potential until the Mound tested me." He leaned back in his chair, eyes sparkling in the lamplight. "Let's see what you can do, then."

Every spell Lazlo had memorized evaporated from his mind in that moment. He took a deep breath, trying to calm his panic. *Think.* He'd planned to try something big, showy, impressive. But right now, the only spell that came to mind was the very first one he'd ever attempted. A simple little spell to cast a light.

Lazlo held out both hands, one palm cupped over the other, and murmured the incantation. An orb appeared between his palms, tiny at first. The more confident he grew, however, the wider and brighter it shone. The center of the orb, like always, glowed a bright, steady white. Outside of it, though, encircling it like a halo, was an orange glow.

With this added light, Lazlo could see the mage's face better. Wrinkles creased his forehead, and laugh-lines encircled his mouth. But it was his eyes Lazlo noticed most of all: bright, sparkling blue. They lit up now, his smile pleased.

"Impressive. Very impressive. You have some talent in conjuration, I see."

Lazlo's light faded as confusion set in. "Conjuration?"

"It's one of the eight schools of magic. You won't have learned those, of course. Unless the books you found were academic textbooks someone smuggled out." The man laughed and turned a hand palm-up. An orange glow appeared around his palm, just like it had around Lazlo's orb. Only, rather than a light, a rose exploded upward from his hand. The man snatched it from the air and laid it on the table. As he did, the orange glow around it slowly faded, until Lazlo would never have known it from an ordinary rose. "Conjuration allows you to conjure real, physical objects—or

14

lights." He shot Lazlo a wink. "It can also help in transporting objects from one place to another."

"Why the orange?" Lazlo asked without thinking.

The man's eyebrows rose. "What do you mean?" He sounded deeply surprised.

Lazlo's face burned. Had he asked something impolite? "I just meant, when I cast the orb, there was an orange glow around it. Same with when you made that rose appear."

The man fell silent for a long, fretful moment. Lazlo regretted speaking. He wished he could snatch his question back and stomp on it. Anything to go back to the easy, comfortable attitude the man had had a moment ago.

Then the man stood, slowly, his blue eyes fixed on Lazlo. "Tell me, son. What do you see when I do this?" He held up both palms and whispered something.

A faint yellow glow lit his hands. Before long, it filled the air between them, pretty as sunlight. But Lazlo couldn't figure out what the man was doing. He saw no other evidence of a spell. "Um... I see a yellow light?" Lazlo replied.

The man exhaled sharply and closed his fists. The yellow glow vanished. In the sudden dark, the man began to laugh.

"I'm sorry. Did I do something wrong?" Lazlo asked, nervous. In his experience, anytime a teacher laughed during an exam, you'd just made a terrible error in judgment—completely misreading a legal text, for example.

But the man across from him sobered, the smile still playing around his mouth. "No, no. Quite the contrary. You've got an exceptionally unusual eye." He stepped forward, drawing close enough to clap a hand on Lazlo's shoulder. "I believe you'll do great things for king and country. Assuming you still want to enlist, of course."

Lazlo's eyes widened, shock and happiness pouring through him in equal measure. "I got the position?"

"Oh, more than just that." The man's hand fell from his shoulder, only to extend in an offer of a handshake. "I'm Master Ebus. Ebus Nordau. I'm an instructor at the Wizards of the Mound Academy."

Lazlo's pulse skipped a beat. He'd heard of the academy, of course. Everyone who was anyone had heard of the Mound. Greater than the Scientia Arcana Academy, older and wiser than the

15

Gagiams Academy of Wizardry, the Mound was the best of the best. The school only the most promising, powerful mages were invited to attend. "Pleasure to meet you, Master Ebus. I'm Lazlo."

Ebus grinned. "Lazlo. Once you're done soldiering in this war, write to me, will you? There will be a place waiting for you at our institution, whenever you're ready to accept it."

Chapter Three

For the dozenth time since he'd received it, Lazlo reread the missive from the Mound. Was it his imagination, or did it sound even more formal than their letters usually did?

Perhaps that was just Muzud's writing style. Very different to Ebus' informal notes.

Still, something about the letter rankled at him. He gazed around his study. His eyes lingered on mementos from his old life—trophies he'd won, awards Ebus had given him. Lazlo stopped when he came to a small portrait on the far wall, an image of him and Ebus together. Ebus' other protégé had cast it for them, an illusion spell that preserved them both in three dimensions, beaming, their arms around one another.

Looking at it now, Lazlo felt a pang.

Pierce. Once, Pierce had been a brother to him, another son to Ebus. Now…

He forced thoughts of him away. He had enough to mourn today, without dwelling on a criminal rotting away in a cell for his crimes. *A cell I put him in.* Lazlo tore his gaze from the illusion and concentrated on the letter once more.

It said nothing about the cause of death. Surely, if anyone on the Mound's council suspected foul play, they would have mentioned it here. That, or someone would have written separately to notify Lazlo. But he hadn't received any other missives from the Mound. Not even condolences from other masters, all of whom must know what Ebus meant to Lazlo.

He scowled.

It must have been natural causes. That, or an accident.

Either way, he'd need to attend the funeral. It was the least he could do for his mentor, after everything Ebus had done for him. Exhaling sharply, he took out a fresh pad of paper and began to write instructions for Guerin.

Hopefully he'd only need to go for a week at most. Guerin had substituted before, anytime Lazlo was ill or needed to leave for a few days. He knew how to instruct the students. Still, the timing couldn't be worse, with all three of their disciplinary reviews at the Mound coming up soon.

He poured over the instructions, making sure to leave plenty of material for them to study and recommendations for which topics they should focus on.

He was still working when Alisa crept into his office, moving as silently as possible in her cat form.

"Yes?" he asked, because even with her nails clipped and her steps near-silent, he could always sense her presence.

Alisa let out a little mewl of protest, then transformed into her natural faerie form. Her forked tail curled around her lavender torso. "You're no fun."

"Not right now, no," he agreed.

Her expression fell. "I'm sorry, my friend."

Lazlo's pen slipped from his fingers. He let it fall, splattering ink across an entire line of the notes he just made. He hung his head, gripping it with both hands. "He's gone, Alisa. He's really gone." A tear trickled down his face, startling him. He wiped it away quickly, almost angrily.

Before he could disguise it, Alisa slipped into his lap, purring loudly. He hesitated for a moment, then reached down to pet the small dragon. "I don't like the idea of you going back there," Alisa murmured, after a while.

"I don't like it either, but I have to," he said, voice harder than necessary. He took a deep breath, gentling his tone. "I need closure. I need to say goodbye."

Alisa cracked one golden eye to study him. "You need answers, more like."

He sighed. "That too."

"Sometimes mortals just die," Alisa said. "Even powerful ones like Master Ebus."

"I know. But..." Lazlo's gaze drifted to the letter from Acting Headmaster Muzud again. "Something's off. I can feel it."

"All the more reason not to put yourself in harm's way." Alisa let out a tiny spurt of steam in frustration. When he didn't respond, she flicked her tail. "At least let me come with you. Provide backup. If anything happens, like it did last time—"

"That will never happen again," Lazlo interjected firmly. "I made certain of it." *By locking up one of my oldest friends.* He pushed the thought aside again.

"Sounds familiar. Someone's always convinced he doesn't need backup. Just like when we first met..." Alisa gave him an arch look.

Lazlo laughed. "I didn't need it. I defeated that dragon all by myself."

Now, Alisa let out a huffy breath of fumes. "Oh, so my distraction didn't help you at all?"

He'd first met Alisa in the cave of Rimrig the Fierce, an enormous dragon terrorizing a huge swath of King Owain's land. Defeating Rimrig had been Lazlo's greatest accomplishment—a moment that changed the trajectory of his entire life. Alisa's too, since she'd been held captive by the dragon.

He wouldn't call her attempt at distracting the larger dragon *helpful*, though.

"You nearly cost me the fight," Lazlo muttered. But at another sharp look from Alisa, he ruffled her ears. "Thank you for trying to assist me. But now, just like back then, I'll be better off facing this alone. Besides, I need you and Guerin here, minding the castle and the students."

"Speaking of the students." Alisa squinted at him. "Do you plan to share this news with them?"

"None of them knew Headmaster Ebus personally. Though I'm sure news will reach the general public soon enough."

"I don't mean the news. I mean your loss. Your connection to Ebus." Alisa tutted. "You always keep things so close to your chest."

"Why bother? It won't change anything." Lazlo pushed out of his seat, disrupting Alisa's perch. She flapped to the ground, only to weave indignantly around his feet as he crossed the small study to a side door, one he usually kept locked.

He needed to start packing.

"It might help you to open up. Talk about him." When he didn't response, Alisa flew over to block his path. "The academy is full of bad memories for you. I know that. But how long will you keep holding onto your pain? It can't heal if you don't expose it to fresh air."

"My business is my business. No one else's. You of all people should know that."

"Not a people," Alisa reminded him, laughing.

But when he gestured, she obediently flew out of the way. He touched the doorknob. It opened at once, recognizing his energy. Inside was a small armory: circular, with a table in the center and weapons lining the walls. It almost resembled a shrine—he certainly tended to it the way some priests tended their temples.

Lazlo strode past the table and the covered sphere perched atop it. Instead, he walked to the west side of the room, where a large iron and wood chest stood, etched with elaborate carvings and inscriptions. Lazlo gestured and whispered something under his breath. The chest popped open.

The mage contemplated the chest for a moment, fists clenched.

His mentor's old advice played in his mind. *You can be mad at a situation or a person. But in the end, you have to let go or you'll never find peace.*

Slowly, Lazlo's rigid stance relaxed. He exhaled and bowed his head. "I'm sorry, Alisa. I didn't mean to be so curt with you."

"You're hurting. Just remember: we all want to help. We care about you." She paused. "That's why I worry about you going to the academy alone. You've got so many ghosts there, and there's no way you'll confide in anyone back at the school."

Lazlo wanted to argue, but Alisa knew him better than that. Besides, who was he even still close with back at the Mound? Bishop flitted through his mind, but Lazlo shook his head. Even if they were still friends, he'd never burden Bishop with his problems. They were his to handle.

"If you want me here for the students," Alisa said slowly. "You could take Kazren."

Lazlo's head jerked up.

Before he could protest, Alisa carried on. "She's ready for testing. You know that. If she were back at the Mound instead of here, she'd already have qualified to enter the Spellduel arena. She's learning a lot from you, I can't deny that, but she needs to be pushed. She needs to learn to fight more opponents than just Aire, Jub, or you."

"Her case will be reviewed soon. The school will let her know if they're ready to invite her back. In the meantime—"

"In the meantime, she's nursing resentment at everyone who keeps her here. Yourself included. If you bring her with you, she can prove herself to the other instructors *before* they pass judgment on her. You could sponsor her in the arena. One Spellduel and they'd be forced to readmit her."

"I didn't invite you along because I don't want to burden you with my woes," Lazlo said. "What makes you think it would be appropriate for me to thrust them onto one of my *students* instead?"

"You needn't bring her to the funeral itself. Though, she might be useful. Especially if you suspect foul play. Second pair of eyes, second pair of spell-hands…"

"So, in addition to potentially re-traumatizing her at the Mound, you also want me to put her in harm's way?"

"She's of age," Alisa replied calmly. "Shouldn't the choice be hers? She can decide for herself whether she wants to risk it or not."

Lazlo groaned. He'd planned on a quick journey. In and out. Attend the funeral, allay his suspicions, make sure Ebus was laid to rest well. Then be back here in time for his students' next exam.

Bringing Kazren would complicate things. Especially if his instincts proved correct, and there was something foul afoot at the Wizards of the Mound Academy. *Again.*

"Regardless, you're going to have to tell them all where you're going. Think about it." Alisa nudged him, then padded across the room to circle the weaponry wall. "And bring the stave, won't you? I'll worry at least a little bit less."

Lazlo obediently plucked his stave from the wall of weapons, setting it next to his trunk. He also scooped up a ring of protection he'd once earned from King Owain himself, for services rendered. He added that to his chest, then began piling robes inside—dark crimson, his official robes as an instructor of the Mound. He didn't bother to wear them out here—one of the benefits of being a semi-recluse. He didn't need to stand on formality.

But he'd be expected to put on his best face now. He could already envision the curious stares, the whispered comments. He hadn't set foot on campus in years for a reason. Just the thought of the gossip he'd stir made him want to lock himself in his tower for another decade.

Alas, he thought, as he added writing materials, spellbooks, and a small medical bag to his trunk. *Some duties cannot be avoided.*

Chapter Four

He finished packing and ate the dinner Mia insisted on interrupting him to deliver *"You must remember to eat while you're at that dreadful place. Three solid meals. I don't want you losing a single pound while you're away, hear me?"* Then Lazlo took a seat at table in the center of his armory.

Slowly, he withdrew the black cloth from the center of the table. As the cloth slid away, it revealed a perfectly spherical, clear crystal ball.

The moment Lazlo touched it, the ball lit up. Blue swirling light gathered in its depths, like the sky seen through a haze of cloud.

Divination had never been Lazlo's forte, but practice had much improved his abilities. When he'd first joined the king's army, ignorant of most spells except the scant few he'd taught himself, he'd been assigned to the position of scout.

At first, he'd resented it. He got left behind on most important missions, tasked with divining the right path for the king's warriors and other mages to fight the real battles.

But that was before the king asked him to scry for old Rimrig the Fierce's lair, and Lazlo's knack for divination saved dozens of knights from riding straight into a dragon's clutches. It had also shown Lazlo the exact route he needed to take through Rimrig's unguarded back caverns to defeat the dragon himself, thus proving himself to the king.

Call it paranoia or simply old habit, but since facing that dragon, Lazlo never went anywhere without scrying the terrain first.

Ebus had approved of this practice, drilling it into him further once Lazlo left the king's army and joined the academy. He'd even gone so far as to teach Pierce the method too. He said Lazlo's experience in the war was a good reminder that mages ought to think just as tactically as soldiers.

Of course, Lazlo could not scry directly onto campus. The Wizards of the Mound had cast a spell years ago to remove their academy from the prying eyes of any enemy mages. The screen completely blocked the school from view, so nobody—neither friend nor foe—could see the campus from a distance.

But the screen only extended as far as the outermost dormitories. Beyond that was fair game. Lazlo could examine the roads in and out of the academy, as well as the surrounding forests.

What he was looking for, exactly, he didn't know. Just that he'd recognize anything suspicious when he saw it.

If there's anything to see. If I'm not just letting old wounds torment me. Lazlo closed his eyes, struggling to clear his mind of all other thoughts. He moved his hands in an intricate pattern above the sphere. When he opened his eyes once more, his irises and pupils vanished. His entire eye turned white, as the landscape outside the academy filled his vision.

He watched brooks babble and grassy fields ripple in the breeze. At the heart of his field of vision, a vast blank space gaped. But that was to be expected.

Lazlo carefully moved around the empty area, checking every footpath and major road up to campus. He couldn't see anything. Not even a few students sneaking out to play hooky in the nearby town.

Sighing, he leaned back in his chair and let the scrying drop.

Alisa glanced up at him from where she'd been cleaning her claws in the corner. "See anything?"

"Nothing of note." He pushed himself out of the chair. As he did, he nudged Alisa's bowl, which Mia had filled with the usual choice cuts of meat for the day. "Eat your dinner. I'm going to go check on everybody else."

"Check on them or invite them along?" Alisa arched a brow.

"I think you've given me enough bad ideas for the day, don't you?" He smirked, and Alisa chuckled before she dug into her dinner.

But her words stuck with him all the way down the long, winding staircase to the dining room where Guerin, Mia, and the students normally ate. Much as he hated to admit it, it *would* be a good opportunity for Kazren to demonstrate how much progress she'd made to the other instructors. He knew how deeply his newest student longed to return to campus, and to reclaim her reputation as the most promising mage in her year.

Kazren was brilliant. Not just at magic or spells, but in general. Any textbook he gave her, whether it be spell theory or a treatise on military movements, she devoured in days. Her mind was like a steel trap—no detail, however tiny, evaded her.

She might be useful when it comes to investigating Ebus' death too…

Lazlo hated himself for even considering this. But Alisa was right— Kazren was of age. By the time Lazlo was her age, he'd been volunteering for the king's army, ready to die for his country.

At the entrance to the dining room, Lazlo paused. From here, he could just see into the room where the others were gathered. Aire and Jub were helping Mia stack dishes to bring into the kitchen, while Guerin and Kazren wiped down the table and bundled up the used tablecloths.

His chest tightened at the sight of them all. They'd become a sort of family to him, over the past few years. He hoped they viewed him the same way.

Glancing from Aire to Jub, and finally to Kazren, Lazlo couldn't help but think of Ebus. Would he have been proud to see the way Lazlo carried on his teachings?

Or would he be more like Alisa, disapproving of how much Lazlo hid from his students?

What secrets did you keep from me, Master? Lazlo thought. *Anything that might have put you in danger?*

Kazren looked up, then, her eyes going straight to Lazlo's. He smiled and raised a hand in greeting, stepping into the room. "How was your meal? Sorry to miss it."

"That's all right," said Guerin gruffly. "You had important business to attend. I told 'em as much." There was a note of apology in Guerin's tone, but Lazlo didn't blame him. The students would've asked questions, especially when Lazlo didn't show up for the usual pre-dinner review of the day's work. He had to tell them something.

"I've got to get these washed," Mia said, her arms filled with plates as she headed for the kitchen. "But we'll see you tomorrow for breakfast?"

He heard the unspoken command. *Don't you dare leave without saying goodbye.* He forced a smile. "I'll be there."

Jub and Aire followed Mia into the kitchen, and Guerin took the soiled linens from Kazren to bring to the laundry room. Before long, Kazren and Lazlo were alone in the cavernous dining hall. She glanced at him, uncertain. Then her gaze drifted to the back door.

He knew she often went outside to stargaze at night. She said reading the constellations helped clear her mind and relax her.

"It's a clear night," Lazlo said softly. "Would you mind if I joined you outside?"

Startled, Kazren hesitated for a split second. "No, of course not."

24

They left through the side door together, neither speaking until they'd crossed the dark grass to a circular stone bench near the west tower. Kazren waited for Lazlo to sit, and then perched on the opposite side of the bench, head tilted back to study the sky.

A few patches of wispy clouds marred the black, but otherwise, they had a clear view. Lazlo gazed at a nebula for a long moment, before he cleared his throat. "You might be wondering why I was away all day today. I received some sad news from the academy."

Kazren didn't reply, except for a slight intake of breath.

"My old mentor passed away," Lazlo said quietly. "I need to return to the academy for his funeral."

"Oh." Kazren's shoulders sank a fraction. "I'm so sorry for your loss." A frown line creased her brow. "Wait. Wasn't Headmaster Ebus your mentor?"

Lazlo nodded, and Kazren's eyes widened.

"What happened? How did he…" She caught herself, seeming to realize how insensitive the question was.

But Lazlo shook his head. "I asked myself the same thing. They haven't told me much. It could be nothing—natural causes or an accident." He fell silent.

Kazren let that silence hang for a moment. "But you don't think so?" she finally wagered.

Not that Lazlo picked favorites. But there was a reason he enjoyed his lessons with Kazren best. "I hope there's nothing more to his death. I fear there may be."

Kazren studied him sidelong. "Why are you telling me?"

She was so quick. Too quick, at times. He took a deep breath and squared his shoulders. This might be a terrible idea. But Alisa, damn her, knew exactly how to drill notions into his head. "I was wondering if perhaps… you might want to accompany me."

Kazren's eyes widened. "Yes!" She bit her lip, trying and failing to hide her rush of excitement. "Please. I mean, I would love to be of assistance, in whatever way you—"

"It could be dangerous," he interjected. "Consider that first. If my suspicions prove correct; if something, shall we say, less than natural happened to Ebus…"

Kazren lifted her chin. To her credit, she took his advice to heart. She thought for a long moment before she nodded again, firmly this

25

time. "I'm honored that you would invite me. Yes, I would still like to go, despite the risks."

He allowed himself a small smile. "Good. I'm glad to hear it. While we're there, perhaps we can enroll you in a Spellduel or two."

Her lips parted in surprise. "You mean it?"

"You're more than ready. But I think you know that." He grinned, and she returned it eagerly. "Who knows? Perhaps this visit will even be the nudge the council needs to approve your return to campus. Though we'd all miss you here, I know you want to go back as soon as you can."

Kazren practically vibrated with excitement at the thought, though she was clearly trying not to let it show. He almost laughed. He couldn't remember the last time he'd seen her this thrilled—even if the thought of losing his prized pupil pained him. "Thank you, Master Lazlo," Kazren whispered. "I promise, I won't let you down."

His smile softened. "I know. Now, pack your things. We leave tomorrow after breakfast."

Nodding, Kazren practically bolted up off the bench. Lazlo moved at a more leisurely pace. But by the time Kazren reached the door to the keep and turned back, ready to hold it for her master, he was already gone. Still, that hardly surprised her. Her master moved through his domain like a ghost sometimes.

Chapter Five

The next morning, Lazlo found Mia's mother and sister in the kitchen alongside Guerin and Mia. Her mother, Elena, grinned at Lazlo as he entered. "Don't mind us." She patted Mia's shoulder. "Just here to help these two with the keep while you're away. And to get ready for the baby, of course."

"I'm still months from my due date," Mia complained, although she smiled as she said it, touching her mother's hand briefly before she finished scooping the last egg onto the students' plates. "Kazren requested breakfast in her rooms earlier... Oh, Guerin, could you take these in to Jub and Aire?" She held out two plates, but Lazlo got there first.

"I'll do it. I need to speak to them anyway." He carried both steaming platters into the adjoining dining room. Mia had outdone herself this morning—eggs and bacon as per usual, but also fresh berries and orange slices, a dollop of her famous homemade yogurt, and a fresh baked roll right out of the oven, with a pat of butter from Guerin's dairy cows beside it.

He found both of his other students in the dining room already. Aire was reading a novel while Jub seemed deep in one of his mysterious projects—which more often than not ended in spell-related disasters Lazlo needed to clean up. Kazren hadn't come down yet. He wondered if she was still packing for the trip. Hopefully she hadn't changed her mind?

Lazlo passed Jub and Aire each a plate, smirking as Jub practically flung himself on the food. "I've got something I need to talk to you both about," he said, taking a seat across the table. "I need to return to the Mound for a little while."

That got their attention. Aire froze with her fork in midair and gaped at him.

Jub did a double-take. "Why? I thought you hated—I mean, I thought you didn't like... going there." His ears turned bright red.

27

Lazlo just chuckled. "I don't, that's true. Unfortunately, I received some difficult news. Headmaster Ebus passed away."

"Oh no." Aire's eyes widened. "Wasn't he your mentor? I'm so sorry."

"Shit," said Jub, before clapping a hand over his mouth.

Lazlo decided to let that one slide. "I need you both to stick to your lessons while I'm gone. Guerin and Mia will look after you. If you need anything, or run into any trouble, just tell Alisa. She'll know what to do."

If Jub or Aire thought it strange that Lazlo trusted his cat to report to him, neither of them let it show. They were used to Alisa babysitting them anytime Lazlo and Guerin were both occupied elsewhere. Only Guerin and Lazlo had seen Alisa's true form, but the others had guessed by now that she was no ordinary feline.

Footsteps caught his attention. Lazlo glanced up just as Kazren sidestepped into the room. She flashed him a small, somewhat anxious-looking smile.

"Kazren is going to be coming with me," he added.

Aire's eyebrows rose. "Oh."

"Congrats, Kazren." Jub grinned at her. "I know how much you've been wanting to go back."

Lazlo glanced at Aire. "I'd take all three of you if I could, but it would make the travel more difficult. Not to mention, I need someone to hold down the fort here."

Her shoulders relaxed. "Of course. We'll take care of everything here, Master Lazlo."

He knew Aire didn't really want to return to the Mound, but she also hated to be excluded from anything. Jub, on the other hand, looked eager for the prospect of a week or two without his master's supervision. He left them whispering over their breakfast as he rose from the table, approaching Kazren. "Do you have a minute?"

She nodded. "But I still have a little bit of packing left."

"That's alright. There's something I want to do before we leave." He held out a hand. Kazren took it, and with a quick somatic gesture from Lazlo, the two of them vanished.

They reappeared a couple hundred yards from the keep, on the grasslands that overlooked Bacre Stronghold. From here, they had a clear view of the property—a long slope down into the bowl where the castle sat. The forest stood at its back, and a small brook meandered around its feet, a sort of natural moat.

Lazlo turned away from the view. "Kazren, listen to me carefully. When I say go, I want you to attack me with a spell—any spell, it's your choice. Once I tap your shoulder, you can stop, the test will be over. All right?"

Kazren nodded, an excited smile stealing over her face.

They'd practiced Spelldueling before, of course. But usually in a group lesson, with Aire or Jub facing Kazren instead of him. Jub was an eager fighter, but he telegraphed his every move too easily—even someone without Aursight could guess which hand or what type of spell he was aiming. Aire was smart, defensive, but less aggressive. She almost never attacked, only defended.

Of the three, Kazren showed the most promise in the arena.

Now, though, he wanted to see what Kazren was truly capable of. How far she could push herself with the right motivation. And since she rarely got a chance to duel with Lazlo, he figured this might goad her on.

Lazlo took five careful steps backward, until they stood as far apart as they would have in a regulation arena. An arena like the one at the Mound, where he hoped Kazren might soon be able to compete.

"Ready?" He didn't wait for Kazren to nod again. "Go!"

Kazren raised both hands, fingers spread. Her lips barely moved—she was getting better at disguising the spoken portions of her spells. But the moment her fingertips lit up orange, he knew exactly what she was about to cast.

Spider's web. Lazlo waited until she extended her arms, then lazily sidestepped the web that burst from her fingertips. The spell moved so fast that it blurred the air between them. This gave Lazlo the perfect opening. He launched a counter-strike, dark cyan pooling from his fingertips into the ground. A multi-headed hydra burst from the manicured lawn.

But Kazren didn't even glance at the beast. Her gaze followed the trail of cyan-colored magic past its body, straight to Lazlo. He only had a split second's warning before she fired off another spell— lavender, transmutation. He ducked under the beam of her spell just in time, though he felt it graze the top of his skull. His hair began to grow long and wild, so sudden and thick that it obscured his vision.

Lazlo cast a quick shield spell, and felt another of Kazren's retaliatory blows glance off it harmlessly. Behind the shield, he quickly reversed the effects of her transmutation spell—what did she cast, anyway? Exponential growth? Expansion? He made a mental note to ask her after this.

Kazren launched another spell at him, but Lazlo didn't wait to see how this one would manifest. He stared hard over her shoulder, vanishing before the energy of her spell reached him. In a blink, he reappeared at her shoulder. He reached out to lightly tap her spine, and Kazren let her hands drop.

They were both breathing hard—Lazlo harder than he anticipated, to be honest. Was he getting old? No, surely not. Kazren was just better practiced.

He'd have to start joining in with the students' sparring lessons more often, if he wanted to keep his game at its peak. "That was excellent, Kazren," he said.

"Thanks." She ducked her head, as though shy. But a huge smile spread across her face, and when she raised her head again, her eyes sparked with adrenaline.

"One question. When I cast that illusion spell, how did you find me so quickly?"

Kazren cocked her head, as if she didn't understand the question. "I followed the magic. It was pretty obvious—this dark blue spill of energy pouring out of you. Anyone would have seen you."

One corner of his mouth quirked. *I knew it.* "Not anyone, actually. You've studied Aursight, correct?"

"You mean, the ability you wrote your spellbook on?"

Lazlo paused. He didn't think he'd ever mentioned that to the students... had he? Then again, Kazren had been here a year already, and the others for longer. He might have let a comment slip at some point over dinner, without even realizing it. "Yes. Though, I never published it."

"Why not?" Kazren eyed him curiously. "Is that why you're not allowed to teach on the regular faculty at the academy, because you didn't publish the book? All instructors need to contribute to the general body of magical knowledge before they can teach for the academy, isn't that right?"

"Usually, yes." He'd been granted an exception—or rather, given a position that suited both his existing experience and filled a hole in the faculty. But he'd given it up, and any dreams of teaching, after everything that happened.

"Then why—"

"We're getting off-topic. The reason I wrote about Aursight in my spellbook is because my mentor was one of the only mages in the world to possess that ability. The other apprentice he took on before me had it as well, and... so do I."

Kazren's eyes widened. "You have Aursight?"

"And I believe you do too, Kazren."

Now her jaw actually dropped. "What do you mean?"

"Most mages cannot see magic. Not the way you do. The colors you described seeing when I cast that illusion are actually an aura around the spell itself. Watch." He held out his hand, palm-up, and wriggled all of his fingers. A moment later, his fingertips began to fade from view. But in their place, a faint lavender glow traced the outline of his hand. "Tell me what you see."

"Purple," Kazren said. "Light purple, where your fingers are. Or, were?"

"That's because I used a transmutation spell to turn them invisible. But your Aursight shows you the outline of the spell I'm doing as I'm performing it. Once the spell has finished, however... watch." A moment later, the lavender glow faded. Now, Lazlo's hand appeared fully invisible. He waved it back and forth experimentally, though neither of them could see him doing it.

"So I can see spells while they're being cast?" Kazren asked.

Lazlo nodded. "The different colors determine the different schools. Remember the rhyme?"

"Abjuration is blue, its nature protective of you. Yellow is for divination, about the future this will bring you information. Fuchsia for enchantment, to give others commandments—"

"Very good," he cut her off, before she could go through all eight. "And transmutation is lavender, which resets all parameters."

Her lips parted. "I thought that was just a metaphor."

"To most students, it is." He smiled. "You've got a unique gift, Kazren. I can help you hone it. Teach you when to rely on it. It's especially helpful during Spellduels, since most people are casting active spells the entire battle."

"Wow." Her grin stretched nearly ear-to-ear now. "So you really think I can take on a regular academy student?"

31

"More than just the regular students. I'm sure you're already one of the better duelers on campus, even without this advantage." He winked. "But you still have a lot of work ahead of you."

She nodded eagerly. "I understand. I'm ready to work, Master Lazlo. Whatever it takes to get back to the Mound." She paused, then, and bit her lip. "Not that I don't appreciate your tutoring here, of course. I've learned so much from you—I still hope to."

"It's okay." He smiled. "I know how you feel." Once upon a time, he had dreamt of making a home at the Mound too. He'd *made* said home, in fact.

Then it had been ripped out from under him.

"Here." Lazlo extended a hand. Kazren took it, and he repeated the usual teleportation gesture. Carrying two people was tricky, but over short distances and to places with which he was familiar, it didn't require too much effort. A wink later, Kazren and Lazlo stood in his laboratory. Lazlo blinked a few times, his eyes adjusting to the much dimmer light. Once they did, he released Kazren's hand and stepped over to his bookshelf.

He pulled out a slim leather-bound manual. "Be careful with this," he said. "It's one of only two copies I've made so far." He held out the book. *Aursight and its applications,* read the cover.

Kazren inhaled sharply. "This is your spellbook?"

"The unpublished edition. I'm saving the other copy to submit to the council... someday." *If I ever change my mind.* Part of him felt bad hoarding the knowledge and insights he'd collected to himself. Especially now, with Ebus gone. Lazlo was the only remaining expert in Aursight—at least, if you weren't counting prison populations.

Knowledge is meant to be shared. That was Ebus' philosophy. Lazlo still couldn't bring himself to hand the spellbook to the Wizards of the Mound Academy, though. It felt too much like admitting defeat. Such an action could upset the fragile balance that kept him here, on his own castle, teaching on his own terms.

This, though, sharing with his mentee... This felt right.

Kazren took the book, hugging it to her chest. "I'll read it the whole trip to the academy," she gushed.

Lazlo chuckled, both at her eagerness and at her assumption. "What makes you think we're taking the long way?"

***

Kazren could barely put Lazlo's book down for long enough to finish packing her trunk. She'd toss a shirt in, then sit to skim a page before she reached for another item of clothing.

A soft knock finally drew her from her reverie. She gestured, a wave of magic opening her door—Jub had taught her that trick her first week here.

Aire leaned against the doorframe, smiling. "I brought you snacks for the trip." She held out a brown paper bag, tied with blue ribbon. The smell wafting from the bag could only be Mia's famous ginger cookies.

Kazren's mouth watered. "Thank you." She accepted it with a faint smile. She and Aire got along well enough, but there had always been an undercurrent of tension in their interactions. Kazren could never quite put her finger on why. She hoped Aire didn't view Kazren as her competition for Jub, because nothing could be further from the truth.

"Are you excited?" Aire asked. Her eyes danced around Kazren's room, landing on the open trunk. "What did Master say? Are you going to be getting special training?"

There it is. Kazren knew the last place Aire wanted to go was the academy. But it must be eating her alive to think that she'd miss out on a learning opportunity. "Maybe." Kazren shrugged one shoulder. "Master seems more interested in my Spelldueling capabilities."

"Ugh." Aire wrinkled her nose and stepped into the room. She perched on the corner of Kazren's bed, taking in the space. Her eyes lingered on the leather-bound book in Kazren's hands. "I've never understood the point of that. Except for mages who enlist in His Majesty's army, of course. They need to learn to fight. But why should regular scholars duel? It seems so… *messy.*"

Kazren snapped Lazlo's book shut and stuffed it into the trunk. "I suppose the instructors believe it hones our skills. You need to think on your feet, cast quickly, make split-second decisions…"

"But magic shouldn't be split-second," Aire protested. "It's a dangerous business. We should deliberate any spell we cast carefully, and have proper plans in place in case it fails."

Kazren laughed. "Ideally, sure. But life isn't always careful or planned."

Aire exhaled through her nose. "Well, it *ought* to be." They both paused at the sound of distant laughter. Probably Jub downstairs with Mia and her family. When Aire spoke again, her voice was softer. More subdued. "Is Master okay? He seems even more reclusive than usual since he found out about the headmaster."

Kazren shrugged one shoulder. "He's upset, of course. Who wouldn't be? Ebus was like our Lazlo."

Aire bit her lip. "Exactly. I'd be a mess. But he's walking around planning our lessons and packing for this trip like nothing happened."

"You know how Master is. He doesn't let things show on the surface. Doesn't mean he doesn't feel them, though."

"Take care of him, will you?" Aire looked so sincere that Kazren couldn't help but smile.

"Of course I will." She arched an eyebrow. "And you take care of Jub, huh?"

Aire snorted. "Nobody could handle that job." She rose and extended her arms, surprising Kazren. She could count on one hand the number of times she and Aire had hugged.

She felt bad for her earlier thoughts now. Maybe there wasn't really an awkward distance between them. Maybe Aire was just shier, more reserved than Jub, and Kazren misread that as disinterest. She stepped forward and hugged Aire, the younger girl squeezing her midsection so tight it made Kazren gasp.

"Good luck over there," Aire said as she drew back. She raised a fist and mimed punching the air. "Give those academy kids hell for us, huh?"

Kazren laughed. "I will. Promise."

She listened to Aire's familiar footsteps retreat up the hall. Farther afield, she could hear Jub shouting, and the easy laughter of Mia and her family. Chest tight, Kazren slammed her trunk shut and dragged it off the bed. It was heavy enough that she needed to cast a quick spell to make it float alongside her. Then she ducked out of her room, closing the door behind her.

It's only a weeklong trip, she reminded herself. Somehow, this felt more final than that. As if she were saying goodbye to something permanent.

34

Maybe she was. Maybe this would be her first step back into the person she ought to be: Kazren Drita, First Student in her class at the Wizards of the Mound Academy.

The thought made her smile. But it was bittersweet, to her surprise. Much as she'd resented being tossed out of the academy—and much as she longed to reclaim her place—she had found a home here. A mentor who understood her idiosyncrasies, and other students who welcomed her with open arms.

She squared her shoulders. If this was to be her last trip as a student of Bacre Stronghold, then she would do her duty. She would help her master uncover the truth about Ebus' death.

No matter what it took.

Chapter Six

Lazlo met Kazren in front of the manor. Her trunk floated alongside her, and he noted her use of the levitation spell with an approving smile. He'd used a different spell on his trunk. When he snapped his fingers, his trunk sprouted legs to toddle after him across the lawn.

Guerin, Mia, and her family had come out to say goodbye. Lazlo waved as they walked away, Kazren calling farewells to Jub and Aire, who leaned out of their second-story bedrooms to watch.

The only one Lazlo didn't see was Alisa, but he paid this no mind.

He led the way across the courtyard to the north tower. As per academy specifications, the north tower did not connect to any of the other buildings in the Bacre Stronghold. It stood alone, a tall spire piercing the blue late-morning sky. The entrance was a set of double doors eight feet high, carved with magical runes.

As Lazlo and Kazren approached, the runes began to glow a deep pink color. The enchantment spell that guarded the tower activated.

Strictly speaking, said spell didn't guard the tower, but what it contained. It had taken Lazlo a good deal of trouble—and pretty much all of his remaining favors at the academy council—to get this building installed. The Mound didn't like to let just anyone build something like this—and with good reason.

Inside Lazlo's north tower was a Gate.

He strode to the tall doors. A final symbol appeared, dead center in the heavy oak paneling. The academy crest. Lazlo raised a fist and pressed the iron ring on his finger to the middle of the symbol.

The entire door pulsed a solid blue. With a heavy clanking sound, the doors unlocked and began to creak open. Lazlo flashed Kazren a quick smile. He enjoyed her wide-eyed awe as she took in the tower and the security measures. She'd never been allowed this close to the tower before—none of the students were, for fear they might accidentally trigger some of the defensive mechanisms Lazlo and several council mages had installed.

Lazlo stepped over the threshold into the tower. Once Kazren followed him, the heavy doors swung shut again with a heavy thunk. The moment they did, torches burst into flames along the walls, lighting their path.

Despite its lack of use, the tower was free of cobwebs or dust. Transmutation spells kept it in good shape. Lazlo followed the torch flames across a short entry hall and onto a stone staircase that ran up the wall in a long spiral.

Kazren paused in the middle of the entryway, tipping her head back, lips parted. From the bottom, the top was only just visible as a faint pinprick of sunlight. "Can't we teleport up there?" she asked.

Lazlo grinned. "Where would be the fun in that? Think of it as our morning exercise. We need to get our blood flowing."

Kazren wrinkled her nose. "Is that an actual requirement of the spell, or do you just like torturing yourself?"

Rather than respond, Lazlo ducked under the staircase itself and pushed against what appeared to be a blank stone wall. It made a loud grinding noise and rolled aside, revealing another circular room next door, this one about thirty feet in diameter.

Kazren laughed. "What are the stairs for?"

Lazlo shrugged. "Ambiance." And to give any would-be invaders the climb of their lives, hopefully, before they realized they'd gotten the Gate's location all wrong.

He gestured for Kazren to follow him into the circular room. She did, both of their trunks floating and walking in behind. Once they'd settled in the middle of the room, along with their belongings, Lazlo paused near a clipboard hanging from the wall. He jotted a note in the log: the date, their destination, and both of their names.

After he finished writing, he joined Kazren in the middle of the room. Runes lined the floor here, similar in style to the ones on the door outside, albeit spelling out a different use. He pointed at one rune in particular and whispered an inaudible incantation.

The entire ring flashed a blinding white.

Kazren gasped, blinking hard. Lazlo had closed his eyes just in time, so he only needed to squint as the light faded once more.

"How long does it take?" Kazren asked.

Lazlo grinned. "We're already here. Take a look." He nodded at the wall, in the direction they just came from.

Kazren whirled around. Sure enough, the dark stone walls of the north tower had vanished. In their place, cheery wood paneling lined this new room. It, too, was circular, but it held two large chests and a bulky desk, as well as a set of handsomely carved double doors.

Lazlo paused by the desk to scribble in another log book. As he did, he glanced from Kazren to the double doors. She was just about to reach for the handle. "Wait," he called. "I need to be the one to open it. Since I've got the key."

He stepped forward, putting himself between her and the exit just in case. Sometimes the academy's identity detectors got a little overzealous. These Gates were the only way to teleport onto campus—part of the protective spells that kept the academy warded and hidden from sight.

In recent years, it had become all too obvious why they needed such strict security. You couldn't let just anyone waltz into a place with as much power, knowledge, and young mages as the Wizards of the Mound Academy.

Lazlo extended a hand, brushing the ring along the symbol on the door. The academy crest lit up bright blue in acknowledgement, and a second later, the door clicked open.

***

The first time Lazlo came to the Wizards of the Mound Academy, he'd just slayed a dragon and earning the king's favor. Needless to say, his ego had been at an all-time high.

But the sight of the academy had humbled him almost immediately.

He'd ridden to the Mound with a group of other recently-admitted students. Unlike Lazlo, a law school graduate and war veteran, most of them were fresh out of primary school. Whey-faced, eager teens, all elbows and grins. He envied them. They might have packed more physical baggage than Lazlo, who'd only loaded a single knapsack onto the wagon they were all sharing, but they'd get to experience the academy with fresh-faced optimism.

Then again, he thought, *optimism isn't all it's cracked up to be.*

Still, as they crested the last hill between them and the Mound, the sight of it stole his breath away. The academy sat at the heart of several hundred acres of land. A circular wall, ten feet thick and forty feet high, carved of pure white granite, enclosed the entire school. The grounds outside the wall had all been carefully manicured—lush green grass that rolled all the way to the foot of the mountains that backed the school. To either side, thick forests seemed to cup the school between their palms, like a jewel they were hiding.

"It's beautiful, isn't it?" murmured one of the boys, who Lazlo had grown close to over the trip. He was older than the others, though still a couple years younger than Lazlo. He'd been apprenticed to his father, a blacksmith, when he discovered a late-blooming magical ability.

His story was very similar to Lazlo's. Aside from the fact that he'd been smart enough not to sign up for a war. "Very beautiful," Lazlo agreed.

Another boy beside them snorted. "Beautiful hell, according to my older sister. The teachers like to torture first years especially."

"Don't be ridiculous," said Lazlo's friend.

"Like you have any idea what you're talking about, Pierce," the second boy muttered.

Lazlo ignored their bickering and kicked his horse onward, toward the academy.

A cobblestone street led up to the wall's lone portcullis. A hundred yards from that entrance, a small village had grown. Edgelight, a quiet little agriculture town surrounded by working farms. It and the academy lived in a delicate symbiosis—Edgelight farmers sold food to the academy scholars, and in turn, the scholars sold them healing elixirs for sick cattle and spells to increase crop yields.

No one could enter the Mound without an invitation from the academy council. Each student riding alongside Lazlo had received one in the mail—he knew, because he'd watched them compare letters in the firelight on the journey here.

Only his had an extra stamp over the academy seal—denoting the fact that the king himself had requested Lazlo's invitation.

He shifted, touching his pocket the way he had every ten minutes on their trip, just to be sure the paper was still there. Touching the rough edges didn't ease his nerves, though.

What if they reject me? What if the fancy scholars in this intimidating building took one look at his tattered uniform and stitched-together knapsack and laughed him back onto the road?

Part of him still struggled to believe all of this was real: the dragon battle, the king's approval, even Master Ebus' compliments, back when he'd first tested Lazlo's mage abilities. He was half-convinced he'd wake up in the law school library any moment, having fallen asleep on one of his more tedious textbooks and dreamt the past two years.

The portcullis was grand and imposing, the guard's expression stern. He searched their wagon thoroughly, opening every trunk and bag they'd packed. Finally, he held out a hand for their papers. He took Lazlo's last, and Lazlo held his breath, heart in his throat.

But the guard only smiled and waved him after the other bright-eyed students. "Welcome to the academy."

As he passed through the portcullis, Lazlo's jaw dropped.

The roads inside the academy walls were wide—double the width of the narrow dirt paths he'd ridden to get here. Gardens of flowering bushes and elegant shrubs lined their route to the main building. The colossal structure was lined with columns, a dome crowning its main hall. The road bent into a T-shape here, and Lazlo watched expensive carriages pull up out front, unloading students and supplies alike.

Trying not to stare too obviously, he followed the other students up the marble steps into the foyer. The doors were ten feet tall, and as they neared, footmen opened the doors on their behalf. The whole group walked slowly, not wanting to miss anything.

Inside, the dome looked even more beautiful and arresting than it had outside. Frescos decorated the marble walls and ceiling, gilded with gold and bright, expensive paints. Framed portraits lined the entryway, and all the doorways were tall and arched. Stairs wound lazily here and there, offering glimpses of sumptuously decorated rooms beyond.

Lazlo had never seen anything like it.

"Where do we go?" whispered Pierce, eying him.

Before Lazlo could hazard a guess, a booming voice echoed through the marble foyer. "There you are. Just the man I've been expecting."

Lazlo recognized that voice, though he hadn't heard it in two years. He turned to find Master Ebus descending one of the staircases, arms spread wide. He looked exactly the same as he had in the tent, when he'd summoned Lazlo in to test his abilities. Only today, he wore finer robes than he had while visiting a war camp.

"And you've met some friends. Good." Master Ebus extended his smile to the whole group. "You'll all be in the same class, though once we've discovered your particular talents, you may all be assigned to different mentors."

The boys shifted uneasily. So did Lazlo. He stole a glance at Pierce, both of them obviously worried. He thought he was going to study with Master Ebus. Wasn't that the whole reason he'd come?

As if reading his mind, Ebus shot him a conspiratorial smile. "I'm afraid I've already called dibs on you, Lazlo. Though once the other instructors see what you're capable of, I've no doubt they'll resent me for it."

The other boys all stared at Lazlo. Pierce especially. When Lazlo caught his eye, Pierce flashed a quick thumbs-up, smiling in encouragement.

He turned away again, face flushed. "It will be an honor to learn from you, Master Ebus."

"Yes, yes." Ebus clapped his hands. "But I'm sure you're all tired from your long journey. Here, put these on." He held out a series of bracelets. "Without these, none of you will be able to do a single spell."

When he said that, Lazlo tried to summon his magic. To his shock, it felt like hitting a wall. Something stood between him and the well of power he'd grown to rely on as easily as breathing. His chest tightened with panic. But the moment Ebus handed him the bracelet, his magic flooded back in. He gasped, feeling like he'd just resurfaced from underwater.

To judge by Pierce's wild-eyed expression, he'd experienced the same panic.

"Better, isn't it?" Master Ebus gave them both a knowing wink. "Now, I'll show you where your lodgings are—as well as the mess hall," he added, when one of the boys' stomachs gave a loud gurgle.

They all laughed, their voices echoing off the high ceilings.

Lazlo imagined he could hear those echoes now, as he stepped out of the Gate and into the same foyer that had once so awed him. To judge by her gawking, it was having the same effect on Kazren now.

He chuckled. "Didn't you pass through here during your initiation?" he asked.

Kazren shook herself and clamped her jaw shut. She looked irritated with herself. "Of course." After a moment, she softened again. "Sometimes I just... worried I'd never see it again."

"That makes two of us," Lazlo murmured.

Together, they dragged their trunks out of the Gate. It was rather more difficult to move his without the aid of magic, and Lazlo kicked himself mentally for packing so much. It was only a weeklong visit. What happened to the man who arrived here fresh from a war with only a knapsack to his name?

He didn't want to bring their trunks all the way to administration, so he asked one of the front door guards to mind their bags. Then he led Kazren toward the administration offices. The stone steps echoed underfoot as he approached the east wing.

He hadn't set foot on campus in years—almost a decade—and yet his feet led him up the right staircase, along the right corridor, and straight to the cheery little red door with the *No Loud Noises* sign out front.

Lazlo rapped on the door. Once, twice, a third time. He frowned at the painted wood. Surely the academy knew to expect him. They were the ones who had sent the invitation, after all.

He rubbed his wrist, only now feeling a faint prickle of foreboding.

As part of the campus's security measures, no visitors could access their magic within the academy's wards without a bracelet. The bracelets were tied to the academy's impressive security spells—it let the school know that anyone wearing one was permitted to be here.

Without a bracelet, he and Kazren were as helpless as his parents would be in a Spellduel. Neither Lazlo's mother nor his father had a single ounce of magical potential. Where he got his plentiful stores remained a family mystery.

"Is something wrong?" Kazren asked. She must have picked up on his agitation.

Lazlo forced a smile. "Of course not." He glanced at the nearest window, trying to gauge the angle of the sun. "The administrators are probably at lunch. We'll just have to come back in a bit."

Kazren wrinkled her nose. "What about our trunks?"

"They'll be safe with the guards for now."

As they exited the main building and crossed the huge campus, Lazlo felt as if he were splitting in two. There was present day Lazlo, shoulders tense, startling at every passerby and loud noise. And then there was past Lazlo, the ghost treading these same walkways.

He remembered his first day on campus as an instructor. How gleefully Master Ebus had greeted him. He remembered Pierce grabbing him a huge, crushing hug, one that stole the breath from Lazlo's lungs. "We made it," Pierce shouted in his ear. "Who'd have thunk those two scrawny boys who dragged themselves halfway across the kingdom as first years would someday be masters themselves, eh?"

Master Ebus had clicked his tongue. "You're not masters yet, boys. Just instructors. Only after you take on mentees of your own will you earn my title." But to judge by the satisfied quirk of his mouth, Ebus was just as thrilled as Pierce and Lazlo felt.

All throughout Lazlo's student years, he and Pierce had been a team. When Ebus discovered that Pierce shared his and Lazlo's rare gift for Aursight, their meeting on the way to school had felt like fate.

Maybe it was, Lazlo thought now. But fate was crueler than he'd dared imagine.

Chapter Seven

Luckily, Lazlo and Kazren didn't need to search far to find the solution to their worries. Almost as soon as they'd crossed campus toward the cheerily smoking building that housed the kitchens and dining halls, Master Unihoast came rushing out to meet them.

"Master Lazlo, Miss Dritra. I do apologize for the delay." He patted his pockets, mumbling under his breath. "We only just got word about the Gate activating; I must confess, I did think you'd arrive later in the day. You always were one for sleeping in, Master Lazlo."

Lazlo chuckled. Unihoast had been one of his instructors, what felt like a lifetime ago. "What can I say? Old age has done its work on me."

Master Unihoast wagged a bent finger. "Don't you dare speak to me about *old age*, young master."

Truth be told, Unihoast only had a couple of decades on Lazlo—next to nothing, when it came to wizards' lifespans. But he let it lie, stifling a smile as Unihoast finally located something in his pockets.

Their bracelets jangled as he withdrew them. "Here you are. Everything's in order; we've been expecting you both."

Lazlo slipped his bracelet onto his wrist. The stones set into the metal pulsed as it activated, and he let out a barely-concealed sigh of relief. He hated to be severed from his magic, even for a short time. It made him feel exposed and helpless.

Kazren, too, seemed to relax a little once she'd secured her own bracelet. "Should we fetch our trunks?" she asked Lazlo, but Unihoast waved her off.

"No need. I'll send some porters to pick them up. Now, did anyone give you details on the service yet? Tomorrow afternoon…" While Unihoast fished another piece of paper from his pocket, Lazlo cleared his throat.

"Actually, I've not received details about anything yet. Could you... tell me what happened, exactly? I only know the broad strokes."

Suddenly, Unihoast jerked, as if he'd heard something. He glanced to one side, his gaze unfocused.

Lazlo frowned. "Master Unihoast?"

He shook himself. "Apologies, my friend. I wouldn't want to say anything untoward. Terrible situation, of course, we're all very broken up. I'm sure you most of all."

Lazlo's throat tightened. "Yes. But how did he—"

"Goodness, look at the time," Unihoast practically shouted. He gestured vaguely at the clocktower over the dining hall. "I forgot I have another appointment. Will you be able to find your lodgings all right? The information should be encoded in there." He gestured at the bracelets, which lit up a second time in confirmation.

Lazlo stared at him. "Certainly. I still know my way around. But—"

Unihoast nodded, his gaze distant and distracted. "Wonderful. Then I will leave you to it." He hesitated once more, his eyes not quite meeting Lazlo's. Then he gestured and drifted up into the air, floating toward the administrative offices back in the main hall.

Lazlo watched him go, scratching at his trimmed beard.

"What's wrong?" Kazren asked him.

"Probably nothing." Lazlo tapped his bracelet. "Everyone handles grief differently. Some people prefer not to talk about it."

"He seemed more scared than grief-stricken to me," Kazren murmured, and Lazlo shot her a warning look.

"I'm sure Master Unihoast is fine. Let's figure out where you and I belong." He raised the bracelet to his lips. "Lodging," he said, clearly and firmly. Beside him, Kazren did the same.

The bracelet vibrated subtly. Lazlo's arm seemed to rise of its own accord, pointing the way toward their lodgings for this visit. But when he glanced at Kazren, she was pointing in a different direction. He frowned. "That's odd," he said. "I assumed they would put us both in the caravansary."

The caravansary was a square lined with buildings on the northeast side of campus. Visiting families and friends of students often stayed there. Sure enough, the moment he said the word *caravansary*, Kazren's bracelet lit up bright green. Lazlo's, on the other hand, pulsed red.

"Guess that's where I'm staying." Kazren looked less than thrilled about it. Probably because the last time she'd been on campus, she lived in student housing.

Even students had more luxurious housing than the visitors. After all, they lived here year-round, while visitors only stopped by for a couple of weeks at most.

"Don't worry." Lazlo gave her a reassuring smile. "I'm sure once the council sees what you can do, they'll regret not giving you an entire manor to yourself."

Kazren snorted. "That's uncharacteristically sentimental of you, Master Lazlo."

"I can be a softie sometimes."

"Tell that to our final exams." But Kazren grinned as she said it.

Lazlo checked his bracelet again. "Faculty housing?" he asked. The bracelet flashed red again. "Hmm." Stranger and stranger. "Well, why don't you get yourself settled in, Kazren, while I work out where's home for me this week."

He walked with her to the row of carriages parked outside the dining hall. She stepped into the first carriage and spoke her destination aloud. The carriage trundled off, powered by some unseen spell and linked to her bracelet, so it knew where she should and shouldn't be at any given moment.

Lazlo waited until she'd reached the main road toward the caravansary before he boarded the second carriage in a row. He could waste energy flying around campus until his bracelet lit up, but he'd rather conserve his power while he could.

Something still felt off on campus. First the lack of greeting or security checks when they exited the Gate. Then Master Unihoast's odd behavior.

Not to mention Ebus' death. *Something's very wrong here.*

The back of his neck prickled as he stepped into the carriage. "Lodging," he said. The bracelet vibrated and pointed him west, toward faculty housing. The carriage rattled that direction too. Lazlo frowned, confused. When he'd asked the bracelet earlier if he was in the faculty lodges, it said no.

Suddenly, realization struck. He looked at his bracelet, unsure whether to be apprehensive or thankful. "Headmaster Ebus' manor," he said quietly.

The bracelet lit up a cheerful green.

"Huh." Lazlo leaned back in his seat, still frowning. Back when he'd lived on campus as an instructor, he'd spent more time at Ebus' manor than his own. And if he'd ever visited while his master was still alive, he had no doubt Ebus would've insisted on hosting him.

Still, it felt strange to be escorted there now, knowing there would be nobody to welcome him.

The carriage sped up as it reached one of the larger thoroughfares through campus. He leaned against the window, watching familiar sights roll past. There was the campus green, where students sunbathed, flirted, and tested new spells on one another. There was the quaint pub that served faculty and older students, and there the lake, fed by a hidden spring that provided the Mound with drinking water.

His eyes glazed as they passed first year dormitories and the nicer second- and third-year apartments. Fourth years got houses of their own, which butted up against the faculty manors. Each of the latter was larger and more elaborate than the last, augmented as they'd been over the years by construction and spells alike.

In the distance, far enough afield so as not to pose a danger to any of those buildings, hulked the massive Spelldueling arena. He could just make out the raised stands, each section topped by massive spiked skulls.

Dragon heads, brought to the Mound centuries ago by dragon-hunters of old. Lazlo sized them up. The dragon he'd felled, Rimrig the Fierce, had been large enough. Yet he was nothing in comparison to those mythic beasts.

An unfamiliar sight caught Lazlo's eye then.

He'd heard about the most recent addition to the campus grounds, but he had not visited since construction had been completed. The Black Tower rose against the sky to the south of campus, close to the southeast entrance. The rectangular tower stood four stories high and over four hundred feet around. True to its name, the stones were so black it seemed to swallow all sunlight that touched it.

Lazlo frowned. *Is that etruesten?*

Etruesten was a dark stone, often mistaken for obsidian, but denser. When worn or touched by a mage, it enhanced the effects of magic. Some mages claimed to have doubled or tripled their spells' efficacy with enough etruesten.

If it was, Lazlo had never seen this much etruesten in one place. A single pendant or etruesten bracelet usually cost more than a commoner made in a year. He couldn't even begin to fathom how much that tower must have cost to build. Of course, the Mound was the wealthiest academy on the continent, but still...

The carriage bumped and rolled off the main road onto a cobblestone side street. Lazlo tore his gaze from the Black Tower to study his more immediate surroundings. A few new manors had been added since he last visited, no doubt for new faculty members who'd joined in the meantime.

As headmaster, it seemed natural that Ebus would have a larger manor than most. But in fact, his had been constructed long before his promotion. Unlike previous headmasters, he had opted not to rebuild a new manor when he was promoted. The only addition he'd made was an extra wing in the back, to contain his much-expanded library.

As the carriage pulled into Ebus' front courtyard, Lazlo spotted a few students leaving bundles of flowers along the driveway and around the gate. His chest tightened.

Ebus had been popular when Lazlo was still on campus. It was good to see that he'd remained so, even though headmasters were typically less hands-on with individual students than the masters who taught them every day.

The front door of the manor was already open as Lazlo exited the carriage. A small group of students were carrying a large eraser board and supplies out, loading them onto a nearby carriage. Nearby, another cluster of students had gathered on the lawn to spar.

Observing all this activity, Lazlo approached the front landing. *Was his house always like this?* Or were students taking advantage of the empty property?

He moved aside to let a student carrying a box of textbooks pass, sweat standing out on his brow. *Why doesn't he use a levitation spell?* Before Lazlo could ask, a soft, feminine voice called his name.

"Master Lazlo. It's so good to see you." Mariou Panayiota had not changed a bit in the last decade. Her bright, friendly smile remained as wide as always.

"I didn't realize I'd be joining a party," he said, nodding at the bustling lawn. "Am I interrupting?"

Mariou laughed. "Not at all. In fact, we're the ones intruding, I'm afraid. I had hoped to be done before you arrived. A few of the students volunteered to help us get the manor in shape to host. Headmaster Ebus borrowed quite a few excess items from the academy over the years, and, well... We didn't want you living in an obstacle course." Mariou chuckled.

"Thank you for your consideration, but you didn't need to go to all this trouble for me." Though truth be told, Lazlo wasn't surprised. Ebus had always harbored a bit of a hoarding habit. Or *collecting,* as Ebus called it.

"Oh, it's no trouble. Besides, we would've needed to do it anyway, eventually." Mariou's bright smile drooped at last. "It's still so hard to believe he's gone."

"I know." Lazlo finally let himself take in the house. He had so many happy memories in this building. Chasing Pierce through the halls, both of them firing ill-advised spells at one another. Coming up with a new theory on Aursight and rushing to tell Master Ebus about it right away. Finally finishing his spellbook and basking in Ebus' praise.

But there were other memories too. The night everything fell apart—and the horrible morning after...

His gut clenched.

Mariou touched his arm lightly. "Headmaster Ebus' most recent mentee has been coordinating all his affairs. Would you like me to introduce you two?"

Lazlo's chest did a funny leap at that. *His mentee.* Lazlo had wondered, after the disasters that Pierce and Lazlo had become, whether Ebus would ever take on another mentee. He found he was glad to learn he had. Ebus had been a natural teacher: kind, compassionate, stern when he needed to be, but always quick to encourage his students to their fullest potential.

It wasn't *his* fault what happened...

"I'd like that very much," said Lazlo.

Mariou escorted him to the backyard, where even more students were busily packing away various Spellduel apparatuses and materials. Mariou walked straight up to a tall young man. He was thin, with dark blond hair, and he wore a dark blue sleeveless tunic with black pants and boots.

As Mariou approached, he turned to face her.

"Master Lazlo, this is Eldon Woods. Eldon, Lazlo was once Headmaster Ebus' mentee, now a master himself."

Eldon broke into a broad smile. "That I know." He extended a hand, looking so eager all of a sudden that he seemed much younger than a final-year student. "Headmaster Ebus spoke of you often, Master Lazlo. He held you in very high esteem. I'm afraid I was a poor replacement, myself." He chuckled.

Lazlo grasped Eldon's hand, smiling. "I'm sure that can't be true. Headmaster Ebus was always very choosy about his mentees. If he picked you, you must be a very talented student indeed."

Mariou arched a brow. "If you do say so yourself?"

Lazlo laughed. "I meant to compliment the boy, not myself. But, if the cape fits…"

Mariou tutted. "Eldon, why don't you show Master Lazlo to his rooms? He must be tired after the journey here."

Hardly, thought Lazlo. But he did not mention the Gate. Most of the higher-up faculty knew he'd had one installed in his castle, but he still tried not to broadcast its existence. Especially around students—even ones favored by his old master. One could never be too careful when it came to security. He'd learned that lesson the hard way.

"Only if it's no trouble," Lazlo told the boy. "If you're busy, I can find my own way."

"Not at all." Eldon didn't spare his fellows a second glance. "It'd be an honor." He set off through the yard. Lazlo followed him out a side door and up a flight of stairs.

"Is there a tournament coming up by any chance?" Lazlo asked as they walked.

Eldon glanced up, surprised. "Yes. We're in the middle of one right now, in fact. Qualifiers for the championship."

Good to know. Lazlo wondered if the sign-up phase had already ended, or if he might be able to finagle Kazren an invitation to the qualifying tiers.

"Of course, they paused the tournament until after the ceremony," Eldon added. "Given everything."

"You mean until after Headmaster Ebus' funeral?" Lazlo asked. He knew the entire school would be expected to attend. Not to mention, invitations had gone out across Cicpe to anyone Ebus had known. After a couple hundred years of teaching at the academy, Ebus had deep connections everywhere. Lazlo wouldn't be surprised if the king himself decided to attend.

Eldon nodded. "Yes. And, you know, considering how and where it happened…"

Lazlo stopped short. They'd just reached the second-floor landing, a lushly carpeted hallway lined with portraits of famous mages Ebus admired. "What do you mean?" he asked.

Eldon turned, surprised. "You haven't heard? I thought everybody knew. Since the entire school was there…"

Lazlo's heart sank. Any hopes he'd had of learning his old master died peacefully at home evaporated. "My notification letter was less than forthcoming," he said.

Eldon bit his lip and glanced around, as if searching for someone to help him. "My apologies, Master. I don't know whether I'm the right one to tell you this, but…"

"Please," Lazlo said.

Eldon winced. "Headmaster Ebus died during a Spellduel. In the arena."

Lazlo's jaw dropped. Whatever he'd imagined Eldon might say, it wasn't this. *A Spellduel?* At his age? Typically, Spelldueling championships were reserved for the students and recent graduates. It was a proving ground, a way for trainees to hone and perfect their abilities.

Older mages participated too, but usually just in friendly bouts with one another to keep their instincts sharp, or in demonstrative duels when instructing their students. It wasn't unheard of for the headmaster to duel someone, but it would've been a very rare occasion.

"What—who was he—?" Lazlo's tongue tripped over itself. He wanted to ask several questions at once.

"He was challenged by a Master Grim Krauss, from Scientia Arcana Academy."

Ah. That explained it. The other two academies on the continent, Scientia Arcana Academy (or SAA for short) and the Gagiams' Academy of Wizardry (or GAW), both had very different philosophies regarding the use of magic. For the most part, they kept to themselves. But every so often, upstarts at both academies grew resentful of the Wizards of the Mound's presumed superiority. Such challenges had been issued before, usually once or twice during each headmaster's career.

Lazlo had expected even GAW and SAA to remain quiet in the face of a headmaster of Ebus' caliber. But apparently someone had decided to poke the beast.

And that someone won, apparently.

"What exactly happened?" Lazlo said, once they continued walking. "Tell me everything." He listened with grim interest as Eldon recounted his master's final day. Ebus had started the bout in good form, landing several attacks on his opponent. Then something had changed. People noticed him touching his stomach repeatedly, and several witnesses in the closer stands claimed his color looked off. Paler than usual, with a greenish tinge.

Master Grim had landed an unlucky hit, and Ebus had struggled to rise again. Then...

Eldon shook his head. "It was almost as if he gave up. I was watching him closely at that point—we all were. Master Grim was such an obvious Spelldueler—any novice could've seen his next hit coming. But Headmaster Ebus didn't seem to notice. He was staring at the stands instead. If I didn't know any better, I'd say he saw some phantom or spirit..."

"Phantoms are children's tales," Lazlo chided, albeit gently. "More likely he sustained a head injury from the previous hit. Did you see if he was bleeding anywhere? When they examined him afterward—" He broke off abruptly when he noticed the boy's expression.

Eldon's lips had thinned and his eyes shone a little too brightly in the corners. "I'm sorry," he whispered, dashing a hand over his face. When he inhaled again, it sounded stuffy. "It's just so strange. He was such a powerful mage. Watching him fall that easily was..." He shook his head. "Half the school thought it a trick. We were chanting his name, waiting for him to rise again. It wasn't until the medics charged the field that we realized something was seriously wrong."

Lazlo grimaced. He couldn't imagine what that must have been like. It was hard enough for him to hear about it now. "I apologize if

I seem over-curious. It's only… I understand. I, too, have a difficult time believing he's gone."

Eldon exhaled. "Me too. It just… it doesn't seem right. Not only his death, but…" Eldon shook his head. "I don't know. Perhaps I'm just being paranoid. But Headmaster Ebus was acting strange before he died. He stuck to his rooms, and he sent back several of his favorite dishes. Almost as though he were already ill…"

Suddenly, Eldon stopped walking and nodded ahead. Only now did Lazlo recognize where Eldon had brought him—to the west wing. The master suite.

"Oh, no. I couldn't possibly stay here," he said.

"Headmaster Ebus would want you to have it," Eldon said. "The other rooms will all be full with visitors for the services. Besides, Miss Mariou already changed the bedding and the steward brought your trunk here."

Lazlo scowled. This boy sure knew where the plunge the guilt-dagger. "This is hardly appropriate," he said.

"On the contrary," called Mariou, sweeping into view with a parchment clutched in one fist. "This is the most appropriate place for Headmaster Ebus' favorite student."

"Mariou, I—"

She cut him off by holding out the parchment. "Message arrived for you just now. From the acting headmaster's office." She glanced at Eldon with a fond smile. "Thank you, Eldon, I'll take it from here."

"Pleasure meeting you, Master Lazlo." Eldon ducked his head in a bow, then hurried away.

Mariou lingered by Lazlo's elbow. He gave her a pointed look, then sighed and unfolded the paper. The further he read, the higher his eyebrows rose.

"What is it?" she asked, craning her neck for a glimpse.

Lazlo's stomach gave an unsteady lurch. "An old friend has come to visit me."

Chapter Eight

Tansya looked, if anything, more beautiful than the last time he'd seen her. *How many years has it been?* Lazlo didn't have time to count.

No sooner had he walked up to the guard house just outside the main entrance of the academy than a blur of reddish-blond curls leapt up to embrace him. "Lazlo!"

"Tansya." He wrapped his arms around his friend's waist in a tight squeeze, then released her. He stepped back to take in her constellation of freckles and gray-green eyes. He still couldn't quite believe she was here. "What happened? Why are you... How did you even know I was here?"

Tansya glanced at the gruff-looking guard seated nearby.

In response, he grunted. "You want a private audience, do it off the grounds," he said. "You're the one trying to enter a protected zone without an invitation. We've already done you enough favors, sending that letter."

"Thank you for that," Lazlo interrupted, before Tansya could retort. He'd seen the damage her quick tongue could do when she got out of sorts. "We are old friends, and I will take full responsibility for her being here. On my honor, she means no harm."

"You haven't even heard why I'm here yet," Tansya pointed out, eyes alight with mischief.

He bit back a groan. This was not a time to joke.

Luckily, the guard only rolled his eyes and went back to glaring at the huge portcullis that guarded the academy.

"Let's take a walk," Lazlo suggested. "Edgelight's only ten minutes on foot. We can grab an ale and talk about what brings you to this neck of the woods."

"As long as they serve better attitude than here." Tansya shot a scowl at the guard. At least she waited until they were outside of the house to flash him a rude gesture, though.

Lazlo couldn't help but smile. She hadn't changed at all in the past… gods, how many years had it been?

He'd first met Tansya right after he slayed Rimrig the Fierce. Unbeknownst to him, he'd upset an entire forest ecosystem when he took down that dragon—an ecosystem Tansya was responsible for maintaining, as the local druid of that forest.

Now, like then, she wore the type of attire he'd grown accustomed to seeing on all druids: dark brown boots, dark green pants and jerkin, all in rough, natural fibers. The kind of sturdy outfit you needed to survive in the forest—not on an academy campus.

If not for her attire, Tansya might have passed for a student here. She was lithe and petite, with wide eyes that made her look younger than she actually was. Lazlo had mistaken her for a lost young woman himself, the first time they'd met. Until she started dressing him down in language that'd make most pirates blush, talking about how much damage his dragon-hunting campaign would cause her forest.

She was the reason that, when Lazlo finally learned enough magic at the academy to create a sanctuary, he built his inside Rimrig's old abandoned den. From there, he'd been able to help her introduce other predators to that patch of wilderness. Ones that helped retain the natural order without threatening any human settlements or passersby, naturally.

"I thought you never wanted anything to do with the Wizards of the Mound," Lazlo commented as they strolled toward Edgelight.

Over the years, he'd taken to visiting her anytime he went to his sanctuary. Tansya was forthright and outspoken. She had no problem telling him what she thought about most mages and their dry, formulaic, textbook approach to magic. *Your instructors want you to cast with no soul,* she used to snap. *Magic is meant to be felt, not memorized.*

They'd disagreed there, but Lazlo couldn't deny he'd learned a lot from shadowing Tansya in the forest. Aside from her impressive ability to feral shape into a variety of animals, as well as the ability to tree travel, stepping into a tree trunk in one location and appearing in another one almost instantly, even if it was miles away—Tansya knew more about herbal remedies than any master at the academy. Not to mention, her understanding of animal behavior and communication fascinated him.

After he left the academy, Tansya was one of the few people in his life who wholeheartedly supported the decision. Master Ebus kept asking Lazlo to return, as did most of the other instructors he knew. Even the king seemed disappointed by Lazlo's decision to sequester himself at his castle—though not displeased enough to take the castle away and force him to return to campus.

Given all of that, the academy was the last place he'd expected to run into her.

"I don't." Tansya heaved a sigh. "Unfortunately, you've apparently decided to associate with them again, so, I have no choice."

Lazlo frowned. "What do you mean? Did something happen to the forest?" He couldn't think of any other reason for Tansya to seek him out—it was the only ongoing project they shared.

But Tansya shook her head, going so far as to cast a nervous glance over her shoulder. "You said there's a pub in town? Let's wait."

Lazlo's nerves edged higher. Tansya normally wasn't the cautious type, if her behavior in the guard house was anything to judge by. Whatever was going on, it must have spooked her. He hated to imagine how bad the news must be.

They reached Edgelight before long, and found a quiet pub with the kinds of dark corners that Lazlo normally avoided. Long experience had taught him that nothing good happened in pubs like these. But right now, darkness and anonymity were exactly what they needed.

He bought them both pints of watery ale, then joined Tansya at a table near the back. He sat, as always, with his back against the wall, facing the entrance. His eyes darted around the room, counting the other patrons and tracking their locations.

While he did that, Tansya sipped her ale. "I came because I had a dream about you."

Lazlo stopped scanning the room and stared at her. "A dream?" *Is that all this is about?*

But Tansya looked so worried that he bit back his usual sarcastic response. "Not just any dream. I was doing a ritual for guidance and futuresight."

"Divination?" Lazlo asked, knowing the druids' futuresight was a closely related field.

56

Tansya's nose wrinkled. A hint of her usual attitude flared. "Hardly. Your lot tinker around with toys and gadgets, stealing glimpses of individual moments. We druids work holistically, to perceive the entire web of possibilities to come."

"So, six of one, half dozen of the other," Lazlo muttered.

Tansya ignored him. "I was *trying* to seek guidance about a new batch of wyverns that was just born—oh, the female you introduced finally nested, by the way. I wasn't sure if having all three of her children in the same area would overtax the smaller wildlife, or if we ought to move one or two of the babies to another region once they're past nesting age. But instead of answers, I saw…"

"Me?" Lazlo guessed when Tansya trailed off.

She reached across the table to grab his wrist. Her eyes, always so full of mirth, suddenly looked more serious than he'd ever seen them. "You're in danger here. I don't know who's causing it, or why. But I saw you trapped in a great web, a shadow creeping toward you."

In spite of himself, Lazlo felt a chill creep along his spine. "Dreams can be difficult to interpret," he said, more to himself than her. "Especially during divination rituals. Whatever you saw—"

Tansya cut him off. "You're the one it wants, Lazlo. But you're not the only one in danger. I saw a girl with blond hair, younger than me. She's bound to you somehow, like a child maybe, or a—"

"Kazren?" Lazlo's shoulders tensed. "My mentee. She came to the Mound with me."

Tansya's mouth flattened. "The shadow wants her. But not for her sake. For yours. That's all I know. That, and…" She reached into her pocket and withdrew something. She laid it on the table with a metallic clink.

Lazlo looked down at a bright green pin, painstakingly hammered into shape. When he didn't reach for it, Tansya huffed and picked it up again, leaning over to pin it to his lapel.

"This is for protection. The dream told me you'd need my help."

Lazlo touched it, stifling an unexpected smile. "You came all this way just to give me a pin?"

"No." Tansya balled her fists and gave him a determined look. The moment he saw her expression, he knew he wasn't going to like whatever she said next. "I came because I need you to get me an invitation onto campus. According to my dream, unless I'm there when that thing comes for you..." Tanysa's throat bobbed in a tight swallow. "You'll die, Lazlo."

**

"You want *what*?" Acting Headmaster Muzud Marblebeard looked like he had aged at least a hundred years since Lazlo saw him last.

Not that the dwarf had ever looked young, exactly. But his gray-speckled beard had gone fully white sometime in the last few years, and the crow's feet around his deep-set eyes seemed to have tripled. "It's only temporary," Lazlo said. "For the duration of the funeral ceremonies, that's all."

Muzud whirled around to glare at Mariou Panayiota, as if she and Lazlo had conspired on this plot together. For her part, Mariou looked almost as offended as Muzud.

That, at least, seemed fair. Lazlo hadn't explained what he wanted when he asked Mariou to set up a meeting for him with the acting headmaster. He'd only told her that it was urgent, and begged her to pull any strings she could to get him an audience before the funeral proceedings started tomorrow.

Now, an hour past sundown, Lazlo stood ramrod straight in the headmaster's office while Muzud began to pace.

It was strange to be here without Ebus. Half of the books lining the walls were still his—Lazlo recognized the telltale trace glimmers of the preservation spell Ebus always used. He'd developed his own unique spell, unsatisfied with the existing versions, because they only repelled silverfish or mold or dust individually, not all three.

The carpet underfoot was burgundy, Ebus' favorite color. The pens on the desk were all the brand of quill Ebus preferred, and the ink wells were the make he liked as well.

Finally, there was the row of headmaster portraits on the back wall. Ebus' was the most recent, a stunningly realistic likeness. His eyes seemed to follow Lazlo across the room. Lazlo met them now, silently asking for help.

"Let me get this straight," Muzud said slowly, as though he were speaking to a child. "You want us to extend an official academy invitation to an unknown entity—"

"Druid," Lazlo corrected.

58

"An unknown *magical* entity who does not practice our branches of magic, nor does she respect our method of study or learning. And you want us to invite her onto campus just days after your former mentor passed away, when the campus is already in turmoil. I cannot think of a worse betrayal of our values. Not to mention a complete violation of our security protocols…"

"I'll vouch for her. I've known her for years, Muz—Headmaster." Lazlo caught himself just in time. "I can assure you, she's no danger."

"She could wreak havoc if she came here with ill intentions. There are countless secrets stored on this campus. Not just in the Black Tower, but throughout all of our libraries. Knowledge we've taken years to amass. She could steal books for herself or her forest brethren—not to mention, she might be working for one of the other academies. If the SAA put her up to this, after what they did to Headmaster Ebus…"

"She's no spy," Lazlo snapped.

But Muzud shook his head. "Even without magic, it's too dangerous."

"Ah." Lazlo forced himself not to grimace. "That's the other thing…"

Muzud's eyes looked like they were ready to pop from his head. "You cannot be serious."

"It's imperative that she be able to protect herself on campus. You can give her a bracelet with limited access—she doesn't need permission to use the carriages. You can even lock her out of the libraries if that will ease your mind. But I need her here."

"What on earth for?" Muzud sputtered. "We should all be preparing ourselves for the funeral tomorrow."

Lazlo bit the inside of his cheek. "Exactly that. Headmaster Muzud…" Here, he stole a glance at Mariou. She hadn't stopped glaring at Lazlo since he first made his request of the acting headmaster. But he hoped she would understand why he'd done it now. At the very least, he knew Mariou would hear him out. Take this seriously. "I believe Headmaster Ebus' death was not just a dueling accident."

Muzud's mouth opened and closed several times. Mariou, on the other hand, straightened, her shoulders tensing.

59

She did not, Lazlo think, look quite as surprised. "It's only a hunch now," he added quickly. "But some things aren't adding up. I spoke to one of the students who witnessed the duel, Headmaster Ebus' most recent mentee. He said before Ebus died, he was acting strange."

Muzud exhaled slowly. "Students love rumors. You, of all people, should know that. You've been tutoring one of our biggest rumormongers."

Lazlo resisted the urge to grimace. He'd read the school's claims about Jub: that he'd spread nasty rumors and bullied his classmates. But after listening to Jub's side of the story, Lazlo believed his mentee had been on the receiving end of that behavior, rather than the other way around.

Now wasn't the time to split hairs, though. "This didn't sound like your typical gossip," Lazlo said.

"When people die unexpectedly, we all seek reasons," Muzud replied. "It's natural. We want someone to be responsible, so we can blame and hold them accountable. But I was there, too. I witnessed the duel. And I interrogated Grim Krauss afterward. SAA he may be, but the man was broken up about what happened. He felt absolutely awful. Kept trying to offer to pay the school a grant as an apology— mind you, we did accept his offer to cover the funeral expenses, budget not being what it used to these days..."

"Mariou?" Lazlo had been watching her carefully, ignoring most of Muzud's tirade.

As Headmaster Ebus' steward, Mariou had overseen almost every aspect of the day-to-day management of his manor. Not to mention, she knew the ins and outs of his schedule. She was Ebus' Guerin—if there was something wrong, Mariou would have known.

Now, her brow puckered, her eyes going distant and uncertain. "He... he was ill." She spoke as if in a fog. Like these were distant memories, rather than just a few days ago.

Then again, Lazlo knew how grief muddled time. Made the mundane, everyday world suddenly strange and threatening.

"It seemed like nothing. I didn't think anything of it, after, but, yes." Mariou nodded. The more she spoke, the more certain she seemed to grow. "He was struggling to keep food down. We had him on a bland diet. It only came on a few days before the duel, a stomach bug of some sort..."

Muzud scowls. "While that may explain some of his behavior at the duel—missing that first shot Grim landed, for starters—it does not indicate anything dangerous. Unless your druid plans to visit so she can rid our campus of contaminated vegetables, I fail to see how—"

"It's not just the illness," Lazlo interrupted. "Please, I need you to trust me. I may only have my instincts to guide me right now, but those instincts once earned me a place as the academy's judge."

Muzud glanced from Lazlo to Mariou. He could practically hear the old dwarf's gears churning.

He did not mention Tansya's dreams. If anything, hearing about them would only push the dwarf into another tirade about the unreliability of druids. But he knew how to play Muzud by now. "You have nothing to lose by agreeing, but everything to lose by refusing me. If I uncover no evidence of foul play, then you were right, and we can all go our separate ways. If I do uncover foul play, we can work together to stop whoever did this. But if I'm right and you refuse to let me investigate, more people could get hurt."

Muzud did not reply. Lazlo took the lack of an immediate know as a good sign—or at least, not a bad one.

Mariou, on the other hand, hummed thoughtfully as she looked at Lazlo. "How well do you know this druid? You said you would vouch for her comportment. You must be fairly close."

Lazlo nodded. "I've known her since before I came to the academy. We've worked together closely for years. If anyone can help me uncover the root of this problem, it's Tansya."

Mariou glanced from Lazlo to Muzud. The old dwarf's eyebrows rose when Lazlo said her name.

"Tansya…" The dwarf heaved a sigh. All at once, the fight seemed to leak out of him. His shoulders slumped, and his head drooped. But he groped across the huge headmaster's desk for a pen, nevertheless. "Very well. *Restricted access* only. I'll allow her to access her magic on the grounds in general, but limited within any campus buildings. No library access or use of the carriages either."

Lazlo resisted the urge to pump his fist triumphantly. "That would be very generous," he said evenly. "Thank you, Headmaster."

Muzud grunted at the sound of his title. "Does this Tansya of yours have a surname?" He wetted a pen begrudgingly.

Lazlo peered over his shoulder as the letters took shape on the blank parchment.

The Wizards of the Mound Academy hereby officially extend this invitation to Tansya Limnoreia of Hallowmight Forest...

He'd done it. Lazlo suppressed a broad grin. Despite the victory, though, unease still churned in his gut. He still didn't know what was happening here on campus. Whatever it was, he hoped he didn't just throw one of his oldest friends into danger's path.

Chapter Nine

The morning of the funeral dawned bright and hot. A muggy heat had descended overnight, layering the campus in soupy air.

Kazren met Lazlo outside the cemetery gates, tugging at the neck of her academy robes. Lazlo understood the feeling. He'd sweated through all the clothes he wore underneath the robes—thankfully, the robes were dark enough that if he held them over his shoulders just right, nobody would notice the damp patches.

"Can't someone cast a weather spell or something?" Kazren grumbled under her breath.

"You know we only risk those in extreme cases," Lazlo chided, but his heart wasn't in the scolding. He, too, wished they could make an exception. Weather magic was notoriously risky—changing weather patterns in one part of the continent had the potential to cause enormous damage to other ecosystems in the area.

Naturally, Tansya chose that moment to join them, hurrying up the path from Ebus' manor, where administration had reluctantly allowed her to take a room near Lazlo. Presumably because they wanted him to keep an eye on her, but Lazlo didn't mind. Whatever got her access.

She'd been forced to come to the funeral itself on foot, since Muzud didn't grant her access to the carriages, and druids did not practice any flight magic, that he knew of. Sadly, she was still quick enough on foot and in this heat to catch Kazren's comment.

"Typical mages," Tansya huffed. "Only thinking about yourselves and your own comfort. What about the plants that need this heat to germinate, hmm? Or what if you summoned a nice breeze here that turned into a terrible tornado over in the plains?"

"*This* is your friend?" Kazren asked. Lazlo had filled her in on a few details about Tansya as they walked here from breakfast.

He'd left out the part about her identity, though.

"Since when does the academy admit druids?" she asked.

"Kazren," Lazlo warned, even though her tone sounded more curious than hostile.

"They don't," Tansya replied. "Not that we'd care to apply even if they did." She sniffed, chin lifted. "Your protégé could stand to acquire a few manners." With that, Tansya swept ahead of them through the cemetery gates.

Behind her back, Kazren shot Lazlo a grin. "I see why you like her."

He smiled, but then Kazren began to snicker, and his expression flattened. "I don't—it's not like that, you—" He broke off as Kazren followed Tansya through the gates.

Scowling, he marched after the women. But the moment he entered the cemetery, all thoughts of Kazren's teasing and Tansya's haughty attitude fled.

At least half the academy had already arrived. More trickled in every minute, by each of the four entrances to the relatively small cemetery. Lazlo didn't know how they would all fit by the end, but that wasn't his problem.

His gaze was fixed on the raised marble plinth atop the cemetery's highest hill. Ebus' wife was already entombed beneath it. She'd died long before Lazlo even met his mentor. This afternoon, Ebus would join her.

With difficulty, Lazlo tore his gaze from the plinth and followed the stream of people toward the ceremonial chapel at the heart of the cemetery. Tansya noticed him behind her and slowed, dropping back to his side. Lazlo appreciated the thought, though he'd never admit that aloud.

A moment later, Kazren looked around for him, then did the same. Together, the three of them approached his old master's final event.

The crowd narrowed as it squeezed inside the small chapel. Briefly, he wondered how they would all fit. But once he crossed the threshold, he understood: someone had cast an enlargement spell on the inside. There was plenty of space for the entire campus in here, the little chapel widening and its ceiling growing until it could have rivaled the most beautiful cathedral on the continent.

Ebus didn't pay any mind to the stained-glass windows or elaborate wooden pews, though. Instead, his eyes fell on the dark wood coffin waiting at the front of the chapel, on display for the whole world to see. Heaps of flowers had been placed all around it, as if to soften the stark lines of that box.

Lazlo's chest seized. The coffin looked so... small. Like it couldn't possibly contain the brilliant, neon-bright personality that had been Ebus.

It doesn't, he reminded himself. It was only his body in there. Ebus himself had long passed on to whatever awaited them all in the next realm.

Muzud stood beside the coffin, dressed in funereal black robes. Unihoast hovered beside him, head bowed, apparently deep in meditation. Other faculty members Lazlo recognized dotted the crowd. He caught a glimpse of Bishop's familiar profile and quickly looked away, face flushed.

He had not sought out his old friend since his arrival on campus. He knew that sooner or later, he'd need to pop that particular boil. Face up to what he'd done—and what he hadn't done to fix it, in all the years since. But he had enough on his mind today. He'd save righting that mistake for another time.

Lazlo planned to linger near the back of the crowd, but the moment Muzud caught his eye, he waved Lazlo forward.

Lazlo cast one last worried glance at Tansya, who caught his hand and squeezed. After the favor Muzud granted him yesterday, Lazlo could hardly refuse. He jerked his head toward Kazren, and Tansya silently nodded, agreeing to watch over the girl. Then Lazlo left to take his place beside Muzud at the head of the room.

The entire academy had shut down for the day, to allow all students and faculty to attend. Most of the staff came as well—Lazlo spotted a few familiar faces among the cooks and cleaning crews. Headmaster Ebus had been a rare headmaster, taking interest in every aspect of campus, not just academics and students. When he first got appointed, he'd raised staff wages for the first time in decades. He also took it upon himself to build new staff housing, and to listen to any complaints people had, all the way down to the janitors and prep cooks.

Once every seat in the magically-enlarged chapel had filled, Master Ugast, dean of illusions, stepped forward to begin the eulogy.

Lazlo bowed his head, unable to keep his eyes from misting.

Ugast talked about Ebus' academic achievements, his talented pupils, and the many projects he'd completed both before he became

65

headmaster and afterward. But Ebus had been more than just his academics. He'd been kind, compassionate, a good listener and an even better friend.

Lazlo shut his eyes until Ugast finished speaking, afraid he'd lose any composure he had left otherwise.

But instinct shouted at him to look up again. *You need to pay attention.* If someone had wished his old master harm, then surely there might be clues among the audience.

Steeling himself, Lazlo took a deep breath and lifted his head once more. He scanned the room systematically, starting at the back left and working his way toward the front and right. He took note of all the instructors he recognized—though if any newer hires were missing, he wouldn't know. To his eye, it seemed like the entire academy had turned out.

Some students weren't paying attention. He noticed a cluster of first years whispering at the back, another clump of third years dozing off in front. But for the most part, people seemed respectful, somber.

He accidentally caught Bishop's eye when he reached the front row center. This time, it was Bishop who looked away, bowing his head as if in prayer. Lazlo wasn't fooled. But he kept moving. He couldn't exactly complain—he'd done the same thing earlier.

So we both want to avoid it. Good. That made things a little simpler.

Suddenly, something tweaked his senses. It was almost as if a bad smell seeped into the room—except all Lazlo could really smell were the flowers heaped around the coffin. His eyes tracked the source of the sensation. Far at the back of the chapel, near the little doors that a footman had closed when the ceremony began, he spotted a figure dressed all in black. They were too far away for Lazlo to make out their features. Dark hair, pale skin, that was all he could discern. But something about their posture struck him as odd.

They stood, as did a few other unlucky latecomers who'd missed the chance to snag seats. But this person wasn't leaning against the wall like most other latecomers. Nor were they standing at attention like the guards and employees around the chapel. Instead, they leaned forward, hands behind their back. They looked eager, almost. Like they were hungry to see more of what was happening.

It struck him as odd behavior for a funeral.

Casting a quick glance at Master Ugast—still speaking—Lazlo shoved both hands into his pockets. He moved his fingers in a familiar gesture, mouthing the magic words under his breath. A simple divination spell should enhance his vision, allowing him to see who that person was.

But no sooner had he cast the spell than the figure vanished.

Lazlo's eyes widened. Frantically, he searched the back of the chapel with his newly-enhanced vision. He could make out every single face of the people back there now, yet nowhere did he see the dark-clad figure from a second ago.

His brow puckered. They were still within the academy grounds. Nobody could portal here. Which meant, whoever that was could not have truly vanished in midair, as they seemed to. *Unless...*

Could they have been a conjuration themselves? A projection of someone who wanted to attend the funeral, but not in person?

Lazlo shook his head. Given the school's protective wards, that, too, would be impossible. The only reason he could cast his own divination spell right now was because he was inside the wards, wearing an academy bracelet.

Unless it was someone inside the academy. Somebody with a bracelet, who did not attend the funeral in person...

He scanned the crowd again, but it was useless to try and identify everyone. There must be at least a thousand people here, if not more.

Frustrated, Lazlo dragged his attention back to the ceremony, blinking away the remnants of the divination spell. Ugast was just wrapping up his eulogy. In a moment, Muzud would ask the pallbearers to step forward—of whom Lazlo was one, he'd been informed just last night.

He needed to tell someone to keep an eye out, in case the figure returned. Lazlo scanned the audience again until he found Tansya, seated next to Kazren at the side. He caught her eye and widened his.

Tansya tilted her head, confused.

Lazlo tried to gesture with his eyes, repeatedly looking over at the chapel doors.

Tansya shrugged one shoulder and shook her head. Kazren noticed him looking, now, and glanced between the druid and the mage. He watched Kazren's mouth move, her hands lifting. Lazlo winced—telepathy spells were difficult to cast in secret, since they involved wide, obvious gestures. He could never have gotten away with it up here, in view of the entire academy.

But luckily, most people's eyes were still fixed on Ugast and the coffin. Nobody noticed Kazren gesticulating wildly, except for a couple of seat-mates who shot her dirty looks. Tansya whispered something, probably giving some excuse for Kazren's behavior.

A moment later, Lazlo felt Kazren's presence in his mind. He shut his eyes, quickly undoing the usual mental seals he kept around his mind, to prevent other mages from prying where they didn't belong.

What happened? Is something wrong? Kazren's voice flooded Lazlo's head. He winced, reaching up to rub his ear. He was pretty sure this was Kazren's first time using a spell she'd only read about—not bad for a first attempt, but she hadn't learned to modulate her volume yet.

Concentrating, Lazlo thought, *I noticed someone watching the funeral at the back of the chapel. They were acting suspicious, but when I tried to get a closer look at them, they vanished.*

He waited a moment, hoping that he'd gotten his message across. Telepathy could be a tricky one. Not everybody's thoughts or minds worked the same way, and it could be difficult to translate all of another person's thoughts.

But Kazren had always been a quick study. *We'll keep an eye out,* she said—or to his ear, seemed to shout. He flinched again, relieved when Kazren broke the connection.

Not a moment too soon. Acting Headmaster Muzud stepped forward to take the floor from Ugast. "Will our pallbearers please step forward?"

Head bowed, Lazlo stepped toward the coffin. To his surprise, Bishop rose too, along with Master Ugast and a few other instructors Lazlo vaguely remembered. *When did Ebus get close enough to Bishop to make him a pallbearer?* Lazlo and Bishop avoided eye contact as they took their positions to either side of the head of the coffin.

Muzud recited a prayer, his deep baritone echoing throughout the chapel. Then, at a gesture from him, all of the pallbearers stooped to pick up a handle.

The coffin felt impossibly light. Someone must have spelled it weightless, because even with six of them, Lazlo should have been able to feel more than this featherweight on his shoulder. His throat tightened, threatening to close as he waited for Muzud to finish the last blessing.

Music began to play, a string band hidden somewhere in the eaves. That was their cue. Lazlo fell into step with Bishop and the others.

Even without seeing each other, or giving any sign that either one was aware of the other's presence, they still matched stride so easily after all these years. Lazlo walked up the aisle of the chapel, scanning the crowd. Kazren and Tansya were both dry-eyed, looking around for some sign of the figure, no doubt. But more than a few people sniffled, handkerchiefs pressed to their eyes or mouths.

Lazlo was torn between giving in to his emotions and staying alert. In the end, instinct won out. He swallowed any grief for now— he could process that later. Instead, he studied the faces around the exit they walked toward. But he saw no sign of the figure from earlier. Only bored fourth years, who arrived too late to snag seats.

He felt a shift in the weight of the coffin, and glanced down at Bishop's feet. They were just visible under the smooth oak paneling. He still wore his old boots, the ones he and Lazlo got when they joined the king's army what seemed like a lifetime ago now. Lazlo couldn't help but smirk. *Still a soldier at heart.* Now, instead of guarding the king's troops, Bishop stood guard over the Mound's most prized treasury: The Black Tower.

Lazlo tried not to think about the last time he saw Bishop. The mingled hurt and resentment in his friend's eye. *Was it worth it?* he asked himself, all these years later.

No. Much as he'd liked Osenne at the time, respected her company... No, she wasn't worth losing Bishop over.

But he could hardly change that now.

Two chapel aides in gold cloaks opened the rear doors for the procession. Lazlo and Bishop led the way out into the cemetery. Mages' funeral processions always took place on foot, out of respect for the dead, who could no longer travel the way mages often did— via one spell or another, never needing to do the hard work.

They did it now, for Ebus' sake.

Lazlo and Bishop and the others carried him all the way across the cemetery on foot. Up the hill to the center of the graveyard, where the raised white marble plinth had been erected. Ebus' name had

69

been carved into the headstone already, beside his wife's old, weathered marker.

Lazlo swallowed around a sudden, hard lump. He'd visited this site before. Only once, with Master Ebus. He'd come too early for a study session and found his master leaving the manor. When Lazlo asked where he was going, Ebus said, "I've got an errand. Stay here with Pierce or come along."

Excited to be asked somewhere alone—he and Pierce were constantly vying for Ebus' approval and attention—Lazlo had leapt at the chance. But when they reached the cemetery, his eagerness waned. "Why are we going there?" he'd asked.

Ebus had smiled and produced a bouquet of flowers from beneath his cloak. "Because today is my anniversary, dear boy. Help me celebrate."

So they'd trekked all the way up the hill to this tomb. The plinth wasn't here yet—they'd clearly added that recently, in the headmaster's honor. At the time, it was just a grassy hilltop with a big marble tombstone at the head. Double-size, though only one side had been filled in.

Lazlo remembered squinting at the name and dates. "Who was she?" he'd asked.

"The love of my life," Ebus had said. He'd nestled the flowers against the gravestone with a fond smile.

"I hope you're with her now," Lazlo whispered, as cemetery workers came forward to take the coffin from their shoulders and set it on the plinth. Tonight, he knew, they would open the ground beneath it and slot Ebus under there, next to his love.

For now, the coffin would remain, for anyone who wished to pay their individual respects throughout the day.

Lazlo hung back, letting the other pallbearers go first. One by one, they placed their hands atop the smooth wood, murmuring goodbyes. Some smiled. Others cried. Bishop bent to press his forehead against the coffin for a moment before he straightened and wiped an eyelid.

They must have gotten much closer since Lazlo left campus. He didn't remember Ebus and Bishop operating in the same circles before.

It warmed him to think of them together. No matter how his and Bishop's friendship had ended up, Lazlo still wished him well. He'd been a good friend. Steadfast, loyal. Not forgiving, never that, but... he'd been better to Lazlo than Lazlo had perhaps deserved.

Once Bishop departed, Lazlo stepped forward. Some of the crowd had followed them to the grave from the chapel. He sensed curious eyes on him. But he forced himself to ignore the stares and planted a palm on top of Ebus' coffin instead.

The wood felt warm to the touch. Soft. If he closed his eyes, he could almost imagine he felt it breathing.

"I'm sorry," Lazlo whispered under his breath. "For leaving. And for staying away so long. I can't make up for that, but... I promise I'll find out what really happened to you."

***

He bowed his head, mouthed a quick prayer, and then moved away. He didn't look back until he'd reached the edge of the hill, where the grass sloped back down toward the smaller, less impressive tombs. He turned, chest tight. And he could have sworn, for a split second, he saw a flash of bright blue light flare to life above the coffin.

Chapter Ten

T hat dripping sound was going to drive him mad.

Pierce Vinther, once a celebrated master at the Wizards of the Mound Academy and on track to become the next headmaster in his mentor's stead, scowled at the far side of his dark cell. It must be raining upstairs, on the clifftop town above them. Anytime it rained, they got the runoff down here.

In fact, this whole structure used to serve as a drainage system for the town. Drains crowded the floor around him, remnants of its old purpose. It still acted as a drain—just now there were a few people in the way. Suspended between the muddy streets above and the ocean waves crashing far below, King Owain had built his most secure dungeon yet.

It needed to be, to hold men like Pierce.

Thick slabs of somaritium surrounded the dungeon on all four sides—embedded in the walls, buried beneath the streets overhead, layered into the cement drains under Pierce's feet. The rare metal inhibited magic of all kinds. No teleportation spell or portal ring could fetch him out of this hell.

He had one window, eight feet up the wall and barely large enough to fit a fist through. All he could see through it during the daytime was a slash of blue, or a patch of stars at night. He could hear the waves crashing on the rocks below, though, and seagulls crying for their dinners as they wheeled past his perch.

In his early days, Pierce used to try to lure them in. He'd saved crumbs from his morning meal, threw them up onto the windowsill.

Apparently even the birds didn't like the cook's swill. The rats didn't mind, though, sneaking in from god-knew-where—probably the damned drains—to snatch a taste.

Pierce learned better. Now he ate every morsel he was given.

He sprawled on the cold floor of his cell, trying not to focus on the drip, drip, drip…

If only it would rain harder. Kick up a real thunderstorm—he missed the kind of wild storms they got back at the Mound. Here was all drizzly seaside mist, barely worthy of the title. It seeped into every inch of his cell, infuse it with moisture and mildew and mold, and he didn't even get the wild pleasure of a lightning crack or roll of thunder.

Pierce clapped both hands over his ears and groaned.

His voice echoed back to him. Aside from the three daily visits from his guards, it was the only voice he'd heard in... he'd lost count. Eight months? Nine? He'd been in general pop, until one too many attempts to escape got him labeled high-risk.

They sent him here to languish. *To die.* Nobody ever came back from the solitary cells.

He moaned again, just to hear something different. It reverberated against the metallic walls and the heavy somaritium bars at the entrance of his cell.

When he first came down here, he'd had a neighbor. An old gnome. Pierce didn't even know he was there for the first week. Then he'd heard a noise and followed it, assuming a rat was lurking outside his cell. When he spotted the gnome, the old man had darted away to hide on his cot, burying himself in his blanket like he'd seen a ghost.

A few months ago, the gnome vanished, as silent as ever. Pierce never even caught his name. He did, however, notice the guards cleaning out his cell. The lead guard carried a suspiciously human-sized lump wrapped in a blanket out of it, slung unceremoniously over one shoulder.

That would be him, soon. Pierce could feel it in his bones. It wasn't the damp getting to him, or the cold, or the horrible food. It wasn't even the solitude—Pierce was used to being alone these days.

No. What would kill him would be the fury.

It lingered behind his eyelids every time he shut them. White hot, blazing, like a fire magic spell he didn't know how to douse. Every night, he tucked himself onto the hard wooden cot chained to the wall—on the far side of the cell from the windows, to keep it as dry as possible—and he dreamt of death.

He saw his father torn apart in a hundred different ways. His sister, on the other hand, always died the same way. With her eyes on Pierce's, her lips shaping his name. She looked younger in his

73

dreams than she'd been the day she actually died. More like the girl he'd grown up with. His baby sister, four years younger, always getting into trouble.

He could still remember the day she was born. It was his earliest memory—his mother placing the little screaming bundle into his arms. *You're a big brother now,* his mother said. *It's your job to look out for her.*

He'd failed so spectacularly that he couldn't believe his mother didn't rise from her own grave to drag him into death as punishment.

He'd deserve it. He'd go willingly, if he could, except he had one last thing he needed to do here.

He rubbed his eyelids until red dots flashed across his vision. Behind them, he pictured the Mound on the last day he'd seen it. Ebus' face as Pierce was led away.

Don't let him do this to me, he imagined begging. *Please. You know it's not right.*

It wasn't right, none of it. Nor was it fair. He rotted here, while Lazlo walked free, after what he did? There was no real justice in the world. No great karmic balance on the scales. Shit just happened, and the worst shit always seemed to happen to the best people.

How much more damage had Lazlo caused in the years since? How many more lives had he ruined from his high-and-mighty position on the bench? Who was his next target? Ebus?

Thinking of their old mentor sent a fresh wave of agony through Pierce. He clutched his chest, gasping at the sudden sharpness. *Could you die of a broken heart?*

The telltale jangle of keys interrupted his ruminating. He sat up, blinking stars from his vision. A glance at the window confirmed—it was still bright outside. Nowhere near time for third meal yet, and they'd served the second of the day only an hour ago. So what was this?

Pierce grabbed hold of the cot and used the sturdy wood frame to haul himself to his feet. He stumbled to the narrow cell door. Through a gap in the bars, he could see the whole of his world: a staircase down into the dungeon and two other cells. One long vacant, the other just recently emptied of the old gnome.

Pierce watched, curious, as wavering torchlight descended the stairs. He heard voices—more than one guard. Frowning, he pressed his face against the bars for a better view. He was long past caring about any punishments from the guards. He'd learned they didn't much care what he did, so long as he ate his food and passed them the waste bucket upon command.

For the most part, the guards acted like he didn't even exist. They didn't respond to his questions, or react to his attempts to chat. When he first got moved down here, he'd tried anything to get their attention. He'd thrown things, cursed them, pleaded, cried. He'd asked questions about their families, jobs, names.

Nothing.

Pierce understood, in a sick, appreciative sort of way. Solitary meant *alone*. If the guards spoke to him at all, he wouldn't be anymore.

So, he felt no compunction about watching them now. If they were going to treat him like a non-entity, then he'd treat them like his personal entertainment.

He watched one guard enter and affix his torch to a bracket on the wall. Then he stepped aside for a second guard, who came in with one arm wrapped firmly around a third person's bicep.

Pierce's eyes widened.

The new prisoner was a woman. She wore the same shapeless beige sack Pierce and all the other prisoners were issued. Her feet were bare, her nails shorn into blunt squares. But under the sack, he could see a hint of curves. And they'd allowed her to keep a tangle of shoulder-length brown hair—they'd shaved Pierce and the gnome's head upon arrival, and a barber came through once a month to shave it all off again.

Pierce wondered if they'd do that to the woman, eventually.

He watched as a third guard brought up the rear, shoving the woman none-too-gently toward the cell opposite. The gnome's old digs. Pierce wondered if they'd even bothered to clean, after the last resident passed away in there. His stomach churned sympathetically at the thought.

He hadn't seen a woman in months. Not since he'd been sent to solitary from the main floor, and even up there, women had been rare. Human and non-magical women were sent to another dungeon. Only mages or druids or otherwise magically talented women wound up here, in the dungeon designed to restrain people nobody else could.

Whoever this woman was, she must have power.

Sensing his gaze, the woman looked up, as the guards finished unlocking her cell. Their eyes met. She didn't shy away from his scrutiny. Instead, she returned it, giving him a frank once-over that made him feel even more naked than on wash days, when the guards hauled in buckets of cold water for him to dump over himself.

The first guard interrupted her stare by shoving her, rather unceremoniously, into the cell. The second tossed a wooden bowl after her, which clattered on the stone floor.

"Thanks a lot, assholes," the woman snapped.

None of the guards reacted. They slammed the cell, locking it.

"How long am I going to be down here?" she asked their retreating backs. As usual, no reaction. "Hey! I'm talking to you." Her voice rose an octave, like she was trying to suppress her panic, but not quite succeeding.

Pierce knew the feeling. He offered her a sympathetic grimace. "You get used to it. I'm Pierce, by the way." He said, eager to talk to anyone at this point.

"Doubtful," she muttered. She crouched to pick up her bowl and a small mug for water. She set them on the shelf above her cot, then considered the scratchy blanket on the cot, nose wrinkled in distaste.

"What's your name?" he asked, when she didn't offer.

The ghost of a smile touched the woman's mouth. She must have been quite beautiful, at some point, if she still looked this good down here.

That, or he was just getting desperate, alone in the dark.

"That information will cost you," she joked.

"Cost me what, exactly?" Pierce replied. A kernel of warmth lodged in his chest. Maybe solitary didn't have to be *completely* alone.

"Hmm, let's see." The woman pretended to take a long survey of her cell. "What've you got over there? I'm gonna guess the same shit blanket and splinter-filled bowl."

Pierce fetched his own blanket and bowl, holding them up as proof.

The woman snorted. "Then I guess it'll have to be the old type of payment for me." She dropped cross-legged onto her bunk. From that angle, Pierce could only see her if he remained standing at the cell door.

76

He did. Gave him an excuse to stretch his legs, and besides, the view was better than anything inside the four walls of his own cell. "What type of payment might that be?"

The woman grinned. "Tell me your story and I'll tell you mine."

Pierce's heart warmed. He had a feeling his stay here just got the tiniest bit more survivable. Yet it was years since he had a conversation with anyone, let alone a woman. Most prisoners kept to themselves, an unspoken rule of survival. Yet down here in the dungeon, it was different. It was just the two of them. Pierce knew it was a risk, at this point it was a risk worth taking.

Chapter Eleven

After the ceremony, Lazlo lingered by the cemetery gate. He was itching to reunite with Tansya and Kazren, to discuss what they may or may not have found in the chapel. Before he could, though, he needed to get through the long line of faculty and old friends who stopped by to offer him their condolences.

Acting Headmaster Muzud came first, slapping Lazlo's back and telling him he'd done an honorable job today. Then came Mariou, squeezing his hand and whispering her thanks for bringing Ebus home. Master Edua and Klaern stopped by, as did the Minister of Healing, Erman Vecdi, who Lazlo remembered from his early days at the academy.

Bishop waited until the crowd around Lazlo was several people deep before he strode past, edging widely around the group. Lazlo's heart sank. He'd been hoping to get a moment alone with his old friend.

Noticing his expression, Mariou touched Lazlo's arm. "Bishop does miss you, you know," she murmured, once the others had moved on to talk to one another. "He knows he's got you to thank for recommending him to Headmaster Ebus, too. You're the reason he got hired here and promoted so high. He just doesn't know how to say any of that to you after... well, everything."

Lazlo winced. "He told you what happened?" Thoughts of Osenne weighed heavily on his shoulders.

Mariou sighed softly. "A couple years after you left, Bishop accepted the position as Chief of Shields for the Black Tower."

Lazlo smiled. "I heard through the grapevine, yes. I was happy for him."

"He only accepted the position because Osenne went back to her church," Mariou said. "He wanted to follow her, but she forbade it. She said she'd never give up her sworn path for anyone else, so he shouldn't either."

Lazlo grimaced. To be fair, Osenne had been straightforward with both of them from the start about her desires. She was open-hearted, full of love, and she refused to constrain that love to any one person. And her duty to her church and her god came before any earthbound affairs. "I worried that might happen," Lazlo finally admitted.

Mariou nodded. "He loved her. Maybe too much, but, sometimes we can't help ourselves, can we?" A twinkle entered her eye, and she darted a quick look over her shoulder at where Tansya lingered near the cemetery gate with Kazren.

Lazlo ignored this. "You must be close with Bishop, if he told you all this."

Mariou lifted a hand to wave from side-to-side. "Not very. But he and Ebus grew very close in recent years. They met to play chess every Sunday, without fail. Sometimes Bishop would come to the house for dinners during the week too—not a lot of the other faculty associate with the Black Tower employees. You know how mages can be about non-magical types." Mariou wrinkled her nose.

So did Lazlo. He'd always hated that artificial divide here. Mages holding themselves above everyone else at the Mound, as if they were better just by dint of having been born with more magical aptitude. "Well, I'm glad he had you two to confide in, then," Lazlo said. "And that Master Ebus had another friend toward the end."

Mariou smiled. "I know he's acting prickly now, but..." Her gaze shifted to the distance. Lazlo followed it to watch Bishop marching on foot across campus, while mages whizzed past in carriages or drifted along via flight spells. But that was his friend all over—rather take himself on his own two feet than rely on anyone or anything else. "Please don't give up on him," Mariou murmured. "I know he'd love to reconnect with you. It's just... a difficult subject for him."

Lazlo winced. "I still feel horrible about the whole thing," he admitted. "If I'd known how badly he'd take it..." Lazlo stopped himself. Because he had known, hadn't he? From the start, he'd seen the way Bishop looked at Osenne—and the way Osenne didn't look at Bishop.

He knew what was between them, but when Osenne's gaze fell on him that day, deep into their trek together, Lazlo had caved in to his baser instincts. He'd lied and told himself he couldn't be blamed.

They were open, after all, and Osenne had been straightforward with Bishop from day one about her predilections.

But he'd known what it would do to his friendship. *I knew.*

"I know you must, dear," Mariou was saying, patting his arm.

Lazlo forced a smile. "I will meet with him," he promised. "And thank you for telling me." He smiled and squeezed Mariou's hand one more time, then stepped back to wave while she climbed into her own carriage.

Once the crowd dissipated, Tansya and Kazren stepped forward to join Lazlo. Before Tansya said a word, Lazlo could tell from Tansya's grim expression that they didn't find anything. "I searched everywhere in that chapel," Tansya murmured. "And around the cemetery afterwards. No signs of anyone using any kind of illusion or deception spells. Of course, there were so many people, I could've missed something, but..."

"What did the person look like?" Kazren asked.

Lazlo shook his head. "I was too far away. It could've just been a latecomer anyway. They wore black, but..."

"So did ninety percent of that room," Tansya finished for him. She tapped her chin, deep in thought.

"We're better off pursuing other avenues of investigation," Lazlo said. "For example, I'd love to talk to the SAA master who dueled him."

Kazren arched a brow. "Is that possible? Wouldn't he be all the way back at Scientia Academy now?"

Lazlo shook his head. "They didn't cancel the tournament, according to Ebus' mentee Eldon. They postponed it until after the funeral, but knowing the Mound, that means it will resume again soon. And that SAA master, Krauss, he defeated our headmaster. No way he'd bow out of the tournament now."

"Even after killing a man?" Tansya's jaw dropped. "I always knew mages were heartless, but..."

Kazren stiffened, looking defensive. "It's not heartless. There are rules, proper procedures to follow. What happened to Headmaster Ebus was a terrible accident, but the peacemakers on campus will have investigated the incident thoroughly. If they found no signs of wrongdoing in the Spellduel itself, then I don't see why the tournament shouldn't continue. Everyone knows the risks when they agree to participate."

Lazlo glanced at Kazren, a knowing look in his eye. "Let me guess. You want to enter."

Kazren raised her chin, but she had the good grace not to deny it. "I spoke to the tournament referees. The first round has already been fought, which means I can't enter the general duels and work my way up the brackets. But I could get on the board as a wildcard if I can find someone to accept a direct challenge from me."

Lazlo suddenly realized where this was going. "Kazren..."

"That SAA guy, Master Krauss. Nobody will want to fight him after what happened to the headmaster. But he still hasn't withdrawn from the tournament. He's probably worried that if he backs out now, people will think he's admitting fault. He'd accept a challenge from me, I'm sure of it."

"Absolutely not." Lazlo groaned.

"Why?" Kazren set her jaw. "We can kill two problems with one spell. You need to talk to the guy and figure out if he did anything shady to your old master. I need to get in Spellduel practice—you said so yourself!"

"I meant you should duel other students your own age. Show off a little to the council. Not challenge a master from another university, someone with *years* more experience than you."

"You said I'm ready," Kazren protested.

"Not for this." Lazlo cut her off with a curt gesture. "Enough. We're not discussing this anymore—I forbid you from challenging him."

Kazren's lower lip jutted out. She folded her arms, glaring across the fields toward the massive Spellduel arena dome.

Tansya rested a hand on Kazren's shoulder, trying for sympathy, but Kazren shrugged her off angrily. Tansya sighed. "While I agree with you..." Tansya's gaze cut to Lazlo's. "That does mean we need to find another reason to talk to this man. What was his name? Krauss?"

"Master Grim Krauss," Lazlo replied. "And, I believe I have an idea." Though he wouldn't admit it, Kazren's impassioned speech *had* given him some inspiration. He just hoped his student didn't resent him even more once she heard his plan. "First, though, let's exhaust all our other avenues of pursuit."

***

Lazlo arrived at the academy branch of the peacekeepers a few hours later. He was starting to feel his age—he didn't recognize anyone in the office. It was strange to be back here after so long. His first position had been in an office adjoined to this building—long before he'd been made a member of the teaching staff, Lazlo had worked as a judge for the academy. Given his background as a law student, and his then-newly-discovered magical talent, it made sense.

The judiciary office butted up against the peacemakers'—parallel positions, working closely together but never quite in tandem. The peacemakers were tasked with preventing crimes and catching any criminals they couldn't stop.

Lazlo's job, on the other hand, had been to pass sentence on the ones they caught. He'd always been a little envious of the peacemakers. Their job seemed the easier, more straightforward one. Uncover the truth, ferret out lies. His job felt far more nebulous. Who was he to weigh the human heart and determine its value? What gave him the authority to determine how long someone ought to suffer for their mistakes, or in what manner?

A young peacemaker stepped forward, dragging Lazlo from his reverie. "Welcome, sir. Can I help you with something?" the young man—boy, really—asked. God, he must barely be out of army basic training.

Lazlo cleared his throat. "Yes, I'm Master Lazlo Redthorn. I'd like to talk to whoever is handling Headmaster Ebus' case—the headmaster was a close personal friend," he added, when the boy showed no signs of recognizing his name.

The young peacemaker frowned. "I'm sorry, sir, but I'm not at liberty to—"

"Is that Master Lazlo I hear?" called a familiar voice from the adjacent hallway.

The boy stopped short and whipped around. Lazlo followed his gaze to Master Bekir Halis, the commissioner of the peacekeepers on campus. The boy's eyes widened, and he practically dove out of the commissioner's way, scurrying back to his own desk with his shoulders raised.

"Master Bekir." Lazlo grinned and held out a hand. "I didn't realize you were still here."

The commissioner shook his hand gruffly, grip firm but gentle. "For my sins, yes. Still kicking around." He released Lazlo and beckoned him up the hallway. "Been a long time, my friend. Please, step into my office."

Lazlo followed Bekir into his office. They sat across from one another, Bekir in a plush reclining chair and Lazlo on one of two stuffed visitor's armchairs.

No sooner had Bekir sat than he lurched up again. "Oh, can I get you anything?"

Lazlo waved him off. "No, thanks. I'm fine. Just came by to—"

"Let me guess." Bekir's jaw was set, a grim spark in his eye. "You want to discuss your old master's case?"

"I don't mean to overstep or intrude," Lazlo replied. "It's only... you must understand, the circumstances are all so sudden and strange."

Bekir shook his head, though he didn't seem irritated. "Oh, I understand that, all right." He shifted toward the open office door and called a name loudly.

A moment later, a peacekeeper knocked on the doorframe. "Yes, sir?"

"Fetch me Ebus' file, would you?" Bekir asked. "And a pair of coffees while you're at it."

The clerk nodded and closed the door after himself.

Bekir heaved a sigh that seemed never-ending. "I know how it must look, from the outside," he said. "But we investigated every inch of that arena. We interrogated that Master Grim for hours, too—frankly, he seemed even more shocked than any of us. It really does seem like a terrible accident."

They watched one another in tense silence for a minute, until the clerk knocked, back again with the files. He scurried off for the requested coffees while Bekir passed Lazlo the file. "Have at it," he said.

Lazlo flipped open the cover with a pang of nostalgia. He remembered reading through dozens of cases like this, back when he'd served as judge. He and Bekir would often meet here in this very office to discuss them—Bekir always pushing for harsher sentences, Lazlo arguing for mercy where he found it applicable.

His chest tightened. Sometimes, he was too free with his sympathy. Too eager to extend mercy. Not aware of who he was putting in danger when he did.

He couldn't help but think of the worst judgment he ever made. His biggest mistake—far worse than his fuckup with Bishop and Osenne. At the time, he'd thought he was being fair. Magnanimous. Giving a man another shot at life.

In reality, his mercy sentenced two innocent people to death and a third to prison.

"Lazlo?" Bekir's voice shattered his reverie.

Lazlo squeezed his eyes shut, opened them again. He returned to the file, swallowing hard. "Says here the cause of death was ruled a severe blow to the head?" Lazlo asked.

Bekir nodded. "Sustained when he hit the arena floor the second time."

Lazlo kept reading. He made himself pore over every individual wound Ebus received—the scrapes along his arms, the dirt under his fingernails from when he hauled himself off the arena floor. He read about Ebus' final meal, the half-digested breakfast in his gut.

That gave him pause. "Did you run a toxic substances report?" he asked, remembering what Mariou and Eldon said about Ebus feeling ill for a few days leading up to the duel.

Bekir nodded again. "Ran the standard report. Came back clean."

"Did you speak to his steward or any of his students?" Lazlo frowned.

Bekir hesitated. "Didn't much see the need. He died in the arena; we all saw it."

"Because I'm staying at his manor right now," Lazlo forged on. "And Ebus' current mentee told me that his master had been feeling off for days before the Spellduel. He said it seemed like a stomach bug, or perhaps food poisoning…"

Bekir locked eyes with Lazlo, a line darkening his brow. "I'll have them run the tests again. The more extensive version."

"Don't just check for the deadly poisons," Lazlo advised. "Look for long and slow-acting toxins. The kind that take time to build up and cause any real damage. If whoever did this knew about Ebus' upcoming duel, perhaps they only wanted to weaken him and give Grim an advantage. Or…"

"Or they knew if they got Ebus weak enough, it would only take a stray spell to fell him," Bekir murmured. "Damn. I should've thought of that."

Lazlo offered a faint smile. "That's why I'm here. To think like the worst of the worst."

Bekir snorted. Then he sobered again. "I am sorry, my friend. Headmaster Ebus had no surviving kin, but if anything, you're the closest he had to a son."

And I abandoned him, Lazlo thought. Too scared to return to this campus for fear of all the ghosts haunting it. He hadn't seen Ebus in over a year when his old mentor passed. Hadn't visited him at his manor in many more. Guilt swelled, thickening his throat.

He forced it away, swallowed hard. "I really appreciate your time," he said. "Means the world to me."

Bekir waved him off. "We'll have it done as soon as possible. Tomorrow morning at the outset." He glanced at his wristband. "They won't have interred him yet, but I should probably contact the cemetery just to…"

"Of course." Lazlo pushed out of his chair to stand.

"I'll send word as soon as we get the results." The commissioner stuck out his hand again, and Lazlo shook it once more. But as he backed out of the office, his mind was years away, deep in the worst memory of his life.

Chapter Twelve

Lazlo had spent the night at Master Ebus' manor, up late studying the particulars of a case involving a student who stole from his classmate. Lazlo was inclined to give the boy a light sentence, given the fact that it was his first infraction. Confinement to his dormitory for a semester, his bracelet spelled so he could only attend classes and eat meals?

He'd puzzled over previous similar cases, and dozed off in the wee hours, drooling onto the case books.

Master Ebus had woken him first thing with a carafe of tea and a frown. "Trouble on campus," Master Ebus said. "Best get dressed quickly. The headmaster just sent for you."

Lazlo practically sprinted up to his rooms to change. He'd been working as a judge at the Wizards of the Mound Academy for three years by that point, but he still felt the precariousness of his position. He was an outsider here in more ways than one—a former law student, who grew up thinking himself a magicless human. Then he'd been a king's soldier, hardened in battle, before doing the king such a huge service that the king requested he be given a post here at the Mound, despite his lack of training.

For the last three years, Lazlo had split his time between two lives. In one, he studied alongside his best friend Pierce—working hard, and with a little friendly competition, to earn Master Ebus' favor. In his other life, he served as the campus judge—the only position the headmaster could think to grant him, since Lazlo had nowhere near enough magical training to become a master yet.

He hadn't even graduate from the academy, let alone written the spellbook he'd need to complete before he could become a master like Ebus.

He was an anomaly, and he felt it every time he walked out onto campus. He didn't fit in with the other students, most of whom were a decade younger. He didn't fit in with the masters, either, who'd spent their lives at the Mound, not out soldiering. Nor did he quite fit with the peacemakers and guards employed here, although his life experience more closely aligned with theirs. Because none of them had been taken under Master Ebus' wing; none of them had "more magical potential than half the first years can shake a stick at," as Master Ebus had once embarrassingly put it.

No, Lazlo was alone here. Which was why he worked so hard at his position. He needed to impress the headmaster, make the right judgments, and keep this campus safe. That was his job as the judge.

Lazlo dressed in a flurry of robes and undergarments. He sprinted back downstairs before Master Ebus had even summoned a carriage, out of breath and panting from the effort.

Pierce ran into him at the base of the steps, bleary-eyed from his own late night of studying. "Did you join the fire brigade now too?" Pierce joked, slapping his back. "You look like you're running to stop a blaze."

Lazlo forced a smile and a laugh. "Summons from the office, that's all."

Pierce affected a sigh. "Ah, yes. Important business. Got to ground another student for pilfering from the kitchens—oh, or maybe they've finally caught whoever vandalized the arena last month." Pierce's eyes glittered, but Lazlo knew his teasing wasn't malicious.

Pierce was the closest thing Lazlo had to a brother on campus. An annoying younger brother who always did better on the tests than Lazlo (probably because unlike Lazlo, Pierce was able to devote himself full-time to his studies), but a brother all the same. "You'd better hurry up and get studying," Lazlo shot back. "Or I'm going to obliterate you on the next exam."

Pierce snorted. "In your dreams. I scored five whole points higher last time."

"Because you got bonus points for writing a whole unnecessary essay," Lazlo grumbled. "That's hardly fair. I didn't know that was an option!"

"Spend more time hitting the books and less time sitting on the bench, then," Pierce replied. Then his expression softened. "Seriously, I'll bet Headmaster Agnellus would give you a break if you asked for one. Tell him that juggling the judge's bench and your studies is a bit much. At least during finals."

Lazlo shook his head, stubborn as ever. "I can handle it."

Pierce's frown deepened. "You'd be way ahead of me if you weren't doing both," he said, in a rare burst of honesty. "I hate to see you wasting your talent on a position like that, when you could be—"

"Judges are important," Lazlo interrupted.

"Not as important as masters." Pierce gestured at the soaring roof over their heads. "Don't you want this? A manor of your own, and pupils to tutor? Instead of spending all your time holed up in some stuffy office with peacekeepers…"

"Hey." Lazlo's voice lowered. "They keep this campus safe. Never forget that."

Pierce's nose wrinkled. "This campus keeps itself safe. Come on. There hasn't been any real crime here since that dragon attack back when *Ebus* was young…"

Lazlo straightened and brushed off his clothes. "I've got to go."

Pierce grabbed his arm. "Are you coming to dinner tonight? Dad's steward is making that dish you like, the one from the southlands."

Lazlo smiled. He lived for dinners at the Vinthers. Pierce's father, Master Calputh, was always full of stories about his years serving as a king's mage. And Pierce's younger sister, Asulloa, always sat next to Lazlo at dinner, asking him questions and touching his arm anytime she got the chance. She was cute, Lazlo had to admit, but he didn't have time for anything serious right now—and the last thing he'd want to do was lose his only friend, if Pierce took umbrage with him dating his sister.

Still, visiting the Vinther house was the closest thing Lazlo had gotten to visiting home in ages. Once a year, students at the Mound got a monthlong break when Lazlo traveled to his parents' place. But it didn't feel the same as it had when he was little.

Lazlo's older brother and older sister were rarely in town; they'd both moved out to start their own families in far-flung villages. Lazlo's younger brother was off at law school himself now, and more often than not, Lazlo's father and mother were busy at their shop. Lazlo spent most vacations working alongside them, both proud and a little surprised by how popular their wares had become.

His parents were proud of him too, of course. They made sure to tell him that all the time. But they didn't understand what the Mound was like. How could they? Nobody else in Lazlo's family had a lick of magical talent.

Anytime he tried to explain a new spell he was working on, or his research into Aursight, he got blank stares and polite nods.

Pierce's family, on the other hand, were all mages. His father offered friendly advice about which masters to befriend and what classes might be fun to take. Pierce's older sister was in her last year at the academy, so she was always talking about different career paths and options for mages with academy credentials.

With them, Lazlo had a glimpse of what life could've been like, if he'd grown up aware of his abilities. In a family that knew what to do with him.

But he shook off that feeling now, with a faint sense of disloyalty. He loved his family. They loved him. That was all that really mattered, at the end of the day.

"I'll be there," Lazlo promised Pierce. Then, buoyed by the promise of a square meal and some good stories tonight, he hurried out to catch the carriage to his office.

***

When Lazlo arrived at the judiciary office—a tiny two-room building affixed to the peacekeepers' headquarters—the whole complex was in an uproar. Peacekeepers stood out front, arms at the ready, on guard in a way Lazlo had never seen before.

Inside was even worse. Mages had joined the peacekeepers, some wearing Spellduel battle gear, as if they might burst into spontaneous warfare right here.

Stunned and more than a little worried, Lazlo hurried to his own office. He stepped inside, only to stop dead on the threshold. Headmaster Agnellus Glycas himself sat behind Lazlo's desk, waiting. When he saw Lazlo, he sprang to his feet. "Mas—I mean, Mister Redthorn. Thank you so much for coming so quickly."

Lazlo glanced at the door. Another peacekeeper stood on guard beside it, warstave over one shoulder. "What's going on?" he asked.

"Sit, sit." The headmaster waved Lazlo toward his own visitor's seat, while reclaiming Lazlo's seat for himself. "Don't mind them." He gestured at the peacekeeper, who did not reply, only stared straight ahead, at attention like a soldier. "Everything's under control. We just beefed up security as… insurance. While we deal with this matter."

Lazlo lowered himself into a chair, frowning. "What matter is that, exactly?"

Headmaster Agnellus crossed his arms on the desk and leaned forward. His gaze bored into Lazlo, frank and direct. "My son," he said.

Lazlo blinked, taken aback. "Your... son?" As far as he knew, Headmaster Agnellus had no living relatives, and he and his wife had separated years ago.

The headmaster nodded. "It will be easier to show you than to explain." He lifted a hand, then paused. "If you don't mind?"

Lazlo shook his head. The headmaster moved both hands in a complicated arc. His fingertips trailed sparks of bright magenta, and then Lazlo was plunged alongside the headmaster into a memory.

They stood in a circular cell about eight feet in diameter. It had a single cot in the middle of the room, a dirty bedpan underneath it. Lying on the cot, arms bound in heavy iron manacles that left ugly red welts all the way around both wrists, was a thin man wearing only a loincloth. He was bald and covered in tattoos. As he shivered, goosebumps rose all along his pale chest and narrow arms, making his spiky tattoos look lumpy and misshapen. His stomach sank in on itself, concave, like he'd been starved.

Lazlo couldn't help it—he gasped aloud.

Headmaster Agnellus touched his shoulder. This being a memory, of course, the man lying on the bed could not see them. But Lazlo doubted he would have noticed them even if they were truly standing here. His eyes were glazed over, staring vacantly at the ceiling.

Underneath the grime and unnatural thinness, the man couldn't have been older than Lazlo himself. Maybe younger.

"My son, Andon," the headmaster said sadly. "He was born with hyperpotential." After a quick glance at Lazlo, who shook his head, the headmaster added, "Too much magic. Not enough control. When the outbursts come, he can't rein it in... almost like the magic has a will of its own. It acts through him, impulsively and often destructively."

Lazlo winced. "I'm so sorry." He'd never heard of such a thing.

"It's rare," the headmaster murmured, as if reading his mind. "My wife and I—ex-wife... We both came from families with intense potential. We were warned, when we married, but..." He shook his head ruefully. "Young love." He cleared his throat with difficulty, then gestured at the cell.

On the cot, Andon moaned and raised a manacled hand. He struggled against his bonds, which Lazlo noticed was a curious, dark metal that seemed to swallow the light.

"We sent him here, to the sanitarium, because they said they could *help*." Agnellus spat the last word like a curse. "Those are somaritium bonds on his wrists; they block all access to his magic. The cell, too, is made of somaritium, modeled after the king's dungeons. But they never told any of us about this; they never got our consent to treat my son like a criminal. He hasn't done anything wrong."

Agnellus turned a pleading eye on Lazlo, now, who startled. What did all of this have to do with him?

Agnellus took Lazlo's hands as the scene around them shifted. Now, they watched a memory of Agnellus himself, crouched beside a man in a cloak. The man picked something at the cell entrance—the lock. It swung inward, and Agnellus swooped forward to grab his son. As he picked him up, the manacles on Andon's wrists glowed bright blue with wards. The thief stepped forward to sever the manacles. The chains clattered to the floor, and together, the thief and Agnellus hauled a half-conscious Andon from the cell.

"I brought him here," Agnellus whispered. "I didn't know where else to take him. That sanitarium came highly recommended; I don't know who to trust now…"

Lazlo frowned. "Can you help him here? We have healers on campus."

Agnellus nodded. "That's what I was hoping to do. But, you see…" His memory spell faded, and they stood back in Lazlo's offices again. The peacekeeper beside the door shot them both a suspicious look. "The sanitarium reported me to the peacekeepers," Agnellus said. "They claim I've removed a dangerous criminal from their care and remanded him to regular society. My son never hurt anybody; they claim he attacked medics at the sanitarium, but can you blame him after what they did to him? He's been in and out of consciousness since we left, barely coherent. He must have been scared out of his mind. Of course he lashed out at them."

Lazlo's heart sank. He couldn't imagine how the headmaster must have felt when he saw his son in chains like that. "Clearly, they were mistreating him," he said.

"They want to force him back there," Agnellus replied. "They came with a warrant, a writ of seizure."

Lazlo's frown deepened. "Is it signed by the king?"

"No. They're claiming as a ward of the sanitarium, Andon is under their jurisdiction, but—"

"No private institution has the right to arrest people in other townships without a written warrant from the king," Lazlo said. "They can't take him from you, don't worry.."

"But they can petition the academy to remove him from our grounds, on account of the safety risk he poses. Which they've done." Agnellus grimaced. "They presented a case to the council." Agnellus nudged a file across the desk.

Lazlo took it, his eyebrows rising as he read. According to the file, Andon had done more than just attack a medic in the sanitarium— he'd blown up an entire section of the building, before they reinforced the somaritium in his cell. Two medics had been critically injured in the blast; one later succumbed to his injuries.

"The faculty council are divided," Agnellus went on. "Deadlocked vote. But it doesn't matter; this is a judiciary matter, not a faculty one."

Emotion churned in Lazlo's gut. "How do you mean?"

The headmaster locked eyes with Lazlo. His desperation was palpable. "You could dismiss the case." He pointed to the file in Lazlo's hands. "Andon didn't know what he was doing when that happened; he'd been placed under duress and subjected to awful conditions. If you pardon him, I can assume responsibility for his care. See to it that he gets the help he needs."

Lazlo darted a glance at the peacekeeper by the door. The man's expression went carefully neutral. "Could I do that? The incident happened at the sanitarium, not here. I'm not sure whether—"

"The sanitarium is a private entity, like you said. They have no judiciary branch. Whereas we're a public university, funded by the king, and you're a royally-appointed judge. Your ruling would take precedence."

His mouth went dry, even as the file pages grew damp under his palms. Lazlo had spent his three years here handling small, campus-specific matters. Thefts and minor arguments, Spellduel rules broken and student feuds gone too far. This... this was something else altogether. A real case, of the magnitude he would have studied in school. This could set precedents for the future—not to mention have immediate implications here at the academy now.

He steeled himself, squaring his shoulders. *This is why King Owain sent me here.* To judge the law of the land. Studying under Master Ebus was a welcome bonus, but it wasn't Lazlo's real mission. The king trusted him to know the law and enact it properly.

It was high time he earned his keep here.

"Thank you for bringing this matter to me," Lazlo said slowly. "Of course, I'll need a few days to review the case, and consult the legal files about similar incidents."

"Naturally." The headmaster bobbed his head, trying and failing not to look too eager. "And then...?"

"And then, I'll see what I decide." Lazlo snapped the file shut and rose. "In the meantime, do we have any somaritium on campus?" At the headmaster's flinch, Lazlo added quickly, "I don't want to shackle your son, but if he might be a danger to himself or others, it would be a good idea to have that metal on hand. Keep him confined to your manor for now, and do what you can for him."

Agnellus grabbed Lazlo's hands again, before Lazlo could stop him. "I will. *Thank you,* Lazlo. I'll remember this, I promise."

They both would. But not for the reasons either of them suspected.

Chapter Thirteen

Shaken by old memories stirred up after his visit to the peacemakers, Lazlo found Tansya and suggested they retreat back to Ebus' manor for the day. As his guest, she'd been put up in the same lodgings as him—though she'd made a point of waiting around outside the peacemakers' offices for him anyway, while Kazren went back to where she was rooming in the caravansary.

Before Lazlo did anything drastic, he needed to discuss the idea Kazren had inadvertently given him with Mariou. That, and he figured it wouldn't hurt to give the manor itself another once-over with Eldon's help, either. Perhaps they'd missed something in the hectic days directly following Ebus' death.

But when he and Tansya reached the manor, Lazlo found a very different scene than the bustling one he'd encountered on his arrival.

There was still a crowd of students gathered, but this afternoon, everyone wore various shades of black. They clustered on the lawns out front and in the main dining hall, heads bent, mugs of wine or beer in hand.

Eldon waved when Lazlo entered, beckoning him over. Lazlo exchanged a quick glance with Tansya, who shrugged and nodded.

"What's all this?" Lazlo asked. He took a seat beside the boy and a couple other classmates who looked even younger than Eldon. Tansya lingered near the back of the room—knowing her, she probably felt uncomfortable being indoors already. He gave her twenty minutes before she slipped out back to sit in the manor's backyard instead.

"Unofficial wake," Eldon said. "Since the school only planned that big official ceremony, and..." He shrugged, glancing at his classmates. "That didn't really feel like Headmaster Ebus."

Lazlo smiled. No, his old master had never stood on ceremony—as evidenced by how at home his students felt wandering around his home. A sixth sense itched in the back of his mind. He knew he ought to keep investigating, that he didn't have time for breaks or pleasantries.

But a spark broke through Eldon's grim expression as he considered Lazlo. "Maybe you could tell us some stories about him," he said. "About what he was like before he became headmaster."

"I hear he used to work for the king," said a younger girl.

"And that he recruited mages for the army," a boy interjected. "One of them even slayed a dragon!"

Lazlo chuckled, unable to resist. "One of them did, in fact." He arched a brow. "Me." It was worth delaying his research just for the expressions on their faces now. Even Eldon gaped at him. Tansya just snorted and rolled her eyes.

Mariou appeared in the doorway. She gave Lazlo an approving look, then went to fill him a mug of wine at the sideboard. He exhaled, defeated.

There was no way he was getting out of this without a story. Lazlo leaned back in his chair. "When I was your age, I didn't go to the academy," he said. "In fact, I'd enrolled in law school."

One of the boys laughed. A girl swatted his arm. "Lawyers are important too," she said pertly.

Lazlo grinned at her. "Indeed they are. But fate had other plans for me. I found an old book of spells in the school library, and to my shock, when I tried them, they worked. I thought nothing of it until the war started. The king begged anyone with magical ability, no matter how small, to join his army. Master Ebus assessed me himself. Realizing I had no training but plenty of potential, he assigned me to the king's scouts..."

***

Lazlo bent over the map. Behind him, a bustling army camp sprawled. It took up the majority of the trail for the last league, and trickled off either side of the dirt path into the trees.

And right now, it had come to a standstill.

"We need to get through," King Owain muttered. His top commanders huddled around him. Everyone frowned at the same spot on the map—a mountain pass one league ahead, marked in angry red slashes. One of the commanders had set a small model on the pass, around where the sightings were clustered.

95

Lazlo studied the figurine now. The tiny red clay dragon was far less intimidating than its real-world counterpart.

"We can't risk a press," a commander said. "Not with a dragon that large in our path."

"We have an entire army," the king replied. "Can't we just crush it?"

The commander bent to slide a fingertip along the map. They could all see where the road narrowed. "This is a chokepoint. It's been ambushing supply wagons and military convoys alike here. We can only fit five, maybe six men through at a time. We have no dragon slayers, nobody with experience fighting a beast this large. If we could catch it in the open, surround it, we'd stand a chance, but as it is…"

"We'd be serving the creature our men on a dinner platter," the king finished, mouth curled in distaste. "One appetizer at a time." He turned away from the map and punched a fist against one palm. "Damn it. What's the word from the Mound?"

"Still waiting on a reply, sire," a page interjected.

"What's taking them so damned long?" King Owain whirled around. Behind his back, everyone exchanged worried looks.

Lazlo knew, of course—the majority of the king's mages had been killed in the last six months of this seemingly endless war. Now, at great and terrible cost, they were finally on the brink of victory. One last press through these mountains and they'd be able to route their enemies' lines from behind, end this once and for all.

But to do that, they'd need to slay a dragon first.

"Get me eyes on the target, boy," the king barked at Lazlo.

Long since accustomed to such treatment, Lazlo closed his eyes. To be fair, the king didn't treat the proper Mound-trained wizards any better, so he couldn't complain. He raised both hands and recited the spell Master Ebus had hastily taught him during the world's shortest basic training course ever. Yet he had mastered those spells the master gave him quickly and found many along his travels with the army.

It was still one of the only spells he knew within the divination school. Scrying to get the lay of the land, a few illusion spells to create decoy troops and confuse the enemy, a few defense spells— shields and the like. Not a lot of time to learn anything elaborate when you're at war. The more experienced wizards in his battalion were too busy fighting and dying on the front lines to train a newbie of a few years.

At least he was very experienced at scrying now.

Lazlo's eyes went white as the vision seized him. He'd focused his attention on the map, at the point where the pass narrowed. Now, he blinked into existence on that pass, a ghostly incorporeal version of himself.

"What do you see?" King Owain demanded, voice close to Lazlo's ear.

He didn't lose focus, used to these interruptions. "Nothing yet." Lazlo's scrying self walked up the pass, eyes on the surrounding rocks. He studied every crevice and crag, not entirely sure what he was looking for. He didn't have any experience with dragons, aside from what he'd heard in old stories.

Monstrous great lizards with wings and flames for breath.

He shivered, even though the dragon couldn't harm him in this state.

For a minute, he saw nothing. He walked up the pass, up, up, into the mountain they'd need to cross somehow. Finally, he spotted something—a long, wicked slash on one of the rocks. A few steps later, he saw another, higher up. Claw marks.

At a thought, Lazlo's ghostly form rose from the ground. He drifted up into the rocks, following one of the claw marks. It led to a wide, flat rock, where he saw a dark smear of something suspiciously like blood. The blood turned to spatters a few steps later, as if whatever had dragged its prey along this rock had taken off with it.

Lazlo rose higher, scanning the area.

A thin stream of steam caught his attention. Just beyond the pass, it trickled out of a tiny opening in what appeared to be a solid hillside. Lazlo moved toward it and studied the hill. A grassy top slope led down to a granite cliff face, much like the rocks that lined the narrow mountain pass. Except…

Yes. Lazlo spotted an opening in the rock, half-hidden behind a tangle of ivy.

He moved toward it, passing through the ivy without needing to brush it aside. As he entered the cave, his vision darkened. He wished he knew another spell, something to enhance his night vision perhaps. But he forged on, squinting in the dark.

Two slices of light cut through the pitch black. One was far away to his left, a round, man-sized opening through which he glimpsed trees—another entrance to the cave.

The second source came from overhead, via a tiny pinprick. That must be the hole where he'd seen steam rising earlier. Lazlo followed the light. It didn't show much. Only a heap of rocks. The topmost rock shifted, sinking down. A moment later, it rose again, and Lazlo froze.

Those weren't rocks.

In the dim, the slumbering dragon slowly took shape. Lazlo could barely comprehend its size—ten, no twenty times larger than a human? His eyes widened, his lips parting.

"What is it?" King Owain asked, startling him straight out of the vision.

Lazlo blinked at the sudden, blinding light of the leader's tent. His pulse raced, his breath coming short. "I found him."

"Before the pass or after? If his lair is before the pass, then—"

Lazlo shook his head. "After. Begging your pardon, Your Majesty," he added quickly at the king's sharp look. "Perhaps I could lure the creature out with an illusion?" He'd gotten good enough at faking oncoming squadrons to make a whole enemy battalion swerve off-course last month.

The king's frown deepened. "Not a bad idea. But we'd need to set up an ambush site carefully. That could take a while…" He cursed. "We need to get through this pass tonight, ideally. We're already running late. If the vanguard gets there before us…"

He didn't need to finish that sentence. They all knew what would happen if the other half of their army charged the enemy lines without them in place to provide backup.

The king waved an irritable hand. "Let me think. You're all dismissed for now. Be ready for my summons in an hour or so."

Lazlo stepped out of the tent. Rather than return to his own tent, hastily pitched this afternoon, he wandered through camp, thinking hard. King Owain's spies were the ones who'd reported the dragon problem, after speaking to a few villagers in the surrounding area yesterday. Apparently, the creature, known as Rimrig the Fierce, had been terrorizing this mountain for years now.

In peacetime, the king would have dealt with such a creature ages ago. Now, with the army stretched thin and wizard resources depleted, there was no one to handle basic problems like this one.

Lazlo closed his eyes, picturing the beast again. It was enormous, yes. But also had very limited movement in the cave it called home. Too bad they couldn't stage an ambush there. To do that, they'd need to creep through its territory in utter silence—dragons had supernaturally enhanced hearing.

Mages dispatched dragons all the time, typically in dragon-hunting squads of five or six. Lazlo had heard the older mages tell stories about such fights, back when he hadn't been the king's only remaining war mage.

His chest tightened. Suddenly, the answer seemed glaringly obvious.

Lazlo strode to the tree where he'd tied his horse and took up the reins. *I can handle this.* It was what a real war mage would do. Besides he had learned many new spells, donated from the left-over articles from war mages belongings that never made it back from an engagement, horded spells he kept and learned in secret.

He rode as close to the pass as he dared, then dismounted. He'd learned the silencing spell during basic training, but he hadn't had much cause to use it. It took him a few tries before he managed to muffle his steps. When he moved forward again, his feet made no sound on the rocky ground.

He climbed through the pass, holding his breath every so often and straining his ears for any sign of Rimrig. All he heard were the usual forest noises—birds chirping, squirrels chittering, the rustle of some small animal through underbrush.

That was a good sign. It meant Rimrig was probably still asleep. Most dragons were nocturnal, but they could wake at any time of day—especially if they realized they were under attack.

With a sense of déjà vu, Lazlo climbed along the path he'd envisioned a little over an hour ago in the king's command tent. He tried not to think about worst-case scenarios—dying, for example, and leaving the entire legion without anyone to scry for them at all.

Lazlo swallowed his nerves. He may not be the strongest fighter or best with a sword. He might not fight on the front lines like the war mages who'd taught him and died for their king. But this he could do.

He stepped beyond the pass, heart in his throat. He could see the grassy hill underneath which Rimrig slept now. He crept closer, both hands spread at his sides. He'd brought no weapon except himself— his hands and the spells he'd collected over the course of this war.

He didn't approach the cave's main entrance. Instead, he concentrated on the illusion spell he'd used so often at war. He sent a copy of himself walking toward the main entry, while he continued on past it, creeping toward the left wall, where he'd glimpsed the alternate entrance earlier.

Just before he reached the back entrance, Lazlo cast a second spell—invisibility cloaked him from head to toe. It would only last until something struck him, but it would help for the start of this battle.

Unseen and unheard, he crept into the rear entrance. The cave was even darker than before, the sun much closer to setting than when he'd visited earlier. But he could still see the hulking mass of Rimrig, asleep in the center.

On the far side of the cave, by the main entrance, he watched a perfect copy of himself approach the beast.

Closer to hand, he spotted something else. Glittering bright piles of precious stones, gold, and works of art. He also spotted more than a few weapons. Lazlo was still examining those when a voice boomed through the cavern, shaking dust from the walls.

"You have my attention, wizard."

A pair of burning red eyes the size of a man appeared. They blinked twice, and rose with the huge dragon's head. Rimrig the Fierce swiveled to glare at Lazlo's illusion.

Lazlo concentrated on his doppelganger, while he himself inched toward the dragon's left flank.

"You have gall, I will admit, coming here. What have you come to offer me in exchange for safe passage for your army?"

Lazlo's eyes widened. *He knows we're here.* That meant the dragon had surveyed them, perhaps before they even knew he was in their path. He struggled to keep the surprise from his tone, knowing he'd only get one shot at this. Dragons loved making bargains, but they seldom kept their word. He'd read that they were arrogant and loved compliments, however.

Lazlo spoke through his doppelganger. "Rimrig, I have come to offer great treasure in exchange for safe passage through your domain."

Rimrig drew himself up. Fire built behind his teeth, licking out between them in tiny flames. "That is the best you can do?" Steam rose around him as he spoke, and Lazlo realized that was what he'd seen coming through the topmost hole in the cavern before.

He fought to keep his hands from shaking as he started the next spell. It was the last one he learned in basic, but he'd performed it a few times now, to keep the enemy off their frontline soldiers.

This would be the first time he'd cast it on himself, though.

Lazlo didn't respond to the dragon. He couldn't speak through his doppelganger and cast this at the same time. It was already splitting his concentration something fierce. A pounding headache started in one temple, and he gritted his teeth, straining to hold both spells.

He didn't need to hold them long. Rimrig laughed and released a white-hot gust of flames. It incinerated Lazlo's doppelganger where he stood. Lazlo felt a brief hot spike of pain and then the illusion vanished.

In its place, a blinding wall erupted between Lazlo's true form and the dragon. It was seven layers deep, a multicolored plane of light.

The dragon snarled and whirled on Lazlo, a fresh breath of fire already building behind its teeth. "Lies and deception. What should I have expected from a human?" Rimrig raised his claw to strike, his wings fanning out to either side.

Lazlo bent both knees, ready to run for cover if this failed. *Who am I kidding?* he thought. If this didn't work, he was toast.

"Why don't you pick on someone your own size?" shouted a voice from the far side of the cave.

Lazlo startled and nearly lost control of the 'zone' spell. He stared, wide-eyed, as a second dragon darted into view. It was magnitudes smaller than the first, barely the size of a housecat. But it flapped in Rimrig's face, tiny lavender wings beating fruitless circles around the larger creature.

"Be quiet, you pest," Rimrig snarled.

"Don't hurt him," the smaller dragon said. "And that's Alisa to you."

Rimrig raised a claw to swat her, but Alisa darted out of his path.

Lazlo gritted his teeth. *Damn it.* He needed Rimrig's attention on him, while the spell still held. "Rimrig!" Lazlo hollered. "I came here with a fair offer. Yet you attacked me."

"Not you." Rimrig chuckled. "Your little illusion."

"You didn't know that." Lazlo raised his chin. "I thought dragons dealt fairly with humans."

Rimrig's laughter grew. The cave rumbled around them. "Then you thought wrong," he said.

"Run!" Alisa squeaked from the ceiling.

Lazlo did not run. He planted his feet and raised both palms, as if about to cast another spell.

He wasn't. He couldn't even if he wanted to. This zone spell was draining his every last reserve and then some. *Please, fall for it. Please, please...*

All at once, Rimrig charged. Lazlo's eyes widened. He'd half-expected the old dragon to recognize this spell. Maybe mages who fought dragons didn't do it with zones or defensive magic, though. Lazlo wouldn't know.

As Rimrig hit the first layer of the zone of light, red flames burst across his thick hide. The dragon ignored this—dragons were immune to fire. He kept charging into the second layer of light. Orange acid splashed over his scales, but the dragon barely seemed to notice. At the third layer of light, brown lighting struck the dragon head-on.

The dragon shook his head, answering sparks building in his irises. It only seemed to make him angrier. He roared so loudly the whole cave shook. Stalactites dropped from the ceiling and shattered around Lazlo. He flung his arms over his head, cowering, as Rimrig reached the fourth layer of his zone spell.

A noxious green cloud of poison engulfed the dragon's face. Rimrig kept moving—at the fifth layer, cold wind exploded throughout the cave.

Nothing slowed the monster. Sweat beaded on Lazlo's forehead and trickled down his spine.

Rimrig hit the sixth layer, icicles stabbing through his scales. He bled from one leg, but it didn't even seem to register. He charged headlong into the seventh layer, and Lazlo finally leapt aside, head ducked as he rolled across the piles of treasure underfoot.

Overhead, bright white light flared as Rimrig turned to stone.

Inertia carried his body forward, barreling right through the spot where Lazlo had just been standing. With an enormous crash, the stone dragon collided with the far wall of the cave and shattered into dozens of pieces. Lazlo stared at the wreckage, panting, until a loud cheer ruptured his thoughts.

"Holy hells. That was amazing!" Alisa alighted by his foot, her eyes bright with mischief. "Pretty sure you just saved my life."

Chapter Fourteen

Lazlo stayed up far too late telling stories to Eldon and his friends. After he told the story of Rimrig, they'd all wanted to hear more about the faerie dragon Rimrig had been keeping prisoner in his lair. Before he gave too much about Alisa away, Lazlo begged exhaustion and turned in for the night.

As expected, Tansya had slipped out back long ago. He knocked on the door of the room where Mariou had put Tansya up before he went to bed, but there was no answer. He wondered if she'd wind up sleeping outside too, maybe in the shape of a fox or a hawk, some of her favorite feral shapes to take.

By the next morning, she was back inside for breakfast, greeting him with a grin before she stepped aside to make room for Ebus' students. Lazlo was forced to shake off a dozen curious students over breakfast before he could get on his way again.

But he couldn't afford to lose any more time.

The Spellduel tournament was held, as always, in the arena. On the way there, Lazlo talked Tansya through the rough outline of his plan.

She wrinkled her nose. "I don't love it. But if it's the best idea you've got…"

"It's the only one, right now," he admitted.

She sighed. "Just don't get yourself killed."

Lazlo shot her a look.

Tansya spread her hands. "What? If this guy *was* the murderer, then we already know he plays dirty. Plus, if you die, I'm going to have to babysit Hallowmight all on my lonesome, which is going to be *very* boring…"

Lazlo laughed. "Oh, so that's the only reason I can't die today?"

Tansya caught his eye and held it for a beat longer than strictly necessary. "I might be able to think of a few more… if I really put my mind to it."

Lazlo tore his gaze from hers, shaking his head. But he couldn't deny there was a faint twinge of... something... in his gut. He suppressed it, forcing his attention to the Spellduel arena itself. They'd made some changes since the last time he was here—new referee boxes sat at ground level with the dueling mages, and he glimpsed added wards and protective spells across the sandy expanse.

His heart wrenched. They'd cleaned the place, of course, but as he stepped out onto the packed earth, it wasn't difficult to imagine Ebus' final moments. Staring up at the crowded stands, decorated in the school colors, with all of his colleagues and students watching...

Lazlo swallowed around a lump. He needed to find the challenger board.

Kazren had been right about the tournament—the initial open rounds had ended. From now on, wizards dueled in the bracket into which they'd placed. But individuals could always challenge one another to separate Spellduels—it was how many people settled minor scores on campus.

Lazlo parted from Tansya with a nod—and she shot him one last stern look. Then he strolled across the tournament field, eyes on the brackets.

The other two academies had sent emissaries for the tournament, like always. It wasn't difficult to find their names on the rolls—the Gagiams' Academy of Wizardry entrants were in a different color ink than the Wizards of the Mounds entrants, as were those from the Scientia Arcana Academy.

The students competed in the main tournament. Masters' duels were reserved for demonstration matches or the occasional elite challenge—like Master Grim Krauss's challenge to Ebus.

Lazlo needed to find Krauss and return the favor.

He wandered the field scanning for SAA flags. Finally, he spotted their banner in the stands—apparently, they'd declined to join the second round of the tournament. Perhaps understandable, but Lazlo couldn't allow that to stand.

He moved into the stands, approaching the cluster of students in SAA robes. Lazlo stopped the first one he came across and asked for Master Krauss. The student pointed him toward an older man higher up in the stands, seated alone. He was short, slim, a little sickly-looking—or maybe he was just pale, it was hard to tell. He was bald, with tattoos across his head, but so were many of the SAA graduates. It was a popular way to demonstrate their vows—to put magical learning and improvement above all else in life.

Lazlo set his mouth in a grim line and climbed the rest of the way to the man's side. "Excuse me." The man didn't look up, or even seem to notice his presence. "Are you Master Grim Krauss?"

Slowly, the man lifted his head. He nodded.

"I was Headmaster Ebus' pupil," Lazlo said quietly.

The old man's mouth flattened. "I see."

"You can probably guess why I'm here." Lazlo's gaze darted to the arena below, then back again.

Master Krauss bared his teeth. "Get it over with, if you must. But only if you swear that once I face you, no matter the outcome, no one else will come to me seeking revenge."

Lazlo bowed his head. It seemed a fair deal. "I challenge you to a Spellduel," he said.

***

The arena cleared as Lazlo and Krauss approached. The students who'd been warming up for their own duels hurried out of the way. It was still early in the day, so the stands hadn't filled yet. But as whispers carried, Lazlo noticed more and more people filling the stands, no doubt as their friends alerted them.

He grimaced. He didn't want to put on a show, or make a production out of this. But he needed answers. He needed to understand how this man, who looked like he could barely defeat a first year, had bested his master in combat.

A referee cleared the field and gestured at them to square off.

Lazlo took one end of the arena, Krauss the other. The referee walked between them, one arm lifted. He looked at Lazlo first, who nodded. Then he glanced at Krauss, waiting for the other man to acknowledge the start of the bout as well. Once he did, the referee's arm fell, and he cast a flight spell to drift up and out of their way.

Up in the stands, murmurs rose. More people pressed against the railings, leaning over to watch.

Krauss was fast. His fingers moved faster than any mage Lazlo had ever seen. His gestures were quick and compact, efficient as a soldier's. His verbal commands were the same—his lips hardly moved, no sound audible from here.

But Krauss's impressive subterfuge didn't matter, with Lazlo's Aursight. An orange hue sparked around his opponent's fingertips, and Lazlo raised his hand to counter with a burst of blue.

To outside appearances, nothing seemed to happen at first. Kazren would be able to tell, if she were watching, but nobody else in the arena could see magic itself.

Electricity arced between Krauss's fingertips. He grinned, ready to fire off a bolt, but suddenly, it vanished.

Lazlo smirked. He grabbed a small object from his pouch and tossed the item between his hands, moving them somatically as he spoke the next incantation. Magenta burst from him this time, along with a flash visible to the naked eye.

Krauss dove for cover.

Lazlo pointed at Krauss, and the other man's back arched, his chest jutting out and his arms bent behind him. Krauss's eyes widened as his body drifted five, ten feet off the ground. He hung there, suspended.

Lazlo pointed at him, then made a fist and tossed his hand to the side.

Krauss was flung to the ground with a resounding crash. Groaning, Krauss scrabbled at his own pouch. Orange light covered his body again. Lazlo noticed a shimmering arrow of pure magic form. It flew toward him, too fast to counter.

Instead, Lazlo flung up both arms, crossed in a hasty shield. It deflected the spell, the arrow flying up into the sky only to dissipate against the arena's protective wards.

Krauss staggered to his feet, already forming another spell. But Lazlo was too quick. He sent an illusion of himself sprinting in one direction, while he darted the other. Before Krauss could pinpoint the real him, Lazlo had already cast his next spell. He radiated orange as he thrust a palm toward Krauss.

Three darts flew from his palm, striking Krauss one after the other.

Krauss cried out and dropped to his knees. Lazlo didn't stop, casting spiderweb. He pulled strands from thin air to wrap around the other mage. He pinned Krauss's arms to his side, rendering him helpless.

The rest of the world suddenly flooded back into Lazlo's senses. The crowd roared, spectators stomping on the bleachers and chanting the Mound's song.

More people filed into the bleachers, drawn by the applause and chanting.

Lazlo waved a hand to dispel the webs he'd cast. Krauss groaned and rolled onto his backside. In the distance, Lazlo spotted a few SAA students hurrying toward their master. "How did you really beat him?" Lazlo asked under his breath, before anyone else reached them. "You're quick, but my master was faster. Stronger. He should have defeated you, so..."

"Everyone has off days," Krauss muttered. Something flickered behind his eyes. Remorse? Or guilt. "For what it's worth, I am sorry about what happened. I didn't mean... rules of the duel. I didn't realize how badly he'd taken my first hit until it was too late."

Lazlo's jaw tightened. "He was ill. Did you know that?"

Krauss flinched. "He never said. He accepted the challenge, so I assumed he was fit to duel."

"Who suggested you duel him? Did anyone put you up to it?"

"No!" Krauss drew himself up with difficulty, wincing as he put his weight on one leg. "I know the rules as well as you, I'm sure. Spellduel challenges must be made freely by both participants. Of their own accord. No coercion or bribery allowed. You think I'd risk my position at SAA? For what?" He shook his head. "My glory days are well behind me, son."

Lazlo stared the man down for another minute. Much as he hated to admit it, the old man's surprise seemed genuine. But that didn't rule out sabotage. If someone else knew Krauss was planning to challenge Ebus, perhaps they'd decided to weaken him before the duel. Convenient way to stage an accidental death...

But as Krauss's students swarmed between them, eager to inspect their master, Lazlo relented. Their worried questions reminded him too sharply of how he might have reacted, had he been here for Ebus' match.

He took a step back, giving Krauss one last nod. This was a dead end.

He turned to leave the arena, chants of the school song chasing him all the way out. It didn't matter how many people cheered for him or shouted his name. Lazlo's mood had blackened beyond repair.

Somewhere out there was his master's killer. And Lazlo was no closer to finding them than he'd been when he arrived.

Chapter Fifteen

"You stole my idea." Kazren ambushed Lazlo before he even made it five steps outside the arena. "I was going to duel him."

"And I'm glad I ignored that suggestion," Lazlo replied, rubbing a crick from his neck. "Because I could barely keep up with that bastard."

Kazren huffed. "He didn't seem *that* good. You had him in, what, eight moves?"

"Ten, but who's counting," said Tansya, materializing on Kazren's other side.

"At least I didn't die, right?" Lazlo shot her a pointed look, then rubbed his temples.

Tansya grinned. "You still move pretty quick for an old man."

"Quicker than an ancient man, maybe," Kazren sniffed, and they shot each other grins.

Lazlo did not enjoy this newfound camaraderie. "I need to follow up on some more leads. Why don't you two—"

"Come with you?" Kazren's grin widened.

Lazlo grimaced. The last thing he wanted to do was get Kazren even deeper into this mess—especially when he had no leads and no idea how dangerous this whole situation really was. He had a bad feeling that he'd only begun to scratch the surface of potential enemies here on campus. Grim Krauss was going to be the least of their problems.

Unfortunately, he could think of only one way to distract Kazren now.

"I was going to say, why don't you see about finding a direct challenger in the student tournament," Lazlo said, against his better judgment.

Kazren stopped mid-step. Her eyes widened. Then she let out a little squeal of disbelief. "You mean it?" As soon as it arrived, her enthusiasm waned. "Ugh. But will they even let me join? I'm still technically not a student here on campus…"

"Regardless of where you're studying, you are a student here at the Mound," Lazlo replied. He reached into his pocket, unfolding the piece of paper he'd prepared last night, just in case it came to this. "Plus, a written recommendation from your mentor should help secure you a spot."

Kazren snatched it, eyes lighting up again.

"Be smart about who you challenge, though," Lazlo said. "I'd recommend watching a few of the warm-up rounds before you pick someone. Since you didn't enter the tournament at the entry stages, you'll only get one shot at getting onto the standings."

Kazren nodded eagerly. "I'll pick the right person. Someone good, but not *too* good. I don't want an easy win, but I don't want to rocket to the top of the standings right away either."

Lazlo laughed. "Modest, aren't you?"

Her grin widened. "Always." To his surprise, she darted forward and gave him a quick hug. Before he'd even registered it had happened, she was already bounding away toward the arena without a backward glance.

Lazlo's gaze drifted from Kazren's retreating spine over to Tansya, who watched him with a smirk. "That was nice of you," she said.

He shrugged, voice suddenly gruff. "Yeah, well. She'll be safer at a Spellduel tournament with newly beefed-up security in place than she will trailing after me right now."

Tansya's hand drifted to her belt. He couldn't see them, but he knew she hid a series of knives along its length. "Why, what did you find?"

He shook his head. "Nothing concrete yet. That's what worries me." He took a deep breath. "You said you came here because you had a vision of me in danger. Did you see anything else that—" A bright flash cut him off. He glanced down to see his bracelet blinking rapidly. He winced and clapped a hand over it.

"Ugh." Tansya shielded her eyes. "What's it doing?"

"I've got a message," Lazlo said. He ran a fingertip along the topmost gem on the bracelet, and a vision flooded his mind. He saw a familiar office, and the commissioner bent into view. *We need to talk,* he said, though Lazlo remembered more than heard his voice aloud.

He blinked and the vision disappeared. Lazlo swore under his breath. "I've got to go back to the peacekeepers."

Tansya flinched. "Should I come with you, or…?"

Lazlo hesitated. It had been a fight to get her campus access already. He didn't want to antagonize the peacekeepers more than necessary. On the other hand, Tansya was here for a reason, and if she was going to assist him in this investigation, then he needed the peacekeepers to start respecting her as a colleague. After a long pause, he nodded. "If they have a problem with it, that's on them."

Grinning, Tansya fell into step beside him as they crossed the long expanse of lawn. "You know," Tansya said conversationally, "I could get used to all this walking. Good for the legs. At home I'm just hopping tree trunks every ten feet, but there's something refreshing about traveling the old-fashioned way."

"Speak for yourself," Lazlo mumbled. "I'd kill for just one teleportation spell right now."

They'd only crossed half of the distance when a carriage rolled to a halt beside them. A familiar stout face poked out of the rear. "There you are. I've been looking all over for you," said Headmaster Muzud. He called something to the driverless carriage, then pushed open the door and hopped out. "Heard you were in the Spellduel arena, but I missed you by a minute."

Lazlo and Tansya exchanged glances. "I was just on my way to see the commissioner," Lazlo began.

Muzud ignored this, talking over him. "Have you seen our new tower?"

Lazlo frowned, taken aback. "I…the Black Tower? Yes, it's—"

"Impressive, no? We built it primarily as a vault for some of the more intense magical items on campus—can't be too careful with what you leave lying about."

"No," Lazlo agreed. After a pause, he cleared his throat. "Is there something I can do for you, Headmaster Muzud?"

The old dwarf seemed distracted, his eyes wandering around the scene before settling on Lazlo again. Lazlo hadn't known Muzud all that well back when he'd taught here, but he remembered the man being quick and to-the-point. Perhaps his sudden unexpected

112

promotion to headmaster was adding more stress than he knew how to cope with.

That, Lazlo could relate to.

"Yes, yes," the headmaster murmured. "It's a handsome addition to campus, very practical too…"

"Are you okay?" Lazlo asked. Over Muzud's head, Tansya quirked a brow, clearly also confused.

Muzud shook his head as if ridding himself of a gnat. "Of course. It's nothing. I was only wondering if you might take something to the tower for me. Give it to the Chief of Shields. You're friends, aren't you, with Bishop Wyon?"

Lazlo's stomach tensed. On the other hand, this would give him the excuse he'd been looking for. "He and I knew each other, yes. We met after the war, when I—"

"Excellent." Muzud began to fish in his pockets. He checked his front pockets, then his back, and finally lifted his robes to burrow underneath them. "Ah, here it is." He withdrew a small box and presented it to Lazlo.

"What is it?" Lazlo asked.

"Nothing dangerous. A trivial thing, really…" Suddenly, Muzud's gaze wandered again. He seemed almost frightened this time, a bead of sweat breaking out across his brow.

"Muzud?" Lazlo gripped his shoulder. He glanced at Tansya, who shook her head.

"I don't sense any magic around him," she whispered. "Could be an ailment of some sort… Is he old enough for memory issues yet? I'm not familiar with dwarven physiology." She raised a hand, closing her eyes and humming. One of her druidic spells.

Lazlo left her to it, snapping a finger under Muzud's nose.

Muzud startled, blinking awake as if from a dream. "Goodness. I really need to see about my sleep schedule," the dwarf muttered. "Keep dozing off at the damndest…"

"Are you sure you're alright?" Lazlo peered at him. "You don't seem like yourself."

Muzud chuckled. "You sound like my assistant. She's always mothering me, that one." He clicked his tongue. "Anyway, if you could deliver that to the Chief of Shields, I'd be in your debt. Hope it's no trouble."

Tansya took a half-step back from the dwarf, clearly finished with whatever magic she'd attempted. From the grim press of her lips, it hadn't worked. "Can't you deliver it yourself?" she asked.

Muzud threw back his head, laughing. "She's a funny one, your druid." He winked at Lazlo, who grimaced. Before he could rebuke the old man, Muzud tapped the box he'd given Lazlo. "It's a key, my friend. Backup for the original. Only other key to the tower in existence. They need it by tomorrow…"

Lazlo frowned. "What happened to the original?"

"Lost, I'm afraid. Not Bishop's fault, mind you, mistakes happen. The peacekeepers are helping him investigate. Locator spell indicates it's still on campus, but what with the wards and interferences here, it's impossible to say where exactly. No doubt it'll turn up at the bottom of the lake one of these days." He chuckled, very nonchalant about losing one of only two keys to the most important building on campus.

Something was *definitely* wrong here.

The dwarf took a deep breath and leaned against the carriage. Maybe he really was just sleep-deprived. He did look exhausted.

"No problem, Headmaster," Lazlo said quietly. "Consider it done."

"Good, good." Muzud yawned. "If you'll excuse me…"

"You need rest," Tansya couldn't help interjecting. "And a solid meal. You haven't eaten since yesterday."

Muzud laughed. "Excellent reminder. Don't worry about this old dwarf; just a passing bug, I'm sure."

Lazlo's ears rang. Ebus had had a passing bug, too. Right before he died. Judging by the look on Tansya's face, she was having the same thought. "Headmaster—"

"Hurry along now," Muzud said, already hoisting himself back into his carriage. "I promise to rest and eat if you promise to deliver that."

Lazlo nodded sharply. He lingered as the headmaster's carriage sped off in the direction of his manor, unease bubbling in his gut. "That's not just a bug, is it?" Lazlo murmured.

Tansya tapped her chin. "Hard to say. I didn't sense anything magical around him, but my detection spells aren't foolproof."

Shaking his head, Lazlo pointed across campus. "Let's get going. I want to speak to the commissioner before I deliver this package."

He slid the box, about six inches long and solid wood, into his pocket. They started off again, their steps quicker now.

Before long, they reached the nondescript peacemakers' building. Lazlo waved to the man on guard out front. The guard nodded to Lazlo, then squinted suspiciously at Tansya. She winked and gave him a huge wave, which did not do anything to improve his sneer of distaste.

Inside, a secretary led Lazlo to Bekir Halis' office. Lazlo arrived just as the commissioner was sitting down over a fresh cup of coffee.

"Come in," Bekir said. He set the mug aside. "Have a seat. And thank you for coming so quickly." He spared a glance for Tansya, but if her presence upset him, he didn't let on. "I'm afraid I've got quite serious news."

Lazlo took a deep breath, bracing himself as he slid into a chair. "I appreciate your speed in investigating this matter."

"Least we could do for Ebus." Bekir bowed his head for a moment.

Tansya did not take the other free chair. Instead, she leaned against the back of Lazlo's. Her hair swung down into the top of his vision, and she was close enough he could feel a rush of warmth rolling off her.

He was grateful to have her here, at least. One person unconnected to the academy, who he knew he could trust.

"I've got the secondary report here." Bekir laid a file on the table. "Aside from me and you—and you, miss…?"

"Tansya," she replied without missing a beat.

Bekir arched a brow at Lazlo, as if asking whether he wanted an outsider to hear this. Lazlo nodded, and Bekir relaxed a fraction. "Aside from us, only the employee who performed the scan has seen these results so far. Once I tell you two, that'll be four of us who know. Understood?"

"We'll be the very picture of discretion," Lazlo promised.

Bekir leaned forward. "Now, the reason I warn you, is because our results from this second scan do not match our first. At all."

Lazlo's eyes widened. "You mean—"

"I worked with Master Erman on this. I'm sure you remember him, Minister of Healing?"

Lazlo nodded, recalling him from the funeral.

"Well, when I went back to ask him for a second test, Master Erman admitted that a colleague had performed the first scan. A cleric, but someone who's worked on campus for years. He volunteered, and Erman trusted him, so he agreed. This time, though, Erman did the tests himself." Bekir's mouth flattened to a grim line. He caught Lazlo's gaze and held it. "Ebus' body tested positive for cyanide."

Tansya gasped. Even Lazlo flinched, although he'd suspected something along these lines. Deep down, he'd been hoping against hope he was wrong.

"Based on the way it presented in his hair follicles and nails, we believe he was poisoned slowly. Over the course of a week at least, with small amounts each day. Master Erman thinks that on the last day, the day of the match, Ebus received a much larger dose than the rest. It would have hit right as Ebus stepped out into the arena."

Lazlo shut his eyes. It made sense, given everything. But...

"Who would do something like that?" Tansya whispered. Exactly what he'd been thinking.

Bekir shook his head. "We don't know yet. And it gets stranger. We managed to track down the cleric who assisted Master Erman on the first test of Ebus' body. Not only does he have no memory of doing that, but the poor man's been laid up for the past few days, unable to remember all of the last week."

Lazlo grimaced. "Do you think someone charmed him? Forced him to do it?"

"Most likely. He's with Master Erman and the healers now; they're seeing if they can reverse the memory loss. So far it's not looking promising."

"How advanced is this cleric?" Lazlo murmured.

"You mean, is he a master?" Bekir shook his head. "Graduate student. And he wasn't very proficient at mental shielding. Still, if whoever did this can charm a graduate of the academy..."

"He or she could have charmed other operatives on campus." Lazlo grimaced.

"Could it be Krauss?" Tansya asked. They both looked at her, and she cocked her head. "If the poison was timed to coincide with his duel with Headmaster Ebus, he'd have a motive to want to weaken the headmaster first. Maybe he wasn't even trying to kill him, just win the Spellduel."

"Is an honorary match between SAA and the Mound really worth murdering someone?" Bekir frowned. "I know we love our Spellduels here, but…"

"Doesn't feel right," Lazlo murmured. "We can't eliminate him entirely as a suspect, no. But Krauss seemed genuinely upset about what happened. He could be acting, of course, but somehow, I get the feeling he's not that talented a performer."

Tansya exhaled through her nose. "Then we're back at square one."

"Not quite." Lazlo reached for the report, glancing at Bekir. When the commissioner nodded approval, he slid it toward himself and flipped it open. "We know for certain it was murder now. And we know the method, or at least half of it. Whoever did this must have had access to Ebus' food."

Lazlo pictured the familiar faces he'd glimpsed at the funeral service—all of Ebus' servants and prep cooks and assistant chefs. Ebus ran a large household at the manor, and a fairly loose one. Almost anyone in his employ would've had access to the kitchens—though none more so than the cooks, of course. Still, what motive would they have for something like this? Ebus paid better than any master on campus, and he was generous with free time and sick leave.

Lazlo scowled, his eyes darting across the top of the report again. *Unless someone charmed them too…*

He pushed back his chair so suddenly that Tansya startled away from him. "I need to speak to the cooks at Ebus' manor. See if any of them saw anything suspicious. Or if anybody's suffering from sudden inexplicable memory loss." He caught Bekir's eye, and understanding flashed between them. "Can we keep this between us for now?" Lazlo asked.

"Of course." Bekir set his jaw grimly. "So far, we only have one real advantage." He pointed to the report. "The murderer has no idea we're onto them yet. Let's keep it that way as long as we can."

Lazlo nodded.

"Have you shared your suspicions with anyone else?" Bekir asked.

Lazlo paused, wincing. He regretted telling Kazren now. *How could I be so irresponsible?* "I debated the idea with one of my students, but—"

"Do you trust them to keep quiet?" Bekir interrupted.

"I do. I've already asked her to keep it between us."

"Good. Keep our numbers down, control the flow of information. In the meantime, if you learn anything new, share it with me first. We have to coordinate our actions, so we don't step on each other's toes."

"Agreed," Lazlo replied. He touched his pocket then, the weight reminding him. "Oh. I have one more stop before I can visit the cooks."

Bekir arched a brow. "What else could be so important?"

Lazlo grimaced. "I agreed to run an errand for the acting headmaster. Won't take long. I just need to stop by the Black Tower to see... Bishop Wyon." His voice very nearly faltered on his old friend's name.

"Why?" Bekir blinked.

Lazlo hesitated, then sat back down. "That's the strange thing. Headmaster Muzud asked me to bring Bishop the spare key to the tower. He said we've lost the original, but he didn't seem at all worried about it. In fact, Muzud was acting strange our whole conversation."

Bekir's brow furrowed. "When did you see him?"

"Just now, on my way here."

Bekir shook his head. "I don't like it. The key to our highest security building goes missing, right in the middle of all this?" He gestured at the report on his desk. They both fell silent for a moment, thinking. Then Bekir sighed. "I'll keep an eye on Muzud. You two be careful out there."

Lazlo and Tansya exchanged a look. "We will," Lazlo said.

Chapter Sixteen

Lazlo and Tansya left Bekir Halis' office far more warily than they entered it. Lazlo had suspected something off all along, but suspecting and getting confirmation were two very different things. He studied the entire campus of the academy through fresh eyes now.

The cluster of students sprawled on the lawns studying and sunbathing—were they in danger?

The pair of masters striding across campus, robes swirling around them, expressions dark as thunderclouds—did they know something? Who on campus resented Headmaster Ebus and why?

Not to mention the cleric responsible for faking Ebus' initial tests... Had he really been charmed into doing someone else's bidding? If so, who else might not be themselves?

He couldn't stop thinking about Muzud's strange behavior. Trailing off mid-sentence, acting flighty and erratic.

Tansya's arm brushed against Lazlo's, startling him back to the present. "I recognize that face. You're thinking."

"Not to any avail yet," he replied, molars gritted. "One thing's becoming clear, though. Whoever did this isn't acting alone. Whether they've recruited other people through magic or force, I don't know, but..."

Tansya squinted across the bright, sunny campus. "Perhaps if we discover the *why*, the *who* will become clearer."

Lazlo sighed and scrubbed a hand over his face. Not for the first time, he wished he'd kept in closer touch with Ebus. His gaze drifted to the Black Tower. It was not the tallest building on campus, but it was certainly the most noticeable, with those imposing dark stones that swallowed the sunlight. "Perhaps this visit to Bishop won't be such a bad thing," he murmured.

Clearly, Bishop had been closer to Ebus than Lazlo knew. He'd been here on campus for the last few years. He might have a better idea of Ebus' recent acquaintances, grudges, or problems.

"What's the story there, exactly?" Tansya asked.

Lazlo shot her a look.

She spread her hands, placating. "I'm not trying to pry. Just... I don't believe I ever got the full story. I remember Bishop, of course, when we all helped free that monastery. You two seemed so close back then. Now, you only look at him when you know he isn't watching."

Lazlo exhaled. He'd forgotten how well Tansya could read him. Not just his facial expressions—druids had a way of sensing emotions that he never quite understood. Or maybe that was just Tansya. "It's a long story."

Tansya pointedly eyed the walk ahead of them. The Black Tower was square across campus still, and with the restrictions on her bracelet, they couldn't call a carriage. "Think we've got a minute."

Lazlo's mouth quirked at the edges. "You're going to judge me."

She snorted, looping an arm through his. "I already do that constantly, so no worries there." She tilted her head onto his shoulder, easy and affectionate. The faint scent of floral soap drifted off her curls, and make something twist inside him that he didn't want to examine too closely.

He heaved another sigh, less irritated now than resigned. "Fine."

***

Bishop and Osenne were the first veterans Lazlo saw after he came to the Mound. He might never have met them at all, if he hadn't volunteered to fetch supplies from Edgelight for Master Ebus—now the recently promoted Headmaster Ebus. And Lazlo had only volunteered for that because those days, he leapt at any excuse to get off campus he could find.

It had only been a few months since his whole world fell apart. Since he'd lost his brother, his best friend, and the only other person who'd truly understood what it was like for him at the Mound.

Pierce, of course, lost far more than Lazlo had. But Lazlo couldn't set foot on campus without remembering. Flashbacks haunted him. He stopped going to the library, because he'd imagine their bodies there. He stopped eating at the dining hall, unable to forget Pierce's confrontation. The screams.

He even stopped listening to cases, because the courtroom was the culmination of it all. The place where he finally realized: *It's all my fault.*

Headmaster Ebus had granted him a leave of absence from work, but Lazlo knew he couldn't live like this forever. He needed something, anything, to distract him.

Someone must have finally heard his desperate prayers.

Outside the academy gate that day, a man and woman lingered at the side of the road. They both looked worse for the wear, travelwise, the woman's blond hair tangled and matted, the man's beard scruffy and unkempt.

As a group of students passed in the other direction, Lazlo noticed the man flash them a hand signal.

He straightened, startled. He recognized that gesture. It wasn't a magical gesture—which the students clearly didn't know, as they flinched away from this stranger. It was the call sign of Lazlo's old military unit. Lazlo hurried to flash the counter-sign, yelling, "Pikes up."

"Never fail!" the man shouted, his expression brightening. "I was starting to think nobody would talk to us at all."

They clasped hands, exchanging introductions. The man was Bishop Wyon, the woman Cleric Osenne Thyphainne. They'd come to the Wizards of the Mound seeking assistance with curse removal, but no one would hear them out. The church Osenne served needed help restoring an old monastery that had fallen to dark sorcery.

To Osenne and Bishop's delight, Lazlo arranged a meeting between them and Headmaster Ebus right away. In the meeting, Osenne explained that the monastery was one of, if not the, most powerful worship sites on the continent, because it had been active for over two thousand years, previously dedicated to gods known only as the "Old Ones." Recently, however, pilgrims had not been able to access the site. They reported encountering waves of negative energy rolling off a dark shield around the whole area.

Disturbed by these reports, Headmaster Ebus was determined to help Bishop and Osenne research the problem. Lazlo leapt at the opportunity to accompany them.

Any excuse to get away from campus, right?

It was a long journey to the monastery. They had to travel on foot, since neither Bishop nor Osenne were able to teleport, and Lazlo had never seen the site, so he couldn't simply magic himself there. Frankly, Lazlo was grateful for the delay. Over the course of their weeks-long journey, Lazlo grew close to Bishop. For once, he'd met someone who didn't know the entire sordid story between Lazlo and Pierce, Lazlo and Ebus, Lazlo and the former headmaster and his too-powerful son.

Lazlo could just be himself again, with Bishop. And they discovered they had a lot in common—they'd served in the same regiment in the last war. Bishop, too, had gone to a secular school, like Lazlo's law school.

Now, with his soldiering days behind him, Bishop felt out-of-place just like Lazlo, unsure of his next steps in the world.

Unbeknownst to Bishop, halfway through their journey, Lazlo wrote to Headmaster Ebus, suggesting that the Mound hire Bishop as a security guard or peacemaker on campus.

As for Osenne, she mostly kept to herself, preferring to study or meditate in ritual over telling fireside stories or reminiscing about the war. At night, she slept in Bishop's tent or shared his bed in the inns they visited. Lazlo took care not to mention this, for fear of striking a nerve, but it was Bishop who finally admitted to Lazlo, one drunken night around a campfire near their destination, that he'd fallen for Osenne.

"I know she doesn't feel the same," he'd slurred. They had agreed to finish off their last reserves of alcohol before they reached the outskirts of the monastery site, where they'd need their wits about them. "She's told me time and again, the church is her first love. This is only temporary. But... we've traveled together so long. Months before she and I reached the academy. I can't help thinking... maybe she'll change her mind."

Lazlo had slipped the bottle from Bishop's fingertips, unsure how to respond. He didn't know Osenne well, but he'd seen enough to guess—she was strong-willed, determined, goal-oriented. He doubted she'd give up her dreams for anyone, and he respected her for that.

Hopefully, Bishop would grow to understand that in time.

Finally, after almost two months of hard travel, they reached the monastery. Once they did, they found far more than they bargained for. Not just disgruntled pilgrims or strange phenomena, but a veritable army battalion, all led by a dark-haired woman who reeked of dark sorcery.

That was when Lazlo left to call on Tansya for backup.

"I remember all of this," Tansya said, waving a hand at Lazlo to hurry up. "That crazy bitch Glanna and her chimera. Thank the gods we stopped her before she completed that ritual; I don't want to know what kind of hell-dimension she was about to open up." Then Tansya paused, wincing. "Course, would've been better if we'd been able to stop her before she sacrificed that poor man... What was his name again? You knew him, didn't you?"

Lazlo bit his tongue, his mood darkening. "Andon. Andon Glycas."

If he closed his eyes, he could still picture Agnellus in his stifling office next to the peacemakers' building. Begging Lazlo to have mercy on his son.

He'd tried to save Andon that day. He really did. But part of him—a bigger part than he cared to admit—had been relieved when they'd reached the altar, only to find Andon already gone. Because in between Lazlo releasing Andon to his father's care and Andon's death on Glanna's altar, "that poor man" had ruined half a dozen lives.

All because I enabled him, Lazlo thought.

"Doesn't explain what happened to you two, though." Tansya nudged Lazlo's side. "Last I checked you and Bishop were on track to become lifelong friends. Bonded by battle and all that. What did I miss?"

Lazlo grimaced. They'd almost crossed the whole of campus now. The Black Tower rose up from the manicured lawns a few hundred yards ahead. He squinted at the obsidian façade. Was it his imagination, or was there a face at the window there, peering out?

"We were," Lazlo admitted. It wasn't until the trip home that everything fell apart.

He'd offered to escort Bishop and Osenne anywhere they wanted to go—provided it was somewhere he'd been himself. Tansya, of course, had been able to simply step into a tree trunk and she was off back to the forest where she lived, around Lazlo's sanctuary Hallowmight.

The others, however, were not so lucky.

Lazlo needed to teleport them one at a time, since it took an incredible amount of effort to bring a passenger along for a teleportation spell, and he'd only just mastered taking himself. Bishop had asked to be dropped off first, back at the Mound. He'd received word that the headmaster wanted to meet with him.

Lazlo had taken him home, embracing at the gates. He already suspected that his old master planned to offer Bishop a job in security. He'd been grateful to know that when he returned himself, it would be to a friendly face.

Then he'd returned for Osenne. Her trip home had been trickier. Lazlo had never been to the Church of Partorm, Osenne's home temple. He teleported them relatively close, but they still needed to travel for a few days to reach it.

That night, Osenne had made it clear how she felt about Lazlo. How she'd been feeling about him for weeks.

He didn't mistake it for love. Not like Bishop. But he didn't turn her down, either. Lazlo had always been the pursuer, never the pursued, and it set off something in him. In her arms, he found temporary relief from all the guilt and stress waiting for him back at the Mound.

By the time they parted at Partorm, he'd confessed more of his problems to Osenne than he'd ever admitted to Bishop. In her simple, straightforward, blunt manner, she'd upended his whole world view.

"If you don't want to go back to the academy," she told him, "Don't."

"So, I didn't." Lazlo sighed. They'd reached the foot of the Black Tower now. He lowered his voice as he glanced at Tansya. "I came back just long enough to ask Ebus for an off-campus position, and then I ran. As for Bishop…" Lazlo shook his head. "I'm the one who told him about us. Probably a mistake. One of a million I've made. But I thought honesty would be the best thing…"

Tansya exhaled through her nose. "You did the right thing. It would've been worse if he'd found out from someone else. Osenne herself, maybe, if he'd tried to pursue something with her again." With that, she waved a hand. "Besides, that was years ago. I'm sure he's over her by now. Probably got some new love interest on faculty—I've noticed no shortage of attractive people here."

124

Lazlo arched a wry brow. "Where were you checking people out, at the funeral?"

"Hey, can't blame a girl for *noticing*." When she caught his eye, she held it for a beat longer than he expected. Was there something there? A hint of…

Lazlo shook himself. *No way.* This was Tansya.

He turned to raise the enormous knocker on the Black Tower's main entrance and let it drop with a resounding boom.

***

The exterior doors opened of their own accord—common for most buildings on campus, but here at the tower, it unnerved Lazlo somewhat. The foyer inside was all polished black stone, with dark marble pillars shot through with veins of gold and silver.

It looked very presidential, if a little gothic.

As they entered, guards to either side of the door snapped to attention. But they did not speak to Lazlo or Tansya, or moved to impede their progress.

Lazlo didn't like this. Something about the energy here—there was a faint haze in the air, as if someone had cast a spell just faint enough that he couldn't decipher the color of its aura with his Aursight. Lazlo squinted around, trying to work it out, when suddenly—

"Master Redthorn. Welcome to the Black Tower." A voice boomed throughout the foyer.

Lazlo stopped dead. He'd recognize that voice anywhere. He scanned their surroundings until his gaze landed on a familiar grizzled face, now sporting several new laugh lines.

Bishop stepped off a winding staircase across the foyer, his eyes on them. "And Tansya!" His expression brightened considerably. "Good to see you."

Lazlo noticed he did not say *both*.

But he'd addressed Lazlo directly. Used his name. *Maybe I'm overreacting.* The snub at the funeral could've been a mistake. Or Bishop might be in mourning, distracted. "Thank you, Chief of Shields," Lazlo said, matching Bishop's overly formal tone. "Hopefully our unscheduled visit isn't too much of an inconvenience."

125

He couldn't help but glance overhead. The foyer was four stories high, the same height as the tower itself. From here, a spiral staircase wound around the entire structure, up and up all the way to the arched rooftop. On every level, four different rooms branched off at the cardinal points, but Lazlo couldn't make out any details of those from here.

"Impressive, isn't it?" Bishop asked. A faint smile touched his mouth, and he moved to Lazlo's side, following his gaze.

Beside them, Tansya shrugged. "For a manmade structure. I've seen trees in the deep forest twice as tall."

Bishop barked out a laugh. "Same as ever, I see."

Tansya executed a sarcastic little curtsy. "And may I never change, since I'm perfect as is."

This time, Lazlo joined in the laugh. "Modest, too."

"Naturally." She winked. "Bishop, how are you enjoying your new position? Unimpressive residence aside."

"How long have you been Chief of Shields?" Lazlo asked. "I should've written when I got the news, to congratulate you. I'm sorry, I…"

"Two years now," Bishop interjected. "Best decision I ever made," he added with a nod to Tanya. Then his gaze darted to the guards, both positioned impassively to either side of the entryway. "But let's talk more upstairs, in my office. This way, if you please." He gestured, and Lazlo and Tansya fell into step behind him.

Bishop stayed one pace ahead of them the whole way up past the ground level. His personal office was situated on the first floor, north-facing door. Bishop invited them inside, then set about preparing a couple mugs of tea at the magic-powered kettle along one wall.

Tansya moved to the window, admiring the view across campus. "You can see all the way to the fancy manor houses from here," she said. "Look, Lazlo."

He did not. He was too busy watching Bishop's rigid spine, trying to determine how best to break the ice.

Bishop's office was as sparsely decorated as his tent had been on their trip. All necessary items—the only books Lazlo saw were about security or shielding spells, the only utensils were for eating, drinking, and writing. He did spot a sword mounted on a rear wall, and recognized the sigil embedded in the hilt. His old service weapon, from the years they served in the military.

Lazlo's throat tightened.

"Tea?" Bishop set a mug before him, and offered Tansya the other. Tansya took it with a grateful smile and blew on the steaming liquid.

Lazlo ignored his. "The headmaster asked me to deliver this to you." He fished in his pocket, then produced the wooden case.

"Ah, yes." Bishop picked it up. He held a ring over it, gesturing. Though Bishop had no magical potential of his own, someone must have spelled the ring to loan him some power, because the wooden key box clicked open to reveal a heavy black iron skeleton key. "One of my men misplaced the original." Bishop grimaced. "Unacceptable oversight. But we've got a locksmith in now. We should have new locks installed by next week. In the meantime..." He wriggled the spare key.

"Honestly, Bishop, I was glad when the headmaster asked me to bring it," Lazlo said. "I've been hoping to speak to you at some point."

A heavy silence fell. Bishop looked up. When he met Lazlo's gaze, both men flinched.

Tansya's eyes darted between them. "You know, I could really use the ladies' room. Bishop, could you tell me where...?"

"Ah." Bishop cleared his throat. "Of course. Out and to the right, three doors along."

"Thank you." She took one last gulp of tea and then slipped out into the hallway.

Lazlo watched the door until it clicked shut behind her. "I still feel horrible about it all, Bishop," Lazlo said, the moment it closed.

Bishop's expression shuttered. "About what."

"You know what I mean." Lazlo sat forward in his chair. "About what happened with Osenne." Even from here, across the desk from his friend, Lazlo could see Bishop's mind racing.

After a long pause, Bishop shrugged one shoulder. "That was a long time ago."

"I'm happy that you found a place you like. Somewhere you fit," Lazlo said. "Truly."

"Mm." Bishop grunted. "And I suppose you'll want me to thank you for it next? I know you wrote to Ebus on my behalf. Recommended me for that first security position."

Lazlo raised both hands. "A recommendation, that was all. You're the one who secured the position." He gestured at the office. "No doubt you impressed Headmaster Ebus, too, or he'd never have put you in charge of securing the most important building on campus."

Bishop's eyes narrowed, as if searching for any hint of sarcasm in Lazlo's tone. When he didn't find it, his shoulders slumped a fraction. He eased himself into the chair behind the desk. "Terrible business, all of this. The way Headmaster Ebus went..." He squeezed his eyes shut. "I was there, you know. At the arena. Couldn't get to him in time; none of us could, not even the medics. I just... kept remembering in the war. When you'd watch a man go down, one of your own, but you were too far out to help..."

Lazlo shut his eyes. "I can imagine."

Bishop swallowed audibly. "You know, I *was* mad about Osenne," he said. "Furious, actually." He chuckled. "But that wasn't the worst thing you did, Laz."

Lazlo's eyes flew open, startled by the nickname. That, and Bishop's almost fond tone. "I don't..."

"You left." Bishop leaned forward, glaring at him now. "You recommended me for this position, got me a secure job, somewhere to call home after all those years after the war. And then you up and left me here alone. You knew how isolating the Mound could be; you told me so yourself plenty of times."

"Looks like you managed to do alright for yourself," Lazlo replied, with a pointed look around.

"That's not the point." Bishop shook his head. "It would've been nice to have a friend. Not just for me, either." Bishop tilted his head, his eyes turning shrewd now. "Don't think I haven't heard rumors about you. Disruptive, antisocial... know what the students have nicknamed you? The Miser of Bacre." He clicked his tongue. "That's not the Lazlo I knew."

"Yeah, well. The Lazlo you knew was a front," he muttered.

"The Lazlo I met on the road was recovering from a traumatic experience," Bishop argued. "He was hurt, yes, but he was still in there. And you just let him bury himself."

Lazlo gritted his teeth and pushed out of his chair. "I don't have time for this."

Bishop rose, too. "Let me guess. Because you're here for the same thing that drove you off campus in the first place?"

Lazlo bristled. "I don't know what you—"

"You want revenge, don't you? Admit it." Bishop bared his teeth. "I heard about your Spellduel. Day after Ebus' funeral and you challenge the man who accidentally killed your master to a fight."

"Don't talk to me about Ebus," Lazlo snapped.

"At least I was here for him!" Bishop clenched his fists. "You ran away. You left him behind, you left me behind, you left this entire campus behind. Now you want to come riding back in to play the hero? I don't think so."

So you're just going to let his murderer get away with it? Lazlo barely caught himself in time. The words almost spilled right out. He grimaced. Bekir had *just* asked him to keep Ebus' murder under wraps, and here he was about to blurt the truth to the man responsible for campus security. The man who'd failed to protect Ebus.

That's not fair, whispered a voice in the back of Lazlo's mind.

But it was true. Whether he knew it or not, Bishop had failed in his duties as Chief of Shields.

For a long pause, both men struggled to catch their breaths. Then Lazlo said, "You and Ebus were close." It wasn't a question.

Bishop's eyes narrowed. "In recent years, yes. He was kind to me. Most mages look down on those of us without magical potential, but Ebus—Headmaster Ebus said he valued my work. I appreciated that."

"Do you know if he had any enemies?" Lazlo asked, softer now. "Anyone on campus with a grudge against him?"

Bishop laughed. At Lazlo's expression, though, he sobered again. "Yes and no. Headmaster Ebus is—was—the best headmaster this school has ever seen, I'd wager. Fair-minded, kind, and he always kept his word. But you'd be surprised how many people that pisses off." A faint smile touched his lips. "Especially students with failing grades, or smarmy merchants who try to swindle a wealthy academy."

Lazlo frowned. "Anyone specific?"

Bishop's expression darkened. "Why, looking for more people to challenge in the arena? It was an accident, Lazlo."

"I know that."

"Do you?" Bishop stared hard at him.

Just then, a light knock on the door startled them apart. Tansya slipped back into the room, flashing Bishop a smile. "Cheers for that. Did I miss anything?"

"Not at all," Bishop answered smoothly. "Lazlo was just saying he needed to get back to campus." Bishop raised the key, jingling it. "And now that you've both so kindly delivered this, I need to get back to work."

Chapter Seventeen

Full dark had fallen in the dungeon by the time Pierce finally stopped speaking. His throat throbbed, begging for water, but he'd already drunk his full allowance today—barely two cups full. The guards were getting stingier by the day.

He was lying on his cot now, since he couldn't see across the dungeon in the dark anyway. He could've stood next to his cell door, but the woman in the opposite sell would only be a shadowy outline to him now. He half wondered if she was even still awake, still listening to his story. Somewhere along the way, he'd stopped hearing her responses.

He was too lost in the memories. The pain, the heartache, the betrayal all felt as fresh as it had that very first day. When the gavel came down, and his best friend looked him dead in the eye and locked him away for life.

"Well, shit." Her low feminine voice ruptured the sudden quiet.

Pierce startled. She *was* still listening. "I know," he muttered.

And then, to his confusion, the woman began to laugh. It started out low at first, then built higher, till she sounded borderline hysterical. She gasped for air, let out a whoop, and started all over again. Finally, the laughs died down to giggles, then faint hiccups. "I'm sorry," she breathed, inhaling sharply. It sounded stuffy. "Shit, I am sorry, I shouldn't…"

"It's fine," Pierce replied, teeth gritted. It was not fine. Was she mocking him? He'd just poured his heart out, and—

"It's just that our stories are so similar." He heard a rustling sound, then footsteps on stone.

As if in a trance, he levered himself off of his own cot and padded to the doorway. He was right. It was too dark to make out anything but her outline—a halo of curls rising around her slim shoulders. But he could see one of her pale arms stretched through the bars, her fingertips reaching for him in the dark.

"You and your family were in the wrong place at the wrong time," the woman said. "I know what that feels like."

Pierce's eyes narrowed. "Your turn. I told you my piece. Who are you, and how did you wind up here?"

The woman chuckled. "So you did. I suppose it is my turn." She tilted her head, far enough that he could make out her profile now. A sharp nose, high cheekbones. She was pretty, he'd seen that during the daylight. By night, however, she turned ethereal. "One more question for you, before I speak my piece. You said your old friend threw you in here. That he himself passed your sentence."

"That's right. Lazlo Redthorn." Pierce practically growled his name.

"Mm. And what was your sentence, precisely?"

"Life," Pierce replied. "For murder and two counts of attempted murder."

"And you plan on serving that full sentence?"

Pierce snorted. "I don't know if you've noticed, but the walls here are solid somaritium. So are the cuffs, the bars, everything. It's not like either of us have much of a say in the rest of our lives, darling. As short as those will probably be."

The woman sniffed. "Speak for yourself. Personally, I don't plan on staying here any longer than I absolutely have to."

"Which, if you're down here in the hole with me, is probably life too." Pierce had never heard of anyone coming back from these solitary cells. Hell, he'd never heard of anyone getting out—not from this dungeon, not given the type of people locked up here.

"That's how long they want me here." The woman sounded mischievous. "But my ride out is already on his way. You can stay here or join me, it's up to you. I just wanted to let you know before I tell you my story, because I have a feeling that once you hear it, you're going to want to come along for my next adventure."

Pierce narrowed his eyes. He'd learned long ago not to take anyone at their word in this place. Murderers, thieves, assassins and worse resided in these halls. Even the upstairs dungeon, where they let people mingle in general sometimes, was filled with people who'd shank you for an extra portion of dinner as casually as someone on the outside might shake your hand.

"Start talking and we'll see about that," Pierce replied noncommittally.

The woman let out a soft hum. "We'll start with my name, shall we? It's a pleasure to make your acquaintance, Pierce. You can call me Glanna."

Glanna. He turned the name over in his mind. But no, it didn't ring any bells. "Pleasure," he said, tone laced with sarcasm.

"As for why I'm here, well, fate seems to be shining on our little hellhole this evening. You see, I'm here because at the height of my power, right when I was about to claim my birthright, someone came along and ruined everything. Not only did he sabotage the ritual I'd started, but he killed half my men, murdered my chimera, and got me arrested in the process."

Pierce stiffened. "Ritual?" he asked.

Glanna ignored him. "That man's name, I will never forget. You and I have a common enemy, my dear." Suddenly, Pierce knew, even before she said it. She reached between the bars of her cell again, straining for him in the dark. As she did, her voice dropped into a low, liquid purr. "Lazlo Redthorn put me in here. And the minute I get free, I promise I will make him pay for it."

Chapter Eighteen

Lazlo's steps were dragging by the time he returned to Ebus' manor. Everything he'd learned today swirled in his mind. The poison, the charmed assistant, the misplaced key. Muzud's strange behavior, and Bishop's same old attitude. All of it fit together somehow, he just knew it. Puzzled pieces with jagged edges. But he was missing some. He still couldn't take a step back and see the entire picture.

Not yet.

"Where are we going next?" Tansya kept pace with Lazlo easily. "Do you want to meet with the headmaster again? You could tell him you dropped off the key and use it as an excuse to see if he's still behaving oddly..."

"Later," Lazlo said. The lab results swam in his mind's eye. "First, I have a question. If you wanted to poison someone, slowly, over the course of a week, how would you do it?"

Tansya hummed thoughtfully. "Depends on the type of poison. If it's something that could be absorbed via skin contact, then I might put some sort of powder in a set of their underwear, or line the insides of their socks. If it's something you need to ingest, then, I'd probably gift them a really expensive bottle of their favorite beverage and work on slipping something beneath the seal—"

Lazlo raised a hand to cut her off. "Your mind is a terrifying place, you know that?"

Tansya beamed. "Well, thank you!"

"Wasn't necessarily a compliment," he mumbled. "But no, I was thinking more along the lines of slipping it into someone's food."

Tansya pouted. "Boring. Everyone expects that!"

Lazlo arched a brow. "Do *you* test everything you eat for poison, then?"

Tansya flushed. "Well, no. But I'm a druid. I've built up an immunity to at least three of the most common poison types, and the rest, I could whip up an anecdote pretty quick. Unless it was that one frog toxin, that stops your heart in under five minutes, I'd be hard-pressed to solve that one…."

"I regret asking." Lazlo smirked. "Look, I just think, evil geniuses aside, we have to assume the most likely route of ingestion for Ebus was through his food. Which means we need to speak to the cooks and all the assistants at Ebus' manor—anyone who could have come into contact with his meals on a regular basis."

Tansya frowned. "I've already snuck into to his kitchen. It's massive. Dozen people working in there at any given hour, and nobody keeps a watch posted or anything; the other servants wander in and out as they please for snacks and the like."

Lazlo eyed her. "What were you pilfering?"

Tansya sniffed, faking offense. "I'll have you know, I was merely *sampling* the hard cheeses. They've got a few kinds I've never seen before aging down there; smelled right delicious too. One of them was really smoky, but with this smooth texture." She looked ready to start drooling over it.

A sudden suspicion stole over him. "Tansya. When you say you snuck into the kitchens, do you mean as yourself, or did you…?"

Her eyes sparkled in the sunlight. "*I* didn't technically go near those kitchens. A little mouse may have investigated on my behalf, though."

He groaned and stopped walking. A glance around the main avenue told him nobody else was within earshot. The closest group was a gaggle of students in robes rough-housing about fifty yards away. Even so, he lowered his voice. "Tansya. It's not safe for you to feral shape out in the open here."

"I know that!" She looked far more offended now than when he said he was afraid of her brain. "I'm not daft. I'm aware of how suspicious you wizardly types get about people like me and our abilities."

Lazlo sighed. "It's not their suspicions I'm worried about." He glanced down at their arms, where their matching academy bracelets dangled. "Headmaster Muzud didn't want to let you in here. He especially didn't want to give you one of these, so you could access magic. He agreed to let you in with a limited permissions bracelet, but I very much doubt he knows about your ability to feral shape, or he'd have banned that ability too."

"Lazlo." Tansya waited until he lifted his gaze to hers. Their eyes met, and Tansya's looked greener, somehow, in the direct sunlight. This close, he could make out tiny golden starbursts around the center of her pupils. "I'll be careful, I promise."

He swallowed tightly. "Good." With that, he spun on one heel and started walking again. He moved so fast Tansya had to jog to catch up.

"Though I'll admit, I have thought about hawk shifting a few times on these walks," Tansya muttered under her breath.

Lazlo shot her a look, and she mimed locking her mouth shut and tossing away the key. He bit back a laugh, worried it would send the wrong impression. Because, although he usually appreciated Tansya's sharp wit and sense of humor, he had to admit, it was worrying him now.

I shouldn't have brought her here. Same with Kazren. Something terrible was happening on this campus, and Lazlo didn't understand it yet. Whatever it was, he had a feeling it put anyone close to him in danger.

By the time they reached Ebus' manor again, Lazlo and Tansya had both worked up a sweat. But he waved off Mariou's sympathetic tutting about how he needed to take the carriages more and walk less. Instead, he and Tansya ignore the usual cluster of students in the foyer and lowered their voices.

"Mariou, who is Headmaster Ebus' cook?" Lazlo asked.

Mariou's eyebrows rose, but if she was confused by the question, she didn't protest it. "That'll be Ryfon Heijyre."

"How long has he worked here?" Tansya interjected.

Mariou tilted her head, thinking hard. "At least since Master Ebus expanded the west wing area, so… a little over eighty years, give or take."

"Would you be so kind as to introduce us?" Lazlo smiled.

"Of course." Mariou glanced between them and then waved them after her. Together, the trio descended into the bowels of the manor.

It wasn't a long walk. The kitchen itself was located directly beneath the dining and common room areas on the ground floor, because of the extra heating it provided in winter months to those rooms. A spiral staircase wound down to the basement level, where dug-out windows provided a little sunlight, but for the most part, the cooks relied on enormous braziers and mage-crafted lamps to light the space.

As Tansya had said, the kitchen was enormous. It took up almost the entire basement footprint of the manor, aside from a few closed off rooms which were used as pantries and cold storage areas.

Lazlo couldn't help but note how many staff members they passed on the way inside, either. Not just kitchen staff, like prep cooks and cleaners and the gardeners who brought in fresh produce each day from the manor's small farm plot. There were maids gossiping in the corner here, servers relaxing in between meal shifts, and a pair of valets playing cards at a table near the fireplace.

His heart sank. Looking for one poisoner in this mob was going to be like hunting out a needle in a hayfield—not just any needle, but one placed point-up on the ground, so if you stepped on it, it would stab straight into your heel.

From the corner of his eye, he noticed Tansya flash him a worried glance.

He steeled himself. *First things first.* The cook oversaw this entire operation. He'd know best if anyone on his staff had been acting strangely in the past few weeks.

Mariou led Lazlo through one of the storage areas, then past a couple of short-order cooks readying snacks for the many students upstairs. Finally, she brought him to a table near the deep sink basins, where an older elf sat addressing two staff members.

Mariou waited until he was finished speaking, and then gestured to him. The elf smiled at her and half-rose from his seat before noticing Lazlo and Tansya. He paused halfway up, looking uncertain.

"Mister Heijyre, this is Lazlo Redthorn. Not sure if you remember him; he was Ebus' pupil years ago, before Eldon and the rest. Lazlo, this is Ryfon Heijyre, the manor's chef."

Now that Mariou mentioned it, there was something familiar about the old elf. He had more white hair than the last time Lazlo saw him, and deeper-set wrinkles around his mouth and eyes. But Lazlo recalled his sharp ears and the funny little patchy mustache he'd grown on his upper lip.

Lazlo held out a hand. "Pleasure."

"Likewise, Master Redthorn." The elf shook his hand once, firm and brief. "We were never formally introduced while you were studying with Master Ebus—excuse me, Headmaster Ebus. But I do remember seeing your face around." He gave a lopsided, toothy smile. "You've aged a touch since then, if you don't mind my saying so."

"Not at all." Lazlo laughed. "I was just thinking the same about you." Tansya's gaze darted from the cook to Lazlo and back again. Lazlo took that as a hint. "Oh, and may I also present Tansya Limnoreia. She's here to assist me with… well, a few things, really." He suddenly found himself loathe to admit what he was looking into. The last thing he wanted to do was frighten Ryfon off before their conversation had even gotten started.

The elf gave Tansya a polite bow. "What can I do for you, Master Redthorn?"

"I understand you've cooked for Master Ebus for decades now," Lazlo said. "Did you prepare all of his meals, or did he ever eat at the dining halls on campus?"

Ryfon straightened, his expression going somber. "I'm proud to say he ate every meal here at home. Even when he had meetings or business at the academy, he'd always pop back for lunch or dinner. Master Ebus said I was the best chef he'd ever had the pleasure of being served by. Now…" The tips of the elf's ears colored red. "That may have been somewhat of an exaggeration on his part—you know how free the man was with his compliments."

"Free, perhaps," Lazlo said. "But he never offered them undeserved."

Ryfon relaxed back into a smile.

Good. Lazlo wanted him laid-back. Unsuspecting. "I was speaking to Eldon the other night, and he mentioned that Headmaster Ebus had been feeling under-the-weather in the week before he passed. Did you hear about that?"

Any of Ryfon's good humor vanished in a blink. He stiffened, his eyes going sharp. "I hope you're not suggesting my food may have had anything to do with that." He glanced at Mariou, who raised both hands, placating.

"Of course not, Ryfon—"

"I only use the freshest ingredients. Everything gets tested here before it goes near a plate. We grow most of our own vegetables and herbs in the plot out back. The meat is—"

"I have no doubt you source all of your ingredients wonderfully," Lazlo interjected.

"We're only trying to retract Master Ebus' last steps," Tansya added, trying on her most winning smile. "Just to get a picture of what he did, how he felt that day."

The elf bristled. "I've cooked for Master Ebus for a hundred years, and you dare to accuse me of negligence? What next?" He flung his arms wide. "Go on. Check my kitchen. Search every corner; you'll not find any mold or rot or whatever else you seem to be implying I'd harbor here."

Mariou stepped forward to touch the cook's arm. "Ryfon, could I speak to you? Alone," she added with a sharp glance at Lazlo. *Let me handle this,* she mouthed, when Ryfon's back was turned.

Shoulders still up around his ears, the elf stormed toward the opposite wall of the kitchen without replying. Mariou hurried after him.

Lazlo and Tansya took one look at each other and then slumped into adjacent chairs. "I could've handled that better," Lazlo groaned.

"Loads better." Tansya nodded. "Like maybe next time, don't immediately insinuate that you think his cooking sucks? Or that it, you know, might be full of poison."

Lazlo grimaced and buried his face in his hands.

"Maybe Mariou will talk him into coming back?" Tansya suggested. "Although, he still looks pretty pissed."

Lazlo raised his head and dared a peek across the room. Mariou was standing close to Ryfon, their heads bent in conversation. Ryfon's face was bright red, his brow lowered, eyes bright with fury. Then Lazlo blinked, startled. There was something else, too… A sort of pale purplish haze in the air between them.

Lazlo stood, eyes widening. "Tansya," he murmured. "Do you see anything down here? Fog or… or smoke?"

Tansya squinted around the kitchen, bewildered. "Aside from the flames over under that huge pot, nothing. All the smoke goes up that chimney, so—"

"Damn," Lazlo breathed. He took a step closer to Ryfon, eyes focused now. *Yes.* There was a definite color to the air. His Aursight, picking up on a subtle but active spell. *Purple?* He took another step closer. *No, closer to pink.* Fuchsia, really. Which could only indicate one thing—an enchantment.

"He's being charmed," Lazlo hissed.

Tansya startled, eyes wide. "Are you sure?"

"I can see it working right now. It's faint, but something must have triggered it. Maybe my asking about the food or about Ebus." He cursed under his breath.

Tansya scanned Ryfon too, brows lowered. "I don't see any rings or necklaces. Just the same bracelet we're both wearing." She raised her arm to jangle her Mound bracelet at Lazlo.

"It could be hidden somewhere. And charms can be cast on any object—a coin, a wallet, a hat, a shoe…"

Tansya frowned. "So, we need to strip him?"

Lazlo shook his head as the cook stormed away from Mariou, fists clenched. "Even if we can break the enchantment, it's unlikely he'll remember who cast it on him. Any mage worth his salt would build fail safes into a spell like that. Forgetting charms, memory clearing clauses…"

"So, what, we just let him keep cooking down here and maybe poisoning us?"

Lazlo ignored Tansya and took a deep breath, tapping into his Aursight. For the most part, his ability was passive and always on. He didn't need to try to notice spells—he just saw them. But enchantment charms were a little different. They could be cast to lay dormant until some predetermined trigger activated them. If someone was carrying a charmed coin, but it wasn't currently enchanting them, Lazlo wouldn't know unless he looked at the coin directly.

Still, with a bit more concentration, he should be able to pick up on other active enchantments, if there were any. Even minor background spells were visible with focus.

He studied each and every person present in turn. Most revealed nothing magical about them—standard for servants and kitchen-workers here. Mages from the Mound typically sought more prestigious positions than general staff after graduation.

He noticed a few faint glimmers of mint green—healing spells here and there, but that made sense. Small cuts and scrapes were common in the kitchen. Other than that, he saw no signs of fuchsia.

His eyes met Mariou's last. She was watching him with an apologetic frown, shaking her head. Lazlo held his breath as he assessed her—she was Ebus' steward, a likely candidate for charming, if someone wanted to get to his old master. But after a long scan, Lazlo's shoulders slumped with relief.

Mariou, at least, was clean.

She gestured to the staircase with her head, and Lazlo and Tansya followed her up and out of the kitchen. The whole walk upstairs, his mind raced. He needed to find out who cast that charm... *But how?*

Chapter Nineteen

"Where are we going now?" Tansya asked.

Lazlo hadn't said a word since they left the basement. He held a finger to his lips, checking around them for any signs of eavesdropping servants or students. He couldn't be certain there weren't more charmed people wandering this manor. He was lucky to detect the cook at the right moment, but there could be more enchantments hidden throughout this building, like time bombs waiting to detonate.

When the coast looked clear, he took Tansya's elbow and drew her into a secret panel hidden in the otherwise smooth marble corridor wall. Her eyebrows rose as they stepped into a cool, dark, interior staircase. "Ebus' secret passages?" she whispered. "You told me about these."

"Did I?" Lazlo blinked. He'd sworn never to let anyone know about these panels when Ebus first showed them to him—as far as he knew, only Ebus, Mariou and Ebus' most trusted students knew about them. Likely Eldon, but Lazlo doubted he would have told anyone else. Not after the Pierce debacle. "When was that?"

"When you were building Hallowmight," Tansya said. "You told me you wanted something similar there."

Tansya had helped him build Hallowmight, Lazlo's hidden sanctuary, inside the same cave where he'd defeated the dragon Rimrig. It had seemed a shame to let such a perfect lair go to waste, after all. And most mages kept sanctuaries like it—places hidden away in remote corners of the world, which they could teleport into and out of at a moment's notice. It helped to have somewhere to store his more sensitive possessions.

Master Ebus had a sanctuary, too. He'd taken Lazlo to it once, in the remote foothills of Trismenor. Lazlo didn't remember much— Ebus had only gone for a quick errand to fetch something, but he'd wanted to demonstrate the usefulness of having a sanctuary. Lazlo had built his own sanctuary at Hallowmight using some of the details he recalled from his old master's—including the failsafe booby trap that would destroy most of the items in the sanctuary if triggered. Never hurt to have a backup plan, if someone terrible was about to steal your prized magical possessions.

Now, Lazlo sighed under his breath. Since Tansya mentioned it, he did remember letting something about the passages slip during construction. But he didn't think Tansya was listening—or that she'd remember Ebus' name. Then again, he never imagined she'd have cause to set foot on the Mound's campus, druid as she was.

He gave his past self a light mental kick. Though, did it really matter now? Ebus was gone, and whoever killed him had already invaded his manor. "They run all throughout the manor," Lazlo explained. "But the one I'm looking for is shielded with an extra layer of spellwork…" He ran his hands along the wall as they started up the staircase. Somewhere along here should be…

Ah, yes. He dug his fingers in a groove about halfway up the flight of steps to the next floor. A brick slotted free, and then a glowing blue light illuminated the space around them.

A light only Lazlo could see, however. He studied the abjuration-blue glow. Symbols appeared within it, dozens in a row. He reached out to grasp one, tugging certain symbols forward and pushing others back, as if creating a cipher in midair. Once the line of symbols looked right to him—it had been an awfully long time since he'd done this—Lazlo gave the whole row a light shove.

"What are you doing?" Tansya hissed, just as a deafening crack sounded.

The wall beside them split open to reveal a low-ceilinged room, sandwiched between the lower and upper floors of Ebus' manor.

Tansya's eyes widened. Inside the room, torches flared to life, casting a warm light over their faces. "Whoa."

Lazlo smirked. "Ebus' private study." He stepped in and beckoned Tansya to follow. As they crossed the threshold, a warm sensation spilled over his body. The additional spells Ebus had put in place, detecting intention and identity. If anyone came here with the intent to cause harm, the spells should notice and sound an alarm.

"What are we looking for?" Tansya whispered.

He laughed. "No need to be quiet. There are sound-muffling spells on all the walls."

"Just seems like the kind of place for whispering." Tansya eyed a pair of stuffed armchairs near a fireplace. It, too, had lit itself upon their arrival. The pleasant scent and sounds of crackling wood now filled the room. Bookshelves on the walls displayed plenty of reading material, and Ebus' desk looked like he'd only just left it, planning to return that evening.

Papers lay stacked on one side, and sealed envelopes of outgoing mail rested on the other. Between them, Lazlo spotted a quill lying on its side, next to a pot of ink drying up.

He brushed a fingertip along the quill and glanced at the stack of mail. Personal correspondence, it looked like. He gave the pile a quick skim, but he saw nothing of note. Ebus had been writing letters to some distant cousins about a child they wanted to enroll in the Mound. Another letter talked of a new planned expansion to the manor, while a third mentioned the Black Tower.

This one, Lazlo did read with interest. But it was only a requisition form—Ebus had asked Bishop for permission to move an old textbook to the tower for safekeeping. Bishop had written back to grant permission, and Ebus had marked at the bottom in his tidy hand, indicating he'd made the transfer.

Lazlo sank into his master's chair with a sigh.

But correspondence wasn't why he'd come here. He reached for the bottommost drawer in Ebus' desk. It, too, was warded, but Lazlo made quick work of the lock spell. His pulse sped up as he reached into the drawer.

This was Ebus' pride and joy, an even better-kept secret than this room itself. Lazlo doubted even Mariou knew about it, because it was technically off-regulation. Of course, as headmaster, Ebus would've been permitted to create such an object. But he'd originally crafted it back when he was only another master instructor here, without permission from former Headmaster Agnellus Glycas.

Ebus' crystal ball allowed him to scry across campus, bypassing the wards that protected the academy from prying eyes. It could also detect any spells being cast on creatures and objects. With it, Lazlo would be able to ascertain how many of the household staff were compromised. Depending on how well he remembered the crystal's instructions, he might even be able to divine who cast the spells, if the perpetrator was here on campus.

But when Lazlo finished pulling the drawer all of the way open, his heart sank.

It was definitely the right drawer. Plush-lined with green velvet, it sported a large indentation in the center, circular, where the crystal normally lay. Right now, however, it was empty.

Lazlo cursed.

Tansya's eyebrows rose. "What's wrong?" Lazlo pointed at the drawer. She leaned over the desk for a better view. "Something missing?"

He nodded, mouth set in a grim line. "Whoever's behind this was someone Ebus trusted."

***

Lazlo and Tansya resealed Ebus' hidden chamber, then hurried back to the main house. They reached the foyer just in time to see Kazren chatting with Mariou.

"There you are!" Kazren's eyes lit up when she spotted Lazlo. "I came as soon as the tournament rounds finished for the day." To judge by her eager grin, things had gone in her favor.

Lazlo still had to ask. "And?"

Kazren's eyes practically glittered. "I beat my first challenger. I'm in the standings."

Tansya whooped and gave the girl a quick hug. "That's incredible!"

"Knew you could do it," Lazlo said, unable to repress a proud grin. He offered Kazren a palm, and she slapped it, beaming. "You'll have to give me the play-by-play later. I want all the details."

Something in his tone must have hinted at his underlying stress, though, because Kazren's smile faltered. Her eyes narrowed as she glanced from Tansya to Lazlo and back. "What did I miss here?"

Lazlo's gaze drifted over Kazren's head to scan the foyer. The usual cluster of students were set up in the dining room, and he could see beyond that room into the common area, where more sprawled-on divans and settees, studying. Plus, there were the servants, so adept at playing invisible. Guards stood blank-faced to either side of the main entrance, other servants lingered in the dining area in case students requested meals or help with anything.

His expression tightened. "Not here," he said. *Not anywhere, maybe.* He still wasn't sure how deeply he ought to involve Kazren in this investigation. Knowing her, she wouldn't take no for an answer, wouldn't stop pushing until he shared everything he knew. But the more she knew about this, the more danger she'd be in.

Kazren squinted, obviously displeased at being left in the dark. But when Lazlo invited her to come talk to Eldon with him, she relented, mollified by this inclusion.

They found Eldon with some friends in the back garden of the manor. He was reading something aloud to the other students, but when he spotted Lazlo coming, he set the book aside. Lazlo recognized the cover—one of the old myths Ebus had loved so much.

He smiled faintly. "Do you have a minute, Eldon?"

The boy's eyes widened ever so slightly, as though surprised. "Of course." He pushed back to stand, and the other students fell to chatting around him, their eyes on Lazlo and his motley crew.

Lazlo nodded at the garden. Eldon fell into step beside him and they meandered toward Ebus' hedge maze, Kazren and Tansya on their heels. "I wanted to talk to you about Headmaster Ebus' manor," Lazlo said softly. "I figured you and Mariou probably know the most about the place. Who goes where, who has access to which areas..."

Eldon straightened, puffing up his chest. Obviously, he was proud to be able to offer Lazlo help. "Of course. Headmaster Ebus put me in charge of overseeing a lot of things. Mostly the other students and their lessons, but I worked with him on a few private projects, too."

Lazlo nodded. He'd expected as much. Ebus had done the same for Lazlo and Pierce, back when they were in their final year at the Mound. He said it was the best way for them to learn how to manage people, prioritize their work, and in general just to prepare for the outside world.

"Could I ask you who else Headmaster Ebus entrusted with such duties?" Lazlo murmured. "Especially anything related to the manor itself. There are certain areas not everyone can visit, but in my time, at least, Ebus would allow certain students and trusted friends access..."

Eldon's gaze sharpened. He glanced over his shoulder at Tansya and Kazren, who both looked away, feigning interest in the hedge maze through which they were meandering. Then he shuffled closer to Lazlo and lowered his voice. "If you mean the passages..."

Lazlo nodded. "I do."

Eldon frowned thoughtfully. "As far as I know, I'm the only student in my year who Headmaster Ebus gave the passcode to. But Miss Mariou has access too, for emergencies. And Chief Bishop, of course."

Lazlo tried and failed to keep the surprise from his face. "Chief Bishop has access to the passages?"

Eldon nodded. "He and Headmaster Ebus worked closely together on the Black Tower's security plans. Before the tower was completed, Chief Bishop worked out of here for the most part. The headmaster said it was the next most secure location on campus."

A bad feeling crept into Lazlo's gut. He couldn't deny that Bishop would've had the easiest time orchestrating all of this. He had access to Ebus' secret study, which meant he probably would've known where to find the crystal ball too. Bishop had no magic of his own, but then, the cook hadn't been directly spelled. He was carrying an item with magic embedded in it; that's what charmed him.

How simple would it be for the Chief of Shields to requisition an enchantment spell from any of the mages here? He'd just need to say that it was for security purposes...

Lazlo shook his head. *No.* He refused to believe his old friend would sink so low. *Besides, Bishop had no reason to harm Ebus. They were friends.*

He was looking for someone with a motive. Someone with a grudge against Ebus in particular.

As if reading his mind, Kazren jogged forward to catch up with him and Eldon. "Who else visited Headmaster Ebus often?" she asked. "He must have had friends, other instructors he liked to socialize with."

Eldon paused. "To be honest, the headmaster spent more time with us than other instructors. He went to faculty dinners and the like, of course, but... he said he believed a headmaster needed to maintain some distance between himself and his direct reports."

Lazlo frowned. "That doesn't sound like him." The Ebus he knew had been free with his friendships and his professional associations alike. Granted, he always prioritized teaching and working with students over frivolous social events or playing politics, the way so many other masters here at the Mound did. But he had lots of friends on the faculty too—how else did he secure the promotion to headmaster, after Agnellus stepped down in disgrace?

Eldon sighed. "He said he was learning from someone's past mistakes."

"Whose?" Kazren asked. Always straight to the point, that one.

Eldon shook his head.

But Lazlo could guess. "Probably the previous headmaster."

Eldon's eyes widened. "You were here, right? When Headmaster Disaster was still in charge?"

Headmaster Disaster. Lazlo's mouth flattened, and Eldon winced.

"Sorry, Master Lazlo. I mean, Headmaster Agnellus, of course. Terrible nickname; some of the seniors call him that and it just sort of stuck."

"You wouldn't make light of it if you'd been there," Lazlo replied firmly. "The situation surrounding Headmaster Agnellus' demotion and departure was awful. The worst tragedy to befall this campus in a century."

"What happened?" Kazren asked.

Lazlo hesitated. So did Eldon—clearly, he'd heard some version of the story. Enough to sense what a dangerous topic this was. But Lazlo shouldn't be surprised. One iron-clad rule of people: they talked. Gossip on the Mound spread about the tiniest of infractions; it was hardly any wonder rumors would spread about that mess.

It had been years now since it all went down. Eldon wouldn't have even been a first year yet. But a few of the older students when he first came to the Mound will have witnessed things themselves. Not to mention most of the faculty were still here.

Lazlo's chest tightened. *How much do I tell them?* He'd kept his own involvement in Glycas' departure close to the chest all these years. But there didn't seem much point in denying it now. What's done was done. No matter how often Lazlo wished he could turn back time, there was no spell to undo the kind of damage he'd caused.

He glanced over his shoulder and caught Tansya's eye. Even she didn't know the full story, but he'd shared bits and pieces. Drunk on druid mead at Hallowmight after long days of construction, in the half-dark of the dragon's old lair. It had been strangely easy, there, to admit to things he hid from the light of day.

Tansya nodded, a hint of steel in her gaze. He knew without asking what she was saying: *Tell them. You owe them this, at least.*

Maybe she was right. Maybe he did.

Lazlo paused. They'd reached the center of the hedge maze. Ebus had built a small fountain here, a statue of a leaping mermaid, with water cascading over her fins. Lazlo crossed to it and took a seat on the stone ledge around the fountain's lip. "You'll probably both have heard rumors about this. From other students, or maybe other masters."

Kazren nodded. Eldon hesitated, then did the same.

Tansya crossed the grass to sit cross-legged on the ground by Lazlo's feet. After a moment, Kazren and Eldon copied her.

Lazlo eyed them each in turn, sighing. "Well. I'd probably better take it from the top. Back before I was a master here, the old headmaster, Agnellus Glycas, hired me to serve as a judge on campus. I have a legal background, so it made sense. And it gave me a good reason to live here while I studied with Master Ebus. I was admitted as an older student, so they expected me to work for my room and board. I didn't mind. It was interesting work, mostly calm. I'd been here about three years, working and studying at the same time, when the old headmaster came to me. He had an… unusual request."

Chapter Twenty

The night after Headmaster Agnellus Glycas asked Lazlo to intervene with the court on behalf of his son, Lazlo went to the Vinthers for dinner.

Pierce met him at the door, excited as ever. "You'll never guess what spell I mastered today." He bounced onto his toes, hardly able to contain himself. "Look!" With a wave and a complicated gesture, Pierce bounced higher than his toes—straight up into the air, in fact.

Lazlo grinned as his friend drifted toward his father's ceiling. "Flight already?"

"Master Ebus told me I'm the quickest study he's ever taught. Can you believe it?" Pierce gestured again, and landed catlike on all fours by Lazlo's feet. "I'm going to absolutely destroy in the next tournament. Nobody'll stand a chance in that arena." He brandished a scrawny bicep, which only made Lazlo laugh harder. "What? You want to fight me first?" Pierce fake-punched his arm.

Lazlo waved his friend off. "Not a chance," he said. He'd learned that flight spell last month, in fact, but he didn't want to burst his friend's bubble. Not when he was in such a good mood.

Besides, Lazlo never competed in the Spellduel tournaments. He felt strange doing it—he was almost five years older than the next oldest senior, and a working judge here at the Mound besides. What if someone cheated in a duel with him? Was he supposed to sentence his own opponent to punishment?

No, better to keep his professional life and his school life separate. If that meant missing out on some of the traditional experiences of a student here at the Mound, then so be it.

"Is that Lazlo I hear?" called a voice from the adjoining room.

Lazlo followed Pierce through the foyer and into his father's dining room. Master Calputh, as per usual, was seated at the head of the table, surrounded by stacks of books. He had a pair of spectacles balanced on the tip of his nose, clearly deep in some new research.

"Thought I heard your voice." Master Calputh rose, beckoning him over. "Let's take a look at you. Where's Ebus been hiding you these days? God, you're almost as skinny as my son. We need to get some meat on you." He turned to bellow for his steward, a beleaguered-looking man, and sent the poor steward running down to the kitchens to demand dinner at once.

Meanwhile, Asulloa drifted into the room. "Dinnertime?"

"Just about, darling." Master Calputh spared his daughter a fond smile.

She didn't notice. She was too busy staring at Lazlo. "Lovely to see you again." To judge by the sparkle in her eye, she meant it.

"And you, Asulloa." Lazlo swallowed hard. *Great.* Another night of praying Pierce didn't notice his sister's affections. Lazlo knew his friend well enough by now to guess Pierce would not take kindly to anyone who dated his sister—not even a friend. Pierce might be the younger of the two Vinthers, but he was fiercely protective of Asulloa, ever since a bout of illness nearly killed her when she was just twenty.

Lazlo made sure to take the seat closest to Master Calputh, and thankfully Pierce snagged the chair on his other side.

Unfortunately, this positioned Lazlo directly across from Asulloa, who flashed him a wide, too-knowing grin. "So, what have you boys been up to? Studying hard, I hope."

"Too hard," Pierce grumbled, reaching across the table for a roll. "Though I wouldn't know about this one." He elbowed Lazlo on his way back from the roll-grabbing. "Ebus and I hardly see you anymore. He's too busy judging people for a living, eh, Laz?"

"*Master* Ebus," Pierce's father gently corrected.

"Master Ebus doesn't stand on such ceremonies with us," Pierce said, shooting Lazlo a look. "Right?"

"He is very informal," Lazlo said, in what he hoped was a nonpartial tone. "But I suppose we should remember to use titles outside of the manor."

Pierce wrinkled his nose. "Suck up," he muttered.

Asulloa laughed, until her father shot her a stern look. She quieted again, though she kept smirking at her plate.

"What about you, Lazlo?" Master Calputh gave him a kind, paternal smile. "Working on any interesting new cases lately?"

He paused, fork halfway to his mouth. To be honest, his conversation with the headmaster had been weighing on him all afternoon.

You could dismiss the case… They claim he attacked medics at the sanitarium, but can you blame him after what they did?

Lazlo exhaled slowly.

"Laz?" Pierce nudged him again. "Something wrong?"

Lazlo glanced at his friend, then his friend's father. Across the table, even Asulloa sobered, sensing his mood. Lazlo pressed his lips together, debating how much detail to go into. "What would you do, if you were asked to decide someone's whole future?" he finally said. "All based on one bad thing they did. Something they maybe weren't even aware they were doing."

Pierce frowned. "Depends what the bad thing is. I mean, there's stealing to feed your family, and then there's murdering someone for pissing you off. You know?"

To Lazlo's left, Pierce's father nodded thoughtfully. "I suppose that depends on what you believe about redemption. Second chances. Personally, I think everyone deserves a fair shot at life. If they made a mistake, but it was an honest mistake, and if they're committed to never repeating it…"

Lazlo bit his lip, thinking. "What if they don't even know what they did, though? If they're not fully in control of their own mind?"

"Sounds like a case for the looney bin, not you," Pierce said.

"Pierce." Master Calputh's expression darkened. "That is not a kind word to use. People cannot help how their minds work. Health is a tricky thing; even with the best healers in the world on campus here, sometimes people slip between the cracks of the system. The human mind is vaster and stranger than any spell I've ever mastered."

Asulloa flashed Lazlo a reassuring smile. "Whatever you decide, I'm sure you'll make the right call. You're very thoughtful."

"Remember, you can ask for outside consultants to help you decide on cases," Master Calputh spoke up. "Not to tell you how to do your job, of course, Lazlo, but if you want to speak to a healer or a physician, you are allowed."

Lazlo nodded. It was a good point. He hadn't thought of doing that, but of course, he was always free to summon as many consultants as he needed when deliberating a case. Perhaps

152

tomorrow, he'd do that. Go to the peacekeepers and file a requisition form.

He smiled, shoulders finally relaxing from around his ears. *Yes.* That was a good plan. He always felt better after talking things out with Master Calputh. He knew just what to say to make a complex, all-consuming problem suddenly seem easy to face.

Grinning and joking with his best friend once more, Lazlo finished his dinner in record time.

***

Lazlo awoke first thing the next morning to a campus in chaos.

The sirens startled him out of a dream first—loud, piercing noises he'd never heard before. The academy had bells that tolled each morning to signal the start of classes, and other bells to ring between each class period. But he'd never heard a sound like this.

Lazlo burst out of his bedroom at Master Ebus', where he'd fallen asleep late last night reading old case files of judgments. He hadn't been able to find any cases brought before an academy judge that resembled Andon Glycas' case. In fact, he found no evidence of judges at the Mound ruling about anything related to people's mental or physical health. The closest thing he found was a decades-old case about a student who killed another student's pet after losing a Spellduel in the arena. The student was expelled and banned from campus.

Lazlo was flummoxed. He could ban Andon from campus, of course, but that wouldn't solve the bigger problem. What to do about a mage who could not control his own power? Especially one who did not seem to be in his right mind at the moment...

Pierce burst into view across from Lazlo, his eyes huge as saucers. The sight of his terror-stricken face dragged Lazlo from his thoughts, and made him stand up straighter. "That signal," Pierce gasped. "I never thought I'd... It's the emergency alarm."

Lazlo stiffened. "What does that mean?" He fell into step beside Pierce, who was hurrying downstairs.

"Everyone needs to evacuate the manors and meet at the emergency site near the main hall. It means something's terribly wrong. Either a natural disaster or a... well, an attack."

153

"Attack?" Lazlo's old soldering instincts kicked into high gear. He glanced around Ebus' foyer, desperately wishing his master was fonder of weaponry. "By who?"

Pierce shook his head. "Don't know. But our bracelets should—yes, there." Both of their arms began to vibrate at the same time.

Pierce and Lazlo hurried out front to find a carriage waiting. They hesitated, glancing around, but they didn't see Master Ebus or any of the other students who hung around his manor. "He must have gone ahead already," Pierce said, pointing across the lawns. Even from here, they could see dozens of carriages all rolling toward the same spot—the emergency meeting point, Lazlo supposed. "Come on."

They leapt into the carriage, sandwiching themselves side-by-side. The carriage lurched into motion, taking the cobblestone roads much faster than usual. Lazlo clung to the strap on the roof of the carriage while Pierce careened into him at every corner.

"This has never happened before?" Lazlo asked.

Pierce shook his head. "Dad told me he's only ever heard the alarm once; someone set it off by accident. I can't imagine what's going on now."

Lazlo's mind raced. "The war," he murmured. "Do you think...?"

Pierce's brow furrowed. "What, that it could be an enemy attack? No way. The war ended years ago." He elbowed Lazlo. "You're proof of that, Laz. This is peacetime."

"Then what in the world could be causing this?" Lazlo fell silent. Through the carriage window, it looked like they might have an answer. A column of ugly black smoke appeared on the horizon, drifting over the rooftops of several buildings. "Is that...?"

Lazlo didn't have time to finish his question. Pierce slammed on the carriage roof. "Stop!" The carriage didn't stop, so Pierce hurled himself at the door and flung himself out anyway.

Lazlo leapt after his friend, terror seizing in his throat.

Sure enough, the black smoke cloud was centered above a row of faculty housing. Right in the middle, on the western edge, where Pierce and Lazlo had met for dinner just last night.

"No," Pierce gasped. He started running. Lazlo ran too, at his side, both of them so distraught it didn't occur to them to cast a flight spell instead. They sprinted up the side roads that wove between the faculty manors, along the main drag where all the most popular faculty members kept homes.

As a senior mage on campus, Master Calputh had a lovely manor, situated right near campus. It allowed him easy access to the classrooms where he taught. It was also just a stone's throw from the then-headmaster's manor, an even larger, more impressive building.

Now, both of those manors—as well as several to either side of them—were smoking ruins.

The moment they crested the hill and saw the extent of the destruction, Pierce screamed. Lazlo, on the other hand, stood stock-still, frozen. He didn't understand. He couldn't comprehend what might have caused this. The academy was the most secure place in the world—hundreds of spells protected it from all kinds of attack, magical, natural, or otherwise.

His first thought was an earthquake, but surely the rest of campus would've felt it too? Why only these buildings?

He counted ruins. Six manors in all. His mind could not process the extent of the destruction.

"Where are they?" Pierce gasped, straightening from where he'd sunk to the ground. "Dad. Asulloa. Where... they can't be in there." He charged forward before Lazlo could stop him.

Lazlo raced after Pierce again. "Wait!" The buildings were still smoking, tiny fires burning all around. "It's not safe. We..." He trailed off as Pierce neared his father's manor.

The ceiling had collapsed, sandwiching all four stories into a single flat plane of rubble. Marble, stone, and gold mingled in a smelted heap. Coals glowed among the ruins, as if this were the remnants of some monstrous bonfire celebration, and not the detritus of a life.

Several lives.

Peacemakers and fire mages were already there, sifting through the ruins. As Pierce and Lazlo watched, they raised their arms to quench fires and shift rubble aside.

Pierce darted forward, ready to help, but a peacemaker Lazlo recognized from his office spun to cast a barrier spell, stopping Pierce in his tracks.

"Let me go!" Pierce flung magic at the barrier. It scattered upon touching it, useless.

Lazlo hurried forward. "Officer Engwyn," he called.

The peacemaker turned. "Your Honor. Please, tell your friend to step back. The professionals are handling this."

Lazlo grabbed Pierce's arm. Pierce struggled against him, face twisted in agony. "Can you tell us what happened? This is his father's home. Is Master Calputh—" He went silent at the look on the officer's face.

Pierce froze, too. All at once, the fight went out of him. He sagged against Lazlo like a puppet with his strings cut. Lazlo only barely caught him in time.

"I'm so sorry, son," Officer Engwyn said. "We got here as quick as we could, but the blast…" He shook his head. "We found your father and your sister. A few staff members too. The steward…"

Lazlo's ears rang. His head swam. *No. Impossible.* They were having dinner together just last night, all four of them.

"—makes you feel any better," the officer was saying, "It would've been almost instantaneous. They wouldn't have had time to feel anything. No fear or pain…"

Pierce stiffened. Those words seemed to reawaken his temporarily doused fury. He surged upright again, fisting tears out of his eyes. "Who?" he snarled, so fiercely that even Lazlo took a half-step back. "Who did this?"

"We're still investigating the cause of—"

"Who was it?" Pierce screamed.

The officer blinked. His gaze darted to Lazlo and away again. It was quick, but Lazlo caught it—he knew what happened here.

Unfortunately, Pierce noticed too. He summoned a spell Lazlo had never seen before, bright fuchsia gathering in each fist. He raised them, and Lazlo understood. He was ready to beat the truth out of this man.

Lazlo leapt in before trouble escalated. "Officer. If you don't mind, Headmaster Agnellus asked me to look into the event," he lied smoothly.

The officer's expression shuttered. He glanced from Lazlo to Pierce and back again, eyes hardening. "I very much doubt that, Your Honor," he finally replied, gesturing behind him at the wreckage of half of faculty row. "Seeing as how Agnellus Glycas' son is the one who cast this spell."

***

Lazlo's voice trailed off. He hated this part of the story. Hated the entire story, in fact, but this part was the one he could never quite voice.

It was my fault. He'd released Andon to his father's custody. He'd recommended Agnellus find some somaritium, sure, but he hadn't forced the man back into cuffs. Agnellus himself admitted that Andon had hurt people, attacked people at the sanitarium where he was being held. Yet Lazlo had allowed him to walk free.

He had trusted the headmaster to secure his own son, and now...

Kazren reached out to touch Lazlo's hand. "It wasn't your fault," she said.

Lazlo laughed bitterly. "Weren't you listening? I freed the boy."

"You didn't know what he was going to do," Tansya interjected. "What Andon chose to do is on Andon alone. Not you. It's not even on his father, although the headmaster certainly should have put his son's chains back on. He knew the boy was a danger. He wasn't well, and he'd been tortured, of course he was on-edge…"

"None of that is an excuse," Lazlo snapped. "Andon was brought to me. The case was my responsibility."

They didn't understand. But Pierce did. The moment Pierce learned the full story of what happened, he knew exactly who to blame— Agnellus and Lazlo. Both of them were at fault.

"What did Headmaster Ebus do?" Eldon asked quietly.

"He was made acting headmaster that same day. The council, with him at the helm, voted unanimously to demote Headmaster Agnellus. He was stripped of his title, banned from the Mound, and sent to live in exile on the far side of Cicpe. They debated permanent somaritium chains for him, too, in addition to his boy, but… in the end, Ebus argued for mercy, and the other masters agreed to grant it."

Depriving a mage of his power before casting him out of the only home he'd ever known was akin to a death sentence.

"And Andon?" Kazren asked, eyes wide.

Lazlo's heart throbbed with old, familiar sympathy. "Andon was chained in somaritium again. The original plan had been to restrain him here at the Mound, with our healers, but…"

He shut his eyes. He could still picture the aftermath of the break-in. Healers lying dead or wounded in the corridors, blood streaking the walls. A gaping hole in the rear of the building, still smoking from

157

Andon's infamous blast spells. This one, at least, had been more contained. A direct, precise hit. Because he'd been aware this time, awake and present when he was attacked.

Lazlo swallowed hard. "He escaped. We lost track of him for a while. I tried to find him, and so did Master Ebus, but…" He shut his eyes, thinking of Glanna in her dark sorceress robes. At the monastery with Bishop and Osenne, he'd watched her raise her fists above Andon's prone body, splayed on a funeral slab like a live offering.

What had poor Andon been thinking, in those final moments? Was he afraid of Glanna and her henchmen? How had he wound up in their clutches? By accident or by choice? Did Andon accept death when it reached a bony hand toward him? Perhaps it was a relief, to finally flee his disobedient body…

"We were too late." Lazlo shook his head. "But that's a story for another time," he murmured.

For a moment, silence fell between them. Eldon stared at the grass underfoot. Kazren's forehead scrunched, the way it often did when she was puzzling out a difficult spell. "So, Headmaster Agnellus would've had a motive," she said, after a time. "To hate Master Ebus. Ebus stole the old headmaster's position and banned him from his home."

"Stole is hardly the word I'd use," Lazlo replied. "Still, you have a point." He hadn't considered that possibility. He hadn't thought about Agnellus in years, aside from sparing him the occasional bout of pity. "I can talk to the peacemakers and Chief Bishop. Headmaster Muzud, too. Someone must have an idea of where Agnellus settled after he left the Mound."

"And Pierce?" Eldon asked, finally raising his head from his studious contemplation of the grass.

Lazlo pursed his lips. "It wasn't Pierce."

"How do you know?" Kazren arched a brow.

"Because Pierce would never hurt Ebus," he said. Once Andon was killed, Pierce had reserved all of his fury for one person, and one person alone. "And besides, it would be impossible. Pierce Vinther has been rotting in a dungeon cell for the last decade." *I should know,* Lazlo thought bitterly, fists clenched. *I put him there.*

Chapter Twenty-One

Late that night, alone in Ebus' manor once more, the memories flooded back in. Telling the Vinthers' story earlier had the effect of opening a dam. Lazlo didn't realize how much he'd been avoiding these memories, holding them back, until they all flooded through him at once.

He shut his eyes, tossing in Ebus' large bed. He couldn't get visions of the trial out of his head.

The courtroom had been packed with spectators. The crowd spilled all the way out the doors and onto the surrounding lawns of the academy, because everybody couldn't fit inside the tiny courtroom.

The families of the victims were all lined up on the left side of the courtroom, standing in for those victims who could not be here themselves. Some were still healing from their injuries. Others had died, either in the initial attack or afterward of incurable wounds.

Of course, Pierce's family was nowhere to be found either. He had no living relatives left.

Lazlo perched on the edge of the bench, sweating beneath his heavy robes of office. He did his best not to look in Pierce's direction. If he did, his resolve would shatter.

Today was going to break his heart. But unlike with Andon, Lazlo knew what he needed to do.

This time, he wouldn't make the same mistake twice.

The days between now and Pierce's arrest had all passed in a blur. The last thing Lazlo could clearly remember was five days ago, when the peacemakers pounded on his office door. "We're needed up at the healers' complex," one had shouted. Lazlo had rushed after them, arriving early enough on the scene that it was still a mess.

Healers lay sprawled on the floor. Some did not move. Others gasped as the few remaining uninjured healers put pressure on their wounds. Blood streaked the corridor in four long lines. Fingertips,

Lazlo realized, dragged along the wall as someone hobbled up the hallway.

The far end of the wall was a blown-out hole, gaping onto what should've been the thick external wall that encircled the academy. Except, a hole had been blown straight through that, too—all ten feet of it, so Lazlo could see straight into the woods along their northern border.

One of the peacemakers, Lazlo doesn't remember who, recounted what had happened. His voice was a distant hum in Lazlo's eardrums.

"—call from the lead healer. Got here as fast as we could, but the boy had already fled. Officers are out looking... no signs... father says he has no idea where Andon would go..."

"Andon did this?" Lazlo had finally asked, resurfacing from his daze. *More sins to add to my tally.*

But the officer had shaken his head. "No, Your Honor. Andon was the target. Attacked in the bed he's been confined to. Healers tried to intervene, but..." The officer hung his head. His gaze drifted to an unmoving heap nearby. The remains of a healer, presumably, though he'd been so disfigured by the blast that they'd need to find some other way to identify the body.

"Who attacked him?" Dread had coiled around Lazlo's heart. The officer pointed the opposite way up the hallway. Lazlo could still remember turning, as if in slow motion.

Pierce hung limp between the two arresting officers' arms. His arms were caked in dried blood, his feet trailing red footprints. None of it seemed to be his, though. Sensing Lazlo's gaze, Pierce looked up. His eyes were red-rimmed, bloodshot, with huge bags underneath. He didn't look like he'd slept in days. Or eaten, for that matter.

The moment their eyes met, Pierce bared his teeth. "I did what needed to be done," he snarled. "I won't apologize for it."

Now, Lazlo stared down at his closest friend from the raised dais of the judge's bench. On the opposite wall, a uniformed officer stood in what should've been Agnellus Glycas and Andon Glycas' place. Representing the injured parties in absentia—because Agnellus was permanently banned from campus, and Andon was still on the run, gods knew where.

Pierce lifted his head. The somaritium manacles on his wrists glinted black as he shook out his fists, both clenched tight. He met Lazlo's eye with a fierce, determined set to his jaw.

Master Ebus had taken the seat beside Pierce, in lieu of his father. Lazlo couldn't hear him from this distance, but he could read his master's lips easily enough. "Why, Pierce?" Ebus was whispering. "Why did you do this?"

When Pierce replied, he raised his voice, loud enough to carry all the way to Lazlo. "I won't stand by while my family's murderer walks free."

Gasps around the courtroom, followed by whispers as those near the front repeated his words to those at the back.

Lazlo shut his eyes. Any hope that his friend might have come to his senses evaporated in that instant. The past few days had been hectic, filled with casework and reports from the peacemakers to read. Ebus, too, had kept Lazlo up at night, asking what he planned to do, begging for whatever clemency Lazlo could offer.

They both knew it wouldn't be much. Six of the twelve healers on campus had been wounded in Pierce's attack—not to mention the two who died in Pierce's initial blast into the center. Of those injured, two were hurt by Andon as he fled, but the rest Pierce himself cut down to get at his target.

Pierce had blasted apart half the infirmary. One of the injured healers was still in a coma, her recovery uncertain.

And then there was Pierce's attack on Andon himself. He'd used a deadly blade-spinning spell, one that Ebus claimed he'd never even taught Pierce. No one knew where he'd learned it. The first cut took off Andon's left hand at the wrist—which was the only reason Andon survived the attack. Andon's somaritium cuff came off with his hand, leaving him free to shield himself from Pierce's blows and then blast his way out of both the infirmary and the academy itself.

The trial hadn't even officially begun, and already Pierce was doubling down on his actions.

Lazlo rose as the peacemakers called the courtroom to order. Every eye swiveled his way. But Lazlo had eyes only for his best friend. His brother, in all but blood. "A great injustice was done to your family and to you," Lazlo said, his voice soft. "We all feel your pain like it was our own. But regardless of what unjust torments the world throws our way, we cannot take the law into our own hands."

Pierce bared his teeth. "I wouldn't have had to, if you'd done your job." His head whipped to the side, as he glared at the peacemakers in the building, one by one. "All of you. Andon Glycas should never have been permitted to set foot on this campus, much less unshackled. He is an abomination, a madman. You want to talk innocence? My sister was innocent. My father was innocent. You all let them die."

Lazlo couldn't stop himself. "Your father would not want you to shed blood in his name."

"You don't have any idea what my father would want!" Pierce snarled. "He was my father. Not yours."

Lazlo kept his face impassive. He would not let Pierce see how accurately that blow landed. "Pierce Vinther, the charges that have been laid against you are thus: two counts of murder in the second degree; one count of attempted premeditated murder; six counts of general assault; two counts of assault with occasioned actual bodily harm; and two counts of causing grievous bodily harm with intent. Two counts of damage to physical academy property; seven counts of reckless endangerment of bystanders..."

As Lazlo continued to read charges, Pierce raised his chin. To his credit, he did not lower his head or attempt to avert his gaze. He met every stare direct his way head-on.

Finally, Lazlo exhausted the long list. He looked up. "Do you understand the charges laid against you, Pierce Vinther?"

"I do."

"And how do you plead?"

Ebus reached for Pierce's shoulder. He murmured something, face turned, so Lazlo couldn't read his lips. Whatever it was, Pierce shook his head and drew back.

"Guilty on all counts," Pierce said. "*Your Honor*."

Lazlo flinched. More gasps echoed throughout the chamber. At the back, Lazlo spotted a cluster of boys who had trained with them at Ebus' manor whispering. One smirked and pointed at the back of Pierce's head. Lazlo resisted the urge to hold them in contempt of court.

Even now, he could not completely repress his instincts to protect Pierce.

"Are you sure?" Lazlo asked, softer now.

Pierce eyed him levelly. "I did it. And I'm not sorry about anything... except that those daft healers didn't get out of my way. I warned them, but..." He raised his chin. "If this was what it took to stop Andon's reign of terror, I'd do it all over again."

Lazlo closed his eyes. He'd been afraid of this. He knew Pierce too well—once Pierce settled on a course of action, nothing and no one could change his mind. Even if that course of action was both deadly and illegal.

Slowly, Lazlo opened his eyes once more. The courtroom seemed to hold its breath. Several people leaned forward in their seats, craning their necks for a better view of the accused. Lazlo took a deep breath. "Then, it is the judgment of this court that you are to be remanded to the dungeons of Plephia... where you will remain for the rest of your natural life."

Ebus cried out, as if in physical pain, and gripped the back of his chair. Shouts rang throughout the room. At the same time peacemakers leapt forward to position themselves on either side of Pierce, as though he might make a run for it with half the academy in his way.

For an interminable moment, Pierce just stared at Lazlo. His mouth trembled, his eyes over bright with unshed tears.

Then the bailiffs gripped his elbows, and his momentary peace shattered. The tears streamed over his cheeks as rage filled his eyes. "Life, for trying to stop a murderer?" Pierce shouted. He bared his teeth, wild now. "This is your fault, Lazlo Redthorn. You freed him in the first place. I hold you responsible."

Ebus buried his face in his hands, his shoulders shaking with visible sobs.

The bailiffs dragged Pierce backward bodily. He thrashed in their grip. Not to try to reach the exits, though. His eyes were fixed on Lazlo, his fists clenched so tightly Lazlo spotted blood flecking his shirt cuffs. His nails must have broken skin.

"It's your fault, Lazlo!" Pierce shrieked. "Their deaths are on your head. I'll make you pay!"

Lazlo couldn't move. He couldn't even speak. *He's right.* This was his fault. All of it. Asulloa and Calputh's deaths, Andon's attacks, the dead healers, Pierce's arrest... all of it could've been avoided if Lazlo had just been better. Smarter. More competent at his damned job.

I'm sorry, he mouthed, the words dying on his tongue.

No matter how much he wanted to, he could not fix this. The past was done, settled, finished. There could be no redoes or mistakes mended.

Death was one problem Lazlo could never solve.

Chapter Twenty-Two

Pierce awoke to a subtle shaking sensation. He sat bolt upright, his eyes adjusting to the dark at once. When you lived in a dungeon, you got very good at seeing in the dark. He frowned at his cell, confused. There was the privy chamber, right where he left it. There the blanket he always tossed off in his sleep. There was the window, still dark and speckled with starlight, no hint of dawn brightening it yet.

He frowned, about to lie back down, when it came again. The whole dungeon trembled, as if in an earthquake.

Pierce swung his legs over the side of the bed and stood. Another tremor. He watched the liquid in his bed pan slosh faintly, and wrinkled his nose. He padded to the far side of the cell, pressing his face to the bars. "Glanna?"

No motion from the opposite cell.

"Glanna!" he hissed, louder now. If this really was an earthquake, he didn't want her to sleep through it and possibly suffer a concussion or worse, if the ceiling caved in.

On the bright side, if the earthquake put any cracks in their solid somaritium cells…

Suddenly, an explosion rent the air. Pierce gasped, instinctively dropping to a crouch. In the cell across from him, Glanna rose smoothly from her bed and approached the bars. "Decided what you want to do yet? Clock's ticking."

Understanding washed over him. Pierce studied her in the dark. "Friends of yours?"

"Something like that."

In the distance, they heard shouts, followed by two more explosions in quick succession. They looked at one another, waiting. Doors somewhere overhead crashed open. Footsteps thundered. The footsteps gained in both volume and quantity, followed by more crashing, and then wild screams.

165

Someone opened the dungeon cells upstairs, Pierce realized. Those sounds were the general population of the slightly lower-security dungeon suddenly set free. He heard shouts from guards, screams, bursts of spellwork.

It all sang in his blood, pumped through his veins like a shot of pure adrenaline. He found himself smiling without even realizing it.

"You might want to step back," Glanna said, gliding away from her cell doors until her back was pressed flat against her cell wall.

Pierce did the same, holding his breath as the door down into their private dungeon smashed inward. It crashed into the unoccupied cell between theirs, crumpling the somaritium bars. Through the now-destroyed doors strode a man with a single mage light. He carried a medium-sized book tucked under one arm, and he wore nothing but a loincloth, his beard and hair ragged and unkempt.

He looked like he hadn't bathed in weeks, and hadn't eaten in longer. His stomach sank in on itself, and Pierce wrinkled his nose in distaste, before he realized that he must not look much better himself.

Despite his attire, the man had a commanding air about him. He gestured with his head, and two armored soldiers burst through the doors after him.

He took a seat on the little guard bench near the wall, crossing one leg casually over the other. Then he snapped a finger, and another soldier marched inside with bags of clothing. He dropped them on the floor and dug through them, pulling out clothes: pants, two shirts, a loose-fitting skirt.

While they did that, the man flipped open the book under his arm. The mage light above his head brightened as he began to read. "Pierce Vinther, mage. Crime: murder, attempted murder, assault, blah, blah blah..." The man waved a hand. "Sentence: life imprisonment." He grinned and quirked a brow at Pierce. "Very interesting cellmate you've found yourself, Glanna."

"Thank you." Glanna remained at the back of her cell, concealed in shadow. "Though I didn't exactly have a say in the matter. Are you going to spring me or not, Talon?"

The man chuckled. "Patience, my dear. I've had to exercise quite a bit of it myself." He gestured at himself. "Had to disguise myself as a prisoner and everything to pull this off."

"Poor you," Glanna replied, her voice audibly sneering. "How long did you have to suffer in this hellhole, a week? Two? I've been here *years*, Marcus."

"Well, not this *exact* hole, you haven't," the man—Marcus Talon apparently—answered smoothly.

Glanna groaned. "I thought we had a deal."

"We do, we do. Calm yourself. I'm just giving your friend his options." Marcus turned to face Pierce's cell. Now that Pierce looked closer, he could see that some of the man's gaunt appearance was a show. His stomach regained its normal size when he stopped sucking it in, and when Marcus straightened to his full height, he wasn't nearly as thin as he looked hunched over.

Marcus strode toward Pierce's cell. "You have a choice right now. You can stay here rotting in this cell for the rest of your life—which, from the looks of things around here, hygiene-wise..." Marcus swiped a finger along the wall. It came away caked in slimy mold, and he wrinkled his nose. "Wouldn't be very long. *Or*, you can work for me in exchange for your freedom."

Pierce knew better than to take the first offer he was given. "What's the catch?"

Marcus chuckled. "No catch. Just an honest bargain among thieves."

"How long do we have to work for you? What work are we doing? Where would—"

"Not so fast." Marcus held up a finger. "I'll give you one answer now, the rest after you make up your mind." He glanced up just as another blast shook the dungeon.

Pieces of dirt and dust rained down on all their heads, and Pierce grimaced, brushing them from his hair.

"We don't have all day to chitchat. Peacemakers will get this under control soon enough. So." Marcus leveled Pierce with a frank stare. "One year's work. That's all I ask. I've need of people with the stomach for dirty work. It ain't honest, or easy, but you help me with this, and you're free as an uncaged bird."

Pierce tore his gaze from Marcus to stare the opposite cell. "You going with him, Glanna?"

"Do I look like an idiot?" She barked out a laugh. "Course I am. I've been waiting years for him to get his ass in here."

Pierce hesitated. The thing was, he still didn't consider himself a *criminal.* Not like the other people in this dungeon. He'd committed crimes, yes, he'd pled guilty, even. He knew what he was. But he had a reason. He was trying to protect people. To make sure that nobody else wound-up dead at Andon Glycas' hand.

Nobody saw that. Nobody understood him. Not even his brother, his best friend. So why wouldn't these criminals assume he was one of them? A bloodthirsty killer like all the rest.

Pierce clenched his fists. After years in this hellhole, he'd learned one thing: it didn't matter what you did. Good or bad, everyone was dealt the same shitty cards in life. Terrible things happened to the best people in the world. His sister's face flitted through his mind, followed by his father's.

It had been so long, he was starting to forget details. What color were Asulloa's eyes? Did his father have a beard too or just a mustache?

He squeezed his eyes shut. What was the point in being good, behaving, toeing the line, if everyone wound up dead anyway?

When he opened his eyes again, Pierce had made up his mind. "I'll go," he said.

Marcus's grin lit up his face. "Good man." He snapped his fingers, and the soldiers stepped forward, blast charges in hand. They strapped one to Pierce's cell doors and another to Glanna's. Pierce turned away, shielding the back of his head with both hands and bracing himself for the blast.

Ten minutes later, he strode out of the Plephia dungeon for the first time in years. *A free man again at last.*

Chapter Twenty-Three

Lazlo startled upright, gasping. He'd barely slept. The memories of his last day in the courtroom haunted his nightmares. After Pierce's conviction, Lazlo had gone straight to the peacemakers to tender his resignation.

He couldn't stop seeing the burnt-out shell of the Vinther manor. The wreck of old Headmaster Agnellus' home. Pierce's haunted expression in the courtroom. The way Pierce had collapsed when told about his father and sister's deaths.

The bloodstains on the walls of the healers' ward. The healers clutching wounded arms and dead friends, moaning.

Those scenes blended with older horrors. Bodies broken apart in the war, blood puddled in the mud of a battlefield. Friends dying beside him, Lazlo helpless to save them.

He'd thought he was done with that life. Free, escaped from blood and guts and horror. Instead, he fled right back into the thick of it. Only it was worse, because this time, civilians were dying. Loved ones. People he cared about, who never saw their deaths coming.

At least at war, you expect to face down death. Here…

Master Ebus tried everything to convince him to stay at the Mound. He gave Lazlo a position in his own manor at first. Then, after Lazlo met Bishop and learned about his and Osenne's quest, Ebus granted Lazlo permission to go with them, perhaps sensing that Lazlo needed a break from the campus itself.

But that break had only solidified what Lazlo already knew—he couldn't stay at the Mound. He needed to go somewhere new, somewhere free of the memories that haunted him.

The king had granted him his castle and lands long ago, after Lazlo killed Rimrig. Special payment for services rendered. But it was Master Ebus' idea to repurpose them. Turn Bacre Stronghold into a kind of extended campus for students. Lazlo liked the idea of taking on the troubled ones, the problem kids. Those who might not otherwise have gotten a fair shake out of this institution.

He knew what that felt like, after all.

And maybe, deep down, with every problem student he trained, Lazlo was trying to make up for the one who'd slipped through his fingers. The brother he couldn't save.

Lazlo stumbled downstairs into the manor dining room. Mariou took one look at him and sent a server running for coffee. "Everything all right, Master Lazlo?" She peered at him, visibly concerned.

He waved her off, forcing a smile. "Hard night, that's all."

She did not look convinced, but thankfully, she was too polite to pry. "I hear your young protégée will be taking the field at the arena today. Apparently quite a lot of people are eager to watch her, after her surprise challenge yesterday."

Lazlo's smile shifted, turning more genuine. "Any idea of the schedule for today?" He had quite a long to-do list—he needed to stop by the peacemakers first and ask after Agnellus. Then he ought to pay Bishop another visit. Inform him that Ebus' crystal ball was missing, and let him know about the problem with the cook. In between, though, perhaps he could squeeze in a small recreational visit to the Spellduel arena.

***

The peacemakers were no help regarding the former headmaster. His last known forwarding address was the distant estate to which he'd retreated after leaving the academy in disgrace, but nobody kept in touch with him. Word was he'd become a recluse.

They did offer to send a messenger to check on him, at least, which somewhat allayed Lazlo's concerns. He'd worry about Agnellus if the man did turn up missing. In the meantime…

Lazlo slipped into the highest tier seats at the Spellduel arena. He didn't want to cause a stir or attract attention—too much to do today. But he needn't have worried. Everyone had eyes for Kazren alone.

She strode onto the center of the tournament field, fists raised above her head. A roar answered her in the stands. Lazlo clapped too, grinning. She was a natural at showmanship. Kazren bowed to half the audience, then the other.

Her opponent, a spindly-looking young man wearing a third-year badge, blinked at her for a moment before he followed suit, imitating her bows. He moved quickly, but his motions were jerky, self-conscious.

Lazlo settled into a spare seat, eyes trained on the pair.

Kazren circled the boy, her attention laserlike now that the initial greetings were over with. The referee along the side counted down, then gave them the start signal. Kazren was off like a bomb—she moved so fast Lazlo couldn't even see her hands. All he caught was the bright flash of dark blue—illusion. A giant spiderweb burst from Kazren's fingertips. The boy flung a shield at it, admirably quickly. But Kazren was already casting her next spell—an actual spiderweb, this time appearing behind the boy. As her first illusion dissipated harmlessly against his shield, her second wrapped around him from behind, pinning his arms.

The boy's eyes went wide with shock.

Kazren closed in for the final thrust, but at the last instant, the boy managed to cast a knife spell. Blades burst from his arms to sever the thin spiderweb strands and he rolled out of the way of Kazren's next thrust.

For a moment, brilliant blue light suffused the arena. Kazren cast abjuration after abjuration spell, barriers heading her opponent off at every turn. The boy whirled between them, dodging what he could. He flung something back at her, pale lavender glittering in the morning light. Transmutation. Kazren blocked it easily and returned an enchantment.

The boy froze where he stood. His feet began to tap of their own accord. He flung his arms wide to keep his balance, and Kazren launched another spell. This time, her transmutation spell glittered lavender in the sunlight, wrapping around the boy's knees and ankles.

In a blink, his lower limbs turned to solid stone, which shone white in the sunlight.

The boy shouted in horror and quickly raised his hands to reverse her spell. He moved frantically, though, not able to get his hands into the right position in time. The movement itself threw him off-balance, and he tipped backward, arms cartwheeling.

He hit the sand of the arena with a deafening thunk. As he did, Kazren conjured a dagger, blade glinting in the sunlight. She crouched beside the boy and laid the flat of it bare against his neck, pressing just hard enough to make him go still.

A second later, the boy raised one fist, the universal signal for tapping out in defeat.

Kazren smirked. She surged back to her feet as cheers erupted once more. Lazlo leapt up, too, clapping hard. Although his eyes kept flicking to the blade in her fist. She kept it cast, even after the Spellduel ended. The knife point glittered, a deadly promise.

Effective, he supposed. But he personally wouldn't have risked conjuring such a deadly weapon in close quarters. Especially not for a friendly bout like this. And not after what happened to Master Ebus so recently…

Lazlo would need to have a talk with her later. He sighed. But, risky move aside, he was impressed by his mentee's performance. She was as quick on her feet here as she'd always been back home at Bacre Stronghold—maybe even more so. She seemed buoyed by the crowd, like she fed off of the adrenaline and attention.

His chest tightened. He could see her coming alive here at the Mound. This was a side of Kazren he'd rarely glimpsed. Hard to tell if someone was gregarious, after all, when the total population of her home was six people and one nosy housecat that's secretly a fae dragon.

She belongs here. Which meant, when this investigation finally came to a close, Lazlo would need to let her go.

***

The Black Tower looked, if anything, more imposing the second time Lazlo strode up to its gates. Tansya met him just outside, having spent the morning on personal errands. He was pretty sure that was druid-code for needing a dose of nature. She looked brighter this morning, healthier. As if she'd had her equivalent of his cup of morning coffee.

"Do you trust him?" Tansya asked, eying the structure that loomed above them both.

Lazlo followed her gaze. He didn't need to ask who she meant. "I trust who Bishop used to be. Whether the man in here is still my friend or not…" He couldn't shake what he'd seen in Ebus' manor kitchen. The glow around the cook as he snapped at Lazlo's questions.

He refused to believe Bishop could be a real suspect. He was Ebus' friend; Ebus trusted him. Bishop had no reason to wish Ebus harm. But if he was enchanted, controlled by someone else…

Lazlo squared his shoulders and knocked on the door. Like before, the doors swung inward of their own accord. The same guards stood impassive and blank-faced to either side of the entrance.

Lazlo scanned them both, paying closer attention this time to their pockets, wrists, and necks. If either of them had any enchanted items on them, charming them into doing someone else's bidding, Lazlo couldn't see the glow from the spells.

Shaking off his suspicions, he strode into the Black Tower, Tansya at his side. A steward met them at the foot of the staircase Bishop escorted them up last time. "May I help you?" he asked.

This man, too, seemed clear of any potential charms or enchantment spells. Nevertheless, Lazlo vowed to tread lightly. "I'm here to speak to Bish—Chief Bishop," Lazlo amended quickly. Didn't want to get off on the wrong foot. Not when he was here on such delicate business.

The steward bowed, his expression apologetic. "My apologies, but Chief Bishop is not in residence at this time. If you'd like to leave a message for him…"

Lazlo and Tansya exchanged a glance. "Any idea when he's due back?" Lazlo asked. "It's a matter of some importance, you see. I'm perfectly happy to wait."

The steward's mouth pinched. Clearly, he wasn't happy about the request.

Lazlo leaned forward. The tips of his fingertips glowed a faint pinkish as he summoned a hint of a coercion spell. Not actual mind control or charming, nothing so crass. Just a little hint of charisma, to nudge this employee in his favor. "I'm here on peacemaker business," Lazlo said, imparting as much conviction into his voice as he could. "Very serious matter. Chief Bishop will want to hear the latest updates from me directly. We can wait in his office; I know the way."

Lazlo started toward the stairs. The steward shadowed him for a few steps. "You see, sir, uh, master, Chief Bishop did not inform us when he would be back. We're not certain how long—"

"That's quite alright." Lazlo waved a hand. "We've got time to spare." They didn't; not really. But if he could get into Bishop's office alone, that might be even better than a conversation with the man. He could look for any hint of controlling charms or enchanted objects, all without tipping off Bishop—or whoever might be controlling him, if Bishop had been compromised.

"I really don't—"

"Need to worry at all, right?" Tansya finished for the steward, her voice a low purr. Lazlo had never heard this from her before. He spun to watch as Tansya flashed a crooked grin at the man. "You know us. Bishop and I go way back, the same as him and Lazlo."

The steward went bright red and visibly gulped. "I-I… The chief did mention a previous association."

"Precisely. He'll be glad to see us. In fact, he'll probably thank you for making us wait. He wouldn't want to miss our visit." Tansya winked, then.

Lazlo turned back around, face hot.

The poor steward didn't stand a chance. "O-of course, you're right. Excuse me. It's only, policy, but I… Yes. Let me show you to his office." He started up the stairs, but Tansya laid a hand on his arm.

"We've been there. Don't trouble yourself for us."

Bright red now, the man squeaked out a response, bowed, and then hurried back down the stairs. Lazlo watched him go, surprised not to see steam pouring from his ears. "What did you cast on that poor man?" Lazlo whispered as they started back up the staircase, alone at last.

Tansya snorted. "Nothing. Just good old-fashioned flirtation."

Lazlo shook his head, but he was grinning. Finding Bishop's office was simple enough—he remembered the way from their last visit. It was unlocked, too, which seemed a stroke of good luck.

"For a security chief, he's not awfully secure with his own belongings, is he?" Tansya murmured.

They slipped into the office. The moment they entered, the hairs on the back of Lazlo's neck rose. He couldn't tell if it was this room, or just the Black Tower in general. Something here always made him feel odd, off-center. As if the building itself were awake somehow, and watching them.

He caught himself holding his breath, and forced out a long exhale. "You check the desk." Lazlo nodded at it. "I'll go through the cabinets."

"What are we looking for exactly?" Tansya asked, bee-lining for Bishop's orderly desk.

"Anything out of place. If he's under an enchantment, then whoever cast the spell will need an object here to anchor it. Normally, with charms, you'd want to place them on someone's body, but it depends. If someone only needed to control Bishop's actions when he was inside this room, for example, they might anchor the spell here. It'd be smart, if they were trying to hide the charm from someone like Ebus, with Aursight."

As he spoke, Lazlo began opening cabinets at random. Bishop kept his office as neat as he'd kept his tent when they were traveling. His books were alphabetized, his weapons polished and hung in cases, like they were for display and not actual use.

Lazlo skimmed each of these carefully, making sure to pay attention to any glimmers of magic. He saw enhancement spells on the blades, accuracy spells on the archery equipment. Nothing unusual there. Most weapons made for troops like he and Bishop had been were spelled to enhance their users' abilities.

Since Bishop had no magic of his own, he relied on external devices more than mages would. Lazlo found spell detection rings in one cabinet, and several jars of truth serum in another. But nothing stood out to him as particularly unusual. Not until…

"Lazlo." Tansya's voice was low and tight.

He spun, pulse picking up. One look at her expression told him something was wrong. She knelt beside Bishop's desk, the bottommost drawer open beside her. She was holding something. A slim vial she'd plucked out of the drawer.

Lazlo approached her, glancing at the desk drawer. It held a series of empty glass vials. Each one was marked with a date—six consecutive days in a row, the earliest dated to a little over two weeks ago.

The last one, which Tansya held up for inspection, was not empty. It contained a centimeter of white powder. The date scrawled on the outside was familiar—it was the day Ebus died.

Lazlo's throat tightened. "Is that…?"

Tansya's eyes began to glow a much brighter green than they normally appeared. As they did, she uncorked the vial and held it under one nostril. She took a tiny sniff, not hard enough to disturb the powder itself. Something flowed between them, though—Lazlo caught a shimmer of pale green in the air. The color he'd come to associate with Tansya, which marked all druidic magic she cast.

The light in her eyes faded and she lowered the jar. Even before she said a word, he knew what was coming. She looked utterly broken. "Cyanide," Tansya whispered. "From the looks of it, the same supply that was used to poison Master Ebus."

Chapter Twenty-Four

Marcus Talon, as it transpired, was a master of disguise. In the months since he'd sprung Glanna and Pierce from their old dungeon hellhole, they'd watched Marcus act a pirate, a horse thief, a down-on-his-luck merchant, and even a high-born elven prince for one minor con.

But Pierce had never seen Marcus look *nervous* before.

They huddled around a campfire, several miles outside of Trismenor. Marcus's crew, called the Jade Owls, was large and varied. The cast changed every few weeks, so Pierce had lost track of the minor players. They always seemed to number at least twenty people, sometimes swelling up to as many as forty in their party for larger raids.

Eyepatch Lyndsey was one of the few permanent fixtures, Marcus's righthand woman. She sat beside him now, fixing the fletching on a bundle of arrows. Eyepatch Lyndsey was the best shot in the Jade Owls—possibly the best archer Pierce had ever seen. They didn't have many archers back at the Mound, since mages tended to prefer magic over physical artillery. But he'd seen Eyepatch hit targets with a simple bow that most mages could only dream of hitting with their best Spellduel attacks.

She worked away on the arrows, not bothered by the pitch black around the campfire. Pierce had long since learned that her eyepatch was spelled to let you see great distances, invisible creatures, and just about anything at night.

Marcus watched Lyndsey work for a moment, then cleared his throat. "I won't lie to you," he said, his voice pitched low. The Jade Owls who were present, about ten counting Pierce and Glanna tonight, all crowded closer to listen. "This job is going to be tougher than any we've taken on before."

Glanna stiffened against Pierce's side. They'd huddled together against the chill in the night air, though Pierce was fairly certain Glanna wanted more. She'd been more and more obvious recently with her come ons—including the other night when she pitched her tent directly across from Pierce's, then left her flap open while she changed.

He'd looked away, throat tight. It wasn't that he didn't want her— quite the contrary. But he couldn't lose focus. Not yet. *Lazlo first.* Only after he'd secured his revenge would he allow himself to think about any other kind of life afterward.

"Why is that, exactly?" Glanna asked.

Eyepatch Lyndsey smirked. "Cause it involves orcs."

Across the circle, another member of the Jade Owls scoffed. Knives, Pierce was pretty sure his name was. Or his nickname, anyway. Half of Marcus's associates preferred not to operate under their real names here. "We can handle a few orcs."

"I'm sure you could, just as we've done at times before," Marcus replied amiably. "But this will be more than a few. You see, there's an elvish settlement north of here, just beyond Trismenor. Remote, for their kind, so they rely on trade routes through Trismenor into the neighboring counties to keep them supplied with food and other essential goods. Unfortunately, last winter, a troop of orcs caught wind of this. They moved in five months ago, and they've stopped all trade in and out of Trismenor dead."

Pierce frowned, lifting his head. "How many orcs, exactly?"

"Hard to say," Marcus replied. "This whole area is deep forest, with a lot of cave and tunnel complexes running through it. Orcs tend to favor guerilla campaigns, only sending out as many troops as they need to in order to attack or stop any given supply train. But our best estimate, based on the information we've gotten from the elven settlement up north, is around five hundred troops."

Glanna bolted up from her seat. "Five hundred orcs."

"Give or take." Marcus shrugged, grinning.

"You're out of your mind. That's an entire army." Glanna thrust an arm around the campfire. "We're only..." She trailed off, gaze darting into the dark. Beyond the campfire's circle were the rest of the Jade Owls' tents. Maybe thirty people traveling in their party this time.

Pierce shook his head. "I've got to agree with Glanna. We're outnumbered and outgunned, if those are the odds. Sounds like a suicide mission."

"Which is why I assured the elves that we're just the crew for the job," replied Marcus. "We don't need to route the entire troop, mind. All we need to do is open up a secure route for the elves' merchant caravans to pass."

"If the orcs have been targeting the caravans all along, what's the difference?" Glanna snapped. "Surely they'll send all five hundred troops to stop whatever wagons we try to lead through the forest."

"Ah." Marcus tapped his nose. "But that's where we have the advantage. They don't know how many we are." He caught Pierce's eye, his own sparkling.

Pierce tensed. He had a bad feeling he knew what was coming.

"Between our masterful illusionist here." Marcus gestured at Pierce. "And you, our lovely enchantress." He waved at Glanna. "We should be able to make short work of this. For example, Pierce, if you made it look like we were, say, several hundred stronger than we are; and if you, Glanna, were able to sway even a few of the orcs to join our cause, surely the blow to morale alone will derail the rest of their army."

Marcus studied their grim expressions for a moment. Then he sighed. "Trust me, these orcs do not want to be here anymore than the elves want them here. They're deserters from their own territory out west, fleeing the perpetual war their leaders got them into with Qapreisia. They chose Trismenor because they want easy pickings. That, and orcs have never had any love lost for elves."

Eyepatch Lyndsey nodded in agreement. "We don't have to defeat them; we just need to convince them to move on. Find another patch of ground to torment."

"So, you want us to route the orcs here, just so they can go terrorize some other innocent village or settlement?" Pierce asked.

Glanna shot him a pointed look. "No settlement in the world is entirely innocent, Pierce dear."

Dear. He ignored that, though he noticed Knives and a couple other Jade Owls glance between them at that. Let Glanna spread whatever rumors she wanted. Pierce wasn't ashamed to be associated with her.

He just knew she deserved better. "Of course not," he said. "But why should we free these elves and doom someone else? Where's the justice in letting those orcs go free after they terrorized an entire settlement, restricting food and basic goods?"

179

Glanna ruffled Pierce's hair. "Still focused on fairness. Justice. Where was that when you deserved it, hmm?"

Pierce gritted his teeth. She had a point. But he still had not adjusted to the way the Jade Owls lived. Pierce had shed blood at the Mound, he'd attacked people, yes. But he'd had reason to. He'd been in the right.

Lately, it seemed like it was getting harder and harder to tell right from wrong.

Marcus smirked at Glanna, then Pierce. "Listen to your girl. She's a wise one. As to why we should free these elves…" Marcus slapped his knee and pushed himself upright. "That's an easy one, Pierce. We free them because they're paying us to."

A ragged cheer went up from the group. Knives brandished his namesake, teeth bared. A few others in the party whooped or growled.

The cheers carried on as Marcus strode out of the circle of firelight. "Get some sleep, you lot," he called. "Big day tomorrow."

Pierce shoved to his feet too, starting toward his tent.

Glanna hurried after him. "Pierce."

He stopped walking. He'd made it far enough away from the fire that his face was in shadow now. So was Glanna's, when she touched his arm and turned him back to face her. He couldn't make out her features. Just her eyes, shining in the dark.

"What's wrong?" she asked, her voice pitched low enough that nobody else would overhear.

"Nothing."

Her teeth flashed in the dark. She was smiling. "Look at me."

Pierce groaned. "It doesn't matter."

Her hand found his arm, gripped it. "Does it have something to do with the reason you keep rejecting my advances?"

Pierce went still. While Glanna had been obvious about her desires—more obvious than ever in the past few weeks—she'd never come right out and admitted to them.

"Tell me," she whispered. "Because I've seen you looking at me, Pierce. I know I'm not the only one who feels this way. So tell me what's stopping you."

"It's not you," he finally said, his throat almost as tight as his fists. "I'm sorry." He turned to go, but Glanna was faster. She darted around him, planting herself in his path.

"Not good enough. After all this time, I deserve a real answer."

Pierce caught her eye again. Held it. "This year is a break," he finally said. "A fantasy. It doesn't change what's coming for me. Revenge is my only future. I need to focus on that as soon as we're free of Marcus."

"*We* need to focus on it," Glanna replied, expression darkening. "It's my mission too."

Pierce shook his head. "I can't ask you to go where I'm going. To become who I plan to be."

"I already am that person," she snapped. "I'm not the one worried about who orcs will attack after we stop them here, or constantly questioning the morals of these missions."

Pierce's face flushed. "That's different. Lazlo deserves what's coming to him.

"I don't disagree. But I've been down this road before; I know what needs to be done. Let me help you, Pierce. Between the two of us, that bastard doesn't stand a chance." She looked so fierce in the firelight, then. So ready to throw everything to the wind, caution and all.

"Let me be your guarantee of success," Glanna whispered.

And finally, after months of resisting, Pierce let the excuses go. *Because she's right.* Together, they were more unstoppable than any force he'd encountered—more than enough match for a few hundred orcs. *More than a match for Lazlo Redthorn.*

"Fate brought us together." Glanna stepped closer. This time, when she reached up to loop her arms around Pierce's neck, he let her. "Now we can take it from here."

A slow smile spread across his face as he bent to press his lips to hers.

***

Early the next morning, Pierce ignored the whistles as he crawled out of Glanna's tent. Glanna, for her part, seemed pleased with herself. She flounced to the stream to freshen up, and hummed while she boiled water for their morning breakfast and tea.

Marcus had decided to send Glanna, Pierce, Knives, and a couple other assassins out in a scouting party first. The orcs seemed to have holed up in a cave complex near the main thoroughfare, which culminated in an enormous mountaintop sanctuary. Marcus wanted detailed plans of the sanctuary before they made their moves on the orcs. With Pierce and Glanna tagging along, they should be able to conceal the whole party from detection for as long as it took to map the place.

They left at dawn, wrapped in furs to keep warm. Eyepatch Lyndsey rode along to act as backup, since she was their best talent at ranged attacks.

The other Jade Owls tagging along carried light armor and weapons—anything they could move stealthily while wearing. They rode in silence until they neared the complex, where Glanna and Pierce dismounted to cast quick concealing and muffling spells over the entire party.

Now silence spells to all to cover the sound of their movement, they set off again in single file toward the jagged, rocky trails that circled a small mountain. Knives and another Jade Owl named Ghost took point. Pierce and Glanna followed them, trailed by Eye-patch and a couple of her comrades.

About an hour into their walk, Knives tapped Ghost, who turned to gesture to Glanna. She and Pierce both nodded. Up ahead, they'd spotted a plume of smoke rising into the air. A cooking fire. *Someone's nearby.*

They slowed further, both Pierce and Glanna checking their spells again to be sure the entire party was well within their magical shield. As they crept forward, they spotted a couple more fires dotted along adjacent trails.

Nevertheless, it still took Pierce aback when they passed the first patrol of orcs. It was a small unit, only five of them, but they appeared so suddenly around a bend in the trail. They crouched around a fire, laughing and talking in their gruff, baritone language.

Pierce studied the orcs' expressions as they passed. He held his breath, half expecting one to whirl around and lock eyes with him at any moment. But the orcs showed no signs of even registering their passing.

Still, his shoulders didn't relax from around his ears until they passed the group. Even then, he kept turning to check over his shoulder every few paces, nerves on high alert.

After a while, the party neared a large cave entrance. More orcs were camped out front of it, and Knives gestured to Ghost, who waved to Eyepatch. A moment later, a flaming arrow appeared in the sky, far away from their little band.

One of the orcs cried out, pointing. The others followed suit, and Pierce and Glanna were forced to leap aside, along with the rest of their bands, when the orcs suddenly charged up the path where they stood.

They held their breaths until the orcs' thundering footsteps faded into the distance. Only then did they creep forward again, right up the entrance of the cave.

Knives and Ghost stepped inside, vanishing almost at once in the thick darkness. Glanna and Pierce exchanged looks, then followed. The moment they crossed the threshold, pitch black engulfed Pierce's vision. He stumbled, gasping under his breath. Then he felt Glanna touch his arm, and his pupils shot wide, night vision flooding his senses.

"Thanks," he hissed. She squeezed his arm once, then let go and turned to lead the way after Knives and Ghost.

They moved in fits and starts, advancing, then doubling back at the sight of other orc patrols up ahead. It was slow business, but it gave Pierce time to examine his surroundings. A strange sense of déjà vu had begun to creep over him. At first, he dismissed it—the place probably only felt familiar because he'd spent the past several years on a dungeon that might as well have been a cave. Dank, damp, dripping stalactites from the ceiling and reeking of seagull excrement. Here, it was bat guano, but similar smell…

But the further they got into the place, the more things began to tweak his memories. An old lantern hung from a hook on the wall that seemed familiar. Another scent, like running water with a sharp chemical overtone that tweaked his senses.

Up ahead, Knives gestured. They heard it, then, too: a rising babble of voices. Orcs—a lot of them, and close by.

They crept forward. Still, invisible to outsiders, they peered one by one around the next bend in the cave. Here, the tunnel opened up to a wide, high-ceilinged room. If it had been in a manor, Pierce almost would've called it cozy. Rugs adorned the ground, and someone had brought in furniture.

The furniture, too, tapped something in his mind. It looked antique, scroll-work wrapped around the legs of the chairs and top of the desk. Almost like the sort of furniture you saw at—

"Who's there?" one of the orcs grunted. In common tongue this time, not their usual language.

Pierce stiffened. But Knives and Ghost were already moving, charging forward into the cavern with a scream. The others rushed up behind them to join, and Pierce and Glanna found themselves dragged forward, into the fray.

"Now, mages!" someone yelled—presumably Eyepatch. Arrows whizzed past Pierce's ear and found homes in the nearest orc's heads.

Pierce and Glanna both spread their hands wide. As they focused on other spells, their glamours dropped away, revealing the entire crew to the gathered orcs—maybe fifteen in total. But what advantage the orcs gained in being able to see their opponents, they quickly lost at Pierce and Glanna's onslaught.

He flung conjured bolts at the nearest orc, then cast a spiderweb to tangle an orc charging at Knives. Glanna unleashed a spell he'd never seen before, something that lit up the whole cavern like daylight as great fireballs devoured two of the orcs farther afield.

One swung an axe at Pierce, but he cast a shield and it clattered harmlessly to the ground. Before he could retaliate, Glanna was already there, her magic wrapping around the orc's throat, choking him lifeless.

The battle was over in a matter of minutes. Breathing hard, Pierce stared at their opponents. Twelve dead, the three remaining orcs knocked unconscious and bound together against the desk he'd been examining a moment ago. As for their team, Ghost was cleaning a deep cut in one arm, and Knives groaned as Glanna patched up an arrow that had gone through the meat of her thigh. Other than that, they were unharmed.

"They were guarding wherever that leads," Eyepatch Lyndsey was saying. She pointed with the tip of her Longbow up a short flight of stairs, at the top of which stood a wood and steel door, lit by a torch in a bracket.

All at once, understanding flooded Pierce. He knew where he was. He'd never approached it from this side, of course—not the long way in. He'd only been here once, and he'd been brought via the shortcut.

His lips parted, his mind struggling to catch up. He couldn't quite believe his luck.

Across the room, Glanna caught his eye and quirked a brow. She'd noticed his stricken expression, no doubt. With an effort, Pierce wiped his face clean, though not before he shot her a quick nod. He'd explain later. For now, they had business at hand.

"Any magical seals on it?" Eyepatch was asking, already starting up the short flight of steps to the door.

Pierce hurried over to join her. "Let me scan it."

Eyepatch Lyndsey raised her longbow again, training it on the door. "You take care of any magical traps, I'll handle any human ones. Or, well…" She spared a glance over her shoulder. "Orc, more like."

Or mage, thought Pierce. He ran his hands over the door. Sure enough, a familiar magic touch washed over him. He recognized this spell. Recognized its caster, too, though Pierce never thought he'd experience it again.

Suppressing a smile, he twisted his hands in a complex motion. He knew the combination to this lock, after all. He knew, too, that its caster wouldn't have bothered to change the locks. Not after he helped put Pierce away for life.

With a solid click, the door shuddered and then shifted inward of its own accord.

Eyepatch flashed him a grin. "Nice one." She started forward into the room. Pierce was about to follow her, when Glanna appeared at his side, one hand resting lightly on his shoulder.

She bent close to his ear, one eye on the other Jade Owls, who were still collecting themselves below. "You know where we are, don't you?"

Pierce's smile widened. "I do. Let's just say, this place is the backdoor into exactly where you and I are planning to go."

Chapter Twenty-Five

*B*ishop. He needed to find Bishop.

How could I have missed this? Tansya had warned him her very first day on campus—she'd said someone had it out for Lazlo. Someone with an old grudge against him. But he didn't think Bishop would take it this far...

And why Ebus? That was what Lazlo couldn't work out. From the sounds of it, according to everyone who'd been on campus, Bishop and Ebus were close friends. *What could've made Bishop turn on him?*

Money, perhaps? But Bishop earned a decent salary as the Chief of Shields. He didn't seem the type to covet more—not like some of the masters, greedily saving up coin and constantly demanding raises so they could further expand their already generously-sized manors.

He could still be charmed, Lazlo reminded himself. Enchanted somehow. Then this wouldn't be his fault. But if that were true, then Lazlo should be even more worried. After all, Bishop was in charge of security for the most important building on campus.

What else would someone controlling him want to access?

All these worries spiraled as he raced across campus. He'd split up with Tansya, sending her to the caravansary to find Kazren. The last thing he wanted was for his over-eager student to come looking for him and wind up tangled in a mess of his own making.

He regretted bringing Kazren here. He regretted talking the headmaster into letting Tansya inside, too. The less people who cared about him on campus right now, the better.

He couldn't shake the feeling that this was all his fault. If only he'd noticed something earlier. Talked to Bishop sooner, interrogated him the moment he sensed something off.

Or, no. If only he could go back even further in time. Why had he avoided the academy for so long? If he'd returned to the Mound sooner, before Master Ebus' death, maybe he could have prevented this entire mess from kicking off.

It's all my fault.

Old, familiar guilt wrapped around his limbs. It tensed every muscle in his body, so when the carriage he'd hired to drive him across campus finally stopped, Lazlo practically flung himself out of it. He raced up the steps to the administration offices, taking them double.

He skidded to a halt outside the office, taking a split second to catch his breath before he pounded on the door. He heard shuffling, a remark inside. He pounded a second time. He'd just raised his fist for a third knock when a harried-looking secretary flung the door open.

"What do you—oh, Master Lazlo." Her face reddened. "May I help you?"

"Bishop," he said, and then realized he'd need more details than that. "Trying to find Bishop. He's not at the Black Tower. It's... rather urgent, I'm afraid. Where's his residence?"

The secretary frowned. "Chief Bishop converted one of the rooms in the tower to a residential suite. He lives just above his office."

Lazlo cursed internally. *Think.* "Where else would he go? Did he visit the headmaster recently? Or maybe..."

"Chief Bishop doesn't go out among the staff, much," the woman said, sniffing a little to indicate what she thought of that sort of behavior. "Not even to frequent the dining halls. Only place he normally visits aside from the tower is Headmaster Ebus' manor, of course, though now he—"

Lazlo cursed. "Thank you, miss. Would you do me a favor and send an urgent missive to the headmaster? Tell him there's been a security breach on campus. We need to go into lockdown."

The secretary's eyes shot wide. "Master Lazlo, I—"

"Thank you again!" He sprinted back down the stairs before she could respond. Bishop might be enchanted—or he might have betrayed them all of his own accord. Either way, the Black Tower was compromised. Only Headmaster Muzud had the authority to seal it. Hopefully, he could do that before any more trouble found its way onto the grounds.

Lazlo had asked the carriage to wait for him while he made this pit stop. Now, he flung himself into it and shouted, "Ebus' manor." Not for the first time, he wished there was a way around the campus's security protocols. What he wouldn't give for just a single teleportation spell right now...

As the carriage surged up the hill toward Ebus' manor, Lazlo leaned out the window. Everything still *looked* normal. Which was to be expected. Bishop hadn't been at the tower. He didn't know what Lazlo and Tansya had found. They had the element of surprise, their one advantage now. But how best to take advantage of it...

The carriage wheeled to a halt outside the manor, and Lazlo straightened his jacket, taking a deep breath. *Act calm.* The last thing he wanted to do was give himself away too soon.

He stepped out of the carriage, expression carefully neutral. *Bishop. The cook. Ebus' murder, the cyanide, the missing key to the Black Tower.* Somehow, it all connected. He just couldn't piece it together yet.

Lazlo paced up the steps and into Ebus' home. Inside, the place looked strangely, impossibly normal. Students clustered in the dining room gossiping. More sprawled in the common area, textbooks open on their laps, studying. He spotted Eldon near the others, and crossed to his side.

Eldon grinned up at Lazlo, oblivious and eager. "Master Lazlo. Congratulations are in order, I hear."

"Mm?" Lazlo asked, momentarily thrown.

"Kazren's Spellduel earlier." Eldon punched his arm. "We all saw that show. What a performance. Hope I don't have to face her— though knowing my luck, I'll be out the next round. Facing a real tough next duel..."

Lazlo's expression flickered. "Yes, of course. Great showing." He crouched and lowered his voice. "Eldon, have we had any visitors here today?"

Eldon looked up, perplexed by Lazlo's sudden shift in tone. "Just the usual suspects." He gestured at the students around them.

"I see." Lazlo's pulse ratcheted higher. "You haven't seen Chief Bishop, by any chance, have you?"

Eldon frowned, cocking his head to one side. "Not since the funeral. Might ask Mariou, though. She keeps better track of him." Something about Eldon's tone made it seem like there was an inside joke there, something Lazlo was missing.

He ignored it. "And Mariou is...?"

"Upstairs?" Eldon guessed. "Around this time of day, she's usually checking on the cleaners, ensuring all the rooms are being 'aired out properly.'" He said the last in a passable imitation of Mariou's accent.

"Good lad." Lazlo patted his shoulder and spun on his heel.

"Master Lazlo?" Eldon called.

He hesitated.

"I'm glad you stayed a while. On campus with us. It's been nice getting to know you better. Headmaster Ebus talked about you a lot..."

Lazlo winced. "I'm glad to have met you, too," he said, which was the truth. Although he still couldn't figure out if his being here was helping or hurting everyone. *I have to find Bishop. Stop him.* That would make his visit worthwhile. If he could just ensure nobody else got hurt...

Lazlo hurried upstairs, ears trained for Mariou's voice, or the sound of maids cleaning. He paced the upper hallways, hearing nothing and nobody. But as he neared his own room, his steps faltered.

The door was ajar.

Lazlo approached it slowly, pulse in his ears. "Mariou?" he called.

Silence answered.

Holding his breath, Lazlo raised both hands, ready to cast a shield spell if this turned out to be a trap. He'd been on edge ever since finding those vials of poison, and the silence was only making his nerves worse. At the door, he braced himself, and kicked it open... Then froze.

Inside the room, bound and gagged, was Bishop. His arms were bound behind his back, tied to the chair Lazlo sat on to tie his boots every morning. His head lolled against his chest, his clothes torn and his boots kicked off. Even from here, Lazlo could tell he was sporting a black eye, and a nasty cut somewhere on his scalp dripped red along his collar.

"Bishop!" He hurled himself across the room, pressing a finger to his friend's neck. A pulse thrummed against his fingertip. *Thank god.* He knelt, noticing up close that his friend's chest was still rising and falling in relatively steady breaths. "Bishop?" Lazlo nudged him, and Bishop's head lolled to one side.

A low groan emerged from his friend's throat.

Lazlo hurried to grab a knife from his bedside table, then hacked at the ropes around Bishop's wrists. He was just starting on his friend's ankles, when he noticed a piece of paper tied around Bishop's throat. It fluttered with the breeze of Bishop's breaths.

Lazlo's body tensed.

He paused, calling on his Aursight. He scanned every inch of Bishop's body, especially the piece of paper. But nothing caught his eye—he could see no enchantments lurking, no spelled objects to indicate a trap.

Taking a deep breath, Lazlo snatched the note from around Bishop's neck. He unfolded it, hands only trembling ever so slightly.

Hello, old friend.

Been a long time. Time's been kinder to you than it has to me, but don't worry. I'm here to even the odds.

In this unfortunate man's left pocket, you will find a key. Collect it and come to the Black Tower in one hour, alone. The key will grant you access to the dungeon. Do not tell anyone, and do not bring reinforcements. Trust me, I have something you very much want.

Or should I say someone…?

He'd just crumpled the letter up in one tight fist when shouts rang out downstairs. Lazlo hesitated, glancing at Bishop. He touched the man's shoulder, squeezed just once. "I'll be back," he murmured. Then he hurried out of the room, racing along the corridor toward the commotion.

The source of it was easy enough to find. He'd barely reached the top of the stairs when a leather-clad blur raced up toward him.

"Goodness, what on earth is the matter?" Mariou was shouting downstairs. "You'll startle the children." A cluster of students gathered around her, looking more curious and excited than startled.

Tansya ignored them all. She flung herself up the last step, breathing hard, eyes wild. To judge by the feather drifting from her tunic, Tansya had feral shaped to fly here. Before she even got a word out, Lazlo already knew.

I have someone you want…

"It's Kazren," Tansya gasped. She held out a bracelet Lazlo recognized at once. It matched his own, only this one had been painted with jaunty gold initials. He'd forgotten that tradition, common among the younger students. Decorating your school bracelets, since everyone was forced to wear the same ones. People liked to make their own stand out.

These said, in clear gold ink, *KD*. Kazren Drita.

"She wouldn't take this off," Tansya said, shaking the bracelet. "She's helpless without it, she can't cast, can't fight."

Lazlo unfolded the now wrinkled and stained paper, then thrust the note at Tansya. "Well," he said, voice grim, expression grimmer. "At least we know where she is."

Chapter Twenty-Six

Back at Marcus's camp, Glanna and Pierce slipped off together, to general whistles and whoops from the others. It was handy, he thought, that they'd established their courtship already. Gave the others less room for suspicions.

Outside, Marcus and his Jade Owls sketched out plans to route the rest of the orcs from that cave complex. Based on Eyepatch Lyndsey's report of the room she and Pierce had broken into, Marcus was pretty sure it contained valuable items. "No harm to the elves we're working for if we don't report this section." He chuckled. "Us freelancers are expected to skim a little off the top…"

Meanwhile, alone in Glanna's tent, she and Pierce laid out plans of their own.

He'd intended to keep his promise to Marcus, he really had. But he couldn't ignore an opportunity this good. It was almost as if the universe were offering it to him on a platter. Surely, his path forward was divinely blessed. How else to account for such good fortune?

He hadn't even remembered where the sanctuary was. Master Ebus had only brought him a few times when he was just starting out as an apprentice. Ebus said he'd wanted Pierce to have the lay of it, just in case anything was to happen. He'd even gone so far as to show Pierce where he kept the backup key.

"Best not to tell the headmaster," he remembered Ebus telling him, a chuckle in his voice. "You know how Agnellus can be. So concerned about security that he impedes all practical solutions. Besides, it's one little backdoor, how much harm could it do…"

One little backdoor. A hidden key that opened a portal directly from this, Master Ebus' private mage's sanctuary, into the basement of his manor. His manor on campus at the Wizards Academy of the Mound.

Pierce's grin turned wicked just recounting the details to Glanna. It didn't take long before she was grinning, too.

"So, if I'm understanding you correctly, that portal will take us right onto campus. Where Lazlo Redthorn teaches."

Pierce nodded, still grinning. "Bastard was a judge when I was last there, though it's been years by now. Knowing his rotten good luck, the fool is probably a master already. Living the comfortable life, maybe in line to be tapped as the next headmaster..." He gritted his teeth.

"Not anymore," Glanna purred. "Not if we have anything to say about it." She slid one fingertip under Pierce's chin, tilting his head up to meet her gaze. Her eyes glittered. "We just need to deal with dear old Marcus, first..."

***

In the end, it was depressingly easy to set Marcus up. His plan to route the orcs hinged on Glanna and Pierce's involvement. He directed them to enchant several blast spells and lay them as traps around the cave. Then he asked them to prepare a phosphorus bomb next. It was only a matter of shifting the spell's trajectory by a few degrees, really.

Pierce and Glanna waited, hidden from view, in the same cavern they'd stormed earlier, while Knives, Ghost and the rest lured the orcs on a chase inside. They waited until everyone had gathered in the room, swords drawn and clashing. They scanned the crowd, Jade Owls and orcs alike.

They waited for Marcus to flash them a signal, his smile bold and confident.

Then Glanna and Pierce triggered their traps.

Pierce's exploded in slick grease that covered everything within a ten-foot area. The nearest orcs were blown apart; further ones shrieked and ran, as the grease stuck to their bodies turned acidic and bubbling.

The Jade Owls cheered as they started routing their enemies.

Glanna's trap went off next, a sixty-foot-long, twenty-foot-wide circle of fire. It burned away most of the remaining orcs in a single instant. Others staggered out of the flames, swords raised, only to be cut down by Jade Owl swords and Lyndsey's well-placed arrows.

It snagged on Pierce's grease, too, licking further and further inward, toward the Owls themselves.

"Bit overkill, was that?" Marcus shouted, and then dissolved into a cough as the smoke reached his lungs.

Pierce and Glanna pinned fabric across their mouths and noses before they rose, haloed by flames and the shrieks of dying orcs. "Not really," Pierce said. They flung their arms wide in unison, and blinding blue light poured forth. The nearest Jade Owls shrieked and flung their arms over their eyes.

Marcus's expression changed in an instant, from easy and open to sharp and predatory. "Owls, with me!" He charged forward, fast as always on his feet.

Glanna was faster. Lightning burst from her fingertips and struck Marcus square in the chest. Someone screamed. An arrow shuddered in midair, only inches from Glanna's chest. Pierce had flung up a shield the moment she fired that lightning—thankfully, or Lyndsey would've killed them both already. Her second arrow ricocheted off Pierce's shield and skittered away across the floor.

Pierce grabbed Glanna's hand and hauled her backward up the steps toward the door into Ebus' sanctuary. She fired off another arrow or two, then an entire flurry of them, before Pierce grabbed her waist and flung them both into the sanctuary.

He slammed the door shut after them, though not before he caught a glimpse of the carnage. Bodies everywhere, flames eating the dead and living alike.

Good luck with that, he thought, jamming a chair under the doorknob, just in case anyone survived long enough to make a run for them.

"How long will that hold?" Glanna asked, panting, eyes on the chair.

"Long enough." Pierce hurried across the room. He knew this now, recognized Ebus' style. The type of desks he preferred, the bookshelves he always kept stocked. At the desk, he ran a hand along the underside until he found the spelled latch. A simple twist to get the cipher into the right position, and a drawer at the bottom of the desk popped out.

Pierce smirked. Just like the drawer in Ebus' secret room back at his manor, where he kept his crystal ball hidden. *Oh, the crystal.* That would certainly come in handy for what Pierce had planned...

He crouched to grope inside the drawer. His fingertips found the slim metal ring—the key to the portal. He withdrew it and reached for the wall next. A tap revealed Ebus' armory—magical rings, swords, old pendants and coins Ebus had confiscated from soldiers and students alike over the years.

Pierce's former master had always been fascinated by enchantments, spells that lived in inanimate objects, rather than a caster's mind. Pierce smirked. That would work to his advantage now.

"Grab as many as you can," he told Glanna, snatching up a spare sack nearby to scoop the rings and coins into it.

"What for?" she asked.

"Don't know yet," Pierce said. He paused to examine one coin in particular. Ebus had jotted a helpful label underneath. *Control spell—research the command words?* His smile widened. "But I'm sure we'll find a use for them."

Bags freshly packed with everything useful they could grab, Pierce turned toward the final door in the study, on the opposite wall of the one they'd barricaded. *The portal.*

He'd only taken a step toward it when the door behind them shuddered. Someone threw their body weight against it.

"You backstabbing bastards! Sons of a whore!"

He recognized Lyndsey's voice. Glanna smirked. "Need a diversion?" She held up a hand, and a bright orb appeared above her palm, throwing sparks.

Pierce shook his head. "Leave her. Where we're going, she won't be able to follow."

With that, he and Glanna raced through the remaining door into the portal. As they ran, the beginnings of a plan formed. Pierce knew what he needed to do. How to cut Lazlo right where it hurt. Simply killing Lazlo wasn't enough. Pierce wanted him to suffer. To feel the same pain Pierce had felt, when Lazlo freed that monster Andon and doomed Pierce's family in the process.

One by one, Pierce would take everyone Lazlo loved from him. Beginning with the man they'd both looked up to like a father...

Chapter Twenty-Seven

Bishop groaned as Lazlo eased him off the chair. Between him and Tansya, they were able to maneuver Bishop's weight onto the bed, swinging his legs up under him. "Lazlo," Bishop rasped.

"Shh." Lazlo touched his forehead. Hot. Too hot. He hoped none of those wounds were infected. "Stay here. Rest. I'll send Mariou up with the healers as soon as we—"

Bishop grabbed Lazlo's arm, his grip surprisingly firm for someone who was just unconscious. "That man," he rasped. "He knew you, Lazlo. He called you *Laz*. If I didn't know better, I'd think…"

Lazlo's entire body went rigid. He'd suspected, of course. The moment he saw that note. *Old friend.* Ever since Ebus' death, Lazlo was running out of old friends. There were only two other people left in the world who would really call themselves Lazlo's "old friend." And Bishop, he'd realized as soon as he found the man unconscious and beaten, wasn't the person behind all of this. He couldn't be.

Which only left one real suspect….

"I don't understand," Lazlo muttered, more to himself than Tansya or Bishop. "He's locked away. I put him there. How did he escape the highest security dungeon in the country?"

Bishop wetted his lips. "Who…?"

"Pierce," Lazlo said.

Both Tansya and Bishop flinched. They wouldn't have recognized him—Pierce was already jailed before either of them met Lazlo. But he'd shared enough stories for them to recognize the name and understand what this meant.

Bishop's frown deepened. "Ebus. Do you think he…?"

Lazlo nodded. "Though why, I'm not sure yet." He glanced at Bishop. "What's the last thing you remember?"

"I was in the tower. I'd finished my chores, and I…" He frowned, eyes going distant. "I felt a bit funny. I had this sudden urge to take out the spare key, the one Headmaster Muzud had you bring me, Lazlo. I took it downstairs, and then…" He shook his head. "I don't know. There's a blank spot. Next thing I knew, I was coming here to find you. I don't remember why, but it was urgent. I wanted to tell you something. You weren't here, though, and I went to leave, but a man blocked the door. Something slammed against my head, the man demanding to know how I knew you. *Laz,* he kept saying…"

"Probably a good thing he didn't know we were close," Lazlo muttered. "From the sounds of it." He held out the letter he'd found tied around Bishop's neck. "It seems like whatever he's up to, it's personal."

As Bishop read, his eyes grew wider and wider. "The Black Tower… how did Pierce even get access?"

"I'm guessing he's the one behind your misplaced key." Lazlo bent to reach into Bishop's pocket. Sure enough, he felt the spare key Muzud had given him. He pulled it out, sighing. "Then he wanted to pass the spare along to me, so I'd be able to follow him. He's got Kazren in the tower dungeon."

Bishop's eyes bulged. "Kazren. Your student?" He pushed himself upright. "We need to find Peacemaker Halis."

Gently, Lazlo caught his shoulder and held him in place. "Not in your state. You're in no condition to go anywhere." He stood. "Don't move. I'm going to get some help."

"Way ahead of you," said Tansya from the doorway. Lazlo hadn't even heard her leave. She flashed him a quick smile, then stepped aside to let Mariou rush past her into the bedroom.

"Bishop! My goodness. Are you alright? What happened?" She flung herself onto the bedside and clutched Bishop's hand. Hers were trembling, Lazlo noticed, and he couldn't help but hear Eldon's teasing murmur repeat in his mind again. *Might ask Mariou. She keeps better track of him…*

Oh, Lazlo thought. *I see.* Perhaps tea and meals with Headmaster Ebus weren't the only thing that had drawn Bishop here to the manor frequently. He took a sliding step backward toward Tansya, who was also smirking.

"I'll leave him with you," Lazlo said. "You might want to call the healers about—"

"Already sent a message." Mariou waved a hand, not taking her eyes off Bishop's face. With her free hand, she touched the bruise over his eye, then slid her hand around to find the damp patch along his skull. She tsked under her breath and reached into a side drawer for some bandages. "Your friend sent another to the peacemakers, too."

Lazlo glanced at Tansya, surprised.

She shrugged. "Seemed like we could use the backup."

"But he said I need to go alone." Lazlo's pulse skipped a beat. If anything happened to Kazren...

"Don't worry. I didn't mention the tower. Just said there's been a security breach and we need to lock down what we can."

"Do you know what's going on?" Bishop croaked from the bed, ignoring Mariou's attempts to shush him. His eyes bored into Lazlo, desperate and worried.

Lazlo's mouth flattened to a thin line. "I'm afraid I do. I'm so sorry you got hurt, Bishop. It's not fair. This is all my fault—"

"You didn't hit me," Bishop replied, mouth quirking at the edges. "Though I was tempted to do the reverse at times..."

"I'm sorry." Lazlo stepped back into the room. Whatever else he'd done, whatever mistakes he'd made, this one, at least, he could address now. "For what I did back in the day. Betraying you with Osenne. It was selfish, and I knew it'd hurt you, but I did it anyway."

Relief and amusement flooded Bishop's expression. "It's alright. I was a fool, head over my heels. But you did me a favor, really. I'd have needed to get over her one way or another."

"Still. I shouldn't..." Lazlo's face flushed, but he forced himself on. "I shouldn't have abandoned you here. Same with Ebus. I should've come back sooner, I should've—"

Bishop lurched upright off the bed, over Mariou's protestations. He stepped closer, unsteady on his feet, but managing. Then, to Lazlo's shock, he wrapped his arms around his friend in a tight hug. "You're here now," Bishop said, voice gruff in Lazlo's ear. "That's what really matters." He slapped Lazlo's back, then took a half-step back.

Mariou watched them both, her eyes shining with unshed tears. Beside Lazlo, Tansya's little grin had widened to a self-satisfied smirk.

"Now, go get your protégée," Bishop said. "You know Ebus would want you to prioritize her over everything else."

198

Lazlo nodded stiffly. That was the kind of master Ebus had been. The kind of master Lazlo hoped to be himself, someday. If he could ever fill his old mentor's shoes. He stole a quick glance at Mariou, who kept her worried gaze trained on Bishop's spine. Then Lazlo cleared his throat. "Before I go, though… would you be able to draw me a map of the tower?"

Bishop tilted his head, frowning. "What are you thinking?" he asked, even as he staggered toward the desk in the corner. Mariou leapt up to fetch him pencils and paper.

"I'm thinking that if I walk in the front door," Lazlo replied, "He's going to ambush me, slap somaritium cuffs on me, and then drag me down to that dungeon to watch whatever he plans to do to Kazren in front of me."

Bishop grimaced. "It's probably what I would do, were I in the shoes of a madman bent on revenge."

"So." Lazlo glanced at Tansya. "That's what I'll do."

Her eyes widened. "What, just walk straight into a trap?"

He nodded. "But a trap we know is there. A trap we can plan around." He beckoned her forward. Together, they bent over the rough map Bishop had begun to sketch of the Black Tower. "Now, tell me, Bishop. Are there any secret passages inside the tower?"

Bishop barked out a laugh. "It was designed by your academy. What do you think?"

Chapter Twenty-Eight

Lazlo knew this plan was irresponsible. Maybe even suicidal. But he couldn't see another option that wouldn't put Kazren in danger.

At least this way, the only life he'd be risking was his own.

He crept as close to the Black Tower as he dared to get, moving along the grass itself, rather than up the official pathway to the tower. The grass around the base of the tower itself was overgrown—just like Bishop had warned him it would be, since the gardener who normally tended this section of the academy campus had been home sick for weeks. Lazlo scanned the surface of the tower. At a glance, it all looked like the same impermeable, smooth black obsidian stone.

But Bishop had told him what to look for. Holding his breath, one eye on the windows of the tower overhead to be sure that no lights flicked on or faces appeared in the glass, Lazlo crept sideways along the tower's circumference. About fifty feet from the main entrance, he finally spotted it—a telltale blue glow indicated the abjuration spell that guarded the hidden rear entrance.

In Lazlo's pocket was the skeleton key he'd taken from Bishop. Before Lazlo left Bishop in Mariou's care at Ebus' manor, Bishop had taken the key and whispered a few words, until the object began to glow with a similar light to this door.

"The back-entrance trigger," Bishop had explained. "Pierce knows this key opens the front door, but he doesn't know about the back."

According to Bishop, once Lazlo used this key to unlock the rear door, the front door would unlock too, just as Pierce would be expecting. Lazlo would need to time this illusion perfectly—even more perfectly than he had when he used the same trick on Rimrig the Fierce all those years ago. But with any luck, he'd get away with it.

Lazlo took a deep breath to center himself. *You can do this.* Master Ebus had trained him well—he was a master of the illusion.

He'd used it to his advantage dozens of times over the years. Fooling Ebus' other mentee would be the hardest part, but…

Pierce has been locked in a dungeon for years, his magic negated by somaritium. He'd be slow, out of practice. Like Lazlo felt in the arena when he faced off against his younger, more agile students.

At least, that was how he reassured himself.

Lazlo shut his eyes and concentrated hard. When he opened them again, he found himself gazing into his own eyes. An exact copy of Lazlo mirrored him now, tilting his head when Lazlo did, lifting a hand to imitate Lazlo's movements.

A faint smile touched his face, as well as his illusion's. *Perfect.* Pierce wouldn't see this coming. He'd send the copy of himself through the front door, while he slipped in the back, Pierce none the wiser. While Pierce was distracted trying to cuff and incapacitate his decoy, Lazlo would hurry down to the dungeon and free Kazren.

Together, he and his student would be more than a match for Pierce. Even if some of the Black Tower guards had been charmed into obeying Pierce—which Lazlo had to imagine they must be—once Pierce was knocked unconscious or forced to use too much of his own magic to defend himself, he'd run out of the juice and concentration to uphold the guards' enchantments.

Lazlo just needed to pull this off, and everything would be sorted. Campus could go back to normal, the Mound safe once more.

He watched his doppelganger march away from him at his command. It walked to the main road, and then approached the front door of the Black Tower. From this angle, Lazlo couldn't see his double anymore, but he could sense the other version of himself raising a hand, an illusion of a key in his hand, matching the one Lazlo held.

Lazlo raised the key to the secret door now. As Bishop had warned him, the moment he drew close enough with the key activated, a keyhole appeared in the wall where before there had only been smooth stone. Lazlo inserted it, feeling his double do the same at the front door.

He turned the key.

The secret door opened silently. He held his breath, hoping that somewhere on the far side of this wall, the front door had just done the same.

Lazlo stepped through the back door into the passages hidden within the Black Tower. A rat burst from the grass beside the door and scurried over his shoe and into the tower, squeaking as it went. Lazlo hesitated for a split second, then forced himself to keep going, following the creature inside.

Mentally, he called up Bishop's map of the place. He could picture the direction this passage took—it looped around the entire tower, hidden within the ten feet of stone between the inner and outer walls. Lazlo veered left, toward the wall opposite the main entrance. That was where the staircase down to the dungeon began.

He'd need to slip out of this passage and into the dungeon's only entrance, but he could cast an invisibility spell on himself easily enough.

He held his breath, moving fast. Through the walls, he heard shouts, a scuffle. He felt his doppelganger being grabbed, manhandled. Nobody hit him, thankfully—Lazlo's double would remain solid and three dimensional until someone attacked it magically. Then it would dissipate into smoke and give the entire game away.

Luckily, whatever Pierce was doing seemed to be purely physical for the time being.

Lazlo reached the door he needed. A few steps and he'd be out in the main foyer of the Black Tower, able to see what Pierce was doing to his poor double. He paused to cast a quick invisibility spell, feeling the familiar cool spill of it over his head and shoulders.

Then he pushed through the door and into chaos.

Across the foyer, two Black Tower guards restrained his doppelganger by both arms. Lazlo's double bared his teeth and struggled in a fairly passable imitation of what he would've done in its stead.

He scanned his surroundings, holding his breath. If Pierce sent the guards to do what he needed to do, then everything was about to fall apart. But...

There.

He spotted Pierce striding confidently toward the front entrance, a telltale smirk on his face. The sight of Pierce momentarily unbalanced Lazlo, his head swimming. He'd known, of course, that he'd be coming face-to-face with him. But he hadn't been prepared for Pierce's appearance.

He was older, of course. But he looked even older than Lazlo himself—the dungeons where he'd been imprisoned clearly had not been kind to him. His formerly deep brown hair had gone white around the temples, his scraggly beard shot through with gray. But it was Pierce's eyes that haunted him.

Deep-set, bright with an almost feverish hatred. His smirk curled up into a veritable snarl as he approached Not-Lazlo by the entrance. Even from here, Lazlo could sense the hatred exuding from his pores.

"Lazlo. I knew you'd come," Pierce said, his voice booming.

Lazlo concentrated on his doppelganger, until the double raised its head. "Let Kazren go," Lazlo said through his double. "She's innocent." At the same time, he began to inch backward toward the dungeon entrance. It was only fifteen feet away from him. Now ten, now five…

"Very convincing." Pierce stepped closer to his double, he stood next to his duplicate. "Did you really think that argument would persuade me? Innocence doesn't matter. If it did, my sister and my father would still be here."

Lazlo turned his back on the scene, even as he made his doppelganger speak again. "Doing this won't bring them back."

At the same time, he finally reached the entrance to the dungeon. Pierce must have left it unlocked and open when he charged across the foyer to the front door. Lazlo elbowed through the door, letting the scuffle in the foyer fade behind him. As he did, he let the skeleton key fall from his pocket. He wouldn't need it anymore, but someone would. He waited until he heard the faint skitter of nails and then stepped forward into the dungeon.

Darkness suffused his vision. He let the invisibility fall away so that he had the capacity to cast night vision on himself.

The darkness bled away, until his surroundings looked as bright as if he'd turned on the lights. Like Bishop's maps said, the dungeon staircase curved back on itself as it plunged down to the basement level of the Black Tower.

Lazlo hurried down the steps as fast as he dared, one ear tuned to the murmur of voices up above. This far away, he couldn't hear what Pierce was saying, but he felt the reverberation as Pierce struck his doppelganger. Lazlo made his double cough and choke—all the better to disguise its lack of ability to speak.

203

The farther Lazlo got from it, the harder maintaining the illusion would be. But he only needed a minute at most. He had the skeleton key in hand, which was capable of opening all the manacles Bishop kept down here in the dungeons too. One twist of it in Kazren's lock, and she'd be home free, able to sprint after Lazlo back up the stairs.

If they were lucky, they'd make it back to the foyer in time to ambush Pierce from behind, while he was still distracted by Lazlo's double.

Lazlo reached the ground floor of the dungeon, heart pounding, adrenaline coursing through his veins. *Almost there. Just a little further…*

Suddenly, piercing pain lanced through his entire body. Someone stepped from the shadows underneath the staircase, just as a second bludgeoning spell hit Lazlo dead in the sternum.

He sagged to his knees, gasping for breath. He could feel his concentration waver, his night vision flickering in and out as he desperately tried to hold onto his illusion upstairs. He lifted his head, eyes only half-focused, and froze.

He was staring into Pierce's eyes.

Pierce smirked, sharp and vicious. "So predictable, big brother. Glad to see I still know all your tricks." Then he thrust an arm out. Something black and circular wrapped around Lazlo's wrist, followed by a searing pain, worse than anything Lazlo had experienced. All his connection to his magic snuffed out at once, making him scream.

Pierce's fist crashed into his temple, and Lazlo went down hard, the entire world fading to black.

***

Lazlo came to slowly, his vision swimming. He blinked hard. That didn't help. The whole world swirled around him, making it hard to focus on any one thing. *Tansya,* was his first thought, followed hard by, *Kazren.* Something was wrong, wasn't there? There was something he needed to do…

Wake up, growled a voice, low and guttural, far too close to his ear.

Lazlo jerked upright, and found he could only move so far. Chains rattled at both wrists, as well as around his waist. He thrashed, inhaling sharply, and looked down to find himself bound upright against a slab of wood.

The rest of the world slowly came into focus. It was dark, low-ceilinged, and reeked of an acrid, chemical smell. Directly in front of him was a brazier holding a single torch, flame burning so high it licked the ceiling and stained it charcoal black in patches.

To his left were a couple more wooden posts like the one he'd been bound to, and to his right…

"Kazren." Lazlo's voice came out raspy, choked. Belatedly, he looked down at himself. Telltale pitch black chains wrapped around his torso and legs, all the way down each arm. He even felt one digging into his neck. *Somaritium.* That explained the strange void in his chest, a heavy absence where his magic ought to be.

It made his breath come faster, his pulse race. He'd never been without magic in his life. Even before Lazlo knew it was there, he'd had it—he just didn't know what it was. That secret core of strength he used to tap into—reserves of extra energy to study at law school, the strength to power through long nights. He hadn't known, yet, what magic was or how much lived in his body. But it had been there with him. Propping him up, lending him strength.

Now, it was gone.

Just like any hopes he'd had of making it out of this dungeon with Kazren unharmed. Looking at her now, his student seemed smaller than she'd ever been. Drained, the same way Lazlo felt—no surprise, given the heavy somaritium chains he saw looped around her wrists and midsection. Her head lolled against her chest, though he could tell that at least it still rose and fell in regular intervals.

Was she unconscious, or just defeated? Hard to tell.

"Kazren?" he hissed again, and she stirred faintly. He watched her, heart in his throat, as she raised her head. It looked like it took a visible effort. "Are you alright?"

She blew a long strand of hair from her face, shaking her head. "Master Lazlo…" Her voice sounded like his, rough and whispered. She shook her head again, harder, and finally lifted her face far enough to meet his gaze. "You can't be here."

Lazlo held her gaze. "I'm not leaving you alone here, Kazren."

Her expression tightened, pinched with worry. "That's what he wants. He told me. His plan was to use me to lure you here, and you fell right into it. You have to get out of here, get help."

Lazlo winced. "There is no help, Kazren. He's got plants all around campus. Surely you've seen the enchantments he's using on the guards—"

"The pendant," Kazren hissed. "Around his neck. It's what he's been using to control everyone. I see him whisper into it right before the guards march off on his orders. If you can just get a hold of that, then—" She broke off in a shriek.

Lazlo's entire body went rigid, as electric sparks flew from Kazren's chains.

A deep cackle ruptured the otherwise quiet dungeon. It grew louder, followed by the slam of a metallic door. Pierce, approaching from overhead, his feet heavy on the staircase down to the ground floor. "The favorite son finally awakens," Pierce said, his voice so loud in the gloom that it made Lazlo wince.

He squinted, peering past the boundary of the torchlight. "Pierce." Again, his voice came out gruff, but at least it had gained a little bit of command by now.

Silence answered him. The footsteps vanished. Lazlo held his breath, straining his ears. All he could hear was his own breathing and Kazren's labored, wheezing breaths as she whimpered, still recovering from whatever electric shock had gone through her body.

Suddenly, a chuckle sounded, far too close for comfort. Lazlo steeled himself to keep from startling.

Pierce stepped around his body and into the torchlight. His sneer turned his prematurely aged face angular and ugly. He looked exactly like his doppelganger had upstairs—for that's what had approached and attacked Lazlo's own double, it had to be. Pierce noticed the direction Lazlo glanced, up at the damp ceiling overhead, and chuckled. "Yes. I know all your same tricks. I can do the same things you can, because I learned from the same bastard."

Lazlo bared his teeth. "Don't you dare talk about Ebus. Not after what you did."

"What, after I poisoned him?" Pierce barked out a laugh. "The old man should've seen that coming. But he never was one for keeping his guard up. Always so trusting, our dear mentor. So concerned about making sure his students were safe and secure and well-tutored... except for when it mattered most."

"Ebus had nothing to do with what happened to your family," Lazlo spat. "You murdered an innocent man."

"Innocent?" Pierce cried. His laugh turned louder, borderline hysterical. "*Innocent*? Don't make me laugh. Ebus is the one who stood by while you put me away for life."

"It was my decision, not his," Lazlo replied. By some act of superhuman strength, he managed to keep any quiver from his voice.

"He enabled you," Pierce snarled. "You were always the favorite. Talented Lazlo, perfect Lazlo, why can't you be more like Lazlo…"

"Ebus thought of you like a son." Lazlo glared at him.

"Well, I'm not his son. I never was. I'm my father's son." Pierce rose to his full height. "And he did nothing when my father was killed. He didn't intervene to get Andon arrested for his crimes. He didn't stand up for me at my trial. He let you lock me away, all for seeking justice."

"You killed innocent people!" Lazlo cried.

"Hardly." Pierce bared his teeth. "Anyone who protects a murderer is every bit as culpable."

Kazren scoffed. "Pathetic. Is that the best you've got?"

Pierce whirled on her, and Lazlo's heart stilled in his chest. "Don't," Lazlo barked. "Your fight is with me, Pierce. She's blameless in all of this."

"Exactly." Pierce's smile flashed white in the torchlight. "I want you to feel what I did, Laz." As if to emphasize the betrayal inherent in that nickname, Pierce raised his hand, palm out. Another blast of electricity shocked through Kazren's body again. Her spine arched and she let out a soft involuntary cry.

That, more than anything, broke Lazlo. He knew Kazren. He knew how much she hated to show vulnerability in any situation. And now, it had been forced out of her. "Stop!" he growled, even though he knew it was the wrong thing to say, knew it would only spur Pierce on to more and worse punishment.

Pierce's hands dropped. Kazren sagged with him, collapsing into her chains. They were the only things holding her up.

Lazlo's chest ached. He could do nothing, bound as he was. All he could do was watch and beg Pierce for mercy—something he already knew Pierce would never show.

"This is what it felt like," Pierce said. He stepped closer to Lazlo again, bent until his mouth was close enough to Lazlo's ear that Lazlo felt the hot gust of his breath. "This is the same pain that I felt when I saw their bodies."

Lazlo squeezed his eyes shut. Behind his eyelids, he pictured the Vinthers. Calputh's kind eyes and warm smile. Asulloa's sparkling, mischief-filled face, young and bright, with her whole life ahead of her. "They would be ashamed of who you've become," Lazlo whispered.

Pierce snarled, animalistic. He flung out a hand again, ready to strike.

Lazlo flung himself forward, trying to intervene. He couldn't reach Pierce, though, couldn't get between him and Kazren in time. Another bolt of lightning cracked in the dim room, and Kazren shrieked, her whole body lighting up. When the light faded, Lazlo caught the scent of singed hair, Kazren's desperate pants. But she was still breathing, still alive.

Think, Lazlo. He trained his gaze on the ceiling. "I'm sorry for what happened to your family," he said. "But doing this, getting revenge on me, hurting others in the process... it won't bring them back, Pierce."

Pierce laughed again, not an ounce of humor in it. "Trust me, I know. I don't care about that anymore. The one faint silver lining of their deaths is that I'm free now. I have no one left to let down, no one left to pretend for. I can do exactly what I want, to whoever I want."

Lazlo caught Pierce's gaze. Held it. "Then I truly do pity you," he said.

At that moment, a shrieking alarm went off somewhere overhead. Pierce's eyes went wide and shot toward the ceiling. At the same instant, the cell doors all around them began to pop open, one by one, with loud clangs.

Pierce cursed and raced toward the nearest cell, just as Lazlo felt the somaritium cuffs on his wrists pop open. Across the dungeon, Kazren's opened too and she collapsed to the floor, boneless and unconscious.

Lazlo stepped toward her, power flooding his body as his chains fell away. For the first time since he set foot in the dungeon, he smiled. A smile almost as sharp and vicious as Pierce's own. *She did it.*

Chapter Twenty-Nine

Tansya's whiskers twitched. She could smell far more in her feral shapes than she was used to in her regular form. Now, a host of unfamiliar scents washed over her—mold and damp and dust, mingled with droppings from rats and mice and a half dozen other creatures. The back passages here were not well-kept, something Bishop had left out when he'd briefed Lazlo and Tansya on the details of the Black Tower's security protocols.

Then again, she supposed he'd have no experience with these passages at her height right now, a little less than five inches off the floor.

The moment she'd raced ahead of Lazlo into the Black Tower, disguised as a common household rat, all of her senses had shifted to high alert. She heard voices through the thick wall in the foyer—Lazlo's doppelganger and hopefully Pierce, racing to stop him.

She followed the real Lazlo through the secret passage until he reached the exit to the foyer. There, she watched him cross to the dungeon. It was open, unlocked, so Lazlo let the skeleton key slip between his fingers, as planned.

Tansya darted forward and snatched it up in her teeth. The key was heavy for her in this size, the metallic taste cold and unpleasant on her tongue. But she ignored it and surged back the way she'd come, into the hidden passages once more.

There, safely away from the eyes of Pierce or any guards he might have enchanted, Tansya feral shaped back to her regular body. She plucked the key from her teeth, jammed it into her pocket, and took off running. Bishop's directions were embedded in her memory, the map he'd drawn visible whenever she closed her eyes.

She followed the passage further around the curved exterior wall of the tower, and then slowed to run her hands along both walls at once. As promised, she felt the texture of the stone change under her right palm, from smooth obsidian to rough and almost brick-like.

Tansya withdrew the key from her pocket. Unlike Lazlo, she didn't have Aursight, so she couldn't see any hue to indicate if the key's abjuration spell was still activated. But Bishop had promised them that once he turned it on, it would remain activated until Bishop himself shut it off again.

It was their one advantage over Pierce—he might have the other key to the Black Tower, but he didn't know how to activate it, which meant he couldn't access these back passages. These contained the hidden, innermost security of the tower, known only to Bishop and Headmaster Ebus before his passing.

Tansya pressed the key to the rough brick wall. She held her breath, waiting. A moment later, something clunked overhead, and the entire wall shuddered faintly.

An opening appeared, where before there had been only solid brick. Tansya stepped through, and as she did, torches along the staircase it revealed flared to life. She raced up the stairs, in the opposite direction to Lazlo, praying that wherever he was far below her, he'd already sprung Kazren's chains and was hauling them both toward freedom.

In case he hadn't, Tansya would be his backup security.

She reached the second-floor turnoff and kept going. She needed the topmost floor. By the third staircase, her breathing grew heavier. She paused in mid-step to feral shape into a hawk instead, her night vision much better in this body, the key now clutched between her talons. She sailed higher, following the spiral of the steps to the fourth floor, the uppermost.

There, she shaped back to her regular form again and pressed the key to the blank wall. Once again, the bricks trembled and winked out of existence. She stepped through an arched opening into a small, perfectly round room. In the center of it was a raised plinth surrounded by a series of complex markings.

As she approached, key in hand, the marks began to glow.

She didn't read whatever ancient script these were written in. But that didn't matter. Bishop had taught her the symbols she'd need to touch, and in what order.

Tansya reached out with the tip of the skeleton key and touched first once symbol, then the next. After five had been selected, they shone brighter than the rest. The cipher was active now. Just one more step.

Tansya took a deep breath. This was what Bishop had called the "emergency override." The moment she shut it down, all the locks in the building would open—including the dungeon cell doors and the somaritium cuffs stored down there, produced by the Black Tower itself.

Of course, this was a gamble. If Pierce had brought his own somaritium chains from somewhere else, the override would have no effect on those. It only deactivated the devices that had been created by and for the Black Tower. But Lazlo had seemed confident Pierce wouldn't go that extra mile.

Pierce had been a smart student, he'd said, but he cut corners wherever possible, always taking the easiest, most direct solution to problems. "If there's somaritium already provided in the tower, he won't go to the trouble of sourcing outside chains as well," Lazlo had told both Bishop and her.

Tansya hoped he was right. That after all these years, Lazlo still knew his former friend. She grasped the glowing symbols of the cipher and twisted, counter-clockwise the way Bishop told her.

For a second, nothing happened.

She shut her eyes, cursing internally. But then she heard a soft whisper of a click. She whirled around and noticed storage cabinets around the room unlocking, one by one.

A slow smile split her face. *We did it.* But there was no time to savor the victory. The hidden doors to these passages would open at this override too. She needed to get downstairs and find Lazlo, now. Either he'd escaped before she triggered this, or…

Tansya spun on her heel, ready to feral shape into a hawk and speed down to find him again. Before she could move a muscle, however, a bolt of energy shot through her body, making her scream, her back arched as she hit the ground.

"Well, well," murmured a soft, feminine voice from the doorway. A voice that sounded familiar, though Tansya couldn't place it yet. "What do we have here? A hidden chamber, and inside it, an uninvited guest."

She lifted her head, vision swimming, and felt her blood turn to ice. She knew the woman striding into the room. But this didn't make any sense. She should be rotting in a dungeon somewhere far, far away. Tansya's eyes narrowed, trying to make sense of this tableau. "Glanna?" she croaked.

The other woman just laughed and raised her fist.

211

Lazlo flung up a fist, casting a shield around him and Kazren just in time. Pierce's first volley of spells bounced harmlessly off the shield, but he knew it wouldn't hold forever. Lazlo flung himself down at Kazren's side. "Come on, Kazren." He patted her cheek, grasping her shoulder to lift her bodily off the floor.

Kazren groaned, her eyelids fluttering.

Lazlo lightly slapped her cheek this time, inwardly apologizing. "Wake up. We need to go."

Kazren's eyes finally opened. They focused on Lazlo first, then the shield glimmering around them. With a gasp, she bolted upright, whirling around just as Pierce fired another volley of attacks into Lazlo's shield.

He gritted his teeth and groaned with the effort of supporting it.

To her credit, wounded and confused though she was, Kazren remained a quick study. She grabbed Lazlo's wrist and raised her palms, adding her magic to his. Fresh juice flowed into the shield, which was lucky, because Pierce flung a bolt of lightning at it that same instant. The dungeon exploded in sparks.

Pierce cackled. "You can't hold that forever."

Lazlo ignored him and tightened his grip on Kazren's wrist. "On my mark, I'll drop the shield. Remember your latest Spellduel?" He hoped she understood what he meant.

"Got it," Kazren replied, she took a deep breath.

"Face me like a real mage," Pierce was yelling. Excess lightning sparked around his hands, his eyes bright with fury that bordered on madness.

"Now," Lazlo hissed.

The shield vanished. Pierce grinned viciously, lifting both palms facing up in a somatic gesture. Before he could move, however, Kazren's spell wrapped around his lower limbs, turning his feet to stone. At the same time, Lazlo launched a move he'd practiced so many times, he could do it in his sleep. A tight web wrapped around Pierce's body, pinning his arms to his side, sticking to his jaw.

Pierce gave a muffled cry as he struggled. Just like Kazren's dueling opponent, the motion unbalanced him. He tipped backward, hitting the dungeon floor with a resounding crash.

Lazlo darted forward. Just like Kazren promised, he found a chain around Pierce's neck. He yanked hard, snapping the chain, and pulled a pendant out from under Pierce's tunic. It glittered silver in the dim torchlight.

Pierce's eyes bulged. He struggled harder, letting out a wordless, half-muffled shout.

Lazlo didn't stick around to find out what would happen once he freed himself. Unlike Pierce, Lazlo's revenge could wait—he had other priorities right now. Chief among them, getting Kazren to safety.

"Come on." Lazlo shoved her toward the exit, racing after her. He clenched the pendant in his fist. If Kazren was right and this was the source of Pierce's charms, the control center of the enchanted objects he'd planted on people all over campus, then all Lazlo needed to do was destroy it.

"We're just going to leave him?" Kazren hesitated on the threshold of the exit.

Lazlo shoved her bodily toward it. "Yes. Your safety is more important." He'd learned the hard way what came of prioritizing missions over lives. People got hurt. People died.

He wouldn't let Kazren face the same fate as Master Ebus.

"But—"

Lazlo kept pushing Kazren up the stairs. Tansya had managed to engage the override, just as Bishop had instructed, which meant they should have a clear shot up out of the dungeon and across to the main exit. As they ran, Lazlo muttered a spell under his breath, one hand fisted around the coin. The metal warmed in his grip, then grew hotter, scorching. He gritted his teeth, ignoring the pain, and kept turning up the heat.

He could feel whatever spell the pendant contained fighting back. Other magic shuddered against his own, darker and stronger than Lazlo expected. He knew Pierce's signature, had seen Pierce's style as he fought. This pendant did not feel like something Pierce made. It was darker, stranger, more powerful than anything he'd seen Pierce cast before.

Is Pierce working with someone else?

Lazlo shook his head. Didn't matter. All he needed to do was finish destroying this pendant, get Kazren out of here, and the peacemakers could take over from here.

They reached the top of the stairs. Light flooded Lazlo's vision, making him wince after the relative darkness of the dungeon. He flung up a free hand to shade his eyes, as he and Kazren spilled into the foyer.

The pendant was so hot in his fist he couldn't hold it anymore; he could feel burns forming on his skin. Lazlo flung it to the ground and sent one last wave of heat magic coursing through the metal. It melted against the stone, puddling into bright liquid silver. A flash made his eyes water, as the spell shattered.

He grinned. "Not far now." He grabbed Kazren's arm again, ready to pull her forward. But Kazren remained rooted to the spot, eyes wide. "What's wrong?" Lazlo glanced at Kazren, then slowly followed her gaze across the foyer of the Black Tower.

Standing across the foyer, barring the main exit to the tower, stood two familiar figures. A semi-conscious Tansya, gripped in a stranglehold with a blade to her throat. And behind her, robed in all black, her smile as terrifying as it had been the very first day he came across her in that dark forest convent, ready to sacrifice a life…

Lazlo swore under his breath. "Glanna."

Glanna's smile widened. "You remember me. I'm flattered." She shifted, the blade digging harder into Tansya's neck, drawing a trickle of blood. "Nobody moves," she added, her tone light and conversational. "Or your girlfriend here dies."

Chapter Thirty

Lazlo's eyes darted around the foyer. He couldn't see any of the guards. Maybe they'd run when the locks disengaged? Or maybe Glanna had done something to them. He'd broken the enchantment, so hopefully wherever they were, they were coming back to their senses. But in the meantime…

Lazlo slowly lifted both hands in surrender. Beside him, Kazren did the same. "Relax," Lazlo said softly. "Nobody needs to get hurt."

"Of course they don't *need* to." Glanna snorted. "That's the point." She twisted her wrist, and both Lazlo and Kazren flinched. Tansya, to her credit, didn't bat an eyelash.

She caught Lazlo's eye and mouthed something. He frowned, trying not to make it obvious that he was studying the motion of her lips. What was she saying? *Bite? Fight?*

"Hey, crazy lady," Kazren snapped. "Let her go."

Lazlo shot Kazren a look, but she was staring right back at him, her eyes wide. All at once, he realized what she was doing. Drawing Glanna's attention so he could focus on Tansya. He glanced back at Tansya, who mouthed again, slower this time. *Light.*

That he could do.

"Don't worry, I'll deal with you next," Glanna was snarling in Kazren's general direction.

Lazlo flung both hands into the air, his eyes shut tight. A blinding flash of light engulfed the room. He didn't have time to warn Kazren, unfortunately, and he felt her recoil beside him. He grabbed her arm and pulled her forward, just as they both heard Glanna gasp. A series of curses followed, as Lazlo and Kazren raced past her, both firing quick spells in her direction.

Glanna stumbled and fell.

Lazlo's vision was clear now, the light having faded fast. Glanna was obviously still blinking stars from her eyes, but Tansya was nowhere to be seen. He'd just have to trust her to do whatever she'd signaled him for. He pulled Kazren toward the door. Kazren stumbled, still dazed by the flash too, and Lazlo muttered a quick apology and then scooped her off her feet and slung her over his shoulder. He raced out of the tower and into the tall grass, just in time.

Behind them, they heard a roar from the direction of the dungeon staircase. Pierce, recovered and infuriated, charging their direction.

Lazlo raced across the darkened lawns of the academy. Kazren bounced uncomfortably over his shoulder until she slapped his back.

"I'm okay now; I can see."

He set her down and they both took off running. "Aim for the tree line," Lazlo barked. The nearest row of trees was a narrow band of apple trees that the groundskeepers maintained for stocking the dining halls. "They won't be able to track us as well in the shadows, and we can cross under the trees and call a carriage from the road on the far side."

As he spoke, they could hear the quiet gallop of a large cat bounding on their position, a panther. Lazlo and Kazren froze as the creature began to expand, rising higher and stretching. Kazren started to shout in alarm, but Lazlo clapped a hand over her mouth until Tansya finished feral shaping back to herself.

Kazren fell silent, eyes still wide. Together, the three of them finished racing to the tree line.

Behind them, they heard shouts, and caught flashes of light as Glanna and Pierce began to cast spells. The field they'd just crossed illuminated, but Lazlo didn't let the others stop. Tansya dragged them both onward, all three of them dodging roots and ducking branches, as Tansya guided them.

They burst out from beneath the orchard trees onto a gravel path, only a few paces from the main road. Lazlo could see a carriage parked nearby, since this road led to several popular study spots for the students. He tapped his bracelet to summon the carriage and it quickly came to life. It pivoted, executing a neat three-point turn and then trundling toward them.

Lazlo pushed Kazren and Tansya into the carriage first, hauling himself up after. "Ebus' manor," he shouted. "Faculty override on the speed, as fast as you can." His bracelet flashed as the carriage's spells verified that he had the authority to ask it to go that quickly.

A second later, the carriage raced off, so fast that Kazren and Tansya both shouted and grabbed the straps overhead.

Another flash lit up the sky behind them. Kazren's eyes were still wide, and he could see the latent terror coming over her. But she had the presence of mind to turn to Tansya, eyebrows lifted. "How did you do that?" she asked. "The... changing thing."

Tansya laughed. "First time meeting a druid?"

Kazren flushed. "Actually, yes."

Tansya grinned. "I'll explain it later."

Lazlo leaned out the window of the carriage to check the path ahead. "We'll reach Ebus' manor in another minute. With any luck, it'll take Glanna and Pierce a minute to work out where we've gone, but they won't be far behind. Hopefully now that we've broken Pierce's enchantment, the staff will be awake and back to themselves. We need to get everyone out—you two will be in charge of leading the staff to the main exit from campus—"

"I'm not leaving you alone," Tansya said, at the same time that Kazren said, "Like hell we will."

Lazlo shot the latter a sharp look. "We're not discussing this. I want you off campus and somewhere safe as soon as possible. You heard both of them back there. All they care about is hurting me, and they'll go through anyone they need to in order to do that."

"So that's a reason to leave you all alone against them?" Kazren replied, one eyebrow arched. "We can take the two of them. Together, all of us can—"

"No," Lazlo interjected.

Tansya leaned across to touch Kazren's wrist. "He's right. It's admirable that you want to help defend us both, but let the adults handle this."

Kazren's eyes flashed, and Lazlo winced internally. It was the exact wrong thing to say to a student like Kazren—someone who constantly worked to prove herself against all odds, and identified with being the best, most talented student. She'd interpret any talk about *adults handling things* as a direct attack on her identity.

"What she means is that..." But Lazlo didn't have time to finish explaining. The carriage jerked to a halt, and he glanced outside, realizing they'd already reached Ebus'. "Just, trust me, Kazren. Please." He nodded at the door, just as the carriage popped it open automatically.

Kazren shot him a dirty look, but at least she leapt out of the carriage, Tansya following hard on her heels. Lazlo jumped out behind them, and nearly collided with Tansya's spine.

After a second, he realized why.

Together, the three of them took in the sight of several dozen bodies splayed on Ebus' lawn. One was sprawled on the steps up into the manor, and there was another lying in the doorway. Lazlo's heart caught in his throat. *Students.* He recognized the academy robes one limp figure wore, and the stack of books clutched under another figure's arm.

He rushed to the nearest figure and bent to press a fingertip to their neck. He held his breath, eyes wide. But a moment later, he felt the steady thrum of a pulse under the pad of his finger. Relief rocked through him.

"They're alive," he murmured.

Tansya bent over another still figure, one fingertip beneath the student's nostrils. "They're sleeping," she said softly, her tone curious.

Lazlo's brow furrowed. "What the hell is going on?" He lifted his head to consider the manor itself. Lights were still on inside. The students couldn't have been like this for long—he could just see into the dining room from here, where half-eaten meals waited on plates, and bodies slumped onto the table beside their food.

"Do you think Bishop...?" Tansya didn't finish her sentence. She and Lazlo traded terrified glances, and then Lazlo raced up the stairs and into the manor.

"Hello?" he called. "Is anybody here?"

A thud answered them from overhead, followed by footsteps racing away. Tansya and Lazlo exchanged looks. Tansya gestured at Kazren to stay where she was, as the two of them started toward the staircase up to the second floor.

He was halfway up the steps when a familiar face peered around the corner.

"Oh, thank goodness. It's Master Lazlo!" Mariou called over her shoulder. She hurried down the steps to meet him, her eyes wild, breath coming short. When she reached him, she grabbed his arm, as if to make sure he was really there. "We thought you were in trouble. All the students fell asleep where they were standing, and then we went downstairs and found most of the staff in the same state..."

"Laz?" Bishop appeared at the top of the steps. Mariou had finished patching his wounds and given him a cane to lean on. He looked better than he had when Lazlo left an hour ago—more color in his cheeks, and a spring to his step. But he clearly wasn't out of the woods entirely yet. "What happened?"

Lazlo winced. "It is Pierce," he said. "But he's not alone." As quickly as he could, he summarized everything that had happened in the dungeon, starting with how Bishop's instructions had helped him overcome Pierce, and ending with Glanna's appearance. "We destroyed the charm Pierce was using to control people. I thought it would free anyone he'd been influencing, but I'm not sure how to tell…"

Bishop's eyes widened. "Oh my god. The students."

"What?" Lazlo glanced down the steps again at the figures sprawled in the foyer.

"They must have all been under his influence," Bishop whispered. "I don't know how familiar you are with enchantments—"

"Not my specialty," Lazlo said.

"But this reaction is common if someone's been under another mage's influence for a considerable amount of time." Bishop scanned the foyer, his expression stricken. "I've never heard of anyone enchanting this many people at once, but… Typically, once someone's released from a mind-control charm, they need a… reset of sorts. A time period where their minds can shut off and recover from the imposition."

At the top of the stairs, Mariou gasped. "I've heard about that before. But… I never imagined that could explain something this widespread. Does that mean he knows everything we've spoken about with any of these people?"

Bishop shook his head. "He can't be controlling this many people in depth. More likely he was just influencing them all, nudging them to do things they might otherwise not have thought to do. There may be a few people like the cook, who he was controlling more directly, but for most of these poor students, it should've been a general influence, more than a direct command of their every memory and thought…"

Lazlo groaned. "Either way, it's bad news for us. Pierce and Glanna are right on our heels, Bishop. We need a plan—and we need to get Kazren out of here, somewhere safe." He met his friend's eye, grateful to see a flash of understanding.

"We've got time," Bishop said. "Let's do this."

***

"What about this?" Bishop held up a ring. He and Lazlo were in Ebus' innermost secret room, sorting through what useful magical items they could find that Pierce hadn't already raided.

Based on the amount of missing items—not just Ebus' crystal ball, but several important magical tomes and amplifiers that Ebus had acquired over the years—they knew Pierce wouldn't be an easy opponent to defeat. But he'd left plenty behind, probably because he knew he couldn't remove every single important magical item from Ebus' manor without raising suspicions.

As far as Bishop and Lazlo could tell, based on their combined experience of how large-scale spells and specifically enchantments worked, Pierce didn't have the capacity to hoodwink everyone on campus at once. He needed to keep his manipulations to small things, for most of his victims. He could nudge them into small deeds or into misplacing items they didn't truly know were important. But he couldn't have convinced, say, Eldon to steal Ebus' crystal ball. Eldon knew how important that crystal was to his mentor, and he wasn't fully under Pierce's sway—not like the poor cook, who had no magical talent of his own or ability to resist Pierce's mental control.

For the big jobs, Pierce would've needed to come here himself. Which meant, he could only remove what he could conceivably carry out of Ebus' study himself—things he needed to hope neither Mariou nor Eldon missed in the interim.

So, Lazlo and Bishop were hoping against hope that they could find enough useful items to cobble together a defense from here.

Lazlo squinted at the ring Bishop held up. "Local anesthetic spell. For healers, mainly."

"Damn." Bishop set it aside and kept digging.

So did Lazlo, rooting through Ebus' storage cabinets and trying to ignore his rising pulse. Tansya had volunteered to take Kazren down to Ebus' private portal in the basement. It must have been the route Pierce took to sneak onto campus in the first place, which made it

220

dangerous—but they knew where Pierce was now. He wouldn't be anywhere near Ebus' secret hidden sanctuary, which Lazlo knew was located deep inside a cave complex in Trismenor.

Tansya would escort Kazren out of the cave, using Lazlo's directions, and then use her tree travel ability to bring Kazren safely home to Bacre Stronghold. Tansya would then hurry back here—per her own insistence, though Lazlo secretly hoped she wouldn't make it back in time for the final confrontation.

The less people he cared about who were here to face down Pierce, the better. He didn't want any more deaths on his hands.

Lazlo paused halfway through the next drawer he was searching. "Oh." He reached for an object he only vaguely recognized from his student days. "Is this what I think it is?" He held it out to Bishop.

Bishop's eyebrows rose too. "A Sphere of Dead Magic?"

When thrown at a target, this sphere activated on impact. It created a dead zone for magic within a twenty-foot sphere. It only lasted a minute, but for that duration, all magic within the sphere was dispelled.

"Could come in handy." Lazlo pocketed it and kept moving. "What've you got?"

"Couple flash bombs, a shield ring that's not as strong as anything you or I could cast... but it could still help as a backup." Bishop sighed. "At this rate, I'd be better off raiding the sword drawer."

Lazlo waved. "Get to it, then. I'll handle the magical items." Anything that would help Bishop cast spells would be a big help—Bishop didn't have any magic of himself. Not like Lazlo or Pierce.

And no matter how hard Lazlo had tried, he couldn't convince his old friend to sit this battle out. *We may not have fought side-by-side in the war, but we were in the same unit. Your fight is my fight, brother.*

Lazlo could hardly argue with that.

Bishop strode across the study to check Ebus' less magical armory, while Lazlo kept digging. Something caught his eye—a familiar leather cover with a curlicue design inscribed on it. His eyebrows rose. "My old spellbook," he murmured. He'd written this one while he was still at the academy.

Since then, he'd written many more. But this one he remembered reviewing with Ebus himself. For a moment, he felt the ghost of his mentor peering over his shoulder as he picked up the book and flicked open the leather cover. *This is a very promising first effort,* he could hear Ebus saying. *Very promising indeed. Especially this section...*

Lazlo's hands moved as if of their own accord. He flipped to the middle of the spellbook, a section he remembered he'd worked particularly hard to develop. His gaze landed on a familiar spell. *The invisibility bubble.* His smile widened. He'd first worked that out right here in Ebus' manor, with his mentor's help.

Unlike the typical invisibility spell, it cast a wide dome of invisibility between the user and their opponents, almost like a shield spell. It meant that within that dome, other mages could still see one another. Unlike traditional invisibility, which rendered a mage invisible to foe and friend alike, with this spell, if one aimed it right, one could remain visible to their allies while they jointly approached their foe.

The only downside was that the invisibility dome was nowhere near as durable as a shield spell. One hit, from either side, and it would vanish. Which meant, you couldn't maintain your invisibility while attacking the enemy. But it could be useful for a first foray. One well-placed surprise ambush attack from the front...

Lazlo tore the page out of the spellbook and stuffed it into his back pocket. Not that he needed the reminder, but it never hurt, in case Mariou or something else might need to utilize it.

He was about to close the spellbook when he heard a sharp whistle from the adjoining room. Bishop. That signal meant that Pierce had just tripped the exterior wards Mariou had set up and linked to Bishop's bracelet.

Showtime.

Chapter Thirty-One

Lazlo and Bishop met at the head of the staircase down to the foyer. Their eyes met and they nodded. They'd only have one chance at their first approach. "Stay close to me," Lazlo said, watching the foyer below, and the still-closed front door. "I'm going to make us invisible to them, but it will only last until we strike. We need to make it count."

Bishop nodded again. He raised both hands, held fresh rings and gemstones. Each one held a hidden spell, which even a non-mage like Bishop could easily trigger. "The girls get out okay?" he asked.

Lazlo grunted an affirmative. "Mariou?"

"Safely out the back door." Bishop's eyes flicked his direction. "I'm glad we hashed things out, me and you. In case…"

"In case nothing." Lazlo punched his bicep lightly. "We'll be fine. You and I have faced far worse monsters than Pierce Vinther."

Bishop's mouth quirked into a smile. "You can say that again."

Downstairs, a deafening crash interrupted them. The door blew inward and crashed onto the marble floor of the foyer. Lazlo swung his hands up and the invisibility dome shimmered into place around them. Thanks to his Aursight, it was easy to tell that it was working. But Pierce had Aursight too. Lazlo held his breath, not moving an inch until the energy from casting the spell faded. Once he could no longer see the shimmering residue the dome spell left, he gave Bishop another nod.

Pierce wouldn't sense anything now. Together, they crept forward, down the stairs into the foyer.

At the same time, Pierce strode through the blown-out door, Glanna on his heels. Lazlo balled his fists. The man had some gall, walking through Ebus' home like he owned the place. He couldn't believe he'd once considered Pierce his brother.

You killed Ebus, Lazlo thought, fists balled, glaring hard at him. *You tortured Kazren. You tried to hurt Tansya too. All because you hate me for seeing justice done.*

He'd failed with Andon. Lazlo had made the wrong call, he knew that now. Freeing Andon to his father's care had wrought terrible destruction at the school. But Pierce had done so much worse since then. Killing those healers, mutilating others, poisoning Ebus, all in his mad quest for revenge.

The Pierce Lazlo knew was gone. This man was a stranger. And the only possible response to his madness was to stop him before he hurt anyone else Lazlo cared about.

Safely hidden behind their bubble, Bishop and Lazlo inched closer to Pierce and Glanna. They watched Pierce glare around at the foyer, the adjoining rooms, the steps. Lazlo froze for a split second when Pierce's gaze landed on him. But Pierce only glanced away again, sensing nothing.

"They're not here," Glanna said, her lip curled. "I told you they wouldn't be stupid enough to come straight back here."

Pierce shook his head. "They are. I saw something out front. Wards, I think. They'll have set them up to alert whoever's in here when we arrived."

Glanna heaved a sigh. She looked more annoyed than ready to fight for her life. "Well, then, we'd better set about finding them, hadn't we?" She moved forward, ducking under the foyer and into the dining room.

Pierce stared after her for a moment, lips pursed. Whatever he wanted to say, he swallowed again, and turned to the steps. He started forward, and Bishop and Lazlo traded glances. They raised their fists, ready to fire the first spell the moment Pierce reached the edge of their dome. He was fifty feet away—now forty, thirty…

Suddenly, a triumphant shout interrupted. Pierce's head whipped around just as a bolt of lightning struck his spine.

"Let's see how you like a taste of your own medicine," someone snarled, still just out of sight beyond the front entrance.

Lazlo's heart lurched. *Oh no.* He recognized that voice. He'd just heard it an hour ago, sending the speaker off to safety. He'd hoped to never hear it in a situation like this again.

Pierce stumbled, but caught himself on the railing, whipping around just as Glanna reappeared in the dining room foyer. She raised her fists, a deadly knife-throwing spell gathering around her knuckles, as Kazren stormed back into the manor.

Nothing for it. Bishop and Lazlo raised their arms too, and cast every spell in their arsenal at Pierce.

***

Lazlo's first volley struck harmlessly against a shield Pierce must have cast in advance. Like Lazlo, he would've known that Lazlo's Aursight would show him any active shields he cast. Pierce had prepared before he walked into Ebus' manor—Lazlo had to give him grudging credit there.

But he wasn't prepared for Bishop.

Instead of throwing a spell, Bishop threw a dagger from his left boot. Tipped in somaritium, the dagger flew straight through Pierce's shield and struck him behind the knee. Pierce yelled and sagged to one leg.

At the same time, Glanna launched another attack at Kazren, who'd only narrowly dodged her first throw, to judge by the bleeding cut on Kazren's cheek. Bishop was twisting a ring, too, one with a binding spell that would've easily incapacitated Pierce.

But if Lazlo let Bishop's throw hit, he had no doubt Glanna's would land too. And Glanna's would be deadly.

Left with no other option, Lazlo threw the sphere of dead magic in between them all. It went off with a flash only he, Pierce, and Kazren could see. All three of them yelled in pain, blinking through the all-encompassing flare of magic. As it faded, however, Glanna's hands hung open and empty. So did Bishop's, his ring slipping off deactivated to clatter on the ground.

Pierce whirled on Lazlo just as Glanna charged at Kazren, fists raised. Lazlo and Bishop traded a single glance, but that was all they needed. They were old soldiers, after all. Accustomed to fighting without the help of magic.

Bishop charged at Pierce, fists raised, while Lazlo leapt over the side of the staircase to land between Glanna and Kazren. Glanna screamed and charged him, a knife in her fist. Lazlo dodged easily, grabbing her wrist as she passed and using it to flip her off balance. She flew over his shoulder, landing on her back with a resounding crack.

"Stay down," Lazlo growled. "I don't want to hurt you."

"That makes one of us." Glanna sneered. He noticed the flash in her fist at the last instant as she brought her blade up, straight for his gut.

Before it struck, Kazren shoved Lazlo out of the way. The blade sank into Kazren's upper arm, and she screamed.

Lazlo grabbed the blade he'd knocked from Glanna's hand earlier and moved on instinct. All he saw was red—Kazren's blood, Glanna's bloodshot eyes. He didn't stop; couldn't stop now.

He drove the blade deep into Glanna's throat.

Those eyes of her bulged, her hands scrabbling weakly at her throat. Kazren screamed again, more in horror than pain.

"Look away," Lazlo told her. He waited until Kazren covered her eyes—until he couldn't see the tears staining her cheeks anymore. Then he wrenched the blade out.

Glanna gurgled horribly. He ignored her and spun toward the staircase, where Bishop and Pierce were still struggling.

Pierce must have learned to fight somewhere—perhaps the dungeon where he'd spent the past several years. He dodged Bishop's strikes easily, a wild grin on his face.

Then again, Bishop was still weak, recovering from his beating earlier.

Lazlo hurried toward the stairs as Bishop swung at Pierce again, faking with his left fist before jabbing Pierce's gut with his right. Pierce groaned and doubled over. Bishop moved in to kick him, but Pierce sprang upright again, a knife in his hand now. He swung at Bishop's stomach, only barely missing.

"It's over, Pierce," Lazlo yelled. "Stop."

Pierce glanced at Lazlo. Then his eyes found Glanna's body, and widened. Pain and shock mingled on his features. "Murderer!" he shouted. He swung a fist again, the blade glittering in his fist. Bishop stumbled on the stairs as he dodged, then tripped backward into the railing.

Pierce lunged for the kill, but Lazlo got there first. He landed a solid punch on the side of Pierce's head. Pierce yelled, his fingers opening. The blade dropped.

Lazlo grabbed him, locking one arm around his throat. "I said stop," he shouted. "You don't need to die for this. You can still just… stop." He tightened his grip. He could do this. Choke Pierce out and arrest him. There was no need to spill more blood. He could

226

still see Glanna's flaked on his fingertips, and swallowed against a surge of bile.

"Laz." Bishop's voice ruptured Lazlo's focus. He glanced up, but Bishop wasn't looking at him. He was staring over the railing at the foyer below. Kazren hovered over Glanna's body, her hands bright green with what looked like an attempt at a healing spell.

A spell. Which meant....

Pierce let out a loud cackle, no doubt realizing the same thing at the same instant. Lazlo only had a split second to prepare before heat burst from Pierce's body in all directions. Searing hot flames erupted from his back, his arms, his hands, his feet.

Lazlo shouted and lost his grip on Pierce's throat. Burns snaked up both his arms, and his tunic had caught fire. Bishop ran forward to pull him away from Pierce, as the latter raised both hands. More flames poured from his fingertips, his palms.

Lazlo knew this spell. He'd never seen it cast, though, not even in the Spellduel arena, because it was suicide. A last-resort spell. Self-immolation in exchange for the ability to burn anything and everything in sight.

"No," he whispered.

Pierce aimed two torrents of flame at Lazlo and Bishop. At the last second, Lazlo snapped out of his shock enough to raise a shield. The flames at through it in an instant. They licked along the banister and over the carpets. Fire raced up the wallpaper and along the roof of Ebus' manor. Something overhead exploded in a shower of sparks.

Another torrent of flame poured from Pierce's fists, only to meet a stream of water.

Lazlo flung the only water spell he knew at Pierce. It was traditionally used for dousing fires in mundane settings—house fires or the like. But it was all he could think to cast now.

His water collided in midair with Pierce's flames. He gritted his teeth. Lazlo was strong, but Pierce had thrown everything he had into this spell—every ounce of his magical potential. Pierce knew he'd destroy himself, but he was willing to, if it meant taking Lazlo down with him.

For a moment, the two streams, fire and water, trembled in midair. Then the fire began to inch forward, the water evaporating in steamy clouds. Pierce was stronger, he was winning... Until...

A second stream of water appeared in another direction. Lazlo spared a quick glance for Kazren, who'd finally turned away from Glanna's body. She'd copied Lazlo's stance and cast the same spell, one he'd only reviewed with her once or twice in years.

A faint, proud smile touched his mouth. *She really is such a quick study.*

Then a third stream appeared from the direction of the front entrance. Lazlo tilted his head to see Tansya striding back into the manor. Her lips were a thin line as she surveyed the damage— Glanna's body, Kazren's still-bleeding right arm, the knife protruding from her shoulder.

And flames licking along the walls, devouring the staircase to the upper floors, all pouring from the flaming inferno that used to be Pierce.

I'm sorry, Tansya mouthed, the moment her eyes met Lazlo's. For letting Kazren give her the slip, no doubt. Or maybe for taking this long to follow Kazren back here.

Lazlo shook his head. *Not your fault.* It wasn't.

And he finally realized it wasn't his either. You couldn't shoulder responsibility for other people's actions. All he could truly control was what he did. How he behaved.

More confident now, Lazlo spun back to Pierce. He redoubled his efforts. Water poured in from three directions, surrounding Pierce's inferno. The latter let out a scream, which transitioned into something like a howl.

In the end, it wasn't really the fire that killed him. It was his own fury, burning him alive.

With one final shriek, the flames vanished. In their place, Lazlo caught a quick glimpse of a blackened, charred body, before the torrents of water still pouring from him, Kazren, and Tansya washed the ashes into a heap that collapsed onto the steps.

Lazlo collapsed with them, sagging onto his knees and gasping. *It's over. It's finally over.*

Chapter Thirty-Two

Putting out the remnants of Pierce's fire took the better part of the evening. Luckily, shortly after Pierce's death, the formerly enchanted and charmed students and staff of the house began to awaken. They pitched in, hauling buckets of water and casting dousing spells of their own, since Lazlo and Kazren and Tansya had drained all their energy.

The peacemakers must have awoken, too, because several arrived before long, worried looks on their faces. They demanded an explanation about what had happened here. Lazlo was too exhausted to explain, but luckily Bishop intervened. He sat them down, along with Acting Headmaster Muzud, and talked them through it all.

Apparently Muzud, too, had been charmed, almost as thoroughly as Ebus' poor cook. He barely remembered the past month, including Ebus' death.

Pierce's plans had run deeper than even they had realized.

Thankfully, the fire hadn't damaged the manor any more than superficially. Mariou surveyed the damage and promised Bishop and Lazlo that she'd be able to repair it within a few weeks. As for the missing items Pierce and Glanna had stolen from the manor, the guards at the Black Tower had already located them all, including Ebus' crystal ball.

Everything had been moved to a new location for now, somewhere secure the peacemakers would be in charge of, until the security measures at the Black Tower could be revised and strengthened once more.

Bishop was going to have his work cut out for him going forward. They all were. But at least there was a future to plan for now. A light at the end of the tunnel, at long last.

Retracing Pierce's steps, they realized he must have entered Ebus' manor through Master Ebus' old secret portal. From there, he would've been able to steal all the supplies he needed to pull off his plan. Then it was only a matter of enchanting the right guards at the

Black Tower to get past Bishop's security measures and into the most protected, powerful place on campus.

It was a sobering reminder—no matter how high or efficiently you build your walls, you needed to keep your guard up.

Commissioner Halis promised to round up everyone affected by Pierce's enchantments and ensure they'd all recovered. Hopefully there wouldn't be any lasting damage from his charms. But Halis seemed hopeful—everyone who'd woken up so far seemed like themselves, and maintained at least some memories from the past few months, though some people had forgotten more than others.

In time, everyone should make a full recovery.

Acting Headmaster Muzud himself was being treated by the healers, but he sent a letter to Ebus' manor, by care of Mariou. He requested a meeting with "everyone involved in freeing our campus of this plague."

Mariou decided brunch would be the best solution. The head cook was still at the healing center, too, since he'd been more affected by Pierce's mind-control than most others. But several assistant cooks were all too happy to step up and fill his shoes for the time being.

They planned an elaborate meal for the next morning. The staff at Ebus' manor pulled out all the stops, doing their best to get it back into presentable shape. The staircase near the front hallway, as well as the first-floor landing, were blocked off behind loops of draped fabric, since those would take longer to prepare. But Lazlo was impressed by how decent they were able to get the dining room looking on such short notice—especially after what the place had been through.

Late the next morning, Acting Headmaster Muzud Marblebeard's carriage drew up out front, followed by Master Halis'. Lazlo and Kazren met them at the doorway, along with Eldon and Mariou. Bishop and Tansya had opted to wait in the dining room. Tansya, especially, felt unsure about whether she should go—she'd come here to protect Lazlo, she said, and her work was done.

But Lazlo insisted she stay, at least until they heard what Muzud wanted to talk to them all about. She'd been just as instrumental in helping to stop Pierce as the rest, after all.

To Lazlo's surprise—but apparently not Mariou's—a string of additional faculty members trailed Muzud inside. Kazren shot him a wide-eyed, nervous look. Underneath it, though, Lazlo could practically feel the hope oozing off of her.

If Muzud himself didn't bring it up, Lazlo resolved to speak to him about Kazren's future. Much as Lazlo wanted to continue mentoring his student, he also needed to do what was best for her. The last thing he'd want to do was hold such a brilliant, promising student back.

Once everyone had settled in the dining room, and a decently passable series of egg dishes and fruit platters had been served, Muzud folded his hands on the tabletop. "There are three topics we wish to address today," Muzud said, looking at Kazren, then Bishop, then Lazlo. "First, the status and future of former Headmaster Ebus' manor. Second, we should discuss any additional concerns regarding the situation that occurred with Pierce Vinther and Glanna Treworgy. And finally, we should examine Ebus' sanctuary—clearly, for security reasons, we'll need to develop a more permanent solution to the back-door problem it poses."

Lazlo's eyes flicked toward Kazren. "I may have a few additional points to touch on."

Muzud bowed his head. "Of course. Shall we get to those afterwards?"

"By all means." Lazlo gestured to the headmaster.

The old dwarf cleared his throat. "Regarding Headmaster Ebus' manor." His gaze shifted to meet Mariou's. Some flicker of understanding passed between them. "I'd like to offer you the manor," Muzud said. "As an incentive to return to campus and teach here."

Across the table, Kazren inhaled sharply.

Lazlo glanced at her, then around at the other faculty members' expressions. Everyone looked solemn, but approving. "What would happen to my students?" he asked.

The headmaster seemed taken aback by the question. "You would continue teaching your mentees as you see fit, naturally."

Kazren was practically vibrating now.

The headmaster didn't notice. He was staring at Lazlo instead. "Don't answer right away. We understand how you feel. But we have more to discuss before you make your decision." He leaned forward. "This isn't just about the enormous service you've done this school, although please know, we're well aware of that. You're the last person who worked closely with Headmaster Ebus. We don't want to lose your knowledge, your resources."

Lazlo's chest tightened. He understood that, he did, but…

Muzud waved a hand. "Give yourself time to consider it. A month, let's say?"

Relief flooded his system. Lazlo nodded, grateful he wouldn't need to decide one way or another right now. But across the table, he noticed Kazren slump in her chair, visibly disappointed.

"Wonderful. Tabling that topic for now, then. Glanna and Pierce… We've been piecing together where they met, and how they escaped. We believe a third party freed them from the dungeon in Plephia, yet we haven't been able to trace that third party down. They were known as the Jade Owls, but it appears they went silent a few months ago. We're still working on locating their leader."

They all nodded grimly.

The headmaster sighed. "In the meantime, just so you're all aware, Glanna's body is being returned to her hometown for burial. As for Pierce… we will likely inter his ashes here, unless you have a better suggestion."

Lazlo flinched. He didn't want to think about Pierce at the end, all bitter flames and hatred. Instead, he thought about the Pierce he'd met on his very first day at the academy. Bright eyed and eager to learn everything he could about magic. "You should bury him with his family," Lazlo said. Twisted and warped though his pain had been, Pierce had believed he was fighting for their sake all these years.

The headmaster nodded. So did the other faculty members around the breakfast table. "Our thoughts as well." He flashed Lazlo a smile. "Final topic, then. About Ebus' sanctuary… would it be possible for you to show it to us?"

Lazlo's eyebrows rose. "All of you?"

A pause followed. The headmaster glanced at his compatriots. Finally, his gaze settled on Commissioner Halis. They traded nods. "Just us, then."

"Of course."

The headmaster and the commissioner rose.

"Now?" Lazlo asked. When they nodded, he cast Tansya and Bishop a look, then shrugged. *No time like the present.*

***

Lazlo led Headmaster Muzud and Commissioner Halis to the Ebus'
secret study, and from there to the mantel above the fireplace. He
tipped over a thick, hardcover book—*Encyclopedia of
Transmutation, Vols 1-8,* the boring title better to discourage idle
browsing. As it moved, the entire fireplace shifted, too.

It ground and rolled until a hollow large enough for a man to duck
through had opened. Lazlo went first, casting a mage light to float
above their heads.

Halis and Muzud followed.

Inside, familiar sights and sensations struck Lazlo. It wasn't the
same as it had been the last time he'd seen it—Pierce had done a
number on the place, raiding various cabinets here and there, leaving
magical items and books strewn about. Even so, the old place was
still stately and impressive, both in its size and in the carefully
organized style Ebus had used to decorate it.

Lazlo's throat tightened. Here, even more so than in his manor or
his private study, Lazlo could sense his old master's style.
Everything was just the way he liked it—the bowls, the tables, the
trays of magical items arranged by use and point of origin.

"Don't touch anything," Lazlo warned.

Halis was gazing at the ceiling. "I sense a lot of magical potential
in here. The room itself has some functions, doesn't it?" He gestured
at the walls. "Beyond just the mage lights." Those had activated the
moment they'd crossed the threshold via the portal.

Lazlo nodded, and led the party deeper into the sanctuary. The
faint sounds of bubbling water rose up. He led them to a small break
in the cave, through which a sliver of water was visible—the ocean
outside, waves crashing far below. He loved the view from here. It
was so unexpected, since the other side of the cave complex where
Ebus had built his sanctuary was all forest and mountain. This felt
like his own private sea.

Muzud's steps trailed off as he meandered through the other turn
offs in the caves. He and Halis took some time surveying the place—
it had more rooms than even Lazlo had explored yet. He didn't know
how far Ebus had built into the mountain—he seemed to have
expanded the sanctuary since the last time Lazlo had visited it.

233

Finally, they made their way back to the central area. Muzud pointed out a large, circular area, with far higher ceilings and a wider central section than any other rooms. It felt almost as large as the Spellduel arena, though it was difficult to tell with the roof overhead, enclosing the whole thing. "I think Ebus hosted some large guests," he said. "Possibly even a dragon."

"A dragon?" Halis' eyebrows rose.

"Look at the markings on the floor." Muzud paced across this open expanse. "Here, and here." He pointed to runes carved in the floor, hundreds of feet apart. "Yes, Ebus entertained some very large guests indeed..." Muzud looked up sharply at Lazlo. "Do you know where we are?"

Lazlo shook his head.

"This is another portal." Muzud tapped the ground underfoot. "We either need to shut it off, or we need to know what's on the other side. The academy won't be secure until we do."

Halis nodded fervently. "My suggestion would be to seal off this entire complex, headmaster. One person already used it to their own terrible ends. There's no telling what other trouble might slip through it."

Lazlo winced. "But there's so much research stored down here. Ebus' projects... we could learn so much from studying this place."

"Enough to be worth risking the lives of the entire Mound?" countered Halis.

Headmaster Muzud cleared his throat. "Such discussions are a matter for the entire council, not just our little group. But both of your points have merit."

"Ebus usually documented all of his projects," Lazlo said. "If you give me some time, I can find the plans for this one. It might give us a clue as to where this portal leads, and why he built it. But in the meantime, I think I have a working solution..." He strode forward, considering the floor.

Muzud was right. Now that he knew what to look for, he recognized Ebus' style of portal-building. The only reason he hadn't noticed this one earlier was because of how spaced out each individual rune was. He paced across the room, reaching for a rune here, a glowing symbol there. Before long, Ebus' cipher floated in midair, activated.

Lazlo manipulated the cipher, spinning the symbols until they flashed green. The whole stone circle flashed green too, then faded to a bright, reassuring blue. "There," he said. "It's off now. No one can access it until we reactivate it from this end."

Muzud and Halis' shoulders both slumped in relief. "Thank you," Muzud told him.

As they walked back through the complex toward the portal to Ebus' manor, Muzud drew up alongside Lazlo. "I don't want to pressure or sway you in any one direction," he said. "But we could use your help here, too. Not just at the academy, but helping us to investigate and study Headmaster Ebus' sanctuary here. You know what he was like; he always had a dozen or more projects going at once. You could help us uncover them again, finish what he started."

Lazlo's throat tightened.

Muzud clapped a hand onto his shoulder. "We understand how many terrible memories you have here. More now, no doubt." He looked genuinely sympathetic. "Just know, if you return, you'll have the whole faculty here to support you."

Hearing that meant more than Lazlo could bring himself to admit.

Chapter Thirty-Three

A few days later, Lazlo and Kazren packed for their return trip to Lazlo's castle. They said little all morning. Lazlo's mind was filled with his home and all the duties that would be waiting for him when he reached it.

Kazren, on the other hand, suffered from mixed feelings. She'd already collected her belongings from the caravansary, and bid tearful goodbyes to the other students she'd met while staying there.

Now, she lingered in the foyer of Ebus' manor, watching workers chip away blackened wood from the ceiling and replace it with shiny new beams.

Her heart sank. She'd found acceptance here. She'd made friends with Eldon and some of Ebus' other former students. She'd fought in a Spellduel tournament—and she'd won her bouts! Unfortunately, the rest of the tournament had been canceled, after Pierce's attacks, so she'd never find out if she could have won the entire thing. But still.

She finally felt like she belonged at the Mound.

While she missed Aire, Jub, Guerin, Mia, and even Alisa, she'd found a new group. Accolades and a way to make her talent shine. She didn't want to go back to hiding her light under a bushel—or in this case, inside a castle a long way from what now felt like home.

Her chest tightened as she cast one last longing look around Ebus' manor. For all the trauma she'd faced here—all the danger she'd confronted head-on and conquered—she still didn't want to leave. She'd defended this campus with everything in her power.

Sure, Lazlo had given her the dressing-down of her life for disobeying his orders and escaping back here to fight, putting both herself and Tansya in danger. But Kazren couldn't bring herself to be sorry for it. Not when she'd protected Lazlo and helped defeat that awful Pierce and Glanna in the process.

Alas, Kazren was still a student. For all her accomplishments and bravery, she still had next to no say in how her life progressed. If the academy didn't officially invite her back here, then she couldn't stay, no matter what she wanted.

Shoulders slumped, she followed Lazlo out of Ebus' manor and into their waiting carriage. Bishop and Mariou helped carry their luggage out. Bishop, Kazren couldn't help but notice, had been here at Ebus' manor suspiciously early and late, anytime Kazren visited. She wondered if he'd returned to the Black Tower at all since the attacks, or if he'd taken to staying here with Mariou at every given opportunity.

She hid a smirk as they all waved farewell to one another. Bishop and Lazlo lingered together for an extra minute, saying something she couldn't parse in low voices—not for lack of trying. Kazren's eavesdropping skills were improving, too.

Tansya had already left a couple days ago. Before going, she'd come to the caravansary to bid Kazren farewell. Their hug had been long and fierce, and Tansya had whispered something Kazren couldn't forget. "Look after him for me," she'd said.

Kazren didn't need to ask who Tansya meant. It was obvious—to her anyway—how Tansya felt about Kazren's mentor. But Kazren had no idea if Lazlo returned the sentiments. He was so difficult to read sometimes, especially about emotional things like this.

Kazren assumed Tansya had told Lazlo goodbye, too. But when she'd mentioned seeing her off at dinner the night after Tansya left, Lazlo had gone pale and stammered in response. *Maybe she didn't tell him she was leaving?*

Kazren didn't have the headspace to puzzle over adults' relationship dramas now, though. She had a journey ahead of her— not a physically long one, but emotionally, it felt immense.

She and Lazlo entered the administration building and retraced their steps to the gate room, where they'd first portaled to campus what felt like an eternity ago. The room looked smaller to her now, somehow. Shrunken in on itself.

This time, unlike at their strange arrival, two gate caretakers greeted them. Lazlo and Kazren each shook off their school-issued bracelets and handed them over. A cold wash of disquiet settled over Kazren when she removed hers, and she felt her power wink out.

She hated this feeling even more now, after the somaritium cuffs. It made her feel powerless, trapped all over again in that dungeon while Pierce laughed and sent his bolts of lightning through her spine.

She shivered, wrapping her arms around her midsection. Lazlo noticed, and rested a comforting hand on her shoulder.

He understood, she realized. Probably better than anyone. After all, he'd been in that dungeon too. They shared a long, commiserating look. Then, with his arm still wrapped around Kazren's shoulder protectively, Lazlo led her into the gate.

The caretakers shut the door behind them, with one last wave. Kazren couldn't bring herself to return it. She was still too heartsick to admit she was really leaving.

The journey was over in a blink. A bright flash of the runes, a twisting sensation in her gut, and then she and Lazlo were back where it all began. Darker stone walls circled them now. Lazlo crossed to a clipboard hanging from the wall, brushed off a few cobwebs, and jotted a note on it, the same way he'd done when they first traveled to the academy.

Kazren and Lazlo's trunks floated after them as they strode through the blank stone wall, which rumbled and grinded out of their way as they neared. Torches burst to life, illuminating the dim interior of the north tower. It, too, seemed smaller somehow. Diminished in comparison to the massive Black Tower on campus— but also less threatening, too.

Kazren suppressed a shiver, grateful when Lazlo pushed open the exterior doors and bright morning sunlight flooded the expanse.

Cold air rushed through the tower, invigorating her. She caught the faint scent of snow in that breeze. The seasons had begun to change. She stepped outside, tipping her head back to savor the feel of the sun on her face. Behind her, Lazlo performed the locking spell on the gate—now a requirement of the academy, thanks to the increased protections after Pierce's attack.

Then he joined Kazren outside and performed a second spell to lock the exterior gates.

Just as he was finishing that, they heard a shout. Kazren lowered her face to see a veritable mob running toward them. Aire was in the lead, but when she shouted again, Jub leapt up from where he'd obviously been lounging outside to join her. Alisa appeared as if by magic, her bell jingling as the tiny cat raced across the lawns.

The latter summoned Guerin and Mia, who looked even more pregnant now than she had when Kazren and Lazlo first departed. Mia didn't race their way, but Guerin did, and Mia waved him on, laughing and smiling.

Aire reached Kazren first, nearly bowling her over in a hug. Jub joined them soon after, and Alisa wound circles around their feet mewling.

"Tell us everything!" Aire gasped.

"I hear you fought in the arena?" Jub cried.

"In it and outside of it," Kazren replied.

"I hope you took good care of her," said Guerin, the latter directed almost harshly at Lazlo. But when Kazren looked over, she noted the sparkle of good humor in the old steward's gaze.

"I tried my best," Lazlo said, giving Kazren a knowing smirk. Alisa gave an indignant howl, and Lazlo bent to scoop her up, scratching the cat behind her ears. "I'm very sorry again for leaving you behind," he told Alisa. "But thank you for taking good care of everyone in my absence."

Kazren exchanged pointed looks with Aire and Jub. He always spoke to that cat as if she understood everything he said. Then again, maybe she did—the cat was awfully perceptive, they'd noticed.

Guerin hugged Kazren next, and then Mia, once she finally made her way to their huddle. Slowly, the motley assembly made their way back down the hill from the north tower toward the manor. *My family,* Kazren caught herself thinking, and she couldn't help but smile.

As sad as it had made her to leave the academy, she was glad to come back here. Their welcome made everything better.

Aire and Jub continued to badger her for more details about the academy—and to ask if she'd brought them any souvenirs back, of course. Guerin jogged ahead to open the doors for them, while Lazlo manipulated his and Kazren's bags to float inside.

"Are you two hungry?" Mia asked. "We can whip up anything you like. Whatever you've been missing."

"Coffee," Lazlo practically groaned. "The stuff they serve at the academy was a miserable excuse for the way you brew your cups, Mia."

She smiled. "And you?" Her gaze shifted to Kazren.

"Breakfast," Kazren replied. "Anything you like—I've missed your cooking."

Mia grinned. "Coming right up." She bustled into the kitchen, waving a hand as she went. "Aire, Jub, come give me a hand. Let's let our two weary travelers settle back in."

"Not like they had a long journey," Jub protested, but one sharp look from both Aire and Mia quelled him. "Alright, alright, coming." He jogged off after the other two, while Guerin went to settle Lazlo and Kazren's luggage overhead.

Kazren turned to Lazlo, and he patted her shoulder. "Go on, get your things settled. I need a minute."

She frowned, confused by his tone, but she hurried upstairs nevertheless. She was exhausted—she felt like they'd walked the whole way here from the academy, instead of portaling right up to the front door. A few minutes' rest would do her some good.

***

Lazlo paced through the foyer, listening to the distant hum of Mia, Aire, and Jub's voices. Then he strode upstairs, toward the class tower. As he went, Alisa transformed and flew onto his shoulder.

"Penny for your thoughts?" she whispered.

His lip twitched into a smile, despite himself. "I'm thinking about change. Whether it's worth the risk."

Alisa hummed thoughtfully. "Depends on what you're changing and what you'd be risking to do it, I suppose."

"Wise as always, Alisa." Lazlo scratched her ear again and pushed through the doorway into his students' study room. He examined the projects they'd worked on in his absence. He paused to skim Aire and Jub's progress on their individual spellbooks. At some point, Alisa made a cooing sound, and he looked up to find her staring at him from the desk.

"You're crying," she said.

He touched his cheeks, surprised to discover she was right.

He'd been thinking about Master Ebus. About lost time and missed opportunities. About the best way to do as much good in the world as he could.

Downstairs, he heard a distant shout. Mia, no doubt, alerting them that breakfast was served. He waved, and Alisa transformed back into her feline form, trotting after him downstairs. Lazlo paused outside the kitchen door to compose himself, then strode inside, shoulders squared.

He took a seat at the breakfast table. Jub set a steaming plate of eggs and bacon before him, then matching ones before each of the others' plates. Aire forced Mia to let her carry the drink pitchers back into the dining room—Mia was getting a little slower on her feet, as her time neared, though she still had two months before the baby would arrive. According to Guerin, she'd insist on working right up "until the child pops out of her."

Lazlo would need to team up with Guerin to talk her into taking it easier. But that was a discussion for another day.

For now, he reveled in being home again. In sitting down at this familiar table with his favorite people in the world, each of them bright-eyed and eager to see what today would bring. For a while, they just ate and talked. Kazren told the others all about her Spellduel, with Lazlo filling in occasional commentary on how impressive her form had been, or where she'd accidentally left her guard open for a split second.

Then Lazlo told everyone about his reunion with Bishop, his investigations into what happened to Ebus—leaving out the more gruesome details for now, for Jub and Aire's sakes—and about Tansya's visit.

"Wow." Aire whistled. "A real-life druid. I wish I'd gotten to meet her."

"She was the best," Kazren said. Her gaze darted to Lazlo, something he couldn't quite read in her expression. "You should invite her to visit us. I'm sure she'd love to see Bacre Stronghold. Meet everybody."

Lazlo steeled his expression smooth, though internally, he flinched. "That would be nice," he replied noncommittally. He didn't want to admit how much it had stung when he'd learned that Tansya left the academy without stopping by to tell him goodbye. Of course, he could visit his own sanctuary anytime and see her, but… it felt too much like chasing someone who might not want the pursuit.

He shook off the sensation, focusing on here and now. His family was together again—that was what mattered. And he needed to talk to them about something. "I have a question for all of you." He waited until they quieted, their gazes all shifting to meet his. "How would you all feel about... dividing our time between Bacre Stronghold and the academy?"

For a moment, no one moved or spoke.

Aire and Kazren's eyes shifted first, glancing at one another, and then at Jub. Kazren's eyes, especially, went wide with shock.

"How would that work?" asked Jub.

"Well, I've been offered a position back at the academy," Lazlo said. "In Master Ebus' old manor, which is currently being redone. I was thinking we could live there for two weeks, then take the gate back here for another two weeks. Back and forth."

Kazren's eyes flicked between the other two. "Yes," she said, too breathy and fast. She took a deep breath, obviously struggling to calm herself. "I'm in. I'd love that."

"But what about our rooms at the manor?" Aire looked worried. "We have projects we're working on here; we can't just abandon everything."

"I'm not about to go anywhere," Mia interjected gently. "Not in my state. And Guerin here can't. As the steward, his responsibility is the maintenance of this building and its grounds."

Alisa gave a loud meow. Lazlo grinned at her. "And of course, Alisa can ensure nobody tampers with any of your ongoing projects, Aire."

"It'll be great." Kazren spun to face Aire, beaming. "I can show you what I was talking about—how neat the caravansary and the study halls are, and how big the library is. Oh, Jub, you could join the next Spellduel tournament with me!"

That suggestion perked him up a little. He lifted his eyebrows at Aire, however, as though he'd prefer to wait for her reply first.

Aire chewed on her lower lip. "I suppose access to a larger library would be helpful with my studies..."

Kazren let out a squeal of excitement. Jub pumped his fist.

"Plus, I could really use all of your help," Lazlo added. "I've been given a research project at Ebus' manor. You three are close to finishing your first drafts of your spellbooks—I think this added experience would really be helpful to you."

Kazren and Jub were both beaming now.

"Will we stay at the manor?" Aire asked. "With you? Not... not in the dorms or anywhere strange?"

Lazlo smiled. "Of course. That's where I need your help the most." He lifted a finger. "But keep in mind, it won't be all fun and games."

Even as he said it, Aire finally broke into a smile wide enough to match the other two's. "Alright."

Kazren leapt from her seat, pumping a fist in the air. Mia and Guerin laughed, while Jub whooped and hugged Aire from behind.

"We'll talk more logistics during class tomorrow," Lazlo said, smiling. He loved his students. They were his family now. *Perhaps one day, I'll be to them what Ebus was to me.* For now, he wasn't sure. *I've still got a lot to learn from you, old man.* "For now—"

But a ringing sound interrupted Lazlo's train of thought. He frowned, first at Guerin, then at Mia. "Is your family still here?" he asked Mia, because that sounded like the doorbell. But nobody ever rang the doorbell of Bacre Stronghold. Even Mia's family usually just barged right in like they lived here—which for a few weeks a year of visits, they did.

Mia shook her head. "They went home for a week for my father's birthday. They won't return until next weekend."

"So who...?" Lazlo frowned, puzzled, as Guerin rose to answer the door.

But Kazren grabbed Guerin's arm, to everyone's surprise. "Let Lazlo answer it," Kazren said.

He looked at his student, suspicion rising. "Who is it, Kazren?"

Kazren lifted one shoulder, her face the perfect study of innocence. "I don't know. Honestly, I don't," she added, when he narrowed his eyes. "But... I have a pretty strong suspicion."

Ominous. Still, Lazlo shrugged and pushed from his seat, just as the bell sounded again. "Finish eating, you lot." He gestured at them to get back in their seats. Once Guerin did, Lazlo strode out of the dining room and up the hallway, through the main foyer.

At the door, he paused. A latent sense of nerves stole over him. He was almost tempted to cast a shield. *What if Pierce didn't die? What if he faked his death, what if he's still out there, what if—*

"Lazlo?" called a voice from outside, muffled by the thick wood of the door. A voice he recognized.

Lazlo undid the lock and flung the front door open. Sure enough, Tansya stood on the stoop, her hair mussed, her cloak coated with leaves and moss, the way it always got when she tree traveled long distances. But she was smiling, blinking up at him with those clear, bright green eyes. Eyes that always reminded him of the forest where they met.

"Tansya?" he asked, redundantly. But he wasn't sure what else to say. He wasn't sure, either, why his tongue suddenly felt heavy and twisted in his mouth, like it was struggling to connect to his brain.

"Hi." Tansya's smile, too, looked almost as sheepish as Lazlo felt. She ran a hand through her hair, further tangling her red-tinged curls. "I... wanted to stop by."

"I can see that," he said, when she didn't say anything for another moment.

"I felt bad leaving without saying goodbye. It's just, after everything we went through in the past few weeks, it was hard to... well, to say that to you." She avoided his eye, looking anywhere but directly at him. "Goodbye, I mean. I didn't want to... I *don't* want to... leave you."

He blinked. Slowly, his eyebrows rose. A complicated feeling arose in his stomach. A mixture of adrenaline and hope and mild disbelief. "Tansya, I..."

She stepped forward and pressed a fingertip to his lips, shocking him quiet and frozen. "You don't have to say anything. We don't have to talk about this now. I just..." She took a deep breath, squaring her shoulders, and finally, finally met his gaze again. "I'm happier when I'm around you. So. Could I stay here, for a while?"

Lazlo held her gaze. He let himself drink in the sight of her, wind-mussed and travel-weary. He was certain he must look the same way. That made him smile. They matched, the two of them. In more ways than just the external ones. Tansya let her fingertip drop from his mouth, and Lazlo caught her hand on its way down, intertwining their fingers to squeeze hers gently. "Of course, Tansya. In fact, I'd like that very much."

About the Author

Ray Clifford Martinez II loves movies and is fan of anything fantasy or science fiction. Recently retired from a twenty-two-year military career, and relocated to Maine. Currently working on a science fiction novel. Ray believes the best art imitates life, especially when seen through a wide lens, and this extends to his writing.